Praise for Will Shindler

'Riveting'
The Sunday Times

'Excellent'
Weekend Sport

'Unmissable'
Sunday Express Magazine

'Gripping'
Heat

'This is the best kind of police procedural'
Literary Review

WILL SHINDLER

The Cold Case

HODDER &
STOUGHTON

First published in Great Britain in 2023 by Hodder & Stoughton Limited
An Hachette UK company

This paperback edition published in 2024

1

Copyright © Will Shindler 2023

A CIP catalogue record for this title is available from the British Library

Paperback ISBN 978 1 529 38389 8
ebook ISBN 978 1 529 38387 4

Typeset in Plantin Light by Hewer Text UK Ltd, Edinburgh
Printed and bound in Great Britain by Clays Ltd, Elcograf S.p.A.

Hodder & Stoughton policy is to use papers that are natural, renewable
and recyclable products and made from wood grown in sustainable
forests. The logging and manufacturing processes are expected to
conform to the environmental regulations of the country of origin.

Hodder & Stoughton Limited
Carmelite House
50 Victoria Embankment
London EC4Y 0DZ

www.hodder.co.uk

I sometimes hold it half a sin
To put in words the grief I feel:
For words, like Nature, half reveal
And half conceal the Soul within.

Alfred Tennyson

PROLOGUE

2009

The air itself felt suffocating. It was half past four in the afternoon and the summer heatwave was showing no signs of mercy. The three of them weren't rushing. No one was rushing anywhere at the moment. They were in the happy corridor between the end of another school day and an evening full of homework. Billy Rickson resented the very principle of homework. White, eighteen, with a sharp angular face, as far as he was concerned his schooldays were almost over – homework, revision and everything else that came with it was very nearly history. With the end in sight the same old routine felt like an imposition.

'It's too hot to be outside,' whined Lee Ellis. They were classmates at the same secondary school in South Croydon. With a shock of styled black hair above cobalt blue eyes and flushed pink cheeks, Lee was a favourite with the school's female population even if he was already taken.

Some way up the pavement was his girlfriend Jemma Vickers, a tall young Black teen from the same class who was striding towards the entrance of a small corner shop. She turned round and gave them both a withering glare.

'I'm not buying yours as well if that's what you're both thinking,' she shouted loudly. Lee and Billy exchanged a smile. She'd always been something of a tomboy right from their first days at school – now she was a tomboy with almost fashion-model looks – at least that's what Billy thought.

She possessed long dark hair, a finely chiselled face and soulful brown eyes – which right now were regarding them both with mild contempt. He loved her a little bit, which both she and her boyfriend knew. It was a crush he'd struggled with at times, but since Lee and Jemma had got together the previous year there was a general assumption that his feelings had gone away. It wasn't true of course, but pride kept him from letting them know that. Now that university beckoned, a little bit of him was selfishly hoping that going separate ways might help split the pair up.

'What are we getting?' said Lee as they caught up with her.

'Beer,' said Jemma firmly.

'I want cider,' said Billy.

She rolled her eyes.

'We'll get both,' said Lee and they all grinned.

A few minutes later they emerged from the shop carrying a four-pack of beer, a two-litre bottle of cider and multiple packets of crisps, which they began stuffing into their school bags. Lee wiped the sweat from his brow.

'Do you know what – I might just go home,' he said, suddenly tired. 'Right now, all I want is a cold shower.'

'No, you don't,' said Jemma, striding ahead without waiting for a response. She marched on while Lee waited with Billy, as he tried to find space in his sports bag for the beer.

'I just want to get out of this heat,' panted Lee.

'So do I but why are you in such a rush to go home?' said Billy as he watched Jemma turn a bend and disappear from view. Why would anyone want to rush away from *her*? he thought. 'Come on,' he continued. 'It's not like we haven't got somewhere to go, is it? And it'll be cool *in there*,' he added conspiratorially.

Lee knew exactly where he meant. They'd found a disused electrical substation up in the woods near Addington Hills and had made it their own over the summer. A place where all their appetites could be indulged without prying eyes.

The boys turned the corner and stopped in sudden shock at the sight that greeted them. A white van was parked by the pavement, its back door wide open. Jemma was lying on the ground motionless while a man in a ski mask knelt next to her. Bizarrely, Billy's first thought wasn't for his friend – more how anyone could be wearing a covering like that in this heat. The man turned and rose to his feet. Before they could react, he was sprinting straight at them holding something up.

Billy heard a spray and felt a fine mist surround his face. For a fraction of a second, it was almost welcome – cooling and wet. Then there was pain and the smell of something like chilli pepper. His eyes immediately began streaming and he started to cough violently. With it came terror, the realisation that he was utterly defenceless now. He swung out a hand, but it didn't connect with anything, and he fell to his knees, furiously rubbing at his eyes.

All he could see were bright kaleidoscoping colours. He was coughing so hard he thought he might throw up. Something was happening though; he was aware of that even if he couldn't see it. He could also hear a voice now, calling out. Someone was running towards him, a young woman by the sounds of her. He heard a door slamming, and blurrily he saw the van accelerate away. He tried to speak but all that came out of his mouth was a dry croak.

Today

'Fucking hell it's cold,' said Detective Inspector Alex Finn. Dressed in full running gear, he was bent forwards, hands on

3

his hips, panting hard. Clapham Common was shrouded in early morning darkness, the falling snow visible under the yellow street lamps. He looked up at his companion, who was barely suppressing a smirk. 'And don't tell me this is *bracing* or normal for where you come from,' he added, balefully. The tall track-suited figure looked over at him pityingly.

'Christ on a bike, don't coppers have to pass bleep tests or something?' he said in a dry Glaswegian accent. Murray Saunders might just slowly have become one of Finn's closest friends. They were of a similar age, both in their late forties, though Murray certainly looked the more battle-hardened of the two. He ran an Alcoholics Anonymous Group close to Cedar House, the station where Finn worked, and possessed an insight into human nature that the policeman had come to value. He was also someone who thoroughly enjoyed poking fun at his rather uptight façade.

'I'm as fit as I've ever been, thanks – it's just too bloody arctic for this today,' said Finn straightening up.

'Exercise is good for you. Good for your body, good for your brain and good for your soul,' said Murray more seriously.

Finn knew what he meant. They'd started this tradition a few weeks before, an early morning run together before work. It was in part a response to a recent loss Finn had suffered. Detective Sergeant Jackie Ojo had died in the line of duty and her death was something Finn felt personally responsible for. She'd been more than just a member of his team; she'd been a good friend too. She'd never let rank get in the way of saying what needed to be said to him and he missed her greatly. It was the second major bereavement he'd been forced to go through in recent times. His wife Karin had died three years earlier and he'd just been emerging from that long dark shadow when he'd been hit by this latest tragedy.

4

It had been Murray's idea to go running together – he thought, correctly, it might help prevent Finn from retreating inside himself again in response to his loss. The two had first met when Finn's grief had been at its lowest ebb, and the counsellor had helped him find a way through, something the policeman would always be grateful for. However, here, now – in the falling snow at silly o'clock in the morning – all he wanted was a warm shower and a large breakfast. He held out his hands in surrender.

'Seriously – is this doing either of us any good?'

Murray smiled.

'It is a little on the fresh side – I'll give you that,' he said. 'Do you fancy grabbing a coffee instead?'

Finn nodded in relief.

'I thought you'd never ask.'

They turned and began trudging towards the main drag of shops on the other side of the common. The rush hour traffic was just starting to build on the South Circular and the smell of petrol fumes was drifting over.

'We haven't talked about Jackie for a while – don't think I haven't noticed,' said Murray casually.

'It's still a bit raw, mate,' said Finn.

'I get that – but I also know what you're like. What you show the world and what you're feeling aren't always the same thing are they?'

'I promise if I need to talk, then I'll be in touch . . . and then I'll try and get a word in edgeways. That's usually how it works,' said Finn. Before he could add any more his smart-watch lit up. He checked the incoming message and his expression turned serious.

'We'll have to postpone that coffee, I'm afraid. Something's come up.'

'A dead body I take it?'

Finn nodded ruefully.

'You know the drill.'

And then his watch flashed with a second message and this time he stopped still to take in what it was telling him.

'Oh no,' he murmured.

A short while later, following the swiftest of showers and shaves, Finn parked up in the snow and looked at his reflection in the car mirror. A gaunt, pale face stared back at him. Carefully moisturised skin and expensive designer glasses projected a sensitive, almost scholarly look. But there were bags under his eyes that spoke of the recent lack of sleep and near-permanent fatigue he was experiencing.

He took a deep breath, snapped on some nitrile gloves and stepped out into the cold. He was parked in a back street in Tooting, out of the way of the morning rush hour. He felt his foot immediately slide on the icy pavement and slowed down – the gritters had, as usual, stuck only to the main thorough-fares. Ahead he could see the police cordon tape sealing off a road that wound into a tunnel beneath a railway bridge. He knew what he was about to see, *who* he was about to find and wrapped his coat tightly around him. It was important to park his emotions and keep things dispassionate. He used to be good at that.

The freezing wind whipped sharply around his cheeks as he flashed his warrant card at the PC manning the cordon and dipped under the tape. He walked down towards the forensic tent, which had been set up on the pavement ahead of the tunnel's entrance. The forensics operation was only just in the process of beginning. Ahead, he could see the familiar silhouette of DC Sami Dattani talking to the forensic patholo-gist. Another member of his team at Cedar House, even Sami's usual boyish demeanour seemed to have altered in the past few months. An easy-going enthusiasm replaced by something quieter and more brooding. The DC looked around, saw Finn approaching and came over to join him.

'Rigor mortis hasn't set in yet, so it looks like the time of death would have been within the last six hours or so,' he said.

Finn checked his watch. It was only just past eight in the morning.

'Likely cause of death?' he asked.

'You better come and see for yourself,' replied Dattani. Finn went over to a crate by the cordon's entrance and helped himself to the necessary forensic apparel and slipped into it. He followed the DC over to the tent's entrance and peered inside. A Black female who looked to be in her early thirties was lying on the ground face up. Blood had pooled around her head and there was a cut on her face. She seemed to be staring back up at them with an almost glassy disappointment.

'Pathologist thinks there might have been a fight of some sort. There appears to be two sets of footprints in places – it could be a mugging gone wrong in these conditions. A high chance there was a struggle – she slipped and smashed her head on the pavement, though obviously, we'll have to wait for the post-mortem to firm that up,' said Dattani.

'Was anything taken?' asked Finn but Dattani shook his head.

'The attacker might have been too freaked out when he saw her head smash open.'

'Maybe.'

'Uniform found her driving licence in her pocket, which they identified her with,' added Dattani, slightly hesitantly. 'They said that you knew this woman, guv – when they called to inform you?'

'Yes,' Finn replied quietly. 'Her name was Jemma Vickers.' He almost added something else but then stopped, his gaze not shifting from the body.

7

Dattani looked at him uncertainly as if waiting for more.

'She was somebody I let down once, Sami.' He faltered. 'Someone *else* I let down. If the DCI asks, tell him I'll be with Lee Ellis. He'll know who he is and why I've gone to see him.'

Without waiting for a reply, he turned on his heels and walked back to his car.

Ten minutes later Finn pulled up in a small street in the hinterland between Croydon and South Norwood. It was mainly a strip of 1930s terraced houses with a newsagent and a pub at one end and, midway down, where Finn was parking up, a small cafe. As he shut the car door behind him, he briefly surveyed the place – it wasn't your classic greasy spoon.

Written across the frontage in large navy-blue lettering was the word *Randelli's*. Money had clearly been spent and although not exactly spacious it looked clean and pleasant inside. The windows were partially steamed up and he could see a handful of punters enjoying their breakfasts. As he entered, he was hit by the smell of fried bacon and good coffee, and he felt his stomach rumble. In the background, a radio was loudly blasting out Magic FM. The place looked like it had recently been redecorated, all brilliant white brickwork with framed pictures of what looked like the Inter Milan football team on the walls.

Behind the counter was a muscly, olive-skinned man in his twenties with slick black hair. He greeted Finn with a cheery smile.

'Yes chief – what can I get you?' he said.

Finn produced his warrant card and introduced himself.

'I'm here to see Lee Ellis,' he said, and the man's face darkened. 'It's alright, he's not in any trouble. Tell him it's Alex Finn – he knows who I am.'

The man looked at Finn curiously, then turned and opened a small door that led into the cafe's kitchen area.

'Lee, there's some copper here to see you. Says he knows you,' he shouted. Finn looked around – the rest of the clientele didn't seem bothered, and the steady chink of cutlery on china continued unabated.

After a moment, a man Finn hadn't seen for a long while slowly emerged. He was wearing a white T-shirt and jeans covered by a chef's apron and had a fully shaven scalp that gave him an almost skeletal appearance. Sharp cobalt blue eyes locked on to Finn straight away but there was no warmth in them. There seemed to be even more tattoos than he remembered from their last encounter. Intricate blue-green designs laced both arms and there was something that resembled a Japanese dragon around his throat. But the marking Finn remembered the most – the spiral of psychedelic colour that grew out of his neck and across one side of his face – was as startling as ever.

'What are you doing here?' he said tonelessly.

Finn braced himself and looked at him levelly.

'I'm sorry, Lee – it's about Jemma . . .' Those laser blue eyes immediately flared at the name. 'I'm afraid she's dead – we found her body earlier this morning.'

Lee stood motionless as he received the news.

'How?' he rasped.

'We don't know yet. We're still investigating the circumstances. Maybe a robbery that went wrong – there were signs of a second person there . . .'

The younger man's breathing had become shallow, the pain starting to spread out across his face.

'I'm so sorry,' said Finn gently.

Lee didn't reply but slowly one hand moved as if to scratch the small of his back. When he brought it back around Finn saw a gun was being pointed at him – now it was his turn to be shocked.

'What the fuck . . .' said the man behind the counter, reacting first.

'*EVERYBODY OUT – NOW!*'screamed Lee suddenly. The rest of the cafe stopped and looked at him, not entirely sure whether this was for real or not. Lee waved the gun at them, his eyes blazing. '*I SAID OUT,*' he yelled again.

Now they understood. Two workmen in orange high-vis jackets didn't need asking a third time and ran for the door. A pensioner who'd been studying the racing tips in the paper scuttled after them. Only a well-built man in painter's overalls didn't seem fazed by what was happening. He rose to his feet slowly and took a step forward.

'Don't be a mug, mate,' he said in a low voice.

'Just do as he says,' said Finn urgently, recognising a have-a-go hero the situation didn't need. The man in overalls ignored him and kept his eyes on Lee instead.

'You're not going to shoot me – you ain't got the balls. So put that thing down and don't be a dick.'

Lee instantly fired the weapon, and the deafening sound of the shot whip-cracked around the room. For a moment the only noise was George Michael singing 'Wake me up before you go-go' on the radio, then the man fell to the floor and began howling in agony.

'Marco – turn that fucking thing off,' said Lee and his terrified colleague ran over and killed the sound. Lee turned to Finn. 'It's the same guy isn't it – the one who took us before? He's killed Jemma.'

Finn tried to find the words, still shocked at what was unfolding in front of him. 'Lee . . .' he began but the other man cut him off.

'This is your fault. This is on *you.*'

He raised the gun and pointed it at Finn's head.

I

'Can I get you anything else?' said the waitress with a casual smile.

Detective Sergeant Mattie Paulsen glared up at her.

'I asked for a soya latte.' She prodded a large mug of coffee with her finger. 'This has dairy milk in it,' she said as if the drink itself had just murdered someone. If the waitress was bothered, she didn't show it.

'So sorry – I'll sort that out for you,' she said pleasantly, removing the offending cup. Paulsen watched her leave with a sour glare. In her early thirties, she was tall, gangly with a shiny black bob of hair and spoke with a mild Scandinavian lilt to her accent. Though raised in London, her dad was Swedish, and her mum was Jamaican. And it was her father who was the reason she was eating in this rather expensive Islington coffee shop.

Sitting beside her was a warm-faced woman, also in her early thirties, with long blonde tresses. Nancy Deen was Paulsen's long-suffering girlfriend. With them was Paulsen's older brother, Jonas. A teacher in east London, he shared her dark good looks and possessed the same hint of an accent. He'd been the one who'd convened this particular pre-work breakfast meeting.

The siblings' father, Christer Paulsen, had been diagnosed with Alzheimer's some years before.

He'd surprised them all by defying the condition relatively successfully since then, but their luck – as they knew it eventually would – seemed to have run out. In recent months, his condition had begun to decline sharply. The memory loss had become more pronounced, the confusion greater, and most worrying of all there'd been spells of unexpected aggression. A collective decision had been taken with their mother to finally put him into a care home. With a week to go the reality of that was now beginning to dawn on all of them.

'It's the right thing to do, Mattie,' said Jonas. 'There's no point getting cold feet now. We all agreed on it.'

'I know – I'm just starting to think that perhaps we're being a bit premature. He'll be so lonely – he'll hate it and the idea of that *really* upsets me,' said Paulsen, unable to keep the slight catch from her voice.

'Look . . . it's done now. If it doesn't work out, you can reassess things later,' said Nancy diplomatically. 'You decided this needed to happen as a family – you can always change your minds as a family if it comes to it.'

The pair nodded glumly.

'I suppose,' said Paulsen without much conviction.

'So what else is new?' said Jonas.

'We've booked a holiday,' said Nancy, glad to change the subject. 'St Lucia!'

'The Caribbean?' said Jonas unable to contain his reaction. 'How did you afford that?'

'We haven't been anywhere for ages, so we've been saving for a big one. It'll be good to get some sunshine,' said Paulsen.

Jonas sipped at his coffee as he thought about it.

'How long have you two been together now?' he said.

'Longer than you've managed with anyone,' retorted his sister and he smiled. Jonas was a famous commitment-phobe and well used to the jibe.

'I'm sure a wedding would make Mum very happy,' he said. 'Particularly now – she could use a lift.'

Paulsen gave him a filthy look.

'Don't make me throw something at you – not in public.'

Nancy looked across sharply at her partner, unimpressed.

'What?' said Paulsen innocently.

Jonas grinned and finished off his drink.

'I think my work here is done,' he said then checked his watch. 'I better get going. Let's . . .' he threw his hands in the air impotently '. . . *keep talking* about Dad. I'll give Mum a call tonight and see how she's doing.' He stood, grabbed his coat off the back of his chair and pulled out a pair of smart leather gloves from one of the pockets. 'Take care of yourselves, eh? And seriously I'm glad you're getting away. You both deserve it.'

His sister rose and hugged him, and he gave Nancy a quick wave before heading for the door. As he left, the waitress returned with the replacement cup of coffee. She laid it down in front of Paulsen and gathered up Jonas's empty plate and cup. Paulsen pointedly waited in silence for her to leave.

'Don't start,' she said before Nancy could speak.

'Don't be daft. I wasn't really offended, but he has a point – maybe we should start thinking about the future and where we're going? We haven't had a chance to talk properly for a long time.'

Paulsen looked across at her.

'Sorry, Nance – I know I haven't been brilliant company recently.'

Nancy nodded sympathetically.

'It's understandable – after everything that happened.'

Jackie Ojo's death had hit Paulsen particularly hard. They'd been friends, but the older officer had also been something of an unofficial mentor. As two women of colour within the Met, Ojo had helped her navigate her way through an organisation that frequently fielded accusations of both racism and sexism. There was a debt there that could now never be repaid.

Paulsen had been exploring some options for a potential promotion to another station when the vacancy tragically opened at Cedar House. Her elevation to detective sergeant had been supported by Finn and felt like a natural progression. But several months on, the reality was that she hadn't found replacing Ojo easy.

There'd been an unspoken resentment from some of the old dinosaurs that still roamed the station – a sense that she'd stepped just a bit too quickly into a dead colleague's shoes. She hadn't quite found the right balance between curbing her own naturally spiky personality and the necessary people skills either. She was aware there was still a lot of work to do to convince the doubters that she was fit to replace their much-missed friend. Most of all she hadn't quite convinced herself yet.

Nancy knew all of this, of course, and was doing everything she could to support her. But as ever with Mattie Paulsen – others could only help as much as she let them. The holiday had been Nancy's suggestion and she'd been cheered by the level of enthusiasm with which the idea had been taken. But right now, St Lucia felt a long way off. The snow was falling again outside and there was a long line of non-moving traffic stuck on Upper Street.

'I don't want to go to work today,' said Paulsen quietly, almost surprising herself with the words. Nancy reached out a hand and wrapped it around hers. As if on cue, Paulsen's phone vibrated on the table. She looked down at the incoming message and her face fell even further.

'What is it?' asked Nancy.

Paulsen shrugged.

'The usual. Someone, somewhere's had a really bad morning.'

Just after nine, Paulsen arrived at Cedar House. She made her way up to the incident room and ten minutes later found herself summoned to a meeting. DCI John Skegman was a thin, wiry man in his early fifties who looked more like a fussy post office clerk than a senior police detective. Like most bosses, he wasn't particularly popular. His demeanour, quiet and aloof from the rank and file, didn't help. But Paulsen had found a new respect for him in the months since Ojo's death.

It wasn't just her murder at the hands of an organised crime gang that he'd had to contend with. Simultaneously, another officer in his team had confessed to working for the OCG who'd killed her. The two things combined had given Cedar House an unenviable reputation inside and outside of the police service. But far from being destroyed by those events, Skegman seemed to have been revitalised by them. In his own way, Paulsen felt he'd shown real leadership. He'd protected them all as best he could and, as a station, they'd battened down the hatches and got on with it. In the past, she hadn't always felt he'd fully trusted her, but he'd backed her promotion without hesitation, and she'd appreciated that too.

As she entered his office, she unexpectedly found him chatting to an attractive young Black woman wearing a bright purple top. The visitor beamed a large smile in her direction that Paulsen didn't return.

'Mattie – thanks for popping up,' said Skegman and she tried – and failed – to recall the last time she'd heard him use the phrase *'popping up'*. 'This is DC Vanessa Nash – she's the new full-time replacement for . . .' he smiled awkwardly '. . . you.'

That made sense. Her position had been covered by a series of attachments over the last few months and a full-time appointment was overdue. She nodded and shook hands with the newcomer, still not feeling a great desire to return the enthusiastic smile that continued to blaze across Nash's face.

'It's honestly brilliant to be here,' gushed the young woman. 'Sorry about the top – it's probably a bit much for day one, isn't it? I was in uniform before so it's my first day in plain clothes and I haven't had time to sort my wardrobe out.'

The words came tumbling out at about ninety miles an hour with a strong London accent. While others might have found that engaging, Paulsen felt like she was talking to a schoolchild. She could also feel herself getting irritated, aware simultaneously that she was being completely unfair. Breakfast with Jonas, nice as it had been, had also been a reminder of what was happening at home with her father.

'Doesn't matter what you wear – it's what you do that's important,' she replied briskly.

Nash found yet another big smile by way of response.

'Couldn't agree more, sarge.'

Paulsen forced herself from correcting her to 'Detective Sergeant'.

'I know you'll make Vanessa feel very welcome,' said Skegman with a pointed smile of his own. Her coolish demeanour clearly hadn't been lost on him.

'So what's this job that's come in, boss?' said Paulsen, changing the subject.

He turned soberly to Nash.

'Why don't you grab a coffee and make your way down to the incident room? DS Paulsen will join you shortly and introduce you to the rest of the team.'

Nash smiled again.

'Thank you so much, sir – both of you. I can't wait to get cracking,' she said, then nodded pleasantly at them both and left.

Skegman waited for the door to shut behind her.

'Jesus, Mattie – can't you make *some* effort? You were new here once, remember? With far less of a smile on your face as I recall.'

Paulsen shrugged.

'Don't know what you mean – but she seems very nice. Where's she come from?'

'Carberry Road. She was a PC there and I've only heard good things about her. A little bit green maybe, but nothing some hands-on experience won't cure.'

Paulsen nodded, mild guilt beginning to set in – remembering how good Ojo had been with her during her first few weeks at Cedar House.

'So where's the DI?' she asked.

Skegman walked back behind his desk and sat down looking troubled.

'He's . . .' He paused. 'I was about to say with the "next of kin" but that's not quite accurate. He's with someone closely connected to the body we found in Tooting earlier.'

Paulsen took a seat opposite Skegman.

'What's the story?'

Skegman picked up some papers off his desk and glanced over them.

'The victim's name is Jemma Vickers. Fifteen years ago, she was kidnapped with her boyfriend at the time, Lee Ellis, in South Croydon. They were both eighteen and it came just a few days after the abduction of another teenager, Oliver Littlewood, from the same area. It was way before my time, but Alex was here as a DS and worked the investigation. They managed to find and rescue Lee and Jemma, but they were too late to save Oliver.'

'Who took them?' asked Paulsen.

'The perpetrator escaped arrest at the time.' Skegman sifted through the papers again and found another document. 'But seven years later, a man called Dennis Trant – who was serving a sentence at Belmarsh for possession of child pornography – confessed to it.'

Paulsen digested the information for a moment.

'So do we think what happened to Vickers this morning was connected with her abduction fifteen years ago?'

Skegman shrugged.

'At this stage, your guess is as good as mine. But Alex once told me about these kids. It affected him deeply – it was a troubled investigation, I think. I know he stayed in touch with Vickers and Ellis over the years – and that's where he is now – with Lee Ellis.'

'Well, you know the DI, boss. He doesn't take much encouragement to blame himself for stuff,' said Paulsen. There was an awkward silence as she realised what she'd said. No one at Cedar House blamed Finn for Ojo's death but they all knew he felt a personal responsibility for it. 'I didn't mean it like that,' she corrected quickly and Skegman nodded.

'I know. And you're right – he does.'

'So what do you want me to do?'

'Just be aware that this is going to be a difficult one for him – he's got a personal stake in it. You've got a new officer on the team as well and that's going to make things even trickier. Look out for her and keep an eye on your DI.'

Paulsen nodded understandingly, appreciating the trust he was putting in her. It was the sort of thing he would have asked Ojo to do once and a sign of how far their relationship had progressed.

'Of course.'

They were interrupted by a knock at the door. A uniformed PC didn't wait to be invited in.

'Sorry to interrupt, sir, but we've got a hostage situation unfolding in South Norwood. Someone's been shot in a cafe. The guy who called it in said a police officer who matches DI Finn's description was inside when it happened.'

Skegman and Paulsen immediately exchanged a look as the words sank in.

'So much for looking out for the DI . . .' said Paulsen.

2

Lee had deliberately pointed down and shot at the foot of the man in the overalls. At gunpoint, Finn and Marco – the cafe's owner, Finn guessed – had then been made to carry him outside and dump him unceremoniously in the snow. A few yards away he could see one of the men in high-vis jackets who'd been eating their breakfasts only moments before, already on his phone. The shot man was still conscious, and Finn could only hope that help would arrive quickly. Once they were back inside Lee handcuffed Finn to a radiator with his own cuffs. Marco was forced to sit down next to him, and Lee bound his hands and legs together using some industrial plastic ties from the kitchen.

Once he'd got them restrained, Lee bolted the front door shut and began closing the blinds.

As he watched, Marco's shock turned to fury.

'What's this about – what the fuck are you doing?'

Lee ignored him for a few seconds while he checked the cafe was now secure then turned to face them.

'What I should have done years ago.'

His voice was calm and as he crossed the room, he left bloodied footprints on the grey laminate floor. He delved into Marco's pocket, retrieved his phone and then took Finn's together with his smartwatch. He switched them all off and put them behind the counter together with the key to Finn's handcuffs like a haul of confiscated sweets.

'Haven't you got anything to say for yourself? You're a policeman for Christ's sake,' hissed Marco at Finn.

'You need to calm down,' said Finn.

'Are you talking to me or him?' replied Marco.

'You.'

Lee was watching the exchange with little discernible emotion. Finn looked again at the gun in his hand. It was a Beretta 9000 pistol, self-loading, chambered for 9-millimetre bullets and designed to be lethal. It was a weapon favoured by many of London's criminal gangs and Finn was well aware of the damage it could do. Lee may deliberately have shot the man in the overalls to injure, not kill – but whether he'd ever walk properly again was another question. Now wasn't the moment to speculate when, where or why Lee had acquired the weapon, though.

'What are you trying to achieve here?' said Finn carefully. His professional instincts were kicking in – he knew he needed to try and stay calm, but that was easier said than done. He was also suddenly feeling extremely nauseous – almost certainly a by-product of the adrenaline coursing through his system.

Lee took a seat at one of the cafe's tables – it was clearly the first opportunity he'd had to actually think about that question himself since he'd pulled the gun on Finn.

'What am I trying to achieve? Closure, I suppose,' he said after a moment.

Finn tried again to compose himself. The radiator he was bound to was scalding hot and he had to stretch forwards to avoid burning his back on it. The heat wasn't helping with the nausea either. He looked up and met Lee's gaze.

'Jemma could have been killed for any number of reasons. If she *was* even murdered – and it's way too early to say if it had anything to do with what happened fifteen years ago—'

Lee crashed his free hand down on the table, sending a salt shaker flying.

'I'll tell you what I want – the investigation into our abductions reopened.'

'Your *what*?' said Marco, confused.

Lee smiled humourlessly.

'Shut up, Marco. Don't try and think – you'll break something.'

Marco strained at the plastic ties around his wrists impotently.

'I wouldn't,' said Lee, gesturing with the gun and Marco stopped.

'Why don't you let him go,' said Finn. 'You don't need him – this is between you and me.'

He knew this man; knew he wasn't genuinely violent by nature. Despite everything, he felt confident he could get through to him and end this quickly.

'No, he stays. Your friends – when they come – might be a little less eager if they know there's a member of the public in here too.'

'That's not how these situations work,' said Finn.

'I thought we were mates, Lee,' said Marco, as if he'd only just realised the danger they were in. 'I've always treated you okay – we have a laugh here, don't we? What's all this about?'

Lee stared at him with contempt.

'I barely know you – you only hired me because you needed a cheap chef. I've been here for seven months – that doesn't make us mates.'

He stopped – outside they could hear sirens now.

'There's no investigation to reopen,' said Finn.

Lee shook his head. The noise outside was building into a cacophony. He put the gun down on the table, reached into his pocket and pulled out a small wrap and then placed it next to the firearm. He carefully opened it and with a teaspoon formed a line of fine white powder on the table. He leant forwards and snorted it up, before raising his head like a lion about to roar.

'There's blood on your hands,' he said to Finn before wiping his nose clean with his fingers. 'So I'd get comfortable if I were you – because no one's leaving here until I finally get some answers.'

The police operation outside didn't take long to swing into action. The road was immediately cordoned off at both ends and a team of a dozen armed officers swiftly arrived on the scene following the report of a discharged firearm. The marksmen took up positions covering the front, rear and sides of the cafe, while others moved into vantage points high up on the buildings opposite.

The pub at the end of the street – The Greyhound – was commandeered as the designated rendezvous point or RVP. By the time the man overseeing the operation, DCI Vincent Walsh, arrived, the early morning snow flurries had finally stopped, and the ominous grey skies were slowly beginning to lighten. The bitter freezing wind hadn't let up though and Walsh could feel it cutting through his protective layers for fun. In his mid-fifties with a thick grey beard, he greeted the men setting up outside the cafe with a gentle Ulster accent.

He sized up the front of the building, which was at the centre of everyone's attention. The white blinds were down, and it would have looked unremarkable if not for the blood-spattered patches of snow where the shot man had been left. He'd been helped clear of the immediate vicinity before the emergency services arrived and there was a visible scarlet trail that followed his escape route up the pavement.

There were also several dog handlers on the scene together with a uniformed response team. A unit from the Territorial Support Group was on standby and Walsh could see two ambulances parked up opposite the pub in readiness for any eventuality. In the sky, a police drone was gently circling the area. Walsh stood in the centre of the road and slowly turned a full 360 degrees to make sure everything was as it should be.

After checking in with the tactical commander of the firearms unit, he made his way to the RVP at the pub and swung the door open.

'Jesus wept,' he muttered as he entered, thinking twice about taking his coat off. It seemed even colder inside than it was outside. The saloon was in the process of being converted into an operations centre. The bar's normal tables and chairs had been stacked at the side while uniformed and plain-clothed officers were bringing in a steady stream of equipment.

'That's the price of energy bills for you,' said a warm crystal-cut voice behind him. He turned to see a smartly dressed woman in her mid-thirties smiling pleasantly at him.

'DCI Walsh? I'm Acting DI Rachel Howe,' she said. 'The negotiator coordinator.'

'Energy bills?' he replied, shaking her outstretched hand.

'The pub landlord's been pretty cooperative, but he doesn't want us landing him with a huge gas bill if this goes on for a bit.'

Walsh rolled his eyes.

'Heaven forfend. So what do we know? Have we firmed up if there's one of ours in there yet?'

Howe nodded.

'Yes – a DI Finn from Cedar House's MIT. He'd picked up a job in Tooting earlier this morning and came here to meet with someone connected to the victim – the cafe's chef, Lee Ellis. Some of the punters heard him introduce himself to the place's owner ...' She checked her pocketbook. 'Marco Randelli – who we believe is still in there too.'

Walsh commandeered a desk and perched on it with a sigh.

'Two confirmed hostages then. Do we know if there are potentially any more?'

Howe shook her head.

'Not for certain.'

'What about the guy who was shot?'

'He's probably lost a toe according to the paramedics.'

Walsh pulled a face.

'Nasty. What about the media?'

'No sign yet – but stuff's beginning to appear on social media, so I'm guessing it won't be long. The officers manning the cordon are keeping an eye. From what the witnesses who were in there have told us the hostage taker was almost certainly Ellis. They all say he was armed with a single hand-gun – possibly a Beretta 9000 from the descriptions.'

'And do we have any idea what this is about yet?' asked Walsh.

Howe nodded.

'Maybe. Cedar House has fed me some background on Ellis.' She explained to him about Lee and Jemma's abduction fifteen years before and Finn's role in the investigation back then. Walsh absorbed the information for a moment.

'So was the death in Tooting this morning a firearms incident?' he asked, and Rachel shook her head.

'No. She'd cracked her head open on the ice and Cedar House are still trying to establish what happened.'

'So this could be a reaction. Finn goes to break the news to Ellis – he takes it very badly and starts blasting people's toes off. Though why a chef making bacon sarnies in a greasy spoon is also carrying a gun is another question. Have we made contact with him yet?'

'No. I was waiting for you to arrive first. It never hurts to give these situations a little breathing space either.'

Walsh clapped his hands together.

'Well, this sounds like a right old heap of messy bollocks.' He produced a toothy smile. 'I don't suppose the landlord of this fine establishment would allow us to turn his coffee machine on?'

Inside the cafe, Marco was pleading with Lee now, as Finn sat motionless, straining to stop his back from falling against the boiling radiator.

'You've got to let me go – please,' said Marco, holding up his bound hands.

'Bloody hell. Didn't think you'd be begging this quickly,' said Lee with an amused smile. He was still sitting opposite them at one of the cafe's tables, the gun resting idly in one hand.

'I'm not,' said Marco with genuine anger. 'My mum's got a hospital appointment later this morning – you *know* that. How could you do this to me today?'

'She can still make that without you,' said Lee, unmoved.

'I was going to drive her.'

'So she can call an Uber. Just relax – you're not going anywhere.'

Marco gave a cry of frustration and slumped backwards.

Lee turned his attention to Finn. 'So what's going on out there – it's all gone a bit quiet, hasn't it?'

Finn considered his answer. He saw no reason to deceive Lee; in fact, quite the opposite. Having an idea of the police operation underway might just focus his mind.

'There'll be about a dozen marksmen in place now, covering every side of this building. Somewhere close – possibly the newsagent or the pub I saw up the road – will have been

26

commandeered as a base of operations. And you can expect a call from a hostage negotiator soon.'

Lee nodded quickly, his eyes blazing, which Finn suspected was the coke making itself felt.

'All good,' he said. 'Excellent in fact – because that's all I want, to talk to someone.'

Finn pursed his lips. It wasn't the answer he'd been looking for.

'Lee – I honestly don't know what you're trying to do. If Jemma was murdered – it *can't* have been the same person who abducted you in 2009. Dennis Trant is dead. He died of cancer in Belmarsh prison six years ago.'

'And as I've told you before – I don't believe Trant did it.'

Finn could hear how tightly wound the man was, though again that was probably chemically enhanced now. He looked across the room. There was a framed picture of the Duomo in Milan on the wall opposite – huge and magnificent in bright sunshine against a cloudless blue sky. He centred himself on it for a second before trying again.

'It *has* to have been Trant. I interviewed him myself. Not only did he admit to it, but he knew things only the abductor *could* have known. Precise details of the room you were kept in, the van used to move you. The wounds you—'

'Shut up,' interrupted Lee in a dangerously low voice.

'You'll also remember that he was in there for possession of child porn,' continued Finn.

'I said shut up,' shouted Lee, standing now. 'You bought his bullshit story far too easily. You *wanted* it to be him. To make *you* feel better – because you fucked up that day.'

Finn's head fell. He wasn't sure Lee was right about Trant, but nor could he be certain that there wasn't some truth to that accusation either.

'You've never told me *why* you don't believe it was him,' he responded.

Lee looked across as if he were dealing with an idiot.

'A whole bunch of reasons. He lived in Shoreditch – why did he randomly pick on one tiny, very specific corner of south London to kidnap three teenagers? And physically he wasn't right. Trant looked stocky in the pictures; the bloke that took us . . .' He faltered.

'Was what?' said Finn. Lee began to look scared as he took himself back. 'That's the problem with the memory – particularly with traumatic events. It's *unreliable*,' continued Finn.

With a sudden roar, Lee grabbed a plate, still with the remnants of an unfinished fry-up on it and hurled it against the nearest wall, smearing the white brickwork with grease and ketchup.

'No, you don't,' he said furiously. He strode up to Finn and pushed the gun sharply up against his forehead. 'You let him go that day – and he's still out there. He's *always* been out there.'

Finn could feel the cold edge of the metal pushing hard against his skin. Far more terrifyingly he could now see the rage and torment in Lee's bloodshot eyes.

'You need to listen to me – I was a different man back then,' Finn said.

Lee snorted with derision.

'Yeah, we're all different people now – aren't we?'

3

'I want to speak to your DI,' said the angry woman standing in front of Detective Sergeant Alex Finn. He looked over her shoulder down the length of one of Cedar House's grey corridors and tried to keep his cool. That wasn't easy in the current heatwave – the bowels of the building felt more like the bottom shelf of an oven – and he could feel the sweat patches under his shirt clinging to his armpits.

'He's busy,' he said, not making much of an effort to hide the gritted teeth he was speaking through.

'I don't care. You kept me waiting for two hours before I could see my client—'

'Yes, I did. It's called due process,' interrupted Finn quickly, deliberately matching her tone exactly. She shot him a look of undiluted vitriol.

'And then when we began, the way you conducted the interview was frankly disrespectful and borderline unprofessional.'

She was trouble, this duty solicitor, Finn thought. In her mid-thirties with short brown hair and an attractive face, she was somebody he always felt he *should* get on with and yet, never quite did. She looked the sort of person who was probably very popular away from the job, with an active social life and a wide circle of friends. The semi-anglicised German

29

accent completed the ensemble and made her sound slightly frostier than he suspected she actually was. She seemed to really have a problem with him too – that was something else he'd picked up on. He wasn't sure why. They hadn't got off on a good footing when she'd first started several weeks before and things had descended from there.

He smiled disingenuously back at her.

'I would point out that you were constantly interrupting during the interview, asking your own questions, and answering on your client's behalf—'

'I was trying to get the damn thing back on track,' she bellowed, cutting him short.

Down the corridor, Finn saw two uniformed constables turn to look at what the commotion was. He wiped a bead of sweat off his upper lip and felt a desperate urge to get out of this sweltering corridor and find some cold water to drink.

'DI Culley's in a meeting,' he lied. 'But I'll be happy to relay your concerns to him. When I get a moment.'

Karin Bergmann held up her hands in surrender. She'd clearly had enough of this too.

'Whatever. I'll catch him later and be assured a conversation *will* be had.'

She turned to leave, took a step then turned back, the irritation visible on her face.

'You know the problem with you, DS Finn? You're so far up your arse you could probably have a conversation with your own kidneys.'

The insult took Finn by surprise, and he had to fight against the slight smile he could feel developing at the absurd image she'd just conjured. For a brief moment, he thought he could see one forming on Karin's face too, but her expression hardened into one final glare of contempt before she marched away. He watched as her footsteps tip-tapped on the hard corridor floor in sync with her fury.

'That sounded fun,' said an amused voice behind him.

'Don't think I didn't notice you make a run for it as soon as the interview finished,' said Finn before looking round at the man who'd joined him. DC Jack Barton was in his late forties with lined, craggy features and greying brown hair. He was holding a paper cup of water and took a sip from it with a twinkle in his eye.

'Toilet break,' he said innocently.

'Yeah, right,' replied Finn belligerently. 'Coward.'

Barton's grin widened.

'You're the DS; I'm just a humble detective constable. You earn the extra bucks – so dealing with stroppy solicitors is your privilege.'

Finn rolled his eyes.

'Can we please get out of this sodding corridor before I melt?' he said.

Barton turned serious.

'We need to go upstairs anyway. I've just been collared by the boss – there's shit going down.'

DI Chris Culley was a man defined by his rank, Finn always felt. For some people policing was a job – for others, like Culley, it seemed to go far deeper. He often thought you couldn't even ask him if he wanted a cup of tea without his brain trying to process how, he – a detective inspector – should respond to such an offer from one of the lower orders. In his late thirties with red, piggy eyes, he was relatively small in stature with a band of neatly trimmed blond hair surrounding a bald egg-shaped head. His relentlessly humourless disposition made him hard work as far as Finn was concerned – it was like answering to a permanently irritable robot. As he and Barton entered the incident room, Culley greeted them like a pair of errant schoolboys.

31

'Where've you been skulking, Alex? I've been trying to get hold of you – two teenagers have just been taken in broad daylight. They're the same age and from the same area as Oliver Littlewood.'

Finn immediately began to realise the gravity of the situation. Oliver was eighteen and had gone missing three days earlier after a night out with friends. There'd been no witnesses and despite exhaustive efforts no clues had been found as to his whereabouts. The early assessments that he was recovering from a hangover or with someone he'd hooked up with were already being revised. To all intents and purposes, he'd disappeared into thin air. These new abductions – if they were linked to his – reframed everything.

'I was in Interview Room One – talking to the suspect in the McEvoy inquiry—' said Finn, responding to Culley's volley.

The DI held up an open palm.

'That can wait – this is the priority now. I'm about to head down to South Croydon – I want you two with me to liaise with the search teams and talk to the families.'

'Sir,' replied Finn curtly. Out of Culley's line of sight, he saw Barton make a smacked-hand gesture. Finn shot him a murderous look and made for the door.

'You're on the naughty step now,' muttered the DC under his breath as he caught up.

'You can drive,' said Finn, not bothering to hold the door for him.

By the time they arrived in the small patch of suburbia where Lee Ellis and Jemma Vickers had been taken it wasn't just police officers who were out on the streets looking. The time was now approaching half past five in the afternoon and the sun was still blazing down. It seemed like most of the local residents were out on the streets in force helping with the search. From a distance, Finn thought you might be forgiven for thinking you were looking at some sort of summer street party or fete.

It was only when you saw the expressions on their faces more closely that you could appreciate the gravity of what was happening. Some were gathered in clusters talking amongst themselves, others were taking direction from the shirt-sleeved officers also out in numbers. The worst part of it was that Finn had seen all this before just days earlier when Oliver Littlewood went missing. Now there were two more sets of parents in the same predicament and a community petrified by the implications. He noticed a lot of unhappy-looking children out with the adults. Nobody's kids were being left at home alone right now.

As he and Barton left their car, a red-faced, sweat-soaked PC hurried over to join them and brought them up to speed with what they knew – which wasn't a great deal. There were two witnesses. The schoolfriend of the abducted teenagers and a young woman who'd come to his aid just as the incident was ending.

'And where is this lad – Billy – now?' asked Barton.

'He was taken to hospital with his parents as a precaution – sounds like he got a face full of pepper spray. The doctors are giving him the once-over. There's an officer with them who took the initial account of what happened, but I'm told the kid's pretty shaken up,' said the PC.

'And the other witness?'

'A woman who was on her way back home from work – she saw the van leave but that was about it.'

Finn nodded.

'Her presence might just explain why they didn't take Billy too. We'll need to talk to him properly just as soon as he's capable. What about the parents of the other two kids – where are they?' he said.

The PC turned and pointed at a middle-aged man with black hair in the middle distance who was standing with another officer and a huddle of concerned onlookers. The distraught expression on his face told Finn all he needed to know.

'That's Terry Ellis – Lee Ellis's father,' said the constable.

'And the mother?' said Finn.

'At home. We've got people with her. But she's . . . not good.'

'And Jemma Vickers – where are her parents?' said Barton.

'In Venice – they were having a romantic getaway. They're trying to get a flight home now obviously.'

Finn pulled a face.

'Messy. What else do we know?'

'Both kids go to the same school – and are in a relationship, apparently.'

'Which school?'

The PC checked his notebook. 'Thomas Downey Secondary School – it's just a couple of miles from here.'

'I know it – so not the same school as Oliver,' noted Finn, looking around properly for the first time. 'Do Jemma and Lee live close to each other?' he said and the PC nodded.

'The Ellises live in that crescent over there.' He pointed at a neat semicircle of new builds on the other side of the road. 'Jemma Vickers lives just a couple of streets away – in Trenholm Road.'

Finn digested this.

'And Oliver lives only around another half mile north from there,' he observed, then thanked the PC who promptly left to re-join the search operation.

'So what do you reckon?' said Barton.

'There's a few things bothering me already,' replied Finn. 'Paedophiles don't tend to want to draw attention to themselves. Abducting three schoolkids in one week from the same neck of the woods doesn't exactly achieve that, does it?'

Barton looked unsure.

'Paedophiles? They're teenagers – virtually adults.'

'They're young enough, Jack. For some – but I agree, if that was the motive these aren't obvious targets,' said Finn.

Barton nodded and thought about it for a moment.

'Maybe he was being opportunistic? He's driving along, sees these three alone and can't resist, for whatever reason.'

'True – but *three* of them together? Hardly easy and one of them got away. If we're lucky this kid, Billy, might even have got a partial plate number off the van. It doesn't make sense to me.' He shrugged. 'And above all, if it's not about sex – then *why* were they taken?'

Barton was about to respond when Finn saw a woman striding towards them. Tall, in her late thirties, in normal circumstances she'd probably cut a striking figure. Instead, she looked wild and wretched. The make-up on her face had run, while her long black hair was tangled and unkempt. Like everyone else, there was a sheen of sweat glistening on her face. Dressed in a stained white T-shirt with jeans and battered trainers she was accompanied by a tear-streaked girl who looked around ten or eleven years old.

'What the fuck are you people doing?' she screamed directly at him as she got closer. 'It's been three days since Ollie was taken and you've let it happen again. What are you *actually doing*?'

The words hung in the humid air for a moment and heads turned across the street to look at them.

'I can imagine how distressing this must be for you,' began Finn. He'd last spoken directly to Sarah Littlewood on the day of her son's disappearance and her anger was understandable. They'd made no progress tracing Oliver, had no idea if he was even still alive.

'You can *imagine*, can you?' she said. She turned to the young girl by her side. 'Did you hear that, Ella? He can *imagine* how distressed we are.'

Now that she was standing in front of him it was more obvious how tired they both were. The girl, Ella, was Oliver's younger sister and looked utterly traumatised. The heat wouldn't have helped either. Nobody was sleeping properly right now, and the last couple of nights must have been hellish for these two. It didn't help that Sarah was having to deal with this on her own, either. She was divorced from her children's father, and he hadn't played any part in their upbringing as far as Finn knew. He wondered how that particular choice was playing out with him right now.

'You're right,' he said, looking at Sarah directly. 'I can't put myself in your shoes. And I don't know if what's happened this afternoon is connected yet, but—'

'Of course it's connected,' Sarah erupted. Suddenly, just as quickly the fury drained out of her, and the tears began to come. 'This is a nightmare. My little boy . . .' Ella also began to cry as if triggered by her mother, and Sarah pulled her close, hugging her tightly.

Finn watched them helplessly, saw Barton glancing at him now too. He knew why – they needed to get a shift on.

'I promise you – I will do everything in my power to find Ollie. And these other two now – whatever it takes,' he said.

Despite his best efforts to inject conviction into what he was saying, there was something missing from his tone and even he could hear it. Far from sounding reassuring, the words sounded strangely empty.

Through her tears, Sarah met his gaze and he felt utterly inadequate. Later he'd remember both his promise, the look in her eyes and her response.

'I'm scared,' she said, 'that your best isn't going to be good enough.'

The inside of the van had felt like a microwave oven. Hot and dark, it smelt of damp clothing and coppery metal. First, their abductor had tied their hands and legs with plastic cord, then when they'd finished spluttering from the effects of the pepper spray, he'd gagged them both. All Lee could hear as they drove on was Jemma's grunting attempts to communicate through the dirty rags that had been stuffed into their mouths. He'd responded the same way. It didn't matter that they couldn't understand anything – just the fact they could hear one another in the pitch-black was a comfort.

The van eventually stopped, and Lee heard the driver's door open, and then slam shut. He'd braced himself for whatever was about to happen. But nothing happened. They simply stayed there in the dark and the melting heat, just about breathing through their noses. It felt like they were there for hours – it was impossible to judge. All Lee could think of was those dogs that were left in the back of cars that ended up dying, roasted alive. Was that what this bloke was trying to do – kill them like a pair of dogs?

After a while, Jemma went quiet and Lee wriggled forwards with his bound feet to try and make contact. He felt his shoe touch something soft but there was no reaction and again he tried to speak through the gag. Briefly, he feared that she was actually dead but eventually there came a sound that might have been whimpering. After that, the appalling temperature became too much, and Lee passed out.

When he woke, he was still tied up, but the gag had been removed. Beautiful, cold water was being poured into his mouth almost tenderly from a plastic bottle, and he lapped at it greedily. It was the man in the mask still. They were out of the vehicle now and Lee looked around, taking in his new surroundings – it looked like a basement or a cellar of some kind. It was gloomy but not the complete blackout of the van, and mercifully cooler too.

He tried to sit up and his head reeled, and it was then he realised just how weak he felt. The man was now letting Jemma drink too. She attempted to speak as the liquid dribbled down her chin.

'What do you want? Why have you—'

But she was cut off as their captor suddenly slapped her hard across the face. The shock of it made Lee jump as well. The man seemed to freeze and then he stepped forward.

'*Shhh,*' he said.

4

Sarah Littlewood stared out of the window and tried to gauge how many inches of snow she could see on the branches of the trees outside. Just shy of her fifty-fourth birthday, her long dark hair was speckled with silver these days. She hugged herself, pulling down the thick roll-neck jumper she was wearing, but she wasn't shivering because of the temperature.

'I should have bought de-icer. I saw the forecast yesterday,' she murmured almost to herself.

'Where do you want to go? I could call you an Uber?' said a concerned voice in reply.

On the sofa behind her was Ella, now in her mid-twenties. Tall and slim, she'd inherited her mother's high cheekbones and good looks. She was gently rocking a sleeping baby who was wearing a bobble hat. As Sarah turned to look at them, the pensive expression on her face gave way to a small smile at the sight of her granddaughter.

'It's okay, I was just thinking aloud. I'll give Terry Ellis a call. I imagine he's probably heard about Jemma now as well.'

A police officer had called a little while earlier to tell them. The news had hit Sarah hard – she wasn't surprised to learn that it had been Alex Finn who'd asked for her to be informed. Some debts lasted forever.

39

'I still can't believe it,' said Ella. 'After everything Jemma's been through.'

Sarah looked down at Kaitlyn, the baby in Ella's arms, and watched her scrunched little face twitch slightly.

'Does she need changing?' she asked.

Ella assessed the child and took a cautious sniff.

'No, she's fine. Just dreaming I think.' She looked up at her mother. 'How are you feeling? You and Jemma were close.'

Sarah realised she wasn't actually sure how she felt; she hadn't really processed the news properly yet. There were so many different emotions, so much from back then that she'd buried over the years that she could feel stirring once again. It wasn't as if they were new feelings – they were always there but she'd got used to keeping them under lock and key.

'I don't know. Very sad, obviously. But I think it's going to take a while to absorb this properly. How about you?'

Ella pursed her lips and carried on rocking Kaitlyn.

'It's so unfair – she was such a kind person.' She shook her head. 'Amazing, really – how she recovered from it all.' Her face turned pensive. 'What about Billy – do you think the police have told him too?'

'I don't know,' said Sarah. 'Do you want to tell him, or . . .?'

Ella sighed.

'Since we split up, he's been so short-tempered with me – even about the most simple things to do with Kaitlyn.'

'It's okay – I can deal with it,' said Sarah interrupting. 'He should know what's happened.'

Ella nodded and looked down, her gaze focused solely now on her daughter.

'Why would anybody want to do this to Jemma?' she said.

Sarah came and sat down on the sofa opposite Ella and picked up the TV remote control. 'I wonder if it's made the news yet.'

She turned on the large widescreen in the corner of the room and flicked through the channels until she found Sky News. They watched for a few minutes as the presenter discussed interest rates with a financial journalist. As he wrapped it up, he suddenly seemed to change course.

'Before we bring you the morning's sports news, we're just receiving word of an unfolding situation in south London. A man's reportedly been shot, and it's thought that at least two people have been taken hostage in a cafe in South Norwood.' He stopped again, apparently receiving more information in his ear. 'And there are unconfirmed reports that one of those being held is a serving Metropolitan police officer. Details are still scarce, but we'll bring you more just as soon as we have it.'

Sarah switched the television off and looked straight over at her daughter, both of them immediately thinking the same thing.

'Oh, Lee . . . what have you done?' she murmured.

At the RVP in the pub, DCI Walsh had settled in. He was sitting at a table with a laptop open and several mobile phones laid out next to it. As it turned out, no one could work out how to operate the coffee machine behind the bar and a DC had been dispatched to get a round of hot drinks from elsewhere. They were being handed out as Rachel came over to join him.

'We've got a mobile number for Lee Ellis now – his father just gave it to us.'

'And how did Mr Ellis take the news about his son?'

'Not well. He was already pretty shell-shocked about Jemma Vickers's death.'

Walsh looked surprised.

'How did he know about that already?'

'DI Finn called him, apparently. Before he left the crime scene in Tooting.'

'Interesting,' said Walsh. 'And did he have any idea why his son might have shot a random builder's toe off or why he's taken two people hostage?'

'Only that Lee was very close to Jemma. He thinks this must be a reaction to what's happened rather than something else. We've sent a car over to pick him up – he might be able to help us. One other thing. Lee's ex-army apparently – it's probably how he procured the firearm, though why he was carrying it today I don't know.'

Walsh pulled a face.

'Jesus – so he'll probably know how to handle it then,' he said. 'When you say *close* to Jemma Vickers . . . the type of close that could turn violent? I mean he may not have shot her but that doesn't mean he's not her killer – we're still a long way from establishing timelines this morning for either of them.'

Rachel shrugged helplessly.

'I think now's the right moment to make contact – find out what he wants.'

'Before you do, and apologies if I'm stating the obvious, but I take it someone's attempted to call DI Finn?'

'Yes,' said Rachel. 'Cedar House has been trying all morning but everything's going straight to voicemail.'

'Okay – then let's give it a go,' he replied.

Rachel nodded and went over to her desk.

'Can we have a bit of hush please,' Walsh bellowed to the rest of the team.

Rachel waited until it was quiet then selected a mobile from her desk. Cross-checking with her pocketbook she dialled a number and put the call on speaker as it began to ring. The answer came almost immediately.

'Lee?' she said pleasantly.

'Who's asking?' came the response. The voice was terse but calm.

'I'm Acting DI Rachel Howe, but you can call me Rachel.'

She kept her tone warm and fluid. There were several agendas already at play. The most important one was to make sure the gun wasn't fired again. There was also the need to gather information and the key to both was to be reassuring. She needed him to feel there was an easy, peaceful route out of this.

'*Acting* DI?' he said.

The truth was Rachel had only recently received her negotiation training as part of the Met's Accelerated Promotion Scheme. She was an experienced officer in her own right but today was her first live active negotiation. With resources thin and time short there hadn't been time to deploy a more seasoned officer, and she guessed the consideration hadn't even been made. If you were ready, you were ready.

'It's just a title. I'm here to see what we can do to sort this out. Can you tell me who else is with you and if anyone requires medical attention?'

Lee confirmed Finn and Marco's presence and that all three of them were, for the moment, okay. Rachel and Walsh looked at one another.

'Can we speak to DI Finn – just to make sure that he's alright?'

'No,' replied Lee tersely. 'I've already told you, he's fine.'

The DCI shrugged – they had little choice but to take him at his word. He motioned at Rachel to continue.

'So what's this all about and how do we bring it to an end?' she said.

'That's easy,' he answered. 'You know that Jemma and I were abducted fifteen years ago?'

'Yes – we've been looking through the files at what happened.'

'Good. Well, I don't believe Dennis Trant was our abductor. I think it was someone else – and I think that person has just murdered Jemma. What I want is the original investigation reopened to find the bastard.'

'I'm sure that what happened back then will form part of the inquiry into Jemma's death,' she began.

'That's not enough,' he interrupted with a crackle of emotion. Walsh gave her a warning look and Rachel nodded in acknowledgement. 'I don't just want it reopened; I want a name. I want to know *who* did this to us – or I swear to God, I'll shoot them both.'

Inside the cafe, Lee threw the phone down on the table, rose to his feet still clutching the gun and began to pace the room. There was a wild look on his face and Finn could see that Marco now understood that the threat to them was very real.

'When was the last time you saw Jemma?' said Finn quietly.

'What's that got to do with anything?' said Lee.

'Because I know how close you two were. You're still in shock about what's happened to her.'

The words seemed to get through and Lee looked down, crestfallen. His expression reminded Finn of the teenager they'd rescued fifteen years ago, the young man he'd kept in touch with over the years. He recognised that vulnerability on his face because he'd seen it before.

'*Will* they reopen the investigation?' said Lee.

'They'll take what you just said to them seriously,' replied Finn, truthfully. 'I know I would in their shoes.'

'And how the fuck do we know that *he* didn't kill this woman?' said Marco.

Lee shook his head slowly and smiled.

Marco turned to Finn. 'I mean *look* at him.'

Finn could understand where he was coming from. The coked-up man standing in front of them had just threatened to kill them, had already shot one person today.

'Because that's the one thing I'm certain *didn't* happen,' he replied.

Lee turned and looked him in the eye, and just for a second the two men seemed to have an understanding.

'Let me get this straight,' said Walsh, running a hand through his mane of silver-grey hair. 'There's a dead fella who confessed to these abductions years ago and your man in there doesn't think he's the guilty party? And if we don't conjure someone out of thin air who does fit the bill then he's going to execute two people. Is there something in there that I've missed?'

Rachel shook her head.

'Given the trauma he's been through and the shock he's in over Jemma Vickers, I think the threat's a very credible one,' she said.

'And what's his problem with Finn? As far as I can see the man's gone out of his way to help this guy over the years. Over and above by the looks of it.'

'I don't think he *does* have a problem with him per se – I think he's just at his wits' end.'

They were interrupted by two newcomers coming through the pub's main door. One was a small, shifty-looking man dwarfed by the hefty overcoat he was wearing. The other, a tall young woman with a black bob who was looking around the pub with an air of indifferent disdain.

'Who the hell are these two?' muttered Walsh to Rachel.

A plain-clothed DC led them through and made the introductions.

'Guv – this is DCI Skegman and DS Paulsen from Cedar House.'

Walsh remembered where he'd heard Skegman's name before and realised he should have put it together earlier. That business with the corrupt DC, a DS who'd been murdered a few months earlier. This was their commanding officer. He could see Skegman had picked up on his hesitancy and knew exactly what was going through his mind.

'You must be worried sick,' said Walsh quickly. 'I'm afraid we've just had formal confirmation that DI Finn is one of the hostages in there.'

Paulsen nodded.

'We'd pretty much assumed that was the case,' she said briskly.

Did she have some sort of attitude or was this her natural demeanour, he wondered? Either way, it was slightly disconcerting.

'What about the other hostage – what do we know about him?' said Skegman.

'His name's Marco Randelli. The cafe's owner according to the Companies House website – we ran a background check on him earlier, but nothing flagged up,' said Rachel after introducing herself. 'He lives with an elderly mother in Norbury.'

Skegman nodded, while Paulsen said nothing. Both were unreadable. They were scared, Walsh thought. That was the reason they were so subdued. It was easy to get so caught up in procedure, the language of the job, that you missed the blindingly obvious. They didn't want to lose someone else.

'We'll do everything we can to de-escalate this situation as quickly as possible,' he said.

Skegman seemed to size him up for a moment then nodded with what appeared to be genuine appreciation.

'Thank you. As you may know, DI Finn has an established prior relationship with Lee Ellis. I think that can only benefit you,' he said.

'I agree,' said Rachel. 'I know it's early days, but is there anything you can tell us yet about the Vickers investigation? It feels like it's inextricably linked to this – anything you have that may help me when I'm talking to Lee,' she said and Paulsen nodded.

'We're treating her death as suspicious – there was a second set of footprints in the snow at the crime scene and we don't yet know who that person was or what they were doing there. We're still doing house-to-house inquiries, going through the CCTV and waiting on forensics. But it is, as you say, early days.'

'Could it have been Lee? It seems very odd that he just happened to be carrying a gun on the morning this happened,' said Walsh.

'I think, given his history with Jemma, we can't rule anything out at this point. Have you made contact with him yet?'

Walsh explained the conversation they'd just had with Lee and also the demands that had been made.

Skegman and Paulsen looked despondently at one another.

'You *can* tell him we'll be looking at the abductions again. That's not untrue,' said Skegman carefully. Everyone in the room knew that was semantics. One way or another re-examining that investigation was something that was naturally going to happen anyway. Whether it would be enough to end this was another matter.

'So how do you want to divvy this up?' said Walsh.

'Let's keep things simple. You handle the situation here; we'll investigate Jemma Vickers's death,' replied Skegman. 'I'll send one of my officers over to join you – if we find out anything that can help you, he can make sure you know it as soon as we do.'

'Sounds a plan,' agreed Walsh. 'One more thing, Lee's father is coming over shortly. He may be able to help with this – if he gives us anything useful, we'll reciprocate.'

Skegman nodded.

'What was your assessment of Lee's mental state when you spoke to him?' he said.

Walsh and Rachel exchanged a look.

'That bad?' said Paulsen.

'He was emotional, angry and grief-stricken. It's not a great cocktail for a man holding a gun,' said Rachel.

Walsh shot her a look, wondering if she was aware of the recent history at Cedar House.

'Shall we break the good news to Lee?' said Walsh. 'You can get a sense of him yourself then.'

The Cedar House pair nodded and once again Rachel returned to her table and went through the same procedure as earlier. She put the call on speaker and the four of them waited as it connected.

'Lee . . . I've got some good news,' she began. 'The investigation into your abduction *is* being reopened. There's a new team of detectives who'll be looking at it all with fresh eyes.' There was no immediate response and Rachel glanced over at the other three. 'Obviously, the most important witness is *you*. And you can help us an awful lot better out here than in there,' she added.

'I'm not going anywhere,' he replied finally. There was no anger in his voice this time. If anything, his tone was dead and listless. 'It's not just about reopening the case – I want an arrest. This only ends when I can look the bastard in the eye – do you understand?'

The line went dead.

5

The sun had come out and it was turning into a crisp winter's morning. Sarah Littlewood had been walking for around ten minutes or so but couldn't remember a single thing since she'd left her house. She'd been thinking instead about Lee Ellis and DI Alex Finn. Of Jemma Vickers, too. The thread that connected all their lives may have become stretched over the years, but it was still strong. More robust even than her relationship with Ollie and Ella's father – he'd moved abroad years ago to start a new life. That was one way of dealing with what had happened – but not something she'd ever seriously countenanced herself. Bar Christmas and birthdays it was as if his family in the UK didn't exist any more.

She made her way to a battered wooden door between a fish and chip shop and a launderette, and pressed one of the buzzers. There was no immediate response, and she checked her watch – it was just coming up to ten now. She heard a clatter of footsteps from inside, the door slowly opened, and she saw the pale face of Billy Rickson staring back at her. A square-jawed young man in his thirties, wearing a training top and jeans, he greeted her with a look of weary confusion.

'Can we talk?' she said gently.

A few moments later, she was sitting on a leather sofa in a small – and very cold – one-bedroom flat. It smelt of stale frying oil and unwashed bodies and she wondered when it had last seen a proper clean. It hadn't been that long since he'd been living under her roof, laughing around the dinner table with his wife and child, looking to the future.

'Is there something wrong with Kaitlyn?' he asked. He was looking at her awkwardly and she could feel his discomfort.

'No – she's fine,' replied Sarah and smiled back reassuringly.

Billy had never moved away from the area. It had always seemed to Sarah that he'd been anchored by those events from 2009, unable to quite shake them off. She'd stayed close to his family – as she had with all those caught up in what happened back then. They'd supported each other, almost like a survivor's group, and when Billy and Ella had begun a relationship, it had felt like a natural progression. When Kaitlyn had come along, there was a sense that some good had finally come from all of this.

But a couple of months ago Billy's father had died suddenly and he'd sunk into a deep depression. He'd closed himself off from Ella before announcing he wanted some time and space alone and found himself this flat. Sarah more than anyone knew what effect sudden bereavement could have and had believed it would probably only be a temporary split. He still visited their home regularly to see his daughter but seemed on edge and uncomfortable around the Littlewoods.

And as she looked around this cold and empty flat she could see that his mental state hadn't improved since the loss of his dad – and now a new bombshell was about to land.

'I wasn't sure if I'd catch you – I didn't know what your shift was today,' she said.

He shook his head.

'I'm not on until this afternoon.'

He worked at the local Sainsbury's supermarket, and often worked nights. Seeing him bleary-eyed and tired wasn't unusual.

'So what do you want?' he said.

Now she was here, and he was in front of her, she didn't know how to say it. So she just said it.

'It's Jemma. I'm really sorry, Billy – but she's dead.'

He reacted as if she'd just told him about a minor alteration to the train timetables. There was a long silence, and she couldn't tell whether he was looking at her or through her while he absorbed the news.

'What do you mean dead? How?' he whispered.

She wondered why Finn hadn't called him earlier as well. But then Billy had always been the outlier, the forgotten member of that trio. It wasn't fair because he'd been marked by those events too in his own way. Survivor's guilt was something she shared with him.

'I don't know exactly what the details are. I got a call from Alex Finn – they found her this morning in Tooting. It sounds like someone might have killed her.' Billy flinched as if she'd screamed the words at him. Sarah braced herself. 'And there's something else I need to tell you. About Lee . . .'

She explained what she'd seen on the news earlier and that produced a very different reaction – there was almost a pleading in his eyes as he listened. She recognised that too – the wish for the world to stop heaping ever more pain on shoulders that had borne quite enough already. 'I'm so sorry,' she said finally. 'I just thought you needed, *deserved* to know what was happening.'

'Lee *shot* someone? Where did he even get a gun from – did he kill them?' said Billy.

Sarah shrugged helplessly.

'I don't think so,' she said.

She didn't know what else to add and he nodded slowly at her.

'Thanks for coming round and telling me – I appreciate that,' he said.

'It's okay. I'm here for you – so's Ella. We both are – if you need someone to talk to. Someone who understands.'

She tried to smile, but he just looked at her warily.

Mattie Paulsen surveyed the incident room and wondered if they'd finally reached rock bottom. She'd thought they had a few months before, but the Murder Investigation Team had rallied round then. They all knew what Jackie Ojo would have said if they hadn't. There was much talk at the time about *'doing it for Jacks'*. And *'showing people what we're all about'*. But the events unfolding at the cafe in South Norwood had visibly rocked them all.

She looked across at the new girl. DC Vanessa Nash was sitting at a desk, cross-checking some paperwork against something on her screen. In fairness to her, she'd stopped all that over-the-top grinning now and had dived straight into the deep end of the investigation. In some ways, the situation worked to Vanessa's advantage. The usual suspects didn't have time to sit and gossip about the latest addition; they were all far too focused on more important matters.

John Skegman swept in and gathered everyone together. There was something different about him too this morning, Paulsen thought – a gravity that didn't show itself too often.

'I know this is going to be a particularly difficult day for everyone,' he began, 'on top of what's already been a very difficult year, so I just wanted to say a few words before we get into it.' He stopped to check that he had everybody's undivided attention. 'It's important you try and put what's going on in that cafe out of your minds. Everyone's concentration needs to be on the Jemma Vickers inquiry. That's the most constructive thing we can do right now.'

Paulsen was pleased to see more than a few heads nodding in agreement.

'Some nuts and bolts to begin with,' he continued. 'I've asked Mattie to lead this investigation – think of her as the unofficial acting DI on this until Alex is back, okay?' He glanced around with just a hint of warning in his eyes, which Paulsen didn't appreciate. She didn't need any extra assistance but saw no signs of resistance to the instruction either. One team, one problem today.

Skegman then motioned at Dattani. 'Sami – I want you to head over to South Norwood and join DCI Walsh at the RVP. You'll be the point man between this investigation and their operation.'

Dattani nodded and Skegman turned to Paulsen. 'So where do you want to start this, Mattie?'

'Same place as always,' she replied automatically. 'Let's take a deep dive into Jemma's life and not make any assumptions about what's happened. Vanessa – you've been looking at her recent history. Is there anything that stands out?'

Every head turned – they might not be gossiping yet, but that didn't mean there wasn't any interest in the new girl.

'I've found nothing out of the ordinary so far,' she said loudly. 'She lived in Streatham, was married with a three-year-old kid and worked as an IT administrator at the HSBC bank in Tooting.'

They waited for her to continue but nothing else was forthcoming.

'Any more?' said Paulsen. It was all information you could have found from a cursory scan of the woman's social media.

Vanessa flashed that wide smile again.

'Not yet. But I've got calls in.'

Paulsen resisted the temptation to say something – she wasn't going to publicly embarrass her on the morning of her first day. She could see too some early scepticism in the eyes of one or two others in the room. Judgements didn't take long to form in this environment.

'Forensics are still working the crime scene and I've had an update from them in the last few minutes,' she said, moving on. 'Whatever happened, happened under the railway bridge so it's been reasonably well protected from the conditions. The footprints there *do* indicate a second person was present and it looks like they exited via the south entrance to the tunnel – so we're checking the CCTV on the surrounding roads that side,' she said looking around the room as she spoke. 'This could just be a simple mugging gone wrong – and that's certainly a high possibility at this point.'

'Could it have been Lee Ellis?' said Nash suddenly. 'I mean why's a bloke cooking fried breakfasts also carrying a gun and why's he upset enough to take a police officer hostage?'

All eyes were on her again.

'Because he and Jemma used to be in a relationship and went through the same traumatic experience of being kidnapped together when they were teenagers?' said Paulsen as if it were obvious, but then nodded in acknowledgement. 'But you're right – there's a chance it was him. At this point *everything's* on the table – and that's how we treat this.'

'So what about the abductions from 2009 – how far back into that do we want to look?' asked Dattani.

'Let's treat it effectively as a cold case,' said Paulsen. 'And for the moment let's forget Dennis Trant's confession as well. I want to see if anything *was* missed back then. We'll come back to Trant as and when.'

'I'll deal with Assistant Commissioner Culley,' said Skegman carefully. 'He was the SIO back then. We'll need to talk to him, and I've already put in a call to his office.'

'An AC? He's not going to appreciate having all this exhumed,' said Dattani.

'As I say, I'll deal with him, Sami,' repeated Skegman, his voice firm. 'He's a professional and he'll understand why we want to talk to him.' He looked around the room once again. 'Let's not waste any more time, but I want to reiterate: the best way to help Alex Finn is not to let yourselves be distracted by what's going on in that cafe. Rest assured I'll keep you all up to date with any developments that occur there. Alex is an experienced officer, he knows Lee Ellis very well, and until this morning the man has had no documented history of violence. There's every chance this will end quickly and peacefully.'

But even as he spoke, Paulsen saw the worry behind his eyes.

The conversation with Billy had left Sarah feeling restless. She left his flat with random memories of 2009 flashing through her mind. The day her son disappeared would always be the second worst one of her life. When Ollie hadn't come home and didn't respond to her texts or calls, she'd initially assumed it was just a teenage boy being a teenage boy. But within hours just about every worst-case scenario she could conjure was running through her mind.

Even so, the police had taken some time to convince that this was serious. She could tell they thought he was probably with a girl or lying hungover on a sofa somewhere. But she hadn't believed that – she knew her son, knew he'd worry that *she'd* be worrying. If he was getting laid, or drunk – or both – he'd have found a lie to spin her at least. By the time the police were properly mobilised she'd already convinced herself of the worst.

She looked up at the morning sun now – felt its warmth on her face, the cold air on her cheeks. She closed her eyes for a moment and banished the memories. In the beginning, as part of her recovery, she'd tried to force herself to look forwards not backwards, but that was a lot easier said than done. These were events you couldn't just erase from your mind, and she'd learnt over the years to live side by side with the pain. Of a fashion, anyway. She opened her eyes again – she wasn't ready to go home yet, and there was one more stop she wanted to make.

A short while later she walked up to a small semi-detached house with a neatly maintained front garden. There was a police car parked outside the front door and she steeled herself before ringing the bell. The man who answered was stick thin and white as a sheet. In his late fifties, he looked considerably older than his years. Terry Ellis had never managed to find a way to live with what had happened. The events of 2009 had visibly sucked the life out of him and destroyed his marriage. They'd made him ill as well. He'd suffered a heart attack not long afterwards, which many people were convinced had been brought on by the abductions.

'Hello, Terry,' she said. 'I thought you could use a friend.' He tried to form some words but couldn't and instinctively she stepped forwards and hugged him. He didn't resist and buried his head in her shoulder instead. Inside, she could see a female PC constable watching them uncertainly from the hallway. Slowly Sarah disengaged.

'I'm so scared,' he murmured. 'They've got armed men there – Lee's going to get himself killed if he's not careful.'

'Stay calm, nothing's happened yet,' she said as reassuringly as she could manage. 'You know how close Lee and Jemma were – he must be devastated. When he calms down, he'll come to his senses, and this will end. That's what the police will be after too – they don't want to hurt him.'

'They've asked me to go there, Sarah – to talk to him,' he said, flustered.

57

'I think that's a good idea.'

His eyes flashed with alarm.

'Will you come with me? I don't think I can do this on my own.'

She nodded immediately.

'Of course, I will – if they'll let me.'

Terry spun round to face the constable behind them.

'My friend's coming with us, okay?' he said with an unexpected sharpness. 'If you want me to do this, she's coming. This is Sarah Littlewood, and she has *every* right to be involved.' The PC didn't argue with him, and Terry turned back to Sarah.

'Will Lee even listen? I mean, he stopped listening to me years ago.'

'Of course, he will,' she replied. 'Since his mum died you're all he's got left – who else is he going to listen to?'

He looked ashen.

'That's what worries me the most, Sarah – I don't think he's got anything left to lose now.'

6

2009

The light – and the heat – held for much of the evening but the search for the missing teenagers turned up nothing useful. The white van they'd been taken away in had seemingly melted away into the rush hour traffic. The abductions had occurred in a quiet street without cameras and nearby CCTV had only provided false leads so far. White vans weren't exactly at a premium in south London and valuable time had been exhausted without making a breakthrough.

The following morning Finn and Jack Barton returned to the same corner of South Croydon to interview the only witness. The search was continuing apace, though there were fewer residents out on the streets helping this time. People had lives to resume and jobs to go to – but Finn could sense a tangible atmosphere of anxiety as they drove through. Those who had come out were watching the police activity with concern. Extra uniformed patrols had been deployed overnight to try and provide some reassurance but until an arrest was made no one in these parts was going to feel comfortable.

Finn and Barton had decided to let Billy recover from his ordeal before questioning him. With the weather so fine, Finn had suggested holding the conversation in the Ricksons' back garden. It was peaceful and private, and he hoped the familiar surroundings would help to relax him. Billy's father George had joined them at a large rattan table out on the patio. His mother had stayed indoors, deciding to sit this one out. Finn could imagine they'd already had a very similar conversation as a family the previous night. She'd looked sick with worry when they'd arrived, and he could empathise with that. Sometimes huge relief could be just as overwhelming as great anguish.

George Rickson on the other hand reminded him of one of those overzealous fathers you found on the touchline at school football matches. An electrician by trade, there was a smugness about him that mildly rubbed Finn up the wrong way. It was as if he thought his son was somehow superior because he'd managed to escape the same fate as his friends. There was a breeziness about him as well, which didn't sit quite right, though that could have been a front to cover his concern.

Billy simply looked stricken, and it was already obvious he was going to need a lot of long-term help to get over this.

'Any of the questions we ask you – there are no right or wrongs so don't feel under pressure,' began Barton. 'We know how hard this is for you. Lee and Jemma are your mates.'

'He'll be fine, won't you, son?' said George.

'Are they dead?' said Billy simply.

Finn and Barton exchanged a look.

'We've found absolutely no evidence that any harm has come to them,' said Finn. 'We simply want to find them – that's the most important thing, and that's why we need your help.'

Billy nodded, but still looked distant, as if not quite plugged into where he was or what he was doing.

'Where were you going when it happened?' said Barton.

'We'd stayed late at school,' recalled Billy slowly. 'Mr Quilter had wanted to talk to Jemma and Lee, and I stuck around to wait for them.'

'He's their form master,' explained George.

'Why did he want to see you after school?' said Finn.

'To talk about university and what to expect there,' said Billy.

'He's given them a lot of advice about careers and stuff,' said George, cutting in again.

'Do you know what you want to do yet?' said Barton with a friendly smile. Finn knew he was trying to relax the boy. But Billy just shrugged, the effort of explaining almost too much for him.

'So where were you going after you left school?' said Finn, getting back on track.

'To the park,' said Billy. 'We'd bought some booze . . .' He tailed off as if embarrassed by the admission.

'Had you begun drinking it?' asked Finn, concerned. If they'd all been pissed it added another dimension to this.

Billy shook his head and then looked up suddenly.

'What's he taken them *for*?' he whispered. The numbness was turning into something more haunted now. 'What's he *doing* to them? You must have an idea?'

The ferocity of the question took them all by surprise. Barton leant in.

'You can't torture yourself, Billy. If you think about things like that – it won't do any good. It'll just upset you even more. The best way to help them is to help us.' He said the words patiently and slowly to punctuate their significance.

Billy nodded but looked close to tears.

'Which park were you going to – did you tell anyone where you were going?' said Finn gently.

The schoolboy took in a lungful of air and then shook his head.

'No, no one knew. We were going to Lloyd Park. Jemma and Lee have spent a lot of time up there this summer,' he said, as if it explained something obvious.

'Is there any particular reason for that?' said Finn.

'They're boyfriend and girlfriend as I understand it,' said George, cutting in.

'There's a disused old electrical substation up there. It's abandoned so it's a good place for privacy.'

Barton smiled conspiratorially.

'It was behind the bike sheds in my day,' he said.

'You gave one of my colleagues a description of the man you saw yesterday. Is there anything else you've remembered about him overnight?' said Finn. 'Some more details about his clothes or the van, perhaps?'

It was clear from his expression that he'd thought about nothing else.

'No, I'm sorry. I'm *really* sorry,' he said helplessly. 'That stuff he sprayed at me – it really hurt, and I couldn't see a thing. He was wearing black and had this mask on – the van was white and that's all I know for sure.'

'You know there's another boy from round here who went missing a few days ago? Oliver Littlewood. Did you know him – did any of you?' said Barton.

Billy shook his head blankly.

'No – I'd never seen his face before until it was on the news,' he replied.

They asked him some more questions to try and prompt his memory – whether the man was short or tall, thin or fat, whether he'd seen any of the numbers or letters on the van's licence plate, but the response was the same. They stopped when it became clear Billy had reached the end of his tether. He looked tormented now – as if his inability to remember anything useful constituted a critical failure that would exact a terrible price on his friends.

'It's alright,' said Finn quickly. 'There are no rights or wrongs, remember?'

The youngster slumped back into his seat. The sun was shining down from a cloudless blue sky and the air smelt sweet with the fragrance of flowers, but everything about this felt barren and dark to Finn.

As they were leaving, they found a familiar face waiting in the Ricksons' living room. Sarah Littlewood had heard Finn and Barton were there and had wasted no time coming straight over. She was sitting on the sofa with Billy's mum, patiently waiting for them as they emerged from the garden. Just as she had done the previous evening she looked thoroughly strung out and Finn wished he could give her a morsel of something positive to cling to.

'I wondered if there'd been any developments – if your night team had found something new?' she asked hopefully.

Her eyes were bloodshot, and Finn couldn't tell whether that was from lack of sleep or from crying. Both, most probably.

'I'm sorry, but we don't actually *have* a night team,' he explained. 'There just aren't those kinds of resources any more. But I can assure you there is an extensive police operation underway to find your son and these two missing teenagers.'

Sarah breathed heavily as she absorbed the information.

'You promised me yesterday – *"whatever it takes,"* you said.'

'And I meant it,' he replied.

'The only thing keeping me going is the thought that you people are throwing *everything* at finding Ollie,' she said in a low voice. 'That you're working twenty-four-seven on it – and now you're telling me that you're *not*?'

The disbelief in her voice was total.

'We're leaving no stone unturned. I promise you,' he said,

struggling to avoid a cliché, unable to find anything better. But it wasn't the disgust on her face that caught his eye. Billy had been listening to the whole exchange and was regarding him with equal horror. Two people now, who'd just lost faith in him, he thought.

'Trust me,' said Finn, addressing them both now. 'There's some of the most experienced officers in the Met out there looking. We *will* find something.'

He wanted to say more but couldn't – aware he was already treading dangerously close to the line of promising what he might not be able to deliver. Billy had heard enough and ran for the stairs. There was a second as they all heard him hurtle up to his bedroom, its door slamming behind him. Sarah held Finn's gaze for a moment longer, then made her own exit.

'You must have something?' said Chris Culley a little while later in the incident room.

His piggy little eyes were looking at Finn and Barton with something bordering on contempt and Finn could feel his temper starting to fray. The conversations with Sarah and Billy had got under his skin, but Culley's inability to understand even the basics of the job never failed to rile him. The man was experienced enough to know how these investigations worked.

'Not yet,' he said patiently. 'But we're still working through the witness statements and waiting on some forensic results. And there's still hours more CCTV from the surrounding roads to go through too—'

'This might be helpful,' said Jack Barton, jumping in quickly. He held up a couple of sheets of A4. 'I've been going through the system looking at some of the people in the area with known criminal records.'

Culley squinted at him as if he were stupid.

'Jack, we put that together straight after Oliver Littlewood went missing,' said Culley, ignoring Finn.

Barton held up a hand.

'I know, guv – but these aren't just the sex offenders. I broadened it out to anyone with a history worth looking at. It covers most of south London and out into the Surrey borders too.'

'And?' said Culley.

Barton passed him the sheets of paper.

'These are the ones whose previous I think makes them of interest.'

Culley scanned the list of names.

'I take it back – good work, Jack,' he murmured. Barton winked at Finn, who rolled his eyes. 'This one's interesting – Eddie Knox. He was convicted in 2006 for kidnapping a guy who owed him money and then torturing him in a lock-up for forty-eight hours. He did eighteen months inside for it.'

'Quite a few other nasty-looking priors on top of that as well,' said Culley, his eyes on the paperwork. 'And he lives right slap bang in the middle of the area where all three of those kids live.'

'Have you spoken to him?' said Finn cautiously.

Barton nodded.

'It was just a phone inquiry – but he claimed he was working on each occasion. He couldn't offer any firm evidence to back that up though.'

Culley glanced up.

'Well, he's certainly worth a chat – what are you waiting for? Bring him in.'

'You just have to know how to handle people like Culley,' said Barton as he and Finn descended the staircase from the incident room to Cedar House's main entrance.

'There's "handling" and then there's brown-nosing,' said Finn acidly.

Barton grinned.

'Develop a workable set of social skills, mate, and you'll be fine.'

Finn gave him a cheerful middle-fingered salute.

'Seriously, the man has all the creative imagination of a bag of crisps,' he said.

'Yeah, but I bet Culley interviews well – that's how he's climbed the ladder. It's his strength; he knows how to play the game.'

'It's not a *game* though, is it?' said Finn indignantly and Barton laughed.

'And that right there is why you'll never be a DCI, Al,' he said.

'Thank heavens for small mercies,' came a sarcastic voice.

Finn saw Karin Bergmann at the foot of the stairs and felt a sudden rush of guilt. Things had got rather petty between them the previous day and he'd felt bad about their row later. Fortunately, there seemed to be a hint of a smile on her face now, so maybe she'd arrived at the same conclusion too. He joined her, saw Barton out of the corner of his eye maintaining a discreet distance and mentally cursed him.

'Look . . . let me say something about yesterday,' he began. 'I'm sorry. You were right; I could have handled that interview a bit better. A *lot* better, actually. I can only assure you that there won't be a repeat. I'll try and learn from it moving forward,' he declared solemnly. The solicitor looked at him, inscrutable for a second, then burst out laughing.

'*What?*' he said, indignantly.

'It's just your face – you were being *so* serious.'

'I was apologising,' said Finn, outraged.

'You certainly were,' she replied, then promptly headed

straight past him and up the stairs. Finn watched her go then turned to look at Barton.

'What the hell?' he mouthed.

'I think she must like you,' he said.

Finn looked even more bamboozled, then scowled at him.

'Oh, fuck off,' he said and strode off towards the main doors. Barton chuckled and followed in his wake.

The cellar had been cold overnight. It was odd, thought Lee, because he knew how hot it probably was outside. But still in his sweat-soaked school shirt and trousers, he'd been shivering at times. He also knew that might not be down to the temperature. He and Jemma had both been shackled to some rusting pipes with thick metal chains. It was like a medieval dungeon from a children's story. Both of them had been too scared to call for help – they weren't even sure anyone would hear them through the thick brickwork. Besides, they didn't want to bring *him* down again.

They'd talked for a while – grateful for each other's company in the dark, then Jemma had dozed off. Lee envied her – he was too scared to sleep. The conversation had been morbid; they'd gone through all the different things that could happen to them. But this wasn't like some of the horror movies they'd watched at the cinema together – this was real and any of those scenarios could unfold at any moment. The possibility that the motive for this could be sexual had also hung over their conversation, though neither of them had raised it directly – but he was certain she was thinking about it too. It was hard not to.

He also felt ashamed – he was her boyfriend and he hadn't been able to protect her. As hard as he'd tried to, he'd also been unable to hide his fear and the memory of that burnt. Jemma had comforted hm, sounding more like his mum than his girlfriend. Now, he worried if she'd ever see him in the same way again – if they got out of this. While she slept, he'd cried – tried to think of home, of his parents. Of their cat, of his bedroom – anything that might provide some comfort, but none of it did.

Eventually, her eyes flickered open again in the half-light. Just for an instant, it was as if she'd forgotten where they were. The chains clattered as she propped herself up.

'We're still here then?' she said huskily.

Lee nodded.

'Afraid so,' he said, trying to muster some of his old bravado.

Jemma yawned and looked around. 'What time do you think it is? It feels like the middle of the night.'

'No – we've been here longer than that. I reckon it's morning now – maybe seven or eight.' The truth was they had no way of knowing and the uncertainty only added to their fear. 'Maybe he's just going to leave us here. Maybe *that's* the point of it?' said Lee.

'Why would he do that?'

Lee had no answer for her. He felt sick and wanted to pee.

'Do you think it's the same bloke who took that boy – Oliver Whatshisface?' said Jemma.

Absurd as it was, Lee hadn't even considered that possibility. He'd certainly seen the police out and about searching for him. They'd talked about it at school too, the novelty of seeing the streets they lived in on the evening news.

'It can't be,' he said.

'Why not?'

'Because he'd be down here with us, wouldn't he?'

'Unless he's already ... *finished* with him.' That thought quietened both of them for a moment. 'How far away from home do you think we are?' said Jemma finally.

Lee considered it.

'I passed out in that van because of the heat . . .' he said.

Jemma nodded.

'So did I. That's what I mean – I don't know how long we were in there for.'

Lee began to understand what she was getting at.

'We could have been in there for hours, days – we could be *anywhere* now.'

The implication was terrifying. Suddenly there was a noise and they both jumped, their chains rattling on the hard concrete floor. A door opened above their eyeline and a dazzling shaft of bright light cut across the room. Slowly, someone began to descend the stairs. A man in black, the man in the mask.

7

'I wouldn't bother taking your coat off – this is about as warm as it gets,' said Rachel as Sami Dattani looked around the pub.

'That's alright – I've been freezing my nadgers off all morning; I'm getting used to it,' he said, hugging himself.

She smiled and pointed at one of the pub's rickety tables.

'We've set up a desk for you. Well, when I say a desk . . .'

Dattani smiled wryly.

'Don't worry, it'll do just fine. No chance of a plate of scampi and chips with it, is there?'

Rachel laughed.

'Chance would be a fine thing,' she replied.

A portly man with a grey beard strode across, extending a hand.

'DC Dattani?' he said with a light Irish accent. 'I'm DCI Walsh – first thing I'd like to know . . . is what can you tell me about your governor – and how do you think he's likely to be handling the situation in that cafe?'

Dattani guiltily realised he hadn't spent any proper time considering that in the rush of things. It was now approaching half past ten, so Finn had been held in there for nearly ninety minutes.

'If I know him like I think I do, he'll be calm, trying to use

70

reason and logic to get through to Lee. That's the way he likes to work.'

Walsh nodded but Rachel looked concerned.

'Reason and logic are fine when you're dealing with reasonable and logical people,' she said. 'I'm just not sure how much effect that's going to have in this instance – Lee sounded extremely emotional earlier.'

A uniformed PC came through the saloon doors together with a thin, nervous-looking man and a rather elegant middle-aged woman. The constable brought them over and introduced Terry Ellis to Walsh.

'I'm worried that you're going to shoot my boy dead today,' said Terry by way of greeting.

'That's the last thing any of us want,' replied Walsh immediately. 'But I'm going to be truthful with you – your son's holding a gun on two people, which he's already used once on someone else. He's only at risk of getting hurt if he puts anyone else in danger. That's why you're here, Mr Ellis – I'm hoping you can help us prevent that from happening.'

Terry instinctively seemed to defer to the woman with him, who put a reassuring hand on his shoulder.

Walsh looked at her awkwardly.

'I'm sorry – who are you?'

The woman didn't bat an eyelid and met his gaze head on.

'My name is Sarah Littlewood – I'm Oliver Littlewood's mother,' she said loudly. Every head in the room immediately turned towards her.

'I'm so sorry,' said Walsh recovering quickly. 'I didn't realise – you must know Lee pretty well yourself then?'

Sarah nodded.

'I want her with me – that's non-negotiable,' said Terry quickly, looking at Sarah again who put a hand on his shoulder. Walsh smiled warmly at them both.

'Of course, if that's what you want, Mr Ellis.'

'So how do you want to do this?' said Terry nervously.

'We need you to talk to your son – just a simple phone call. A familiar voice can work wonders in these situations.'

'Whoa,' said Sarah cutting in immediately. 'Let's just give Terry a little bit of time and space before we rush into anything. I'm sure we all want to get this done right.'

Walsh nodded rapidly again.

'I wasn't suggesting we hurry anything. Acting DI Howe is a trained hostage negotiator – she can talk you through this until you're happy, okay?' Sarah and Terry both nodded. 'In the meantime, is there anything we can get either of you?'

'A chair would be good,' said Terry.

Dattani was watching with interest. Lee's father seemed to be breathing quite hard, shivering as well. Sarah had picked up on it too.

'Perhaps we could have some tea too – with plenty of sugar,' she said pointedly. 'And do the radiators in this pub actually work?'

'We're working on that,' said Walsh sheepishly. He looked over at Rachel. 'Can someone have another word with the landlord? We're trying to do a job of work in here.'

But Rachel was looking hard at Terry.

'Are you feeling okay, Mr Ellis?' she said.

The constable who'd brought them in had grabbed a chair and he sank down on it gratefully.

'I think he might be in shock actually – it's been a bit of a day, so far,' said Sarah.

'Give me a few minutes and I'll be fine,' said Terry. 'Can you tell me exactly what my son has said to you so far?'

Walsh explained the conversation they'd had and the demands that had been made.

'I'm sorry,' he said. 'I realise this must be bringing back some bad memories for both of you.'

'Bad?' said Sarah. 'There are other words that come to mind.'

'Do you mind if I ask something?' said Dattani to her, as Walsh looked down, chastened. 'Do *you* think Dennis Trant abducted Lee and Jemma Vickers back then?'

Sarah looked him up and down.

'You mean do I also believe Trant slaughtered my teenage son like an animal?' She crossed her arms defensively. 'Yes, I do, I read his confession, heard the reasons why the police believed him, and have never doubted it.'

For a second Dattani thought he saw a flicker of something in her eyes before her face hardened again. He turned to Terry.

'And you, Mr Ellis?'

Terry rubbed the back of his neck, his pallor now whiter than chalk.

'My son's always thought it was someone else,' he said softly, glancing around at each of them. 'Perhaps it's about time we listened to him?'

And this time even Sarah had no answer.

Paulsen had taken Nash with her as they travelled across south London to speak with Jemma Vickers's partner. To her irritation, Nash hadn't stopped talking since they'd left Cedar House. Paulsen wasn't sure whether that was the nerves of someone trying to make a good impression, a naturally larger-than-life personality, or whether she simply had verbal diarrhoea. The only good thing was that it had served to take her mind off Finn's predicament. Skegman's advice not to think about it was well intentioned but almost impossible to follow.

'So what's your situation then? Have you got a partner?' asked Paulsen casually. If they were going to talk for the entire journey, she might as well make it an information-gathering exercise.

Nash laughed out loud.

'No, I've been single for about three years. My last boyfriend cheated on me, so I haven't been in a rush to dive back in – and you know what? I'm actually loving it. I live at home with my mum and dad – I've got a big family – and I'm fine with that for the moment. The next guy needs to be the *right* guy. What about you?'

Paulsen remembered her breakfast with Jonas again and Nancy's concerned face looking at her across the table. She couldn't stop herself from picturing her father in an anonymous care home bedroom somewhere and shivered at the thought.

'I live with my partner in north London,' she replied concisely.

If Nash thought the answer was a bit abrupt, she didn't show it.

'I mean I'd like to get married and have kids one day – the whole thing, you know?' she replied. 'But right now, I'm just focusing on my career.'

Nash beamed another of those huge smiles.

'So why come to Cedar House? We've got a bit of a reputation these days in case you hadn't noticed,' said Paulsen carefully.

Nash shrugged.

'I don't care about any of that – I was just looking for a chance. I'm really excited to be here, as it goes.'

Paulsen felt a sudden rush of pettiness – despite herself, Nash's relentless good cheer was getting under her skin.

'Just so you're aware, there's a lot of people in that team who are hurting right now. The officer who died . . . was very popular. So you might want to tread carefully to begin with.'

Nash nodded, sensing a change of atmosphere.

'And what about the bent one – was he popular too?' she said slightly more sharply.

Paulsen gave her a side glance.

'He'd been part of the place for a long time. So his betrayal cut deep.'

For a second the only sound was the humming of the car's engine.

'Consider my card marked,' said Nash coolly.

Steve Garland was an attractive young Black man roughly the same age as Paulsen. He and Jemma had lived with their three-year-old son Harry in a smart two-bedroom flat in Streatham. Steve's mother was comforting him when they arrived. A uniformed PC was also present and family liaison officers were on their way, but for now, the atmosphere in the flat was still one of huge shock.

Harry was subdued, instinctively aware that something very wrong had happened even if he didn't understand what yet. His grandmother and the PC took him into a bedroom so that the others could talk uninterrupted. Paulsen, Nash and Steve sat around the kitchen table and for a moment they all looked at each other awkwardly. The flat suddenly felt over-heated, small and claustrophobic.

'I'm so sorry for your loss,' said Paulsen.

'It doesn't feel real if I'm honest,' said Steve, shaking his head.

'Can you tell us why Jemma was in Tooting this morning?'

Steve swallowed.

'I honestly didn't even know she *was* there. She often went to the gym on Streatham High Road before work, so I was used to her leaving early. That's where I thought she'd gone.'

Paulsen and Nash exchanged a glance.

'Did she have any kind of history of keeping things from you?' said Nash.

Paulsen glanced across at her – the question could have been phrased a little more diplomatically.

'No, not in the slightest. We don't – *didn't* – have that kind of relationship,' said Steve. He stopped and suddenly put a hand over his mouth, cutting off a silent scream. In the background, they could hear the muffled sound of his son shouting through the walls. Slowly he took his hand away, took some deep breaths, then motioned at them to continue.

'Sorry,' he said apologetically.

'Could she have gone to meet a work colleague?' said Paulsen.

'Possibly – but she never really talked much about her work. She thought I'd find it boring. I can't honestly think who else she'd have gone to see so early.'

'What time did she leave?' asked Nash.

'About six.'

Paulsen and Nash exchanged a glance. The information significantly narrowed the window for the time of death.

'Can you think of anyone who might have wanted to hurt her?' said Nash.

'No, not at all. She was just a kind, decent human being and after everything she'd been through . . .' He shook his head. 'She didn't deserve this – she should have died an old woman, surrounded by people who loved her.'

Paulsen's mouth felt dry and she cleared her throat.

'Is there any chance that this might be connected to what happened to Jemma in 2009?' she said.

Steve momentarily looked defeated by the question.

'I can't see how – she made an amazing recovery from that.

It was something that she worked hard on – we talked about it a lot in the early days of our relationship. She didn't want what happened back then to mark her life. She just tried to be a good partner and mother.' He wrung his hands together. 'That's what she wanted most.'

Paulsen explained what was happening in South Norwood and the demands that Lee Ellis had made. Steve was visibly shocked by the news.

'Lee's never really been able to live with it the way Jemma was able to.' He stopped, still taking the information on board. 'They were insanely close – I can't say I always liked that. I tolerated it, I suppose.'

'Is that because they used to be in a relationship?' said Paulsen, sensing that this might be important, but Steve shook his head dismissively.

'No – they were just schoolkids then and it ended soon after the abductions. I know she didn't have any romantic feelings for him any more. But there was obviously a connection between them. Jemma was a good influence on him. She could always calm him down when he began to get overwhelmed. I got used to it over the years; Lee calling at all hours of the day, messaging her in the middle of the night, that type of thing. Jemma was always able to get through to him. But sometimes . . . it was like there were three of us in this marriage, that's all.'

It explained a lot to Paulsen – why Lee's reaction to the murder had been so extreme. He hadn't just lost a friend, he'd lost his prop – the one person he felt understood him.

'Lee's made it clear that he doesn't believe Dennis Trant was the man who abducted them. What was Jemma's view on that?' she asked.

Steve shook his head.

'She didn't really talk about it much, but like I say Jemma

always wanted to look forward, while Lee could only look backwards. That was the difference between them.'

Inside the cafe, Marco was getting impatient.

'If you're not going to shoot us – and I still don't believe you are, Lee, then what *are* you going to do?' He pointed at Finn. 'At some point, his mates are going to come crashing in here – and I reckon they'll be carrying bigger guns than you. Seriously, have you thought this through?'

'Have I thought this through?' repeated Lee slowly. He looked at Finn. 'What do you think?'

Finn was aching from leaning forwards and fell back against the scalding radiator for a brief moment.

'I'm pretty certain you've never *stopped* thinking about 2009,' he replied. 'Do you think Jemma would want you to be doing this, though? I knew her too, and I suspect she'd hate this.'

The mention of Jemma's name was deliberate, and it brought a look of anguish to Lee's face. He sank on to his haunches and slowly ran a finger through the puddle of blood that had pooled on the floor from earlier.

'I'm doing this for her as much as I'm doing it for me. Now she's gone I'm the only one who can get answers,' he said.

'I spent hours interviewing you afterwards and you told me what happened,' said Finn carefully. 'But there were certain things – how you got those scars on your face, for example – that you always closed down.'

Lee looked at the blood on his hands and rubbed it absently between his forefinger and thumb.

'We told you everything – you just didn't do your job properly.'

'I've always felt you kept something back,' continued Finn tentatively. He'd never vocalised this before – after Trant's confession, he'd never needed to. There was no hard evidence for the suspicion, just an uneasy feeling that had lurked at the back of his mind.

'That's a bit gaslighty isn't it – trying to imply it was our fault that you didn't catch the right guy?' said Lee.

Finn ignored the jibe.

'Did something *else* happen in that cellar – something you kept between yourselves all this time? If that's the case why not tell me now what it was?' he said.

Lee dragged himself back on to his feet and then walked over to Marco, pointing the gun at him.

'You don't think I'd use this, then? You know nothing,' he said.

He casually ran his blood-soaked finger across Marco's forehead. The blood dripped down into his eyes and with his hands bound there was nothing he could do except blink. Lee turned to Finn.

'And as for you – you need to shut up. What good have you *ever* been?'

Lee's mobile began to ring, the ringtone echoing around the small room. Lee went back to the table where he'd left it and answered the call, his expression changing immediately.

'*Dad . . .*' he murmured.

In the RVP, Walsh, Rachel, Dattani and Sarah Littlewood were crowded around the table where Terry was sitting. As per Sarah's request, they'd talked through the best way of approaching the conversation before making contact. Rachel had steered the discussion, but she hadn't wanted to over-whelm Terry. Ultimately, he was there to be a father and most of her guidance had been about what *not* to say. He was staring at the beer taps at the bar as if they held some deep significance. As before, the call was on speakerphone.

'Hello, son,' he said quietly. 'Are you alright?'

There was the sound of heavy breathing for a moment.

'No, Dad, I'm not.'

There was an audible catch in his voice.

'So how are we going to sort this out then?' There was no reply and Terry looked at the faces around him nervously before resuming. 'I know we haven't always been close – especially since your mum died. But I'm on your side – you know that, don't you?'

'Yeah,' said Lee throatily.

Terry ran a hand through his hair.

'So tell me why you're doing this.'

'You know what it's about,' said Lee. 'Someone murdered Jemma today – and I think it's the same man who took us when we were kids. He's still out there . . . and I have to finally make the police understand that.'

Terry's eyes flicked up to Rachel. She gestured at the rest of the room, and he nodded his understanding.

'If you really think that, then surely this is easier if you work *with* the police. They'll listen to you – there's no need to get yourself killed to make a point.'

Rachel gave him a thumbs up.

'No,' said Lee. 'I've been talking to the cops for fifteen years and they've done nothing. They stopped hearing me years ago and now Jemma's dead and I'm done talking – I've got no choice.'

Terry shook his head.

'There's always a choice.'

'Not this time. I'm sorry – one way or another, this ends today.' He faltered. 'Goodbye, Dad.'

The line went dead.

'Lee?' shouted Terry. He looked at the phone helplessly.

'It's okay, you did brilliantly,' said Rachel.

'No, no ... it's not okay. Didn't you hear him? He was saying *goodbye* to me.' He winced for a moment, as if in pain. He tried to stand and put a hand on his chest. Walsh went to help him, but Terry's face screwed up in silent agony, his legs buckled from under him, and he fell to the floor.

8

Sami Dattani immediately rushed forwards and began to examine Terry. He tilted the stricken man's head back and then looked up with alarm.

'He's not breathing,' he shouted.

Walsh had simultaneously crossed the room and was calling for the paramedics. There were two ambulances parked on the opposite side of the road, but Dattani didn't wait and immediately began chest compressions. In the centre of it all Sarah was watching, frozen to the spot in horror. Within seconds the emergency team were running through, and Dattani jumped back to let them take over.

'Is he going to be okay?' said Sarah.

'I don't know,' replied Dattani. 'To be honest I thought he was already gone.'

Walsh was looking on too, ashen-faced, as the paramedics got to work. They heard a crack as one of Terry's ribs broke. Sarah winced in horror, but Dattani remained impassive. Ribs could be repaired, but there was a real danger they were about to watch a man die in front of them. The paramedics began removing Terry's clothing and placed the two pads of a defibrillator on to his exposed chest.

'This is all my fault,' murmured Sarah.

'No, it's not,' said Dattani, the words coming out harsher than he meant.

She shook her head and they continued to watch transfixed.

There was a controlled urgency to the paramedics' movements as they waited for the device to analyse the unconscious man's heart rhythm, then one of them shouted, *'Clear.'* Everyone moved back as the charge was activated. The lead paramedic began applying CPR again and then checked the readings. They were all watching his face, searching for some clue of which way this was going. He shouted *'clear'* once more, delivered a second charge, and resumed chest compressions. This time Terry's eyes flickered open, and the paramedic swivelled round to give them a thumbs up.

A short time later Terry Ellis was being stretchered towards the open rear door of the waiting ambulance outside. Its proximity had probably saved his life – for now. But he looked far from out of the woods and the concern of the paramedics was self-evident. Sarah insisted on accompanying him to hospital and Walsh assured her he'd call if there were any developments from the cafe. He re-entered the pub with a deep frown of concentration, one hand rubbing absently at his brow. It wasn't hard to guess what was on his mind, thought Dattani.

'Well – this is a nice king-sized cluster of fuck we find ourselves swimming in,' Walsh said to no one in particular. 'An unstable man who's holding two people hostage because his best mate died this morning, and now the only other person he's got in the world might not make it to lunchtime.'

Rachel, who'd been on the phone, finished her call and came over to join them.

'I'll state the blindingly obvious – we can't risk telling Lee about this,' she said.

'You don't think it might make him think twice about what he's doing?' said Dattani.

'Perhaps – but it might also make things a whole lot worse. Do you want to take that risk?' Dattani saw her point and shook his head. 'There's something else,' she added.

'I take it from your face that it's nothing I'm going to like?' said Walsh.

'Cedar House has had uniformed officers searching Lee's flat. I've just been told they found a quantity of marijuana and cocaine inside.'

Walsh blew through his lips.

'Let joy be unconfined,' he said. The words were flippant, but his expression and tone were anything but. 'So we've got an ex-soldier with a gun possibly coked to the tits?'

Slowly Rachel nodded.

Inside the cafe, Lee seemed to have perked up. Finn was trying to work out why. He wondered if it was the adrenaline, pushing his grief about Jemma to one side temporarily. Or maybe it was just the coke. He'd been listening hard to Lee's side of the conversation with his father and been attempting to recall the current state of their relationship. Lee's mother had died from a stroke several years ago, and though he and Terry hadn't fallen out, the weight of tragedy had certainly created some distance between them. The way Lee had said goodbye to his father had felt final – as if a decision had been made, and that's what concerned Finn the most. Was it the sense of a burden lifted that had created the change in his mood?

'Do you want me to turn that radiator off? I'd completely forgotten about it,' he said to Finn, almost affably. 'You must be burning your arse off.'

'Thank you,' said Finn with relief as Lee came over and began to turn the tap. Marco was sitting in sullen silence next to him, keeping his own counsel, his face still stained with the blood that Lee had dabbed on him earlier.

'There's no need to be uncomfortable while we wait. Why don't I make us some bacon sarnies to keep us all going?' offered Lee brightly. 'I mean – we could be here for a while.'

'Knock yourself out,' said Marco.

Lee grinned and headed through to the kitchen. After a few moments they heard the sizzling of a pan, and the smell of frying bacon began to fill the room again. Finn looked across at his fellow hostage – he'd been hoping a moment like this might present itself.

'You need to try and stay calm. Be polite – cooperate with him wherever you can,' he whispered. It was standard advice for these situations, but Marco looked back at him incredulously.

'*Polite?*' he whispered back. 'That coked-up psycho's going to kill us both. Where are your mates with the tear gas and guns?'

'That'll be the last resort – they'll try and talk him down first. And that's something we can help them with.'

Marco took a breath; the logic of what Finn was saying beginning to penetrate.

'Okay. But it's not me I'm thinking about – it's my mum. She'll be worried sick. She's on her own; she's got no one.'

Finn remembered Marco's earlier comment about his mother having a hospital appointment later.

'Is there a problem?' he asked.

Inside the kitchen, they could hear Lee whistling cheerfully now.

'You could say that. She's got a brain tumour.'

The words hit Finn like a hammer. It was the same cancer that had killed his wife, Karin.

'I'm so sorry,' he said.

They were both speaking quickly now, aware Lee could re-join them at any minute.

'She's having surgery today,' he said looking bereft. 'That bastard in there knows it too.'

'Don't be too hard on him,' said Finn. 'You've no idea what he's been through.'

85

'Sounds like you don't, either,' said Marco harshly. That was a fair point, Finn thought. 'Do you really think he'd kill us – or is this all just attention-seeking?' Marco continued. 'I don't know how my mum would cope without me.'

For an instant, Finn tried to imagine how Karin would have managed in her final months without him and the thought was almost unbearable.

'He's not a violent man – or at least he hasn't been to my knowledge. I don't think it's in his nature, despite all the trauma,' said Finn.

Marco shook his head.

'I'm not so sure about that. You know he was in the army? I think something happened to him – in Afghanistan. He's mentioned it a few times – something bad, but I don't know what.'

This was new information to Finn. The sound of frying had stopped, and he could hear the chink of plates now – they didn't have much more time.

'You think he's got PTSD from there, too?' he said.

Marco nodded.

'I'm certain of it – that's what I thought this was all about, to begin with.'

Sami Dattani immediately rang Skegman at Cedar House to tell him about Terry Ellis's heart attack and the news was relayed to the incident room. They also now knew about the drugs that had been found in Lee's flat. None of it had done much to improve the bleak atmosphere. Jackie Ojo would have kicked arse at this point, thought Paulsen – not allowed anyone to feel sorry for themselves or to be distracted. But she couldn't do that, much as she could see that it was needed – she hadn't earned the right yet. If she did try something along those lines, she had a feeling it would probably backfire badly.

'So, there's nothing in Jemma Vickers's recent history that looks unusual?' said Skegman, who'd wandered down from his office for an update.

'Just that her partner didn't know why she was in Tooting so early this morning?' said Nash. 'Which suggests maybe she went there to meet someone and this wasn't a random mugging gone wrong.'

'Do we have a timeline yet?' asked Skegman and Paulsen nodded.

'The body was found just after seven-thirty and, according to Steve, she left home at about six – so the murder must have happened somewhere in that ninety-minute window. Eighty, probably – if you count the time it would have taken her to get there,' she said. 'Digital Forensics is going through her phone, and they've got her laptop to work with now as well – hopefully, they'll find something to tell us why she was there.'

'What about Vanessa's point from earlier – is there any chance that it was Lee Ellis she met, and he killed her? And that the siege is a response to that?' said Skegman. 'The guilt, setting in, maybe?'

Paulsen nodded.

'The picture Steve painted of Lee was of a pretty emotionally disturbed man. He and Jemma were very close though, even after their teen relationship ended. Sounds as if they became a bit more brother and sister after that.'

'And siblings can fall out,' said Nash.

Skegman nodded.

'So it remains a possibility. What's your take, Mattie – how do you want to proceed from here?'

That was the second time he'd deferred to her, she noticed. He really did seem to be giving her the same respect he'd normally afford Finn.

'I think we have three lines of inquiry. One – that what

happened to Jemma this morning was a random one-off event, and the fact she was in Tooting so early was unrelated to that. Two – Lee's right and Dennis Trant *didn't* abduct them fifteen years ago and that individual *is* still out there. And three – that Lee himself might be Jemma's killer, in which case – why and what prompted this?'

Skegman weighed it up.

'Alright, make sure we're going down all three of those avenues thoroughly and let's investigate Trant a bit more deeply too. Does he have any surviving family?'

'I think I read in the file earlier that there was a wife and son,' said Paulsen. 'We'll see if we can track them down.'

'And as for Lee . . .' began Skegman.

'I think I might have something interesting on him,' said Nash interrupting. 'We know he was in the army – I've just been sent through his service record. He joined up in 2010 when he was nineteen.'

'That's only one year after the abductions,' said Paulsen. 'I wonder if joining up was some sort of reaction?'

'Very possibly,' agreed Skegman.

'The thing is – he was given a medical discharge two years later in 2012, just before British forces began leaving Afghanistan,' said Nash. 'Looks like it was pretty sudden – he wasn't injured, so I'm thinking it was to do with his mental health.'

'Didn't the army tell you?' said Skegman.

'All they'd say was that it was a behavioural disorder.'

'Which ties in with what we already know.'

'But did something happen to him out there?' said Nash. 'I mean the more we know about his past, the more it answers some of the questions we're asking, surely?' she said, glancing at both Skegman and Paulsen.

'It does,' agreed Paulsen. 'Is there someone we can talk to?'

Nash nodded.

'They passed on a contact to me – William Owusu, he was in the same battalion and lives in Bexleyheath.'

'Good work, Vanessa,' said Skegman. He looked at the clock – it was now nudging towards eleven. 'Alright, we've got a direction of travel for now, so let's get cracking.'

Paulsen and Nash nodded and rose to their feet.

'Have you got a quick second, Mattie?' said Skegman lightly and waited for Nash to leave before turning to her. 'I just wanted to check that you're okay?'

She glared at him in response.

'Why wouldn't I be?'

'Because I'm not, frankly,' he said, instantly disarming her. 'It's okay to be worried about Alex. And to be missing Jacks, as well.'

She realised what he was saying, and her face softened.

'I'm not letting it get in the way if that's what you're concerned about. At least I don't think so.'

'I'm here if it does,' he said simply.

9

2009

As per DI Culley's instructions, Finn and Barton travelled across south London to interview Eddie Knox. He was renting a basement flat of an old Victorian building just half a mile away from where Jemma and Lee had been taken the previous day. As they arrived it was easy to see how the abducted teenagers might have first caught Knox's eye. He probably shopped in the same supermarkets, used the same transport links and queued in the same fast-food restaurants. If he was involved, there would have been plenty of opportunities for him to have watched from the shadows, formulating a plan.

'So what exactly did this guy do?' said Finn as they got out of the car.

'He's been in and out of various institutions for various drug-related offences. But three years ago, he abducted a low-level dealer who owed him money and held him prisoner for forty-eight hours. He poured boiling hot water on his head, burnt his face with an iron and removed several fingernails.'

'Nice.'

'He did his time and then decided to start a new life in London.'

'Lucky us,' said Finn. 'Any problems since he came down here?'

Barton shook his head.

'None that his probation officer knew of. Model citizen by all accounts.'

'I'm not sold this is our guy,' said Finn, pressing a buzzer on the front door. 'He had a specific reason for what he did before – now he's suddenly become the type to lift three schoolkids off the street in one week? And why? What would he want with three teenagers?'

The door opened and without waiting to be asked he stepped inside.

Knox was a slightly built man in his early forties. He didn't look like the classic stereotype of a violent criminal. Wearing an orange T-shirt, shorts and Birkenstock sandals, there was nothing that made you look twice at him. The one thing that Finn did notice was the intensity behind his gaze. This was a man used to dealing with police and wasn't intimidated.

'Relax, Eddie,' said Barton as they walked into the small living area. 'No one's saying you've done anything wrong – and if you've nothing to hide, you don't need to worry. You have my word on that.'

'Right . . .' said Knox warily. 'So why have you singled me out?'

'Why do you think?' said Finn.

Knox shook his head.

'I said all this on the phone earlier. What I did back in the day, I don't regret. It was business and the bloke I hurt deserved everything that happened to him. You play with fire – you get burnt. It doesn't mean I took these kids,' he growled.

'If you say so,' said Barton. 'Though I'm not sure three years ago counts as "back in the day".'

'What do you do for a living?' said Finn, glancing around the flat. It was smart and tidy, though its size and the sparseness of the décor suggested a man on a limited budget.

'I'm in IT,' he replied with a slight Mancunian twang. 'I can do it all from my laptop, which means I can pretty much work from home full-time.'

'You're self-employed then?'

Knox nodded but there remained just the hint of something behind his eyes. It wasn't hard to imagine that this was someone who could be easily triggered. Barton didn't waste any time asking where he'd been at the time of the abductions.

'I told your colleague on the phone before – this flat becomes unbearable in the heat, so I've been taking my laptop and working in Roundshaw Park. It's only a few minutes up the road from here.'

Finn and Barton exchanged a glance. It was just a fifteen-minute drive from Lloyd Park where the three teenagers had been heading when they were attacked.

'What time were you there yesterday?' said Finn.

Knox gave a resigned shrug.

'Same as I have been all week. I went down after lunch – so about two. And I've been leaving at about half past six each day.'

'Can anyone else corroborate that?' he said.

Knox shook his head and they checked where he'd been the night Oliver Littlewood disappeared.

'Here. Alone,' he replied emphatically. He looked at them both with the expression of a man used to not being believed. 'I saw the news reports last night. You're looking for a white van, right? I don't even have a car – I can't afford one. I'm renting this place and I can barely swing a cat in here. If I took three schoolkids, then where do you think I've put them?' Finn and Barton had no answer, and Knox snorted with derision. 'The trouble with you lot is your suspicion overtakes everything else – even common sense. If I'm the person you're looking for – then how would I have done it? And why for God's sake?'

He wasn't quite squaring up to them physically but there was venom in the final question.

'He's got a point,' said Finn as they left. 'And the more I think about it, the more I reckon there's got to be more than one person involved in this. Dragging two teenagers off the streets isn't exactly easy – even if they have just been pepper-sprayed. And frankly, I *get* this guy – who he is, what he is. He's a piece of shit, but not necessarily the kind of piece of shit that pulls off crimes like this.'

Barton stopped by the car and flicked away a ladybird that had landed on his shirt.

'So are we ruling him out then?'

Finn mulled it.

'Maybe Knox just identifies the targets – and it's someone else who takes them. But it still doesn't explain why.'

Barton shrugged.

'You heard him – he needs money. Perhaps someone else wanted those kids for whatever reason and, like you say, he's the middleman.'

Out of the corner of his eye, there was a movement. Finn turned, and they both saw Knox peering up at them through his curtains before disappearing inside again. Just for a second Finn caught the hatred in those eyes, boring through the glass straight at him.

'Good work,' said Culley, a rare smile on his face as Finn and Barton briefed him on the conversation. 'So this guy's a decent prospect then?'

The incident room was baking, even with all the windows open. The faint smell of sewage was wafting in from some-where to add to the general unpleasantness.

'I think he's worth keeping an eye on for sure – he doesn't have a solid alibi,' said Barton. 'He lives right on top of where these kids went missing and his previous makes him a good fit.'

Culley nodded.

'I agree, so let's put him under surveillance.'

Finn looked less convinced.

'What's the matter, Alex?' said Culley, sourly.

'I think that's a bit hasty. Knox is certainly someone of interest – but there was nothing that made me think we should jump to any quick conclusions. He looked like a man who'd done his time and was more interested in staying under the radar now,' he said.

Finn regretted the use of the word 'hasty' even as it came out of his mouth.

Culley's top lip had curled into a sneer.

'And maybe he's got a very good reason for that, don't you think? Given his history.'

'He might also just be the wrong guy in the right place,' replied Finn straight away.

Culley visibly restrained himself from taking the argument further.

'Are there any other lines of inquiry you want to update me on?'

'We're still working our way through the list of local sex offenders – but nothing's flagged up so far,' said Finn.

'There's another possibility,' said Barton. 'That these three kids have been lifted to be trafficked.'

He and Finn had discussed the idea on the drive back to Cedar House. They might be on the verge of adulthood, but they were still schoolkids – just. And there was always a market for youths that age. The thought was chilling, and they could see from Culley's face that he immediately understood the implications of it too. The local community was already on edge, and this might just push them over.

'DI Culley, can I have a word?' said a loud voice interrupting them.

They all looked around and saw Karin striding across the room.

'Oh, Jesus,' said Culley under his breath. 'Keep looking into Knox,' he added quickly before turning to greet her. 'I hope this is urgent, Ms Bergmann – in case you hadn't noticed, we're trying to find three missing teenagers.'

'I'm aware of that – but there are also other investigations in progress. Other people whose problems are just as pressing. Your job is to make sure everyone gets the same attention.'

Culley's eyes narrowed. Finn was rather enjoying this. It was nice to see someone else get both barrels from the solicitor for a change – especially Culley. Others in the room were looking at them now too.

'I'm very well aware of what my responsibilities are, thank you,' said the DI, his voice becoming slightly nasal, as it tended to when he was riled. 'Which job are you referring to in particular?'

'The McEvoy inquiry. You only have a few more hours before you have to charge or release my client—'

'Again – I'm well aware of that fact,' said Culley. 'And as you know we have another interview scheduled with him shortly. It's why you're here,' he added testily.

'Which is my point. Have you been down to those cells – they're like pressure cookers in this heat. My client says he's not been given any water to drink—'

'There's a sink in his cell,' said Culley, deliberately stretching out the words.

'Which is *broken*,' shouted Karin back at him.

Culley seemed to become aware of how many eyes were on them now and lowered his voice.

'Fine – we'll make sure your client is suitably refreshed and lubricated before we talk to him.' He didn't wait for her response and marched out of the room, shaking his head.

She watched him leave, then turned to Finn.

'That man is a fucking moron,' she said as if it were blindingly obvious, and Finn fought the urge to agree.

'Come on,' he said. 'I'm waiting on a lab report to come back so I've got five minutes. Let's go down to the custody suite.'

He led her to the door, ignoring the look of amusement on Barton's face. The corridor outside was marginally cooler and they both enjoyed the draught for a moment.

'Do you know something?' said Karin as they walked. 'That DI has absolutely no emotional intelligence whatsoever and I've seen a few knuckleheaded inspectors in my time. How did he even get to that rank?'

This time Finn made no effort to hide his chuckle. Culley was striding ahead further down, and it was fifty-fifty whether he could hear them or whether she even cared about that.

'There's a reason his nickname's Rolf,' he said quietly. She looked at him blankly. 'Right 'Orrible Little Fucker . . .'

Now it was Karin who was laughing.

'Suits him perfectly. I'm sorry – it's this heat; it's making me cranky. I shouldn't have shouted at you yesterday or teased you earlier.'

'Don't worry, I think we're all feeling these temperatures at the moment,' he replied.

Culley turned and entered his office, shutting the door firmly behind him.

'Honestly, stupidity like that makes me question why I bother sometimes,' she said, shaking her head. 'I don't just mean a broken sink. At times this job is like wading through treacle. With a rucksack full of bricks on your back.'

'What else would you do?'

'I could give you quite the list actually,' she replied. She was smiling now, her anger beginning to ebb. The expression suited her, he thought.

'Why don't you then?' he said, not entirely sure where the words had come from. 'Over a drink or something,' he added, before instantly regretting it. She looked bamboozled by the suggestion, and he felt utterly mortified. To his surprise, her smile returned.

'Why not?' she replied with a shrug.

The man in the mask had brought down a plastic basin and placed it on the floor of the cellar. Silently he'd unchained Lee and Jemma separately and allowed them to have a much-needed pee. After restraining them once more, he gave them some water, before leaving them in the dark again.

'He doesn't want to hurt us,' said Lee, taking some encouragement. 'And did you see? He looked away while you were pissing. Why would he do that if he was some rapist?'

'Doesn't mean he isn't going to do it later,' said Jemma. 'And if he really gave a shit, he'd have brought us food. My stomach hurts, I'm so hungry.'

As they spoke the words echoed around the empty cellar. All that seemed to be down there was some dusty old furniture covered by a large tarpaulin.

'I'm sorry you're here,' said Lee quietly.

'Thanks,' replied Jemma with a touch of her old sarcasm.

'You know what I mean. I wish that *neither* of us was here.' He looked up at her shyly. 'But I also know that I don't know how I'd cope if I were on my own.'

There was a silence.

'I get it. If I had to be down here with anyone . . . at least it's you,' she said more softly. The words made his eyes sting again, and even now he desperately didn't want to cry in front

97

of her. He fought to hold it together, wanted to protect her somehow but just as quickly felt his defences crumble and his panic rise.

'We're never going to get out of this, are we?' he said, unable to contain it. He was hot now as well, the sweat dripping under his arms. 'I'm scared, Jem, really fucking scared . . .'

'*Shhh,*' she said sharply.

'I don't want to die in here,' said Lee, spiralling.

Jemma was leaning forwards now.

'I said shut up – *listen* . . .'

Lee did as he was told and above, through the ceiling, he could hear the faint, muffled sound of sobbing.

IO

Today

It wasn't hard to tell that William Owusu used to be in the army. Paulsen's first observation was that he was built like the proverbial brick shithouse. Owusu worked as a postman and was wearing a pair of shorts when she and Nash met him at his delivery office.

'You get sweaty doing this job, whatever the weather,' he explained with a shrug as he took them through to a small icy yard at the back of the building where they could talk alone. 'Sorry it's a bit fresh out here but there isn't really anywhere private inside.'

Nash produced what was fast becoming her trademark big smile in response. Paulsen looked around. The area was littered with cigarette stubs, and it wasn't hard to guess what its primary purpose was.

'I can't say I'm surprised about what's going on in that cafe,' said Owusu, getting straight to the point. 'In some ways, I think this has been coming for a long time.'

'What makes you say that?' said Paulsen.

'Whatever happened to Lee when he was kidnapped clearly screwed him up big time. That was obvious, even back then.'

'Obvious in what way?' said Nash.

'He was a crackerjack,' replied Owusu immediately, then when he saw their confused faces: 'Volatile, unpredictable . . .

99

you never quite knew what you were going to get. And in the army, especially out in the field, you don't want that, trust me.'

'Did he ever talk about what happened to him?' said Paulsen.

'A little – but he never went into any detail. The general concern was that it seemed to make him feel invincible – like there was nothing that could hurt him worse than what had already happened.'

'Do you know why he was discharged from the military?' asked Nash.

Owusu nodded slowly and looked across the yard.

'I've got a fair idea. There was an interpreter who worked with us. His name was Hafeez and he was popular with the lads. He had a nice way about him – helped smooth out a few tricky situations with the locals for us. He got kidnapped, ambushed when he was out on his own one day.' Owusu stopped, a combination of sadness in his eyes and anger in his voice. 'We never saw him again.'

'He was murdered by the Taliban?' said Nash.

Owusu nodded.

'Not just that – they tortured him first. Took him to a nearby village, chained him up in a cellar and gave him the full treatment.'

Paulsen and Nash looked at one another.

'I guess it's not hard to see why *that* might have triggered Lee,' said Paulsen. 'How did he take it?'

Owusu exhaled as he remembered.

'He got it into his head that one of the local drivers who worked for us had given Hafeez up. He had no evidence for it – but wouldn't let it go. A few days later the guy was found dead. Someone had beaten his brains in.'

'Lee?' said Nash.

Owusu shrugged.

'It was impossible to prove, and they fudged the investigation – it was easy enough to blame the Taliban. But none of the lads trusted Lee after that – most people thought he was a liability, and he was discharged a few months later.'

'How dangerous do you think he is?' said Paulsen.

There was a long pause while Owusu considered it.

'It's been a long time since I last saw Lee Ellis. But you always feared for how it was going to end for him.' He seemed caught in a memory and then shook his head. 'That's probably the best answer I can give you.'

'This doesn't really change much, does it?' said Nash as they drove back to Cedar House. The earlier sunshine had gone, and the skies were arctic grey again. 'We already knew Lee was pretty unstable.'

'Of course it changes things,' snapped Paulsen. 'He's holding two people at gunpoint and now we know he might well have form for murder.'

Nash looked at Paulsen coolly.

'Does he though? How do we know that the Taliban *didn't* murder that driver? That Lee was just traumatised by seeing someone he liked being taken hostage, tortured and then killed. You, yourself said it was easy to see why that would have upset him. There's a lot of assumptions in what we've just been told.'

Paulsen could feel herself getting irritated by Nash again and tried not to show it. The new DC was definitely grating on her nerves, and she couldn't really pinpoint why.

'It tells me Lee's got a temper that may potentially have turned lethal in the past. And that makes me wonder if he met Jemma in Tooting this morning and whether they might have had a row. One so bad he lost control,' she said.

'Her injuries suggested she *might* have been beaten,' said

Nash slowly as she realised what Paulsen was saying. 'Same as that driver in Afghanistan.'

'Exactly,' said Paulsen as outside it began to snow again.

Inside his flat, Billy Rickson looked out at the wintry street below and hugged himself. His late shift at the supermarket was getting ever closer. Getting to work through the snow wouldn't be an issue – he lived close enough to make the journey on foot, but he was sorely tempted to call in sick. Given what was going on, he really wasn't sure he could get through a full eight hours of the usual crap. Jemma was dead – and he'd loved her for as long as he could remember. It felt like he'd lost a piece of himself that he'd never, ever get back.

Ella was the mother of his daughter, and he'd loved her too, but the intensity of the feelings were nowhere near the same as they'd ever been for Jemma. He'd always held out the irrational hope that someday, some way, fate might yet bring them together. Now that was impossible, and he'd finally have to let go of this crush that he'd carried for so long and it made him feel empty. Briefly, he remembered that summer's day when she and Lee had been taken. He'd often wondered if things would have been different if it had been him instead of Lee who'd been snatched that afternoon. The bond between those two had lasted for life and a small part of him had always been jealous of the connection it had forged between them.

He watched a young woman with a pram battling through the wintry conditions outside and the silhouette made him think of Ella and Kaitlyn. He missed them, particularly his daughter – no one else had quite the same effect of calming him. He remembered Sarah's words earlier to him – *'I'm here for you . . . someone who understands'* and felt his blood boil. She had some nerve, he thought. He reached for his phone and made a call.

'Hello, Ella – can we meet? I need to talk to you.'

Inside the diner Lee had handcuffed Finn to Marco, leaving them each with a free hand to eat the bacon sandwiches he'd made. Marco had responded by throwing his across the room. Finn's was untouched while Lee was sitting at a table, noisily devouring his own.

'You forgot us, didn't you?' he said suddenly.

It took Finn a second to understand what he meant.

'That's not true – you know I stayed in touch with both of you over the years.'

Lee put his sandwich down and ran his tongue over his teeth.

'When did we last meet? September 2021, wasn't it? Admit it, you finally dropped us. How long had you been waiting to do that?'

The tone remained casual, but his body language was tense again, his hand curling around the handle of the gun. Finn wondered how much more coke he had left in his pocket.

'Am I missing something here?' said Marco. 'Why *should* he stay in touch with you? It's not like he's your mum, is it?'

Finn glared at him – he was hardly following his earlier advice to stay polite and cooperative.

'He knows what he did . . .' said Lee.

'What does that mean?' said Marco, but Finn ignored him, keeping his attention purely on Lee.

'My wife died a few years ago,' he said. 'That's not an excuse, but my head wasn't right for a while. I might have let things slip, but I never forgot – I promise you that.' Finn could see the hurt in Lee's eyes as he spoke – exactly the same look he'd seen in that eighteen-year-old version of him once.

'Jemma and I did continue to exchange emails – she kept me up to date. The impression I got was that you were both doing okay?'

'Yeah – she liked to tell people that,' said Lee.

'Are you saying it wasn't true?'

'I'm saying it's never that straightforward, is it? Sometimes things are alright, but a lot of the time they aren't. I reckon Jem was just better than me at hiding it.'

'You both dealt with what happened in very different ways though, didn't you?' said Finn carefully. He hadn't forgotten Marco's earlier comments about Lee's time in the army and was trying to find a way to steer the conversation there.

'We're different people,' said Lee. 'Or at least we were.'

'Jemma did a lot of work on herself afterwards – and you joined the armed forces, didn't you?' said Finn.

'What about it?' said Lee, looking at him suspiciously.

'Is that where you got the gun?'

Lee looked down at the weapon.

'Yeah, through a contact. I've had this for a while, though. I *always* have it on me – as far as I can, anyway. When I was in the army carrying one of these made me feel safe. It was a hard habit to give up when I came home.'

Finn was almost relieved by the explanation, which at least had some logic to it given everything he'd been through. He'd initially feared that Lee had fallen in with one of the local gangs and that's why he was carrying the weapon.

'I get why you signed up,' said Marco unexpectedly, his tone more conciliatory than it had been before. He seemed to have cottoned on to what Finn was trying to do. 'I've got mates who've served – I know how much they took from it.'

Lee nodded.

'It helped for a time. But I couldn't run away from what happened. *You* know what I'm talking about,' he said, directing the words at Finn. 'You were there – in the Red Room.'

And for a second, Finn *was* back there – a jagged flash of a memory, a cellar soaked in blood.

'*Oliver,*' he murmured.

Terry Ellis was whisked away on a gurney into the bowels of Croydon University Hospital leaving Sarah Littlewood standing in a corridor like a spare part. She'd patiently explained to one of the doctors that Terry's only next of kin was currently about a mile away holding a gun on two people in a greasy spoon and she was the next best thing to family. The medic said Terry's condition was critical but stable and though she was welcome to wait, she could be there for a while. The morning suddenly caught up with her and for want of anywhere else to go, she decided to head home.

So much had happened – first and foremost was Jemma Vickers's death, which she still hadn't given herself time to properly think about. There'd been that uneasy conversation with Billy Rickson in his flat and then the sight of Terry falling to the floor clutching his chest. Her own heart felt heavy – Lee Ellis and Alex Finn had played big parts in the story of her life, and she wasn't sure she wanted to think about how that situation might end.

She put her key into the lock of the front door but before she could turn it felt her phone vibrate in her pocket with an incoming message. Stopping she pulled the handset out and froze as she saw the message on the display. There was just a single word:

LIAR

For a moment she didn't move, trying to make sense of it. She could see who'd sent it – and that alone had some very alarming implications. The question now was how to react to it – what to do?

'Mum? Is that you?' Ella called from inside the house. She must have heard the key in the lock. Sarah took a deep breath and went inside. Ella was with her baby in the hallway. Her smile of welcome turning into something more concerned as she saw the expression on her mother's face.

'What is it?

'Nothing,' said Sarah covering quickly, putting the phone back into her pocket.

'Are you sure?'

'A lot's happened this morning,' she said and explained about Terry Ellis and her trip with him first to the RVP and then to the hospital. And as she listened to Ella's shocked reaction she was thinking about the message on her phone and why it had come today – of all days.

11

After she returned to Cedar House, Paulsen sat at her desk for around half an hour but found her concentration wandering. Her eyes kept flicking to the mounted TV screen in the corner of the room, which had been switched to the BBC News Channel. Reporters were now outside the cordon surrounding the cafe in South Norwood but just seemed to be repeating what scant information was already available. In the end, she lost patience and went to see if Skegman had an update.

'There's nothing new to say, Mattie,' he said before she could open her mouth. 'I'm in constant contact with Sami at the RVP. As far as we know it's all quiet inside that cafe.'

Paulsen looked at his wall clock – the time had just passed half past twelve.

'How do you think he's doing in there?' she said.

Skegman arched an eyebrow.

'How would you like to be locked up with Alex Finn? Thoughts and prayers with Lee Ellis at this point.'

Paulsen couldn't help but grin and it felt strangely relaxing – she hadn't had much to smile about since getting out of bed.

There was a knock at the door and Vanessa Nash entered. She looked slightly nervous and was clutching her pocketbook.

'Sorry to interrupt,' she gabbled, but Skegman was already waving her apology away.

'What is it, Vanessa – have you got something?'

She nodded.

'Digital Forensics just called. They've been going through Jemma Vickers's laptop, and it looks like she'd been doing some investigating of her own.'

'Investigating what?' said Paulsen. 'Her abduction in 2009?'

'Sort of . . .' started Nash. She flipped open her pocketbook. 'Have you ever heard the name Red Tide?' Skegman and Paulsen looked at her blankly and shook their heads. 'It's an avatar for an individual who sells niche material on the Dark Web.'

Skegman looked at her warily.

'Neither Jemma nor Lee was sexually abused by their abductor. That much we *do* know – they were examined by a doctor after they were rescued.'

'And Oliver Littlewood wasn't abused either – the post-mortem report was in the file I read earlier,' said Paulsen. 'Though that isn't to say that wasn't the eventual plan for them, I suppose.'

'Don't shoot the messenger – I'm just relaying what they told me they'd found on Jemma's laptop,' said Nash.

'What kind of niche material does he sell exactly? Porn of *some* kind presumably,' said Skegman.

'That's the thing, we're not actually sure. Digital Forensics put in a call earlier to the Online Child Sexual Abuse and Exploitation Unit at Scotland Yard,' said Nash. 'They'd heard of Red Tide, but he's pretty obscure; there's lots of avatars on the Dark Web with similar names. They're trying to find out more but what they do know from the chatter about him in the various forums is what he sells is high-end and expensive.'

'So, what made Jemma focus on him in particular?' said Paulsen.

Nash shook her head.

'We don't know. Also, Red Tide could be based anywhere in the world. The only investigative work that's ever taken place came from police in Copenhagen a couple of years back. They briefly thought they'd found evidence in the electronic chain linking him back here – to south London. But no one was ever able to firm that up. So it's more of a suggestion at this point than hard proof of anything.'

There was a moment while that sank in.

'My first thought is let's not jump to any quick conclusions,' said Skegman.

'Do we know if Red Tide was even operating in 2009?' said Paulsen.

Nash checked her pocketbook again.

'The Exploitation Unit says he *might* have been – the first mention of him in their system is from 2011, but they reckon there's every chance he could have been active before then.'

'So, DI Culley and his team wouldn't have known anything about him when they were investigating at the time,' said Skegman.

'Have Digital Forensics gone through Jemma's mobile phone yet? Is there anything similar on that and do we know who she'd gone to meet in Tooting earlier?' said Paulsen.

Nash shook her head.

'No – she didn't seem to be using her phone to access the Dark Web. The only thing they've flagged up is a call to her from a withheld number made at 7.13 p.m. last night. Even we can't track withheld numbers – so that could be who she arranged to meet, or it could be something completely innocuous.'

For a moment the only sound in the room was the water gurgling through the pipes of Cedar House's ageing radiators.

'For whatever reason Jemma must have thought Red Tide

was connected to her abduction. But if there are few details then maybe she was just trying to find out more. It could also be a blind alley,' said Skegman slowly. 'She wasn't police, and you could understand it if she'd been pursuing every possible lead that might be related to her own situation.'

'Or maybe digging into Red Tide is what got her killed? Did she stumble on something that led to her death?' said Nash.

Skegman reclined back into his seat and rubbed the back of his neck.

'That seems a stretch, but not impossible I suppose. I'm afraid this just brings us back to Dennis Trant again. Why did he confess to the abductions and why was Alex so sure he was telling the truth? Remind me what we know about the original investigation?'

Paulsen shrugged.

'Their prime suspect at the time was an ex-con called Eddie Knox. It looks like they went after him hard but weren't able to pin anything on him.'

'So maybe he's Red Eddie then?' said Nash.

Paulsen gave her a stony look while Skegman simply shook his head. He appeared to come to a decision.

'Alright – in light of this new information, let's give Lee Ellis exactly what he's been asking for. I'm formally reopening the murder investigation into Oliver Littlewood in addition to the original abduction of the other two. Have we found any contact details for Trant's surviving family yet?'

Paulsen nodded.

'Yes, there's a son. Peter Yelland – it looks like he changed his surname.'

'Well, you would – wouldn't you?' said Nash.

'Let's go and talk to him about his dad, find out what he thinks about that confession,' said Skegman. 'And while we're at it, let's find Eddie Knox too and see what he's up to today.'

'Shouldn't we also be speaking to AC Culley since he was the DI on the case?' said Paulsen.

'Yes,' said Skegman. 'We should. But so far, he doesn't seem to be in any kind of hurry to return my calls. Make of that what you will.'

'It's shit biscuit Tuesday, I'm afraid,' said Peter Yelland apologetically as he led Paulsen and Nash through a spacious open-plan office. Tall, smart and in his late twenties, Yelland worked as an insurance account executive at a company in Shoreditch and had seemingly been quite happy to speak to the detectives about his father. A large group of people blocking the corridor were crowded around a table, helping themselves to biscuits from a pile on a paper plate.

'Shit biscuit what?' said Nash, nonplussed as they weaved past.

'It's a bit of a tradition here – every Tuesday someone buys a packet of essential range custard creams for the rest of the office. It helps build team spirit.' He looked at Paulsen and Nash's uncomprehending expressions and shrugged with slight embarrassment. 'It's a thing.'

He led them through to a glass-fronted meeting room and ushered them in.

Given what they were there to talk about he seemed remarkably relaxed. Steve Garland's earlier comments about Jemma's determination to not let the past affect the present came back to Paulsen. She sensed something similar about this man. Yelland shut the door and the three of them sat down around a meeting table.

'I'm so sorry to disturb you at work with this,' said Paulsen.

'That's okay – I'm not uncomfortable discussing my father, but I'd rather the rest of the office didn't know why you're here,' he said, clasping his hands together. 'I've told them you are potential clients if that's okay.' Paulsen nodded understandingly. 'As far as my dad's concerned – I feel so disconnected from him these days that it's like I'm talking about a stranger – so ask me whatever you want.'

Paulsen could see a wedding ring on his finger that he was idly rotating as he spoke.

'It's about the confession he made in prison not long before his death – he claimed to have murdered a teenage boy, Oliver Littlewood, and abducted two others in 2009,' she said and Yelland nodded.

'I thought it was absolute bollocks at the time and I still do,' he replied. 'I pretty much disregarded it to be honest.'

'Why?' said Nash.

There was a burst of laughter outside from where his colleagues were still taking their biscuit break.

'That's a complicated answer,' he said slowly. The earlier, easy-going manner seemed to have given way to something more serious now. 'Living with shame is something that takes a long while to get used to. I meant what I said – I don't find it difficult to have the conversation, but I will admit it's been a journey.'

'It's okay – take your time if you need to,' said Paulsen, pretending it didn't matter. The truth was every second counted for Finn – but Trant's confession was important, and she wanted to form as accurate a picture as she could.

'I was extremely close to my dad as a child. He was a warm and funny man – and those are my earliest memories of him. As far as I could tell, my parents' marriage was rock solid too. But then one day, out of the blue, the police came knocking and they took his computer away. I expect you know what they found on it.'

'Extreme child pornography,' said Nash, nodding.

'*Extreme,*' repeated Yelland. 'I'm not sure that does it justice – it was the worst of the worst. The police told Mum and she told me about it later – because I asked her to. The vilest, most repugnant stuff your imagination could come up with. And not just a few pictures . . . thousands of them, gathered over many years. All those days he was being warm and funny, he was simultaneously . . .' He stopped and shook his head. 'Mum left him straight away. It's astonishing how quickly your own father can be . . . *cancelled.*'

'Were you able to do that too?' said Paulsen, more out of curiosity than a need to know. 'Just cancel him?'

'At first it was hard. But then you think about it. I never saw those photos . . . but the descriptions of them stayed with me – the look on Mum's face, the tone of her voice. And as I got older, had children of my own . . .' He shook his head. 'My father was dead to me a long time before he actually died.'

'If you don't mind me asking – did he ever touch you?' said Nash.

Paulsen glanced over at her – there were more delicate ways of phrasing the question.

'No,' answered Yelland emphatically. 'There was never even a hint of something wrong. He was very effective at keeping his two lives apart.'

'That's not uncommon in these kinds of cases,' said Paulsen.

'But he wasn't a violent man,' said Yelland. 'He was a coward actually – a meek and mild accountant by day, a loving husband and father at home – but someone hiding a pretty dark secret.' He exhaled with a slight tremble that Paulsen noticed. Whatever his earlier assurances that he was comfortable discussing Dennis Trant, she wasn't completely convinced.

'But like you say he kept his two lives separate,' she said. 'So there could have been a more violent side to him that you never saw?'

Yelland shook his head.

'I'm as sure as I can possibly be that he couldn't have murdered that teenager – because what happened was barbaric. I simply don't think he had that in him.'

'Have you ever heard the phrase "Red Tide"?' inquired Nash.

Yelland looked bemused and shook his head again.

'No, should I?'

Paulsen and Nash exchanged a glance.

'Do you know if your father ever filmed any of the stuff that was found on his computer – photographed any of it, himself?' asked Paulsen.

'No. Mum stayed in contact with the police for a long time after his arrest and they kept her informed about their investigation. They were convinced he was just a consumer, downloaded it all off the Dark Web – but his only crime was possession of the stuff. He never shot any of it himself.'

'So why did he make that confession then?' said Paulsen.

One of Yelland's workmates walked past them and gave him a breezy smile through the glass. He returned it and he waited until she was gone.

'Dad made several attempts to get in touch with us. Obviously, we never replied but it didn't stop him from trying – big heartfelt letters of contrition, that sort of thing. The longer it went on the more bitter he seemed to get. I think the reality of what he'd lost had started to bite and he went a bit mad frankly.'

'And you think that's why he confessed? Essentially, because he'd lost the plot?' said Nash. Again, Paulsen winced internally at the bluntness of the question.

'Along those lines – some late bid for notoriety, perhaps.'

'That doesn't quite stack up for me,' said Paulsen. 'He knew details about the cellar where those kids were held – the layout, the contents of it – which only the killer could have known. That's why the police at the time believed him,' she said.

Yelland shrugged.

'I know – but I think that was just a fluke. It was a cellar where a teenage boy was murdered – it's not hard to guess and describe what that might have looked like. I mean – a cellar's a cellar.' Paulsen looked unconvinced and Yelland leant forward. 'I can't give you the hard evidence you're looking for – but I *knew* my father, spent the first part of my life with him. I just don't believe he did it and I can't really explain why he confessed to it. But he's dead now and I think the world should just forget about him.' He sat back again. 'I have.'

12

2009

Finn walked into the incident room carrying two large iced coffees in transparent plastic cups. He put one on Jack Barton's desk, fumbled in his pocket and tossed a handful of sugar sachets after it. Barton gave Finn a side glance.

'A date? You're going on a date?' he said, letting his eyes do the rest of the work.

'I wish I'd never told you now,' growled Finn, before sucking on the straw of his own drink.

'And you're doing this tonight? You don't hang around, do you? I mean there's me thinking you're this repressed, up-your-own-backside, obsessive-compulsive . . .' Finn raised an eyebrow. 'And it turns out you're actually a bit of a dark horse.'

'Can we not talk about this?' said Finn.

'Absolutely. One hundred per cent,' said Barton, tearing open a sugar sachet and tipping its contents into his drink. 'Won't mention it again, I promise.'

He beamed innocently at Finn who glowered back at him.

'What are you doing anyway?'

Barton had a property website open on his PC and quickly closed it down with a guilty expression.

'Taking advantage of a brief lull to do some research.'

Finn squinted at the screen.

'Sidcup – that's out in the sticks isn't it? Are you thinking of moving?'

Barton shrugged.

'Some of us just want the quiet life, Al. I'm not like you – I've got no desire to rise up the ranks. More than happy to stay a DC for the rest of my career, mate. You've got to think of the future.'

'How does Kathy feel about that?'

Kathy was Barton's long-suffering wife and Finn frequently felt a strong empathy with her.

'She's the one driving this and I've learnt not to argue with her. You'll find out when you settle down. *If* you settle down.'

He winked provocatively at Finn who shook his head impatiently.

'Never mind that now; I think I've found something interesting.'

He put his drink down and pulled out a crumpled printout from his back pocket. 'Craig Quilter – he's Lee and Jemma's form master. Remember Billy Rickson told us he was the last person they spoke to before they left school?'

'We're supposed to be looking into Eddie Knox …' protested Barton.

Finn rolled his eyes.

'What is there to look into? We know everything there is to know about Knox. We've spoken to his probation officer – read every file and report available. What else is it Culley thinks we're going to find?'

Barton surrendered.

'Go on then – what have you got?'

Finn unfolded the sheet of A4.

'Quilter was a geography teacher at an academy in Guildford before he came to London. I spoke to the head teacher there. It turns out he left under something of a cloud.'

'What happened?'

'He had a fling with a girl he used to teach.'

Barton raised an eyebrow.

'She wasn't underage but she was an ex-pupil,' continued Finn.

'So? What's the problem – it's icky but it's not illegal.'

'Her parents didn't see it that way and tried to confront him. It got nasty. He broke the father's jaw and put him in hospital. The whole matter was settled before it got to court. But apparently, there'd been concerns about a few of his relationships prior to that as well. This girl wasn't the first.'

'It didn't stop him getting another job?' said Barton.

'No, a criminal record isn't a bar in the teaching profession – but there's a whole lot of things there that I don't like given his direct connection to Lee and Jemma.'

Barton didn't look so convinced.

'He's worth looking into, I suppose.'

'He also lives on his own, a ten-minute walk away from the Littlewoods. And not far from where Lee and Jemma were taken as well. Just like Knox,' he said.

'The difference is – Knox actually has previous convictions,' said Barton. 'This guy just lives local to the school where he works. Besides he's got an alibi, hasn't he? I'm sure I saw a statement somewhere that uniform took from him.'

Finn nodded.

'He said he was at the school doing some marking for another hour after he spoke to the three of them – but there's nobody to corroborate that.'

Barton gave it some thought.

'Aren't you putting a lot on this one incident in Guildford?' he said.

Finn shrugged.

'Possibly – but if he was close to these three, then maybe he knew where they were going after school and also had an idea of the route they might take.'

'So what do you want me to do?' said Barton.

'A bit more digging into his past, then tell me if it's worth having a bigger conversation with him.'

'And Knox?'

'Put him on the back burner for the moment.'

Barton sighed.

'Rolf will do his nut. And you know what they say – "the boss may not always be right, but the boss is always the boss".'

Finn was about to respond when Karin breezed into the incident room. He was unable to prevent himself from glancing across at her, but she ignored him and began talking to one of the DCs in the corner. He quickly swivelled round again.

'On an anthropomorphic level . . .' said Barton. 'You do realise this is absolutely fascinating?'

Finn and Karin met that evening at a tavern in Fitzrovia. It was a busy night, with a large crowd drinking outside in the evening sunshine. There'd been quite a text negotiation throughout the afternoon about the venue. Karin lived in north London while Finn lived south of the river, and in the end, they'd compromised on somewhere central. He'd suggested a wine bar, she'd told him to find a decent pub. After a long day in the heat, there'd been no time for either of them to freshen up, or even get nervous about it.

And now here they were. It was a slightly odd feeling – he remembered Sarah Littlewood's earlier fury that the police weren't doing enough. But he remained on call and knew from experience that giving his brain at least some respite on investigations like this didn't always hurt.

He'd just fought his way back from the bar with their drinks

– white wine for her, red for him – when she went straight for the jugular.

'So why isn't there a Mrs Finn, then?' she asked, taking her drink gratefully.

'It's . . . complicated,' he said, scratching his earlobe for no reason. 'Work's the main reason, I suppose. And I'm also quite fussy – which doesn't help.'

'I'd kind of picked up on that,' she said conspiratorially.

'It's not necessarily the best habit. So what about you – what's your excuse?' he said, happy to turn the conversation around. She seemed to sniff the air for a moment.

'I guess, much the same reasons. Though I also don't think finding someone has been a priority for me, of late,' she said, sipping her drink. 'So back to you.' It felt like they were playing some sort of verbal tennis now, thought Finn. 'Tell me who you are when you're not being a very serious policeman?' she said.

'Is that really how I come across?' he replied, remembering Barton's *'up-your-own backside'* jibe from earlier.

Karin smiled.

'A little bit,' she said, and Finn smiled back at her. Her expression switched from faint amusement to one of genuine curiosity. 'That's better,' she said. 'I knew you had a smile hidden away somewhere. So come on, answer my question – tell me more about yourself.'

Finn looked down at his wine and wished he'd followed his initial impulse and bought a whisky instead.

'I'm a little bit of an introvert, I suppose. You won't find me out clubbing every Friday that's for sure.'

'No shit.'

'Nor will you find me socialising with the rest of my colleagues too often. I like a quiet night in, a good book and I'm a big fan of American sport.'

'Jesus,' said Karin, taking another gulp of wine.

'And catching bad guys,' he added. 'I like doing that too.'

She pulled a face.

'You do know how cheesy that sounds, don't you?'

He grinned, unabashed.

'Totally.'

'Is that why you joined the police, though? I mean, I've met lots of officers through my work. And as I'm sure you're aware, there's quite the spectrum of motivations.'

He nodded – that was certainly true.

'My father was an academic and my mother worked for the Prison Reform Trust. They both cared about social justice, so I suppose it was just the way I was brought up. I wanted to make a difference in some way. I can't actually remember wanting to do anything else.'

'You talk about your parents in the past tense?' said Karin gently and he nodded again.

'They both died when I was relatively young – they had me quite late in life.'

'Any brothers or sisters?'

Finn shook his head.

'So no partner and no family – and evenings spent in . . . reading about baseball. Doesn't that make you rather lonely?' she continued.

He shrugged and seemed genuinely bemused by the question.

'I'm not sure I've ever thought about it like that,' he said.

She regarded him for a moment.

'Interesting.'

The conversation switched to her own background. Karin had been brought up in a city called Stralsund in north-eastern Germany and had always harboured a desire to live and work abroad. She'd come to London in her early twenties, liked it and stayed.

'I'm not sure about English men though,' she said. 'Everyone I've dated has been a bit . . . I don't know – repressed?'

Again, Barton's use of the same word earlier came back to Finn.

'Then what are you doing here, tonight?' he said drily.

She laughed, and their eyes met for a moment.

'Because you don't fool me, Detective Sergeant.'

'And what's that supposed to mean?'

There was a pause as she thought about it.

'When I first met you, I thought you were an arse,' she said.

'Thanks very much,' he replied.

'But I had this suspicion that beneath the exterior was something else. A side you don't necessarily like your colleagues – or even duty solicitors – to see. And then you helped me with that sink in the cell today.'

'So do you still think I'm an arse?'

'The jury's out on that one,' she replied, but the expression on her face was warm. 'We may need another date to find out.'

Lee was asleep when he felt a foot kick at his leg and heard the accompanying clang of chains.

'Who do you think that was crying earlier?' said Jemma not waiting for him to re-adjust.

He blearily hugged himself. The cellar was feeling cool again, which made him think it must be evening now. It seemed to exist in its own bubble – operating to its own laws of time and temperature. The heat was probably sweltering just a few feet up that staircase.

'I don't even know that it *was* someone,' he said. That was the other problem with sitting in the dark like this – it messed with your senses. Every time he tried to remember the sound, it seemed different. 'It could have just been a TV. Or a dog, whimpering,' he said.

'Yeah, because Mr Shitface has puppies up there,' said Jemma.

'Mr Shitface?' said Lee.

They both laughed and for a second they were drinking beers at the park in the sunshine without a care in the world. The feeling disappeared as quickly as it had come.

'What if it's that other boy – Oliver . . .' whispered Jemma.

'Then why keep him separate?'

'Why do you think?'

Lee did think about it and shivered. The sound of footsteps thumped above, and they both listened in silent terror. They waited for the door to crash open again, but it didn't.

'I'm not sure I want to picture that,' said Lee. He could feel his eyes starting to tear up again and this time couldn't stop it. 'He's going to hurt us, isn't he – at some point?' he said in a small voice. The threat of that seemed worse than even the possibility of death.

'You've got to try and stay calm,' said Jemma. 'Do it for me . . .'

Again, he found the sound of her voice a lifeline.

'How are you *not* scared?'

'I *am*. I promise you,' she replied. 'But I know that panicking won't help. And if that fucker tries anything on with me, it's him who'll get hurt.'

Even in the half-light Lee could see the determination on her face, knew it well from experience. She wasn't joking and thought she might even be able to do the guy some proper harm if it came to it.

'Jem . . . can I ask you something?' he said carefully. She didn't reply, so he took that as permission to continue. 'If we get out of here . . .'

'*When* we get out of here,' she cut in.

'When we get out of here,' he said, correcting himself, 'you'll still want to be with me, won't you? This won't affect *us*?'

He could hear her breathing hard before she answered.

'Let's just concentrate on staying alive, Lee. I can't think about anything else right now.'

Without warning the door to the cellar burst open again and bright light daggered in. The man in black began to descend the stairs and this time they could see he was dragging someone with him. Lee strained to get a view. It was like some rubbish was being brought down to be dumped. As the pair reached the bottom of the stairs Lee saw a dirty, terror-stricken face that he recognised at once. He'd seen it before, earlier that week in a photograph on the news – just as Jemma had suspected, the other missing boy – Oliver.

13

Today

By the time Paulsen and Nash returned to the incident room it was approaching half past one. Nash was now working at her desk eating a jacket potato from a polystyrene container. Paulsen felt no such hunger pangs. A cursory glance at the TV showed little had happened at the cafe while they'd been talking to Peter Yelland. She wasn't sure if that was a good thing or not and kept hoping to see the breaking news banner at the bottom of the screen declare the siege over without casualties.

Skegman entered the room and came over to join her. She explained what Yelland had told them about Dennis Trant and his certainty that his father hadn't been the man who'd abducted the three schoolkids fifteen years ago.

'And what's your take on that?' he asked.

For a moment she thought again about her own father, a brief shiver as she imagined him alone in some unfamiliar room – hostage to something altogether different.

'I know my dad inside out. What he's capable of – and what he's not,' she said. 'Yelland was *so* sure that Trant couldn't have murdered Oliver Littlewood and I'm inclined to trust his instinct.' She shrugged. 'But then the man was clearly good at keeping secrets, so I could be wrong.'

Skegman mulled it over. 'If it *isn't* Trant, we're still back to the issue of why he confessed and how he acquired such detailed knowledge of that cellar.'

'I'm wondering if that's because he *had* seen it,' said Paulsen. 'Through a picture he'd been given perhaps – if he was working with someone else?'

Skegman nodded. 'There were no photographs of it in the collection retrieved from his computer. They did another search after his confession and found nothing – but that doesn't rule it out. There's also the question of who might have provided it – this Red Tide character Jemma was investigating perhaps?'

'Maybe – but we know so little about him at the moment. It looks like she did a lot of digging, joined some chat forums and exchanged some exploratory emails with a few people, but there's nothing that gives any detail. The Exploitation Unit are helping us out with that though – they've promised to give me a call when they have a bit more information.'

Nash came over to join them.

'I've got a current address for Eddie Knox. He's moved a few times since the original investigation but still lives locally. And get this, he's had several stints inside since 2009.'

'What for?' asked Skegman.

'Several knifepoint robberies. And a nasty incident where a guy on his way home late at night was violently mugged. He ended up with a fractured skull.'

'Leopards and spots and all that,' said Skegman.

Something was flagging at the back of Paulsen's mind – but she couldn't quite make the connection and the feeling annoyed her.

'The common denominator seems to be money – sounds like he's skint,' continued Nash. 'He's got to be worth pulling in, hasn't he?'

'Hold on, let's not jump the gun, Vanessa,' said Paulsen.

'I'm sure Knox isn't the only person on our patch with form like that and there must have been a good reason why Alex wasn't convinced by him during the original inquiry.'

Nash shot her a waspish look.

'Or maybe he got it wrong back then and we're in danger of repeating his mistake?'

'You don't know the DI – I do. You've been here half a day and you're querying his judgement? You might want to actually meet him before you start doing that,' snapped Paulsen.

'Let's all just take a step back for a moment,' said Skegman. 'The whole point of reopening this investigation is to look at *everything* with fresh eyes – and that's exactly what Alex would do if he were here. So let's go and talk to Knox – then decide whether he's significant or not.'

Nash nodded primly and returned to her desk while Skegman turned to Paulsen.

'I can't tell whether you're giving her a hard time, or whether this is just you being you, Mattie – but do you want to cut her some slack? It's not exactly the easiest first day she's walked into,' he said.

'And she's doing alright,' replied Paulsen, almost spitting the words out.

'But?' said Skegman, sensing there was one.

'But maybe she could also read the room a little better.'

'And perhaps that's something that works both ways?' he replied.

Eddie Knox had been shopping at his local One Stop when the news bulletin playing on the radio behind the counter stopped him in his tracks.

Police have named the woman who died in Tooting this morning as thirty-two-year-old Jemma Vickers. Officers from the Major Investigation Team are still establishing the exact circumstances of the incident and forensic inquiries are ongoing as well as a detailed trawl of CCTV footage. Detectives continue to appeal for any witnesses and would like to hear from anyone who was in the vicinity of Fallows Road between six and seven-thirty this morning.'

Standing in one of the shop's aisles, he'd tried to make sense of it. Perhaps it wasn't *that* Jemma Vickers; then he shook his head. Of course it must be. There were many reasons why this might have occurred, and it could be something completely unrelated to what happened fifteen years ago. Or it might have *everything* to do with it. He left the shop, found a quiet corner, and made a phone call.

'Don't panic,' said a quiet but firm voice. 'Go home and keep your head down. Only call me again if the police get in touch with you.'

And ten minutes later, just after he'd got back to the sanctuary of his flat – he received a call from a DC Vanessa Nash.

As Paulsen and Nash made the drive from Cedar House to Knox's flat in Coulsdon the atmosphere was distinctly frosty – and that had nothing to do with the falling snow outside. Nash was subdued following the spat between them in the incident room earlier. While not necessarily sulking, she'd clearly decided silence was the best policy.

Paulsen was also feeling uncomfortable. It had rankled with her to hear Nash query Finn when she hadn't even met him yet – especially given the situation he was currently in. But she also knew Skegman's words hadn't necessarily been wrong either. She wasn't being particularly fair to the newcomer and didn't seem to be able to stop herself either. Most of all she wasn't even sure *why* she was doing it. Her own shittiness was making her even more bad-tempered as the day progressed – like a self-inflicted feedback loop of shittiness, she thought, gloomily.

As they arrived, she decided to focus on why they were there. The pair walked up to the building where Knox lived, and she surveyed the row of windows on the adjacent flats.

'I wonder how many of his neighbours know about his record,' she said as Nash pressed the buzzer. They waited but there was no reply.

'He was expecting us, wasn't he?' said Paulsen.

Nash nodded and tried a different buzzer. After a few moments, one of the other residents opened the door and let them in once they'd flashed their warrant cards. They walked up a flight of stairs to Knox's door and Paulsen instantly noticed it was ajar.

'Hello?' she called out but there was no answer.

They cautiously entered and saw a dark-haired man sitting on a sofa with his back to them.

'Eddie?' called Paulsen, but the man didn't respond. She walked round and saw the reason why. He was slumped back with what appeared at first glance to be an expression of mild alarm on his face. One hand was casually cupping his stomach in the same way you might after a particularly heavy meal. His midriff was soaking wet and dark viscous liquid was dripping down on to the carpet. As she moved closer, she could see his fingers gently resting on something.

'Oh, Jesus . . .' said Nash, and Paulsen realised what it was she was looking at – the grey-white outline of an intestine that had spilt through the gaping slit in his stomach.

Inside the cafe, Lee had handcuffed Finn back to the radiator and bound Marco's hands again in a fresh set of plastic ties. Now, to both men's dismay, he was standing at the counter snorting more coke.

'Come on, mate, you've only just done a line – that's a waste

129

of good shit,' said Marco. Lee wiped a residue of white powder from his nose and ignored him.

Finn was watching him with mounting concern. He'd also been trying to work out what the likely train of thought would be right now in the RVP. It had felt a while since they'd last been in contact – the investigation on the outside had clearly yet to produce anything meaningful. The longer this went on, the more coked up Lee got and the less well this was likely to end. Marco was shaking his head.

'I still don't understand what this is all about – why am I even here?' he said, almost to himself.

Lee gestured at Finn.

'Don't ask me – ask him.'

As Finn caught Lee's gaze his eyes were then drawn to the elaborate inkwork on the gunman's neck. The vivid colours didn't quite hide the large ugly scars underneath. He could remember the day they found him when the deep cuts were still fresh.

'Maybe I'm getting this wrong,' said Marco. 'But this bloke *saved* you, didn't he? Stayed in touch with you and your mate for years afterwards. Are you sure you're not just blaming him because you *need* someone to blame?'

It was a decent assessment, thought Finn, even if he'd picked entirely the wrong moment to express it. There was a new fire behind Lee's eyes now – which was either righteous fury or the fresh line of coke kicking in.

'No, and I'll tell you why not. Because his mistake back then didn't just cost my friend her life today. The guy who took us has been out there doing the same thing for years – all because *he* won't admit he got it wrong.'

Finn frowned.

'Hold on, that's a bit of a leap. Where do you get that idea from?'

Lee shook his head.

'Don't you know how many teenagers go missing in this part of London? Do you think that's a coincidence? Haven't you heard of Jarrod Thomas?'

Finn sighed as he realised what he meant.

'Of course I've heard of Jarrod Thomas.'

'Who's he?' asked Marco, bemused.

'A fifteen-year-old boy who disappeared just before Christmas,' said Finn. 'There are posters of him all over south London. But that's the point – teenagers go missing all the time. I know the stats – it's my job. A lot of those are runaways. Eighty per cent of them are found within twenty-four hours and ninety-eight per cent are resolved with no harm recorded. The idea that the *same* man's been out doing this, over and over, is absurd. We'd know if that was the case.'

Lee strode over and pushed the barrel of the gun sharply under Finn's chin, jerking his head back. 'Don't you *ever* use that word to me,' he said, almost whispering. 'What happened to us wasn't absurd – and what happened to Oliver Littlewood *definitely* wasn't absurd. Do you understand?'

He dug the gun in deeper.

'You're right,' said Finn calmly. 'So why not set me straight– and tell me exactly what happened in that cellar before we pulled you out of there? Because I think there *is* something you've held back – otherwise I don't think we'd be in here now.'

Lee pulled the gun away, but their eyes remained locked, the years of history occupying the space in between. Marco looked defeated by the whole exchange and held up his bound wrists.

'In the meantime, I could really use a piss,' he said. 'Do you mind?' Lee was breathing hard, still staring at Finn. 'I'm desperate and it's not like there's a window in that bog to jump out of, is there?' he added, nodding towards the back of the cafe. It seemed to Finn like an attempt to break the tension and he was silently grateful.

'Alright,' said Lee finally. 'But don't try anything stupid.'

Putting the gun down he picked up a knife from the counter and cut the plastic ties around Marco's wrists.

Finn saw what was going to happen a fraction of a second before it did. Marco launched himself at Lee, grabbing for the knife. The audaciousness of the move took Lee by surprise, but he recovered quickly. Briefly, the two wrestled for control of the blade, and Finn could see Lee reaching out with his free hand for the gun on the counter. Marco, bigger and stronger, wrenched the knife from his grip but his victory lasted just a split second.

The deafening sound of a shot cracked around the room. Marco flew backwards, his head smashing into the wall, and he slid to the ground, bright red blood smearing down the white brickwork after him.

14

Outside the cafe, the marksmen dotted around the building reacted instantly to the sound of the gunshot. They took up ready positions, leant in and focused on the crosshairs in the sights of their Heckler and Koch rifles. Around them the snow continued to lightly fall, floating down like small white feathers on the breeze.

Inside the RVP, they all heard the gunshot too and immediately crowded around the DC who was monitoring the exterior of the cafe via the feed from one of the cameras they'd set up earlier. They all studied the image on the screen in silence for a moment but there was no sign of any activity.

'Call him,' said Walsh, and Rachel went back to the table she'd used earlier and hit the redial button on her phone. This time there was no instant answer. There was an agonising wait instead, as it rang out until the voicemail kicked in. A tinny voice spoke to them through the speakerphone.

'This is Lee – I can't talk – leave a message and I'll get back to you.'

Rachel cut the call.

'What the hell's just happened in there?' said Walsh.

The noise was still reverberating around Finn's head. There was an acrid smell in the air and for a second, he thought he could hear church bells as well until he realised it was a ringtone. Lee was now crouching down on the floor, still clutching the gun but with his hands over his ears. He was shouting something too that Finn couldn't make out.

As Finn finally got his bearings back, he twisted to look at Marco who'd fallen next to him. With one hand now cuffed to the radiator, he couldn't turn properly but he could hear a gurgling noise that didn't sound good. It looked like Marco had sustained a head wound of some sort and Finn followed the smear of blood up the wall and realised what had happened. He pushed against the cuffs again, feeling them dig into his wrists and swore.

'Lee!' he shouted. 'It's okay – you *didn't* shoot him. He's not dead.'

But the other man was still oblivious. His skeletal face was red with tears, and he seemed to be mumbling something now. The phone, which had fallen on to the floor near him, began ringing again and Finn stared at it in frustration.

'You need to answer that. Marco's not dead – *you didn't shoot him,*' he repeated. With his free hand, he pointed at the brickwork above his head. 'You shot the wall – you can see where the bullet hit. He hurt his head when he fell back against it, and I think he needs medical attention.'

Lee didn't seem to hear him, and the phone stopped ringing. Finn swore again and looked over at Marco who'd stopped moving now.

'Lee, *listen* to me – they'll have heard the shot outside. You need to tell them what's happening in here *fast.*'

Finn was screaming the words now and finally seemed to be getting through. Lee lowered his hands and slowly rose to his feet.

'He shouldn't have tried to take me by surprise,' he said. 'You never do that to a soldier.'

The earlier conversation about Lee's time in the army came

back to Finn. His reaction to what had just happened certainly looked like PTSD. Lee bent over Marco's prone body.

'Careful – it's a head injury,' warned Finn. 'It might be a concussion.' The phone on the floor rang for the third time. 'If you don't tell them what's happening, they'll assume the worst and send a team in,' he said urgently. Again, it seemed to take a second longer than it should for the message to get through, then Lee swiped the phone up and jabbed at the display.

'*Hello?*'

In the RVP, Dattani and Walsh exchanged relieved glances. They still had no idea what was going on but at least Lee had answered the phone.

'What's happening in there, Lee?' said Rachel trying to keep her voice steady. 'We thought we heard a shot?'

'Yeah,' he said, almost monotone.

Walsh held up his hands as if to say, '*What does that mean?*'

'Yes, there *was* a shot?' said Rachel.

'It was an accident . . .'

Sami Dattani felt his heart miss a beat. Jackie Ojo's funeral, the tears of her son, the wake afterwards, the shock at Cedar House – all of it – flashed through his mind. Not again, he thought with rising nausea.

'Is anyone hurt?' said Rachel.

'Yes – Marco, but it's not serious. The bullet didn't hit him – he fell and cut his head, that's all.'

'What about DI Finn – is he okay?' asked Rachel.

'Yeah,' said Lee in the same dead voice and Dattani allowed himself to breathe out.

'*Get him to put Finn on,*' mouthed Walsh and Rachel nodded.

'Can we speak to him, Lee? Just to check he's alright?'

'Why? Don't you believe me?'

'We just want to make sure everyone's safe. Can you put him on – just for a moment?'

Finn had been watching Marco while he listened to the phone call. The cafe owner was still out cold and that wasn't a good sign. It was only on television and in movies that people were knocked out as if they'd been tranquillised. He should have regained consciousness by now and there was a nasty pool of blood beginning to form under his head.

Lee held out the phone.

'They want to talk to you,' he said.

Finn took the phone gratefully with his free hand and put it to his ear, trying to focus, aware they might use the call to try and communicate something important to him.

'This is Finn,' he said and also assumed he was talking to a roomful of people via speakerphone.

'Hello – I'm Acting DI Rachel Howe,' replied a taut voice on the other end. 'Are you okay?'

Finn had seen the name on some paperwork somewhere but couldn't put a face to her.

'I'm fine but there's a man in here who needs urgent medical attention—'

Lee plucked the phone out of Finn's grasp and he felt his heart sink.

'No one's coming in here,' said Lee into the handset. 'It's just a bang to the head. We've got food and water – he'll be fine.'

'He needs a doctor,' called Finn urgently.

'I said no one's coming in,' Lee repeated.

'A first aid kit then – something, anything,' pleaded Finn.

Lee looked down at Marco – saw the quantity of blood now pooling on the floor.

'Alright – a first aid kit,' he said. 'You leave it outside the

136

front. And don't get any ideas about taking pot shots when the door opens because it'll be Finn who'll bring it in – and I'll have *my* gun pointing at him. You phone me when it's there. And understand – nothing's changed. This doesn't end until you find the guy who started all of this. The next time you call, I want updates.'

He hung up as Marco groaned again.

'If he's concussed and it isn't treated – it could do long-term damage. Let him go, Lee,' said Finn.

'Stop being dramatic. It's just a graze – he'll wake up in a minute.' Lee bent over Marco again, pulling a fresh plastic tie from his back pocket. 'You and I have seen a lot worse.'

Paulsen was standing in the snow with her phone to her ear as an incident response vehicle arrived outside Eddie Knox's flat. Nash greeted the two uniformed officers inside, before leading them into the building. Paulsen was talking to John Skegman who'd been updating her with the developments from the cafe.

'What do you mean an accident?' she said, one finger in her ear as she strained to hear him.

'That's what Lee said it was, according to Sami.'

'Guns don't go off accidentally. They have triggers that need to be pulled—'

'Mattie – it's as much as we know,' said Skegman. 'They've spoken briefly to Alex and confirmed he's unhurt.'

'Is he? Or is he only saying that because he's got a gun to his head?' said Paulsen.

'Stop asking me things I can't answer. As I keep repeating, that's a situation we can't influence. Right now, we need to focus on who killed *Eddie Knox*,' he reminded her sharply.

He was right, thought Paulsen, and she took in a lungful of cold air, felt the burn in her throat and exhaled.

'Uniform have just arrived here, and forensics are on their way,' she said. 'We'll start knocking on doors as fast as we can and see if anyone saw or heard anything. The door to the flat was open when we got here too – so Knox must have let his killer in. This can't be coincidental, can it? He gets murdered straight after we get in touch asking to speak with him.'

A police van was now pulling up and parking next to the IRV. Paulsen could see Nash emerging from the front of the building. The two constables she'd just taken inside would protect the crime scene until the forensic team arrived. A uniformed inspector jumped out of the van and immediately began speaking to Nash.

'You're right,' said Skegman. 'The same man Finn investigated over the abductions in 2009 is murdered within hours of Jemma Vickers – there's got to be a connection between the two deaths.'

'Do we know any more about this Red Tide yet? Or why Jemma was investigating him?' said Paulsen, watching as the inspector began organising a cordon around the front of the building. Some of the other residents had noticed the activity now and were coming out to see what was going on.

'Do we really think he's relevant?' said Skegman.

'I don't know. But right now, I'm clutching at straws because I'm struggling to understand who would want to kill both Vickers and Knox – assuming it *is* even the same killer. It doesn't make any sense to me – it's both the original suspect *and* the original victim.'

'We've been talking to Digital Forensics again – Jemma Vickers's interest in Red Tide suddenly stopped a few months ago. So either she ruled him out . . .'

'. . . or she'd found what she was after,' completed Paulsen thoughtfully. 'Are we sure we've got all her phones and hard drives? I know we found material on her laptop but if she was doing a deep dive on the Dark Web then she might have wanted to keep that *very* private and not use any of her usual devices . . .'

'Possibly – but it might be a difficult one to broach with her partner in the circumstances. I'll look into it,' said Skegman.

The inspector was looking over at Paulsen now, clearly wanting to speak with her, and she held up a couple of fingers and mouthed *'two minutes'* to her.

'So, what do you want me to do?' she said into the phone.

'There's something else we've found this end,' said Skegman. 'Alex took a liking to a man called Craig Quilter in 2009. He was one of Lee and Jemma's teachers at Thomas Downey School. He was also the last person who saw them on the day of the abductions.'

'I saw his name in the file earlier – what about him?' said Paulsen.

'One or two things as it happens. He left Thomas Downey in 2011 and moved to a school in Devon. He quit a year later after he was accused of assaulting one of the pupils there.'

'What was that about – do we know?' said Paulsen.

'Sounds like he was slightly *too* interested in the boy's girl-friend – who was roughly the same age as Jemma when she was abducted. He's no longer a teacher and he moved back to south London in 2016. Something similar happened at a school in Guildford before he even came to London and taught Lee and Jemma.'

Paulsen stared across at some snow-dusted wheelie bins on the other side of the road as she tried to make sense of the information.

'Is there anything in his more recent past?'

'Yes, a domestic last year, which uniform attended. His wife said he'd tried to push her down a flight of stairs during an argument. Like Knox, there's a consistent theme.'

'My head's hurting – so has his name come up anywhere else?' said Paulsen.

'Yes – we cross-checked him with Digital Forensics – Jemma seems to have taken an interest in Quilter too. They had a brief exchange of emails just before Christmas. She wanted to meet him for a chat, and Quilter agreed to it.'

'Do we know what that was about? Did she think *he* was Red Tide?' asked Paulsen.

'Good question – that's the only communication between them that they found. But it's suddenly looking like an interesting conversation. I'll text you his address. Let uniform manage the crime scene at Knox's flat – I'll send a couple of DCs down to relieve you. Take Vanessa and go and talk to Quilter.'

Paulsen looked over at Nash who was talking again to the inspector.

'It would really help to be able to speak with someone directly involved in the original investigation, guv. Is there still nothing from AC Culley's office?' she said.

'Not a word,' replied Skegman. 'Anyone would think he's trying to avoid us.'

15

When the call came, things happened quickly. An old man, out in the early morning sunshine working on his allotment, had smelt the smoke first and then saw it and called it in. Finn and Barton were now standing on a patch of wasteland behind the allotments close to Croydon Airport. They were staring at the burnt-out wreckage of a white van. They'd managed to recover a partial number plate and found that it belonged to a local builder who'd reported the vehicle missing eight days previously.

'Are you going to tell me how your date went?' said Barton casually.

'The time frame works,' said Finn, ignoring the question. 'If you were going to abduct three schoolkids then you might want to use a van like this and then burn the evidence afterwards.'

The old man had called the fire brigade as well as the police and they'd done an efficient job of making the smoking wreckage safe. The whole thing smelt appalling though – a toxic mixture of burnt rubber, fuel and smoke.

'It also matches the description of the vehicle Billy Rickson and the other witness gave us,' agreed Barton. 'Was there a little bit of a snog at the end of the night?' he added.

Finn looked around the patch of nowhere where the van had been left.

'I doubt there's a street camera anywhere near here, is there? That's deliberate.'

'Blimey – maybe more than a snog then?'

Finn gave him a weary look.

'You're not funny.'

Barton grinned, then turned serious.

'If this *is* the van that was used to take those kids, then destroying it suggests he might be done – for now at least, anyway.'

'That makes sense,' agreed Finn. 'I still don't understand why he needs three of them, though. Assuming he has Oliver, Jemma and Lee. It feels like a very particular number.'

Barton pondered it for a moment.

'If the intention isn't to kill them – and we haven't found any bodies yet – then three teenagers are quite the handful to keep watered and fed. Not to mention, quiet.'

Finn nodded thoughtfully.

'Every instinct suggests trafficking to me – so why does it feel like there's another layer to this?' he said, staring at the burnt-out vehicle.

Back at Cedar House, Culley was treating the discovery of the van as a major breakthrough.

'We know where Jemma and Lee were abducted. We've narrowed down from street cameras roughly where Oliver Littlewood was probably taken. And now we know where the van, which was most likely used to grab them, was dumped. We also know when and where the van itself was stolen in the first place – so we surely must be able to triangulate where that vehicle's been?' he said, rather pleased with his own logic flow.

The DI was in short sleeves, the two large sweat patches under his arms matching the glistening moisture on the top of his head.

'I can go through the CCTV,' offered Barton. 'As you say, guv, now that we've found the van, there are plenty of new areas we can check.'

Culley's piggy eyes narrowed.

'There's hours of it, Jack, and I need you and Alex working the investigation. I'll allocate someone especially to the job.'

Barton shrugged.

'Are you sure? I don't mind. I've been working this since Oliver went missing, I know pretty much every detail to look out for.'

Culley irritably waved him away.

'I'd much rather you and Alex focused on Eddie Knox. Where have you got with him?'

'We've got some feelers out there,' answered Finn smoothly. 'Should have something for you later, I'd imagine,' he lied, without a hint of guilt.

'Good,' said Culley with satisfaction. 'Let me know what comes back.'

He turned and headed back to his office. Barton raised an eyebrow but as Finn was about to respond he stopped. Over the DC's shoulder, he could see through the incident room window Karin Bergmann making her way to the front entrance of the building. He quickly tried to avert his gaze but it was too late, and Barton turned to see what he was looking at.

'Oh,' he said, turning with a grin.

'Not a word,' said Finn before he could add more. 'Instead of smirking, do you want to tell me what you've found on Craig Quilter?'

'Not much to add to what you discovered. I did a background check, nothing flagged up and his record at Thomas Downey has been exemplary. But I assumed you'd ignore that and want to talk to him anyway – so he's expecting a visit from us this morning.'

Finn smiled.

'I knew there was a reason I liked you,' he said.

It was break time when Finn and Barton arrived at the school. Watching the mini ecosystem of the playground as they walked through, Finn found it hard not to flashback to his own schooldays. There was an impromptu game of football taking place with a tennis ball, huddles of kids shouting and remonstrating at each other. His eyes were scanning for something in particular though, and he made a quick bet with himself that he could find it before they reached the main entrance. Sure enough, he did – two boys standing alone in the shade talking unnoticed, ignoring the rowdy noise and crowd elsewhere. Watch the quiet ones, thought Finn, feeling a certain solidarity.

His first impression of Craig Quilter was that he reminded him a little of Superman's alter ego Clark Kent. Good-looking with a square jaw, glossy black hair, and a smart pair of designer glasses, he seemed to be the only person in south London unaffected by the heatwave. Dressed immaculately in a creaseless check shirt and chinos, there didn't seem to be a hint of sweat on him. They were talking in an empty classroom that felt like a greenhouse as the sun blazed through the windows on one side.

'The kids are still pretty shaken up,' said Quilter. 'I know it might not look like it out there but trust me – it's manifesting in quite subtle ways. I don't suppose there have been any developments in your investigation?'

'I'm afraid not,' said Barton.

'It's kind of why we're here,' said Finn. 'I know you've already been asked about this, but can you clarify for us a few details about the last time you saw Lee and Jemma?'

Quilter nodded.

'Sure – anything I can do to help.'

'What did you talk about with them before they left that day?' said Barton.

The teacher looked surprised.

'As you say, it's all in the statement I gave to one of your constables.'

Finn nodded.

'Just humour us – we only want to make sure nothing important was missed.'

Quilter shrugged.

'I saw them just before they left – Lee, Jemma and Billy. We've been talking a lot about the future. Not just university – not all of them are going – but what they might want to do with themselves, career wise. Their thinking is changing all the time, as it does at that age, and I've been acting as a sounding board really.'

Finn was frowning now, remembering Billy's comment earlier that Quilter had called the meeting.

'Sorry – but at whose instigation was this? Did you summon them, or did they come and find you?'

Quilter blew gently.

'I'm not sure I remember actually.' He paused for a moment. 'Jemma, I think it was – she saw me in the corridor between lessons and I told her to come and find me after school.'

Finn glanced over at Barton but he didn't seem to have clocked the inconsistency.

'And she brought Billy and Lee with her?' said Barton.

'Yes, but that's not unusual. They're a pretty tight trio – they've been mates all the way through.' He smiled unctuously. 'And I think Lee and Jemma were something of an item. They said they were all heading to the park after school to enjoy the sunshine.'

'Did you know which one?'

'Lloyd Park – as I understand it. They seem to have gone there a lot this summer – I've heard them mention it a few times.'

Finn and Barton exchanged a glance.

'And how long were you here yourself afterwards?'

Quilter looked at them awkwardly.

'Why would that matter? Am I under suspicion or something?'

Barton smiled briskly.

'As DS Finn said, we just want to clarify some of the details.'

Quilter didn't look hugely reassured.

'I stayed for about an hour doing some marking. I like to get a chunk done before I go and then finish the rest at home after I've eaten.'

'Can anyone corroborate that?' said Finn.

The atmosphere was distinctly starting to cool now.

'No,' said Quilter.

'So if we look through the camera footage from the school car park, we'll see you leaving when you say you did then?' said Finn.

'No, because I don't have a car. I live locally and I walk to and from work,' he replied, an edge in his voice now.

'Do you know the Littlewoods?' asked Barton. 'You don't live too far from them, I believe.'

'How do you know where I live?' said Quilter sharply, but neither detective responded. He sighed. 'No, I don't know them – I mean I might have encountered them, but I didn't have a clue who they were until I saw their faces in the news when Oliver went missing. He's not a pupil at this school.'

'You were at Cardinal Askew Academy in Guildford before you came here, weren't you?' said Finn.

Quilter's eyes flickered with confusion.

'Yes – why?'

'Wasn't there an incident of some sort there which led to your departure?'

If they thought the question might put Quilter further on the back foot they were wrong. He seemed to visibly relax.

'*Oh* – that's what this is all about. Of course, I can see why you'd be interested in that. It was all a misunderstanding though. There was a former pupil of mine there whose father was an alcoholic. She was having a lot of problems and I was trying to help her. Unfortunately, the father made entirely the wrong conclusions about what I was doing and confronted me. But it was all quite innocent, I can assure you,' he said and smiled.

'Doesn't sound that innocent. You broke his jaw, didn't you?' said Finn but Quilter shook his head dismissively.

'I was just defending myself – it all got rather out of hand.'

'If it was all so harmless, why did you leave? Doesn't it suggest you have a problem with your temper?'

Quilter gave a slightly forced laugh.

'Of course not – I couldn't punch my way out of a paper bag. It was just a very unsavoury isolated incident. But once something like that happens it leaves a cloud – as this conversation rather proves.'

'You don't make a habit of dating teenagers then?' said Finn, persisting.

Quilter looked over at Barton who said nothing.

'My record here is spotless. I have nothing to explain – and I certainly have had *nothing* to do with these abductions,' he said stonily, the helpful façade finally dropping.

'I don't like him, and I don't believe him,' said Finn as he and Barton walked back to their car. Break time was over, and the playground was deserted now.

'I don't understand,' said Barton. 'You're happy to give

Knox – a convicted offender – a free pass. But this guy, a schoolteacher, you don't trust.'

Finn thought about it before he replied.

'Everything was too slick and no answer he gave had any substance to it – we can't prove Jemma instigated the conversation after school, and don't forget Billy told us Quilter asked to see *them*. We can't prove when Quilter left the building that day because he could have slipped out any of the exits on foot. We can't prove he doesn't know Oliver Littlewood and we can't prove what went on in Guildford was as harmless as he says.'

Now it was Barton who was thinking.

'All true – but are you sure you aren't just blinkered because you want to prove Culley wrong about Knox?'

And as they reached the car, Finn had no answer.

Something awful had happened to Oliver Littlewood. Even in the gloom, Lee could see the nasty purple bruise on his face and a smudge of dried blood on his neck. And then there was the trembling; he didn't seem to have stopped since he'd been brought down to the cellar. He might have been good-looking in different circumstances, with boyish features and a thick mop of chestnut brown hair. It looked like he'd been dressed to impress when he was taken – he was wearing a dark navy T-shirt and expensive jeans that were bound with a smart-looking leather belt.

'Are you okay?' asked Jemma but he didn't seem to hear her. She glanced at Lee and then tried again. 'It's Oliver, isn't it? What do your mates call you – Ollie?'

'Yeah,' he said finally. His voice was unexpectedly clear, posh even.

'I'm Jemma and this is Lee. Looks like we're all in this shit together. Have you been here all this time too?'

Oliver nodded.

'Upstairs – some sort of loft. I didn't realise there were others here though . . .'

There was something of the beaten dog about him, thought Lee. He was terrified, almost even of *them*, it seemed.

'How did he get you?' said Jemma.

His face clouded over as he remembered.

'I was on my way home after a night out. I was a bit pissed, and suddenly this bloke grabbed me, tried to drag me towards his van. He caught me by surprise – I tried to fight him off but then he sprayed me with this stuff . . .' He tailed off and shook his head.

'Yeah – that's what happened to us too,' said Jemma. 'Is that how you got those bruises – fighting him off?' she said, and he nodded.

'Has he said anything to you – told you *why* he wants us?' said Lee already feeling himself tense up at the possible reply but the boy could only shake his head again. You could tell Ollie had been held here a couple of days longer – he looked dirtier, more tired, more scared . . . more broken. Lee wondered how long it would take before he and Jemma became like that. They talked for a while, filling in some more of the details about who they all were until the conversation petered out and Lee dozed off after that.

The only food they'd been given since they'd arrived had been some packaged supermarket sandwiches. It was therefore a surprise when their captor returned with something hot a little while later. It was nothing elaborate – just pizza slices, of the dethawed variety, but Lee wolfed his down gratefully. Oliver had been given a knife and fork, but the other two hadn't – the newcomer had also been given his portion on a plate of his own, while Lee and Jemma shared one. Whether that was intentional and what the point of it was, was hard to tell.

When they'd finished the man wordlessly collected their plates. Even after the door closed behind him, they waited for a few seconds before breathing out. Each time he came, it brought a wave of instant terror, each time he left without harming them the relief was indescribable.

'Lee,' whispered Jemma quickly. 'Look.' She pointed over at Oliver. Next to him, lying discarded on the ground was the knife he'd been using.

16

Today

There was something creepy about Craig Quilter, thought Paulsen. For someone who didn't seem to have any discernible income, he'd clearly managed his money well. He lived in a small, well-tended first-floor flat in Purley. But as pleasant as his home was, the man himself seemed to be the epitome of seedy. He'd bleached his hair, had greasy pockmarked skin and wore oversized thick black glasses frames, which magnified his eyes. It was unsettling because you could tell he might have been good-looking once.

It was hard to believe he used to be a schoolteacher. There didn't seem to be much evidence of a woman living in the flat, she noticed, remembering Skegman's information earlier about the domestic incident uniform had attended the previous year.

'What is it I'm supposed to have done?' he asked with an exaggerated weariness.

'We just need to ask you some questions about your movements today,' said Nash.

'My movements?' he said, smirking as if enjoying a private joke.

Paulsen was determined to keep this as functional as possible.

'Where were you between six and seven-thirty this morning?' she said.

'Warm in bed.'

'You live alone here then?' said Nash.

'I'm a single man now, yes,' he replied flatly.

'Have you left the flat at all for any reason today?'

He scowled at them both, the thick glasses giving him the look of a slightly angry owl.

'No.'

'How do you earn your living?' said Paulsen.

'I don't have to bust a gut – I have a lot of savings,' he said. 'Which I top up with private tuition work.'

'You've done well to effectively retire at your age. Where did all those savings come from?' said Nash immediately.

Quilter smiled thinly.

'Mostly inheritance after my mum died. But the pandemic was good to me too – thanks to Zoom I've made a lot of money without needing to leave this room. I'm sure there are clever people who can verify that for you if required,' he added smugly.

'Have you ever heard of a man called Eddie Knox?' said Paulsen, cutting to the chase.

He shook his head blankly.

'What about the name Red Tide – does that mean anything to you?' said Nash.

'Not a clue – is that some sort of detergent?'

Nash looked across at Paulsen.

'Are we done?' said Quilter. 'If so – lovely as this has been, I've got things to be getting on with.'

Paulsen smiled quickly at him.

'One more question, Craig – one of your former pupils at Thomas Downey School got in touch with you before Christmas, didn't she? Jemma Vickers? And we know that you agreed to meet with her.'

For the first time, he looked thrown.

'As far as I'm aware there's no crime in that,' he said, recovering quickly.

'What did she want?'

'Why does it matter?'

'Because Jemma's dead,' said Paulsen and she explained what had happened.

Quilter seemed genuinely shocked.

'You're surely not trying to pin that on me? I was just her geography teacher, a long time ago.'

'We just want to know why she wanted to talk with you?'

He sighed and glanced out of the window for a moment.

'It wasn't some happy school reunion, I'll admit that much. She'd heard about the domestic I was involved in with my ex – someone had found out and posted it on a Facebook group of ex-Thomas Downey pupils she was part of.'

'Why did she want to speak with you specifically about that?' said Nash. 'If I saw something like that about one of my ex-teachers – I can't say my first reaction would be to look them up.'

This time Quilter nodded in agreement.

'Yes – but you weren't abducted by some nutter, were you? She'd got it into her mind that I *might* have been the person who abducted them in 2009. So, she wanted to check for herself. To look at me, hear me – with an adult sensibility, I suppose – and see if it matched with her memories.'

'And did it?' asked Paulsen.

'No. And she accepted that too, even apologised to me afterwards, believe it or not.' He looked at them defiantly. 'A lot's happened over those fifteen years. I wish I could turn back the clock – be that schoolteacher again and maybe make some different choices in life. But I didn't abduct those kids – and for what it's worth I'm sorry about Jemma. Because I liked her.'

★

'I believe him,' said Nash as they walked back to the car afterwards.

'You believe a man who literally can't corroborate a single thing he's just told us,' said Paulsen. 'He might well have murdered Jemma Vickers in Tooting this morning – because maybe she *did* identify him as their abductor.'

Nash stopped.

'Do you mind if I speak my mind?' she said.

'Fine by me,' said Paulsen.

'What's your problem?'

She was looking at her straight in the eye now and her tone was unashamedly aggressive.

'What's that supposed to mean?' replied Paulsen levelly.

'You've been on my back all day. I was just offering an opinion – not a statement of fact. I get that you're worried about your DI. But I've done nothing except support you – so I'm asking you again, *what's your problem?*'

The aggression in her voice took Paulsen by surprise for a moment. For a brand-new DC on her first day, it was certainly ballsy and she looked well up for the confrontation. Paulsen knew the right thing to do would be to meet her halfway. Make some sort of apology – reset their working relationship. It's what Finn would do – what he'd be telling her to do, as well.

'Tell you what – let's have this conversation when we've actually achieved something. Maybe when we've made an arrest, perhaps when your DI's *not* staring down the barrel of a gun?'

'You think I don't care about that?' said Nash.

'I think there's a time and a place for a conversation like this and it isn't now,' said Paulsen, opening the car door and climbing in.

★

Sarah Littlewood reached out and held Steve Garland's hand.

'You didn't have to come over,' he said. 'But I'm glad you did.'

From somewhere, he seemed to find the smallest of smiles. Sarah responded with a sad one of her own. There'd been too much going through her mind to just sit at home doing nothing. She looked carefully at Steve, his pain – iceberg deep – was something she knew only too well. She wanted to reach out and hug the man but saw her own dead expression from fifteen years ago staring back at her.

The Vickers's FLO had given them some privacy and as Sarah looked around the living room, she saw reminders of Jemma everywhere. A pair of leggings on the radiator, a pink coat hanging on a hook and pictures from happier times adorning the mantelpiece. She felt a wave of sudden sadness and realised she hadn't truly absorbed what had happened herself in the rush of things.

When Jemma had returned to the area to settle down with Steve, she and Sarah had become friends – the thread of that shared experience still connecting them after all these years. They hadn't been hugely close but didn't need to be because it felt like the tie would *always* be there. That she'd survived what had happened in 2009, built a successful life for herself and *still* died prematurely was a savage irony.

'How are you coping?' she said.

Steve looked down at the carpet.

'I'm not, really,' he replied and then shook his head.

'What's going on at that cafe – what's Lee *doing* for God's sake? Jemma wouldn't want this.'

She sensed he'd changed the subject to Lee and the cafe because he didn't want to talk about his own feelings.

'Lee's hurting – you know, more than anyone, how much he leant on her.'

He looked at her squarely.

'I've never liked the bloke. Can I say that now?'

Sarah nodded awkwardly – in the circumstances, it wasn't really the moment for an argument.

'I can understand why,' she said diplomatically. 'He's always been pretty intense.'

'More than that – he's damaged – in a way that Jemma never was and I've tried to be tolerant. Of what he went through. God knows I feel sorry for him, but if I never saw him again . . .' He shook his head.

She could easily guess why he felt that way. The rapport between Lee and Jemma would make anyone jealous. The fact that it went back to their schooldays and the shared experience of their abduction – it wasn't hard to understand where his hostility came from. She wasn't here just to console him though. The message she'd received on her phone earlier was still troubling her – as was its implication.

'Lee's obsessed with the idea that their abductor is still out there,' she said carefully.

'Sounds like him. It's paranoid nonsense and I told Jemma that too.'

Sarah looked up sharply and instantly regretted the reaction.

'So, she was suspicious too?'

Steve looked drained as if the day had suddenly caught up with him.

'I'm not sure. Once Dennis Trant confessed, I thought that would be the end of it. We moved away from the area after that – lived in Essex for a while but then, as you know, we came back here to start a family and . . .' He faltered but Sarah was already nodding.

'It brought it all back for her – moving back, didn't it?' she said.

'Yes – it was like a draught you can feel that no one else can, one that just won't leave you alone. As time went by, I could tell it was bothering her, but she didn't want to talk about it with me.'

'So, you don't know whether she ever tried to actively pursue it?' said Sarah, again choosing her words with care.

'Why do you ask?' said Steve.

'In case she and Lee were right – that the bastard who killed my son *is* still out there,' she said.

'Of course,' said Steve. 'It nagged at her. She was on the internet a lot – I know that – digging into it, and I think she rang around a few people just to see what they thought after all these years.'

'Who?'

'Terry Ellis, probably, the Ricksons as well, I think. I know she spoke to George Rickson.' He shook his head. 'Did she not tell you? I'd have thought you'd have been the first person she'd have discussed it with.'

Sarah ran her hand through her hair and tried to find an answer for him.

'Yes – I didn't know what to make of it. I mean – as far as I was concerned, I'd got some closure when Dennis Trant made his confession.'

Steve was starting to lose it again. His eyes were reddening, and he pursed his lips in an effort to contain the emotion.

'As I say – she and Lee were close. How much they talked about it between themselves – I don't know. But now she's dead and Lee seems so sure that this guy might have done it. But surely it's impossible. He can't still be out there – it doesn't make any sense.'

Sarah looked across at the mantelpiece at a picture of Steve and Jemma together, both smiling broadly, his arm round her shoulder. And then she thought about the text she'd received earlier – that single word – *'LIAR'* – jumping out accusingly from the screen. If she was right about what that meant then she doubted that was the last message she'd receive.

'No, it doesn't,' she said with a shiver.

Billy sat on the park bench wrapping his arms around himself and wondered what was going on in the cafe where Lee was holed up. He felt a sudden surge of empathy for his old school-friend and the pain he must be in to take such desperate action. Knowing someone else, only a few miles away, was feeling exactly the same way about Jemma as he was, helped in a funny sort of way. They had that in common, though he wondered if either Lee or Jemma had ever really understood that. Billy had never truly lost his feelings for her. He'd known most of his life that it was never going to happen, but the small spark of hope had always been there, a schoolboy crush that wouldn't fade.

Even after she'd split from Lee in the wake of their abduction her subsequent relationships had never seemed meaningful; men appeared to come and go. Until Steve came along – and she'd moved away from the area to be with him. And even then, against all common sense, he'd always wondered if she'd eventually find her way back to him. Good old Billy, the friend who'd stayed constant. Instead, when she returned to the area pregnant, it seemed she'd genuinely found true happiness.

His own relationship with Ella had begun unexpectedly. She'd chased him after he'd broken up with a previous girl-friend. Initially he'd been unsure about it – for lots of reasons. The connection to the past for one, also the sense that he probably shouldn't rush straight into another relationship. And of course, those stubborn feelings for Jemma that just wouldn't fade. But then Kaitlyn had come along, and everything had changed again. But a little flame of something for

Jemma had still stubbornly flickered somewhere inside of him. Until today.

'Hey,' said a voice and he turned to see Ella, approaching with Kaitlyn in her pram.

He rose to greet her.

'How is she?'

'Asleep – please don't wake her,' she said tersely.

He looked into the pram at his sleeping daughter and felt himself choking up, but her mother's face was unforgiving.

'I don't understand why we had to meet out here – you could have just come over.'

Billy thought about Sarah and shook his head.

'I don't have time – I have to go to work soon. You've heard about Jemma?' he added, and her face softened.

'Of course,' she replied. She parked the pram next to the bench, wiped some snow away with her hand and sat down next to him.

'I'm sorry – you must be really upset,' she said. 'Mum's in bits.'

She hadn't seemed in bits earlier, he thought. Ella had no idea about his feelings for Jemma. No one knew because he'd done such a good job of masking them over the years. He tried to articulate how he was feeling but the words simply wouldn't come. She watched him struggling with it and her face clouded over with concern.

'I hate the thought of you going back on your own to that shitty flat. You look a mess, and you shouldn't be alone today. Why don't you just come home?' she said quietly. He looked at his sleeping daughter, thought about Jemma, remembered too that conversation with Sarah earlier and slowly shook his head.

'I'm sorry – I can't,' he croaked.

She shook her head with instant exasperation.

'*Why?* You've still not explained it to me properly why you walked out on us. Don't you love me any more? Love *us*?' she said, nodding at the pram.

He did love her – but in a completely different way to Jemma and he adored his daughter. But there was no way he could tell her the real reason why he'd left.

'You don't understand,' he began, but she was already on her feet.

'. . . is not the right answer,' she said coldly. 'She'll need feeding soon, and I don't want to hear the same old lame excuses again, Billy.'

'Don't go – stay a bit longer,' he said, mournfully, still looking at his sleeping daughter's face.

'What aren't you telling me?' she pressed but he didn't answer, and she shook her head. 'You're still coming around on Saturday aren't you?' she snapped. He nodded and she began to steer the pram away. 'Fine – I'll see you then.'

He watched them go until they'd disappeared out of sight and only then did he realise his face was wet with tears.

Inside the cafe, the first aid kit had been delivered and Lee had allowed Finn to apply some bandaging to Marco's head. The young cafe owner was awake now but distinctly woozy.

'I feel like I've been hit by a truck,' he muttered. 'How long have I been out?'

'Only a few minutes. What you did was bloody stupid, by the way,' said Finn. 'Do you feel dizzy?'

Marco looked around the cafe. Lee was sitting at one of the tables again, hand still coiled around the gun, watching them both closely.

'Yes.'

'Can you tell me what the time is?' said Finn, pointing at the clock on the wall.

Marco squinted at it.

'Just approaching twenty to two,' he replied and swallowed. 'My mouth's dry – can I have some water?' he said, directing the question at Lee.

'I don't think so,' came the reply. 'Once bitten and all that.'

Finn sighed.

'For God's sake, I think he's concussed and look at him – he's in no fit state to do you any harm.'

'I feel really, really sick,' said Marco to no one in particular. Finn gave Lee an imploring look and finally, the other man rose to his feet. He went over to the sink and filled a teacup from the tap. Still holding the gun with his other hand, he came over and let Marco sip from it. As Finn watched, it looked an oddly tender moment between the two.

'Can't you just let him go?' he said quietly. 'He needs proper medical attention.'

'No,' replied Lee. 'How many times do I have to keep saying it? Today's the day I draw a line. I've learnt how you lot work – you won't act unless you're forced to. If this puts pressure on your mates out there to pull their fingers out, then that's fine by me.' He stood up again, letting the remaining water drip down Marco's shirt. 'Probably the worst that will happen to him is he ends up with a scar.'

Instinctively, the hand holding the gun moved up and brushed the side of his face where his own scars were hidden by the elaborate tattoo there.

'You said your abductor did that to you.'

Again, Lee locked eyes with him. But this time there was no aggression – Finn thought he saw a flash of fear, pain certainly, and also deep sadness.

'Because he did.'

'Beyond that, you've never really talked about it.'

'Did I need to? I told you what happened – the guy cut me; it is what it is.'

Again, Finn felt the suspicion that he didn't quite have the full picture.

'Anything you'd like to add to that now? I mean if you're right, and you really think there's someone out there – then surely, it's in your own interests. If there *is* something you've held back . . .'

For a moment Lee looked like he might have something more to say but his face hardened, and he turned and walked back to the counter.

17

As it turned out Culley wasn't too concerned that Craig Quilter had been added to the list of suspects. He listened carefully as Finn explained the holes in the story that the schoolteacher had given them. For his part, Finn had done a little further digging into Eddie Knox to mollify the DI. Other than learning some more about his background and family, nothing particularly useful had come to light.

Finn and Barton were now in Culley's office as the three of them tried to take stock of where they were. They were all painfully aware that three days had passed since Jemma and Lee's abduction, and they still had no idea who'd snatched these teenagers or any clue of where they'd been taken.

'Both Quilter and Knox are decent fits for this,' said Culley. 'There's no chance Knox was acting as Quilter's spotter, is there? Or vice versa, for that matter?'

Finn hated talking to Culley in his office – it seemed to exacerbate the man's sense of self-importance. It didn't help that it felt like a sauna in there too, right now. He deliberately took the only other chair in the room, leaving Barton on his feet.

'Makes no sense to me, guv,' he replied. 'If it is Quilter, he wouldn't have needed someone to spot those kids – he saw them every day, knew exactly where they were going and what their likely route to the park would have been.'

Culley frowned.

'But he could have passed that information on to Knox who then intercepted them?'

'It's possible,' said Barton. 'But we don't even know if Quilter *is* guilty of anything or that he even knows who Knox is. We've been checking through the obvious possibilities, local GP lists, gyms, clubs – but there's nothing.'

'Doesn't mean they don't know each other – they could have met in the pub?' growled Culley but Barton could only shrug in response. 'So who else could be in the frame then?'

'We're liaising with Scotland Yard to see if there are any viable trafficking links – and we've ruled out most of the local known sex offenders now,' said Barton.

'What's the latest on the van?' said Finn.

'Forensics aren't hopeful of pulling anything off it – the fire was pretty comprehensive,' replied Culley. 'The CCTV search has yielded nothing helpful yet. We've found the van on camera a few times, but we're still trying to identify a pattern to the sightings.'

'It's not a state secret where the CCTV cameras in London are situated. You can find the details online easily enough,' said Barton.

'True,' said Finn slowly. 'But you'd need to be pretty smart to work out a route to avoid all of them. Two separate abductions, transporting the kids to wherever you've taken them and then finding a location to torch the vehicle – all without being traced. This is someone who planned it meticulously.'

Culley shook his head with exasperation.

'Meanwhile, the clock is still ticking, and we've made fuck-all progress.' The room was starting to feel stifling hot to Finn. Culley seemed to have acclimatised to it well enough, possibly because he was a lizard and had cold blood, he idly thought.

'How are the parents bearing up?' said the DI.

'About as well as you'd expect,' replied Finn. 'Sarah Littlewood's literally leaving messages for me every hour. Jemma Vickers's family are on their way back from Venice and the Ellises . . . are not in a good way, put it like that.'

His words hung as heavy as the heat for a moment.

'Aren't we looking at this the wrong way?' said Barton. 'Say the motive isn't sexual or trafficking of some sort – then why *would* you want these kids?'

Finn nodded.

'I agree. I still think there's an element of this that feels unusual – the fact that there's three of them, that they all live so local to each other – it doesn't seem random to me.'

Culley sat back and tossed his pen on to his desk.

'We've done all the standard background checks into the parents – nothing flagged up about any of them if that's what you're suggesting,' he said.

'Just because there isn't anything obvious doesn't mean there isn't *something* that connects them. But so far there's been no ransom demand or communication of any kind from the kidnapper,' said Finn.

Barton sniffed, wiped a bead of sweat off his brow and turned to look at them both.

'We all know the stats,' he said. 'So, I'm just going to put this on the table. After this amount of time, shouldn't we start working from the assumption that we're looking for bodies?'

'That's a bit premature, isn't it?' said Karin. 'Particularly if these kids *have* been taken by traffickers?'

'Possibly,' replied Finn gloomily.

The pair were sitting in YoYo's, a new coffee shop that had sprung up opposite Cedar House the previous month. It had become the go-to place for everyone at the station, largely because in the hinterland of the trading estate where they were based, there *was* nowhere else for them to go. The fabulous rudeness of the proprietor, Yolande, gave it a certain charm and Finn rather admired her zero-fucks-given approach to dealing with customers.

'But Jack's got a point,' he said. 'The more time that passes, the more statistically, the chances of finding these kids alive reduce.'

Yolande tottered over holding two cups.

'Earl Grey?' she snapped. Karin nodded and Yolande placed a cup in front of her.

'The Americano's mine,' said Finn with a pleasant smile.

Yolande glared at him glacially.

'Coffee with milk,' she said and plonked it down.

Karin smiled, largely at Finn's flustered reaction. For an instant, even Yolande seemed to soften.

'Watch this one,' she said, glancing at Finn but directing the comment at Karin. 'A bit too sharp for his own good – can't see what's right in front of his nose. He'll walk into a lamp post one day.' And with that, she left them.

'I reckon she's got your number,' said Karin.

'I don't know how; I've barely spoken to her since this place opened.'

Karin looked over at Yolande who was now serving a uniformed PC at the counter with similar disdain.

'I don't think she misses much.'

'Bit like you then,' said Finn, taking a sip of his coffee. It was thick and bitter, just how he liked it.

Karin's expression turned serious.

'How long have you been single?'

'Really?' said Finn. 'Why spoil a perfectly nice cup of coffee with a question like that?'

'What you told me in the pub before . . . about not noticing if you were lonely . . . it worried me a bit if I'm honest.'

Finn nodded.

'I suppose it's because I'm used to it. Not just because both my parents are gone. I think it's because I lost my brother when I was quite young as well.'

'What happened?' said Karin. Finn put his coffee cup down and looked out of the window for a moment. 'You don't have to tell me if you don't want to,' she added.

'He had a heart defect. There was no preventing what happened. He just . . . *died* one day.'

Briefly, there was nothing but the hubbub of the other people in the room chatting amongst themselves.

'I'm so sorry,' said Karin.

'Don't be,' said Finn, businesslike. 'I probably shouldn't have mentioned it. It hit me pretty hard at the time – I guess I'm not great with loss. It felt so unfair, and I've always thought that in part is where the desire to become a copper came from. I didn't want other people to feel the way I did.' He shook his head. 'You never forget those kinds of emotions. Which I suppose brings us back to these missing kids.'

'No,' said Karin quietly.

'No what?' said Finn, confused.

'You asked me the other night if I still thought you were an insufferable arse.' She smiled and it dazzled him for a second. 'No, you're not, is the answer.'

'That's . . . good,' he replied.

Something seemed to cross her mind.

'By the way – am I right in thinking you're looking for a white van in connection with these abductions?'

Finn nodded.

'We found a burnt-out wreckage of one near Croydon Airport this morning. We think it was the same one that was used to take Lee and Jemma. Why do you ask?'

'It's probably nothing but I thought I'd mention it. Someone

167

in my office saw your appeal and thinks he might have seen it too. He lives quite local.'

Finn looked sceptical.

'There's a lot of white vans in London – what made him think this one was ours?'

'Because he's only seen it twice, speeding down his road on both the evenings in question.'

Jemma had pleaded with Oliver to throw her the knife, but he'd been strangely reluctant.

'I don't think it's a good idea,' he said. 'We should just give it back to him – show willing.'

'Oh, for fuck's sake,' said Jemma. 'We can use this. It's just one man – I'm younger and I'm betting fitter too. Give me that knife and I reckon I could take him.'

Again, Oliver looked uncertain. Jemma glanced at Lee for support, but he wasn't sure either.

'If you get it wrong – he could kill you. Kill all of us. Remember how he hit you when we first arrived. It's not worth the risk,' he said.

Jemma pulled a face.

'He might kill us all anyway – now we've got a way of hurting *him*. That knife might be the only chance we've got of staying alive. Are you going to use it?' she said to Lee, and he didn't reply. She turned back to Oliver. 'What about you – Mr let's-give-it-back-to-him?'

There was silence in the cellar, and she held Oliver's gaze.

'Just throw the fucking thing over,' she demanded.

He looked down at it for a second as if pondering whether he *could* use it if he had to – and then the knife arced across the room and clattered to the ground, agonisingly short.

'Shit,' said Jemma.

Above them, they could hear footsteps once more. They

waited, but the door to the cellar didn't open. She stretched out a foot, but it looked like the knife would be just out of reach – that if she wasn't careful, she'd only succeed in nudging it further away.

'Jem, just leave it there. He'll see when he next comes down and realise he forgot it,' said Lee. He was already imagining a hundred ways in which this could go wrong.

'Like fuck I will,' she muttered and stretched out her leg. Somehow, she managed to find the extra millimetres and curve her toe around it. Gently she dragged the blade towards her until finally she could lean forwards and pick it up. She grinned in triumph.

'Now we can fight back,' she said, tucking the knife under the coil of chains that were holding her. In the dark it was almost impossible to see, but easy enough for her to grab if she needed to. Fear immediately started gnawing at Lee again.

'He must have noticed it was missing though? How could he not – he took the fork. Why did he give it to him in the first place?'

'Calm down, Lee,' whispered Jemma. 'The point is he did – and now *we've* got it.' On the other side of the room, Oliver was shivering – they could see him holding himself, gently rocking. 'I promise I won't use it unless it's life or death,' she said with a glint of steel and he could see the fresh hope it had given her.

If there was some cause for optimism it was quickly shattered. They were sitting quietly when the door above crashed open again. This time there was nothing silent about the man.

'I think we ought to get this party started, don't you?' he boomed. Lee instinctively looked over at Jemma but she looked terrified as well, all her earlier bravado gone. Whatever this was about, whatever reason they'd been taken for – it felt like this was it.

As he came down the stairs, there was a knock each time. A hard blow of wood on wood, slow and deliberate. The reason became immediately clear – there was a baseball bat in his hand, which he was bringing down with each step. As he reached the bottom, he patted the end of the bat on to his palm a couple of times. He was going to beat them to death, right there and then, Lee thought. Jemma's hand was already hovering by the coil of chains where she'd secreted the knife and he willed her not to do anything stupid. The man was smiling now, too. Lee was sure of it – despite the mask, he could *see* it in his eyes.

For a second – which felt like forever – he stood there, happy to let their imaginations go to work. Then, with a sudden speed, he went over to Jemma, turned the bat horizontally and pushed her up against the wall with it. With his free hand, he plucked the blade from under the chains.

It was obvious he knew exactly what had been hidden there and Lee waited for some kind of immediate retribution. Instead, the man said nothing and strode over to Oliver. The fear on his face was like nothing Lee had ever seen before – the boy's eyes were bright and wide and his jaw was slack, though no sound was coming out of his mouth. Their tormentor stood in front of him, bat in one hand, knife in the other.

'Stand up,' he commanded in a clear distinct voice. Oliver didn't move – as if paralysed by the instruction, and the man leant forwards and pulled him to his feet. Stepping behind him, he pushed him hard towards the centre of the cellar and the teenager stumbled forwards still with the same wild staring eyes.

'Ollie . . . would you like to go home now?'

Oliver was shaking, his whole body, juddering.

'Yes . . .' he replied, though it sounded less like a word than a gasp.

'This one,' said the man, pointing at Lee. 'Cut his face and you can go.'

Lee's stomach tightened. He turned to Jemma in terror, but she could only look back at him with the same stricken expression.

'*What?*' said Oliver as if he couldn't quite comprehend what he'd just heard.

'It's very easy. Just like slicing pizza. Cut him and then you can go.' He turned the blade round and held it out. 'You could be back with your mum and your sister – you'd like to see Ella again, wouldn't you?' he cajoled, his voice sweet as honey. Oliver remained frozen to the spot. The man leant in and whispered in his ear, loud enough for the other two to hear.

'Do it – or I'll beat your brains in, right here, right now,' he said, holding up the bat before throwing the knife on to the ground in front of the teenager. After what seemed an eternity Oliver slowly bent down and picked it up. He looked over at Lee, an apologetic expression forming on his face.

'No – for fuck's sake,' screamed Lee, pressing himself against the wall behind him. In his mind's eye, he was willing Oliver to plunge the knife into this demon's neck. Instead, to his horror, he took a step forward.

'Good lad,' said the man, striding across. He savagely grabbed Lee by the hair and yanked his head back. 'Come on, son, you can do this,' he said as if talking to an errant dog. Oliver swallowed, took a few more steps and tentatively raised the blade. Lee tried to twist and turn away but was being held tightly in place. 'That's it – just like slicing into a peach,' purred that voice again. Lee winced as the steel began to cut and his bladder instinctively opened. Oliver's face distorted into something furious, and he felt his flesh splitting – and then the pain hit, and he began to scream.

18

Today

Mattie Paulsen was nervous – which was unusual. She'd never taken a briefing before, but as she looked around the faces in the incident room, she could feel an unspoken resistance. Some of the more experienced officers would doubtless prefer Finn was there doing this; several others almost certainly felt that *they* should be doing it. Nash sat, impassively nursing a cup of coffee. The journey back to Cedar House had been quiet after their confrontation. It was half past two now and it didn't feel like the day was getting any better to Paulsen.

'Before I get into it – I've just had a quick word with Sami at the RVP. They got a brief glimpse of the DI when he came out to pick up the first aid kit. He seemed unharmed from what they could tell – so that's something. If I hear any more, I'll of course let you know.'

She turned to the board behind her where pictures of Jemma Vickers, Eddie Knox and Craig Quilter were all pinned up. Photographs of the two crime scenes were also there – different angles of Jemma's body lying on the ice where it had been left and Knox with that one casual hand on his spilled intestines.

'So, here's what we know,' she said. 'Jemma seems to have shared Lee Ellis's belief that Dennis Trant wasn't their abductor in 2009. It looks like she'd been discreetly investigating it herself in the months leading up to her death. We know she'd been focusing on an individual called Red Tide – a dealer who specialises in selling material on the Dark Web. She also spoke to her former schoolteacher several months ago, Craig Quilter, who's certainly got a very questionable history of his own. We know DI Finn identified Quilter as a possible suspect fifteen years ago – as well as this man, Eddie Knox.' She pointed at Knox's picture. 'The fact that *he* was also killed today when we'd planned to speak with him feels too much of a coincidence – so I'm formally linking the two investigations.'

She knew she shouldn't, but she couldn't stop herself from quickly checking to see if there were any signs of dissent and was pleased to see a fair few nodding heads instead.

'What's our take on Trant then – do we think Jemma and Lee are right?' asked one of the older DCs.

Paulsen nodded.

'We've spoken to his son today, who's also pretty sceptical about the idea that his father killed Oliver Littlewood. We can't say it definitively – but I think for the purposes of our investigation we have to work from the assumption that they might be right.'

'Do we know any more about Red Tide yet?' asked a voice from the back.

Paulsen picked up a printout from the desk next to her.

'A little bit. Part of the problem is that Red Tide is a pretty covert presence – even on the Dark Web, so we still don't know why Jemma took such a specific interest in him. It must stem from her own experience in that cellar in 2009. Something that happened or was said that led her to this individual. What the Exploitation Unit have told us is that they have some evidence that what he deals in is pretty high-end bespoke material. The nature of that is still unclear – and we know none of those kids were sexually abused fifteen years ago.

They're still digging, and I'll keep you posted if they find out more.'

She gathered her thoughts for a moment and then turned back to the boards behind her.

'So, the question is – who would want to kill both Jemma *and* Knox on the same day and why? One person we can now rule out for Knox's murder is Lee because at least we know where he was when it happened. We do have one new development from that crime scene though.'

She held up a piece of paper with a blurry image on it. 'If you check your emails you'll find a hi-res version of this – we pulled it off a store camera on one of the side roads on the south side of the railway tunnel where she was found – it's time-stamped at 7.17 a.m. this morning.'

The picture showed a man in a dark coat wearing a baseball cap with his back to the camera walking up a snow-covered street.

'There are obviously other people who've been caught on the same camera – but this is the only individual either on his own, or whose movements we can't further trace that we've isolated in the relevant time frame. I'd say he's a person of interest – the jacket appears to be a Canada Goose parka and we think the baseball cap is dark green, not black as it looks at first glance. It's a possibility this is the individual whose footsteps we found in the snow near to the body. It's not much – but it's something to go on.'

She looked around the room and saw one or two studying the image more closely on their phones.

'It seems to me, the obvious answer is that Jemma was getting somewhere with her own investigation,' offered Nash suddenly. It seemed as if the room had, as one, turned to look at her. 'And unless there's someone else that she'd identified that we don't know about – then it brings us back to

Red Tide – I mean, is it possible that Canada Goose guy *is* Red Tide?'

The room fell silent for a moment as they all considered it. Paulsen nodded in agreement and then turned to another DC.

'Nishat – you've been with Jemma's partner this morning. Did he shed any light on what she'd been doing?'

DC Nishat Adams was one of the two family liaison officers assigned to Steve Garland. FLOs weren't simply there to support victims of crime, but to discreetly investigate where necessary too.

'That's the interesting thing,' said Adams. 'He knew she had doubts, but it's clear she never discussed the extent of those doubts with him – or the digging she'd been doing. I've put your request to him about doing a discreet search of their flat in case she had another phone or laptop hidden away somewhere. I think he's taking his son and is going to stay with his parents for a few days so we should be okay. I'll let you know when he gets back to me.'

Paulsen nodded.

'The only person – that we know of, anyway – who connects all of this up is Craig Quilter,' said Nash, looking Mattie pointedly in the eye. No one else in the room would know – but it was a very public way of recognising that she understood Paulsen had been right about Quilter earlier. It just made Paulsen feel even worse about the way she'd been treating Nash, an awareness that she'd need to put this right at some point. If the day ever relented, that was.

She nodded in agreement.

'It does look like Jemma might have discovered something – something that got her killed, even if it was a row on the ice that got out of control – and it's also possible Knox may well have known what it was. If it *is* Red Tide who's responsible, then maybe they all knew his identity.' She looked at the picture of Quilter – it was from his school-teaching days, a smarter, cleaner-cut version of the man they'd met earlier.

'I'm sure his flat's clean as a whistle,' she said pointing at it. 'Especially now that we've paid him a visit – but I'd like a warrant to search it, just in case.'

'What about the mugging gone wrong theory?' said a voice at the back.

Paulsen shrugged.

'Still on the table until it isn't . . .'

She was about to continue when John Skegman swept in through the double doors. The room went quiet, and it took Skegman a second to realise why.

'Relax – this isn't about Alex.' He saw their collective relief. 'Sorry for the scare.' He turned to Paulsen. 'I've actually got some good news – AC Culley has finally agreed to talk to us.'

Finn was becoming increasingly confident that Lee had no serious intention of harming either of his hostages. His distraught reaction after he'd thought he'd shot Marco had been revealing. His chief concern now was that Lee didn't end up getting himself killed. There was also frustration kicking in. He was becoming convinced that there was another layer to what had happened in 2009.

Lee was pacing the room once more. He held up his phone. 'Your mates out there have gone very quiet.'

'Good police work takes time,' said Finn patiently. 'Suspects need to be identified, tracked down and interviewed. That's why this is so stupid. End this – let them take Marco to hospital. Help the police investigation – with me – back at the station.'

Marco was lying slumped against the wall now. Even without getting a close view, Finn could see from where he was that his pupils were dilated.

'If I end this now then what's it all been for?' said Lee. 'I don't just mean *this* today – I mean *all* of it – the last fifteen years. Jemma's life.' He shook his head. 'I know what will happen if I stop – more psychiatrists, more people offering to talk, to listen – more of the fucking same.'

He was shouting now, his temper rising.

'That's not true,' said Finn. 'I won't let that happen – I will pursue this. If you're right that it wasn't Trant – then I'll find who did this to you.'

Lee laughed.

'Sorry, if I'm laughing openly at you. But you've had fifteen years and now because there's a gun to your head, you're promising me the world. How stupid do you think I am?'

He was right too, thought Finn. Whatever the right words were to cut through, he wasn't finding them. He felt clumsy and irrelevant – just like he had after Jackie Ojo died.

'*You're panicking,*' said Karin. '*Calm down – the answer's in that cellar.*'

He took a deep breath.

'So, what haven't you told me – because there's something, isn't there?'

Lee stopped pacing and turned his back on Finn.

'That I still hear that voice. When I'm walking home from the pub alone late at night or when I'm lying in bed awake in the morning. Or whenever I generally feel like shit – there *he* is.' He turned to face Finn again. 'I've never forgotten Oliver Littlewood either – or the blood. Do you know what it feels like – to carry that?'

Finn nodded.

'I know the way the dead sometimes won't leave you alone,' he said quietly. 'I also have a few people who keep me awake.'

In his mind's eye, he was running again, towards the open door of a flat in Bethnal Green, barging into a room with

Jackie's dead body lying in the middle of it. Paramedics, watching him helplessly as he yelled at them.

'You think I'm arrogant – don't you?' he said. 'That I don't own a mistake? You couldn't be more wrong.'

Lee dragged a chair over and sat down in front of Finn.

'Do you want to see what your mistakes look like?' he said. He reached out the hand holding the gun and pulled up his T-shirt over his shoulder. He had a dark blue sleeve tattoo going down the entire length of his arm. At the base was a rose, the swirling petals morphing further up into a huge image of a tiger's face.

'What am I looking at?' said Finn and Lee pointed at the rose just above his wrist. As Finn bent forward, he could see scar tissue underneath the ink, a vertical line quite clear.

'That didn't happen in the cellar – that happened much later,' said Lee.

'I'm so sorry,' murmured Finn.

'Do you know who found me – got me to hospital in time?'

'Jemma?' said Finn and Lee nodded.

'She saved my life. And for what? For why?' He motioned at the cafe around them. 'For this? Honestly, day to day, I don't know what the point of any of it is any more.'

'I thought you were in a relationship a while back?' said Finn, trying to remember her name. 'Lara? I thought that was going quite well . . .'

'Her name was Lou. And it didn't last very long. They never do – not when they get to know the real me.'

Beside them, Marco groaned again, and Finn tried not to let his concern show.

'You know I never stopped loving Jem, even after she got married. She was the only one I really wanted to be with.'

'You went through so much together,' said Finn. 'That connection's always been there.'

Lee nodded.

'I think she loved me too in her own way. She had that effect on everyone – I know Billy carried a torch for her too. You knew what she was like – she *burnt* through life.'

It was a good description of her, Finn thought. Lee looked on the brink of tears and for a moment he tried to picture their relationship in recent years. They were both two extremely strong-willed people; he knew that much. But Jemma had always been focused on her recovery while Lee was haunted by the past. Almost like a yin and yang, one pulling one way, as the other pulled in the opposite direction. A thought struck him.

'We've talked about Trant,' he said. 'How often did you discuss him with her?'

He imagined the Jemma he knew wouldn't have wanted to be constantly dragged back there but Lee's reply wasn't what he was expecting.

'She was digging into it. She didn't tell anyone – not even Steve. Not properly, anyway. You were so sure it was all put to bed that we just didn't think you'd listen to us any more. So, she decided to have a go herself – however long it took, whatever she needed to do.'

And then it struck him, and he kicked himself for not seeing it sooner.

'Your certainty that it wasn't him goes beyond just a belief, doesn't it? You *know* something more concrete. Both of you did.'

Lee's eyes flickered up and met his gaze, but he said nothing. The thought that neither of them had trusted Finn enough to reach out to him, hurt. He remembered his near-breakdown over Karin's death – he'd been so wrapped up in his own grief over the last few years that it was possible he *had* neglected Lee and Jemma. Would he have even noticed if they'd approached him? His brain snapped back into the present as the significance of what he was being told dawned on him.

'Did she find something – is that what you're saying? Something that got her killed today?'

Lee shrugged.

'That's the thing – if she did, she didn't tell me. I'm *sure* she discovered something, but for some reason, she didn't share it.'

Finn was confused now.

'That doesn't make any sense. You, of *all* people?'

'We argued about it – but I'm certain that in the last few weeks she kept something back from me.'

Finn's mind was racing through the possibilities.

'To protect you in some way, perhaps?'

Lee shook his head.

'We'll never know now, will we? She's taken that secret to her grave.'

Was it possible Jemma Vickers's own cold-case investigation had uncovered something Finn had missed in 2009? He remembered the way he and Barton used to bitch about Culley – but had they all screwed up back then? Yet more guilt to trowel on to the tally.

'What makes you so sure?'

'Because she became secretive – wouldn't answer any questions about what she was doing, who she was talking to – and we shared *everything*.' Lee pointed at his wrist again. 'This is a woman who saved my life, took every call, answered every message.'

Finn was at a loss to make sense of it, desperate now to be on the outside investigating, not sitting in here handcuffed to a radiator pipe. He wondered who *was* leading the investigation and for an instant had a flash of Jackie Ojo marshalling the troops in the incident room and then wondered if Skegman had given the job to Mattie Paulsen. The thought was intriguing, but he didn't have time to dwell on it.

'I'm sorry – I truly am. If we did miss something – if *I* missed something – then let me try and correct that now,' said Finn.

The words, yet again, seemed to hit a brick wall. Lee looked deflated now and that worried Finn even more than when he'd been raging.

'No, mate. I don't think so,' he said.

'Why not?'

Lee shook his head.

'Because I'm starting to think that one way or another, I'm not sure I want to be on this planet after today.'

19

By ten past three Skegman was parking up inside the Met Police's headquarters at New Scotland Yard. Given the way the investigation was unfolding, and the implicit doubt it was casting over the original inquiry in 2009, he'd wanted to be there for the conversation with Assistant Commissioner Culley. Mattie Paulsen shivered as they walked up the steps to the entrance, past the famous revolving sign outside. In the middle distance behind them was the parliamentary estate. It hadn't been that long ago since she'd helped apprehend a killer there. It wasn't a happy memory – one that would inextricably be linked to the murder of Jackie Ojo just a short time afterwards.

As they walked through the corridors of the building, she became aware of some of the glances Skegman was attracting. The legacy of Ojo's death continued to overshadow both him and Cedar House. With Finn's life still in the balance she could guess people's thinking – to lose one officer in the line of duty was careless; to lose two would be downright negligent. She was surprised to realise that she felt strangely protective of the DCI. When you knew the truth of what had happened, the man was displaying considerable dignity, she thought.

AC Culley greeted them with barely disguised irritation as they were ushered into his office. A squat, balding figure wearing narrow metallic glasses, he looked the classic stereotype of pen-pushing upper-echelon management. It would be interesting to get Finn's perspective on him at some point – assuming he survived the day, she reminded herself guiltily.

'Thank you both for coming at short notice – I'm quite pushed for time,' said Culley as they took their seats opposite him. 'I'm not entirely sure how I'm going to be able to help you with this, though.'

Skegman ran through where they were at. The mention of Eddie Knox's murder produced a definite reaction, Paulsen noticed.

'Given that both Jemma Vickers and Lee Ellis seem convinced that Dennis Trant wasn't their abductor, and given what happened to Knox earlier, we've reopened the investigation into Oliver Littlewood's death and the abduction of the other two,' said Skegman, almost apologetically. He looked uncharacteristically awkward as he spoke, thought Paulsen. Given how low his reputation had sunk in this building, coming here to question an AC about a cold case took balls. The way Culley was looking at him suggested that thought was front and centre in his mind too.

'I interviewed Dennis Trant personally in 2016 – I heard his confession. I have *no* doubt whatsoever that he was the man responsible. If Alex Finn hadn't let him slip on the day we found those two, then maybe there wouldn't be any ambiguity about that.'

Paulsen had read the historical files on the investigation once again before they'd left Cedar House. Finn had been there the day Jemma and Lee were found and had briefly encountered their masked abductor. There'd been a brief skirmish before the man had managed to give him the slip and escape. It had been clear that Finn had prioritised rescuing the hostages over pursuing him and it was a choice any officer in his shoes would have made. Any lingering doubts Paulsen possessed that she hadn't taken to Culley were ended by the dig at Finn. He was one of *those* kinds of guys then – the type who'd throw you under the bus.

'You were very keen on Knox as a suspect at the time, weren't you?' she said.

Culley looked at her as if noticing an unpleasant smell wafting into the room for the first time.

'The man was a convicted sadist. If that finally caught up with him today – then maybe we shouldn't be surprised. Or perhaps there's someone else out there who was triggered by Jemma Vickers's death for some reason. Knox had a lot of enemies as I recall. It doesn't change my view that there's nothing essentially new to see here.' He held up a hand and sighed. 'Look, don't get me wrong – I obviously hope that the situation at the cafe is resolved peacefully and quickly, but don't let Lee Ellis dictate your thinking. We conducted a thorough investigation in 2009 and couldn't find any hard evidence to pin it on a particular suspect – which is precisely why Trant's confession made sense to me. Someone from left field who slipped through the net the first time round.'

'What about the schoolteacher Craig Quilter? You looked at him back then and he's been involved in a few pretty unpleasant situations since,' said Paulsen. 'DI Finn was keen on him as well, wasn't he?'

Culley shook his head dismissively.

'We ruled him out in the end. In my view his alibi was solid – he had no connection to the house where we eventually found those kids and physically, he didn't have the time to be bouncing between the school and that cellar. He wasn't a credible suspect, regardless of what he might have done before or since,' he said dismissively.

Skegman nodded understandingly.

'We're just crossing i's, dotting some t's, sir – in the

circumstances, it's belt and braces to be speaking to the SIO in charge at the time. As I'm sure you understand.'

Much as she felt sympathetic to Skegman, his obsequious tone irritated Paulsen. AC or not, there was no need to excavate a tunnel up the man's arse.

'Does the name Red Tide mean anything to you?' she said.

Culley raised an eyebrow.

'A DS from the Exploitation Unit rang and asked me the same question earlier. Some individual on the Dark Web Jemma Vickers was investigating privately apparently – no, I've never heard the name before. It certainly never cropped up fifteen years ago.'

'We're trying to establish why Jemma was so interested—' started Skegman but Culley was already shaking his head.

'Not to speak ill of the dead – but I'd trust my own trained staff over an amateur, and a victim biased by their own trauma at that. Characters like this Red Tide are ten a penny on the Dark Web. I think we can all guess what kind of material he deals in and I'd also remind you that none of those teenagers were sexually abused.'

'And yet you accepted Trant's confession . . .' said Paulsen provocatively.

Culley looked ready to explode.

'Is there anything at all you can remember that troubled you at the time: any hole in the investigation, anything that came out of the interviews you conducted before or after?' said Skegman quickly. Culley peered over his glasses at him again, his piggy little eyes squinting a bit.

'You're getting too bound up with the past, both of you. Vickers and Knox were killed *today*. I'd concentrate on supporting DCI Walsh at the RVP if I were you. Dennis Trant abducted all three and murdered Oliver Littlewood. You need to work out why someone else might have been inspired by those events. That's a far more useful line of inquiry than looking for mistakes in the original investigation.' He sat back and checked his watch. 'I think we're done here – don't you?'

'Believe it or not, Culley's quite well regarded at senior levels,' said Skegman as they made their way out.

'I know the type,' spat Paulsen. 'Good with flow charts and presentations but all the people skills of a rusty spanner.'

Skegman looked over his shoulder – as usual, discretion wasn't her watchword.

'Mattie – some effort to keep your voice down would be good. Unless you're determined to flush the final fragments of what laughably might be called my career prospects down the toilet.'

She looked at him sheepishly and nodded.

'So, what did you make of that?' she said.

Skegman made an upside-down smile.

'Not much more than I expected. Culley's a man on an upward trajectory – give it another couple of years and I reckon he'll be in the frame for the commissioner's job. If they did fuck up in 2009, one way or another he won't be allowing that to stain his reputation.'

'You didn't think he was hiding anything, then?'

They'd reached the steel turnstiles at the exit and Skegman peered out through the vast glass frontage. It had stopped snowing again, but there was a strong wind blowing across the murky grey waters of the Thames.

'No, I wasn't getting that vibe. More damage limitation, I'd say – he just wanted to shut down even the possibility that the problem might track back to him. It doesn't really help us – or Alex – right now.'

They walked out across the concourse towards the car park

and Paulsen pulled her coat tightly around her as the cold cut through. It felt like it was going right into her bones.

'I think Vanessa's right,' she said. 'The only explanation that makes sense is that Jemma stumbled on to something. Either Red Tide or someone similar – and Knox also knew who that person was.'

'So let's focus on that,' said Skegman.

'It's embarrassing though, isn't it?' said Paulsen. 'I mean I don't want to agree with that man back there – but how could she have found out something we missed?'

'Because we weren't looking in the right areas before, and we are now. There'll be plenty of time later to analyse all that. Put your energies into finding the killer first.'

They'd reached Skegman's car. He unlocked the door and they both climbed inside. Paulsen sighed as she buckled up.

'I just feel like I'm letting the DI down. We're nowhere near to making an arrest and we just don't know what's going through Lee Ellis's mind,' she said.

'You can't think like that,' said Skegman. 'You're searching for a magic bullet to end this, but police work doesn't work to order – you know that. You're not doing anything wrong; in fact, you're doing everything the way Alex would.'

She looked at him, allowing some rare insecurity to show on her face.

'Really?'

He nodded.

'All that anal-retentive, buttoned-up, methodical bollocks of his must have rubbed off on you.'

Paulsen smiled.

'I'll take that as a compliment.'

He made no effort to start the car and his own expression turned more serious.

'People think I'm done, Mattie. That I'm just serving out

time now. But I'm not. I saw how they were glancing at me in there, the way Culley looked down his nose at both of us. I won't be making them happy with an early retirement any time soon. I want to drag Cedar House up by the bootstraps and ram it down their throats. If that makes us their problem child for a bit, then that's fine by me.' He turned and looked at her. 'Just so we're on the same page.'

She nodded.

'We are.'

He smiled.

'Good. Never doubted it,' he said and gunned the engine.

Culley looked out of his office window and saw Skegman's car making its way out on to the Victoria Embankment. He watched as it turned towards Westminster Bridge and headed back over into south London. Skegman and Paulsen had that same attitude he remembered from back in the day from Finn and one or two others at Cedar House. The polite courtesy to his face, the barely disguised contempt lurking not too far beneath the surface. They had some cheek given the disgrace that station had brought on to itself recently. There was also the same streak of self-righteousness that Finn had possessed too. God knows why – there was a reason that man had never progressed beyond the rank of DI and why he was an assistant commissioner.

He went back to his desk and pulled up the files from 2009 on to his computer. Some DC at Cedar House was doubtless, even now, going through them with a fine-toothed comb. He needed to find an hour to refamiliarise himself with every last word of it just in case any further awkward questions came his way. He clicked his mouse and listened to the printer in the corner hum into life.

He wondered what kind of conversations were going on

right now between Alex Finn and Lee Ellis. One way or another there would be fallout from that incident, however it resolved – headlines, journalists digging into Jemma and Lee's story all over again. It wouldn't take them long to realise a current senior officer at New Scotland Yard had been in charge of the original inquiry. He went back to the window and looked out over the Thames. It was time to circle his wagons, he thought, and reached for his phone. Briefly, he pondered the wisdom of what he was about to do. He didn't want to leave a breadcrumb trail for anyone – but better to be safe than sorry. Scrolling through his contacts he found a number and dialled it.

20

'*Stay calm,*' the man on the phone told Craig Quilter. '*Stand your ground and hold your nerve.*' Easy for him to say, thought Quilter afterwards. He wasn't the one the police were hounding. Quilter was in his kitchen now, steeping a camomile teabag in a mug of hot water. Lost in thought over the morning's developments, he watched as the liquid slowly turned yellow. He'd thought his number was up earlier. That those two detectives had come to arrest him and that his afternoon would be spent in a police interview room.

He couldn't get his head around why someone would have wanted to kill Jemma Vickers and the phone call hadn't brought any answers either. He could think of no obvious motive – at least, not after so much time. The fact the police had come to him was a shock though, as was their reference to Red Tide. Where they'd got *that* name from suddenly was interesting, to say the least. Hold your nerve, indeed.

He took his drink into the living room and had just settled down on the sofa when the doorbell rang. He rolled his eyes.

'Fucking police. What now?' he muttered and went to answer it.

Even as he reached for the door that feeling of wariness returned, a sense that he should just ignore this. It could be anyone on the other side, but he also needed information, and curiosity got the better of him. He turned the latch. Standing in front of him was a middle-aged man he'd never seen before.

Large, with closely cropped hair and thick salt-and-pepper stubble on his chin, he greeted Quilter with a genial smile. There was no sign of a warrant card anywhere.

'Expecting someone?' he said with a throaty London accent.

Instantly Quilter tried to close the door, but a meaty hand reached out and stopped him. He felt himself being pulled like a rag doll.

'Who are you?' he stammered.

By way of reply – almost in slow motion – a fist connected with his temple and Quilter's knees buckled from under him. The man dragged him down the stairs and out on to the street. He shepherded him towards a waiting car. The back door was open, and the engine was running. Quilter saw a figure – equally heavyset – behind the wheel. The first man piled in next to him and slammed the door shut.

'Shat yourself yet?' he said with the same friendly smile, baring his teeth. Even as Quilter tried to find an answer the man slapped him hard across the face. 'Why don't you tell us *what* you are?'

'I don't know what you're talking about,' he responded defiantly.

They were on the move now and the man hit him across the face again, this time with his knuckles. It felt like a sledgehammer.

'You like them young, don't you, Craig – your women?' hissed the man.

'You've got this wrong – I'm not some sort of paedophile,' Quilter replied, tasting blood in his mouth.

'Is that right?'

A huge fist crashed down on his groin and he bent forwards in agony as the car picked up speed.

The drive didn't seem to take long. Maybe only ten minutes or so. They pulled up and stopped by a deserted children's play area. Quilter had spent the remainder of the journey doubled up, trying not to vomit, though he wasn't sure whether that was from pain or fear.

'Almost over, sunshine,' said his tormentor before jumping out of the car. He opened the door and roughly pulled him out. As Quilter tried to stand, the man promptly gut-punched him and he instantly threw up the contents of his stomach on to the pavement. The driver came round and joined them. Quilter tried again to look up and see where he was but was in too much pain to even manage that.

'What do you want with me?' he croaked.

He heard a peal of laughter.

'You'll see,' said a deep surly voice, which he realised belonged to the driver. The two of them chair-lifted Quilter up and began to walk. He was in too much pain to even offer token resistance. They turned a corner and he saw a small, deserted footbridge overlooking a railway line close to some warehouses. Realisation hit him almost as hard as the physical blows – what was about to happen and why.

'Don't do this,' he whispered. '*Please* – there's no need. I won't say anything – I can disappear.' Even to his own ears, he sounded pathetic.

'You're going to disappear alright,' said the driver matter-of-factly. They checked that they were alone and began to slowly climb the steps of the bridge. Quilter kicked out, tried to twist out of their grasp but had no chance.

'I'll give you money – I've got plenty of it,' he gasped.

The first man laughed.

'We know. But to be honest, mate – we don't care,' he said. And then they threw him over.

Skegman and Paulsen were on their way back from New Scotland Yard when they heard the call over the radio about the body on the railway line. The immediate assumption had been that it was a suicide – the main priority now, to halt the flow of trains on the line. But Paulsen's ears had pricked up at the location. She'd been in the area only a few hours before visiting the man who was now lying like a rag doll on the tracks. A jogger had spotted the body and called it in, and an ambulance and a police patrol car were both parked close by when they arrived.

'That's Craig Quilter, alright,' she said. The pair were standing by the metal fence overlooking the line not far from the footbridge. Skegman squinted through the gap in the railings at the huddled shape in the centre of the track.

'Are you sure?'

'One hundred per cent. Unless the bleached hair, grey hoodie and jeans combo is a thing around here.'

Skegman rubbed the back of his neck.

'So did he jump or was he pushed?'

Paulsen carried on staring at the body for a moment or two longer. She and Nash might have been the last two people to see Quilter alive.

'I'm wondering if our visit might have prompted this – in which case, why?' she said.

He shrugged.

'Because he'd murdered Jemma Vickers earlier today – and quite possibly Eddie Knox as well? Couldn't live with himself?'

'Maybe. But . . .' She frowned as the wind swirled around them. More emergency vehicles were starting to arrive now.

'But what?' said Skegman.

'What if the same person who killed the other two is responsible for this?' She gestured over at the body. 'As you say – it's ambiguous, isn't it?' She was interrupted by her phone ringing. She pulled it from her jacket pocket and looked at the display. 'That's Nash – I better take this.'

A group of men in orange high-vis jackets bearing the words 'Network Rail' were now on the scene and were hurriedly making their way towards them, together with one of the police constables. Paulsen guessed one of them was the operations manager. It would be his job to organise the removal of the corpse from the line. If the early forensic examination suggested foul play, then there'd be more than a few commuters facing difficult journeys home later.

'I'll deal with them,' said Skegman, already heading away. Paulsen put the phone to her ear, turning, trying to shield herself from the wind.

'What have you got, Vanessa?' she said.

'A bit more on Red Tide,' she replied quickly, and Paulsen could hear the suppressed excitement in her voice. 'The Exploitation Unit has been liaising with some of their foreign counterparts since we spoke to them earlier. They just received some interesting information from a contact in Rotterdam. They don't have any footage yet, but the Dutch police aren't convinced it's pornography Red Tide deals in. At least not the conventional sort.'

Paulsen frowned.

'How do you mean?' she said.

'He doesn't trade very often – but what he does sell is for big sums – all in cryptocurrency.'

'Why don't they think it's porn though?' said Paulsen. She realised she'd made the assumption without ever questioning it.

'Precisely *because* he rarely surfaces. If it was straightforward kiddie porn, that wouldn't be an issue – unfortunately, there's plenty of that out there. They think this is something very niche, made to order.'

'A snuff movie?' said Paulsen. 'Did he murder Oliver Littlewood on camera back then?'

'Possibly. But there's something else to it as well . . .'

Paulsen was watching Skegman talking to the Network Rail officials as she listened. There was a lot of gesticulating going on, both at the footbridge and at the body. For a second her eyes settled on Quilter again. It looked almost like he'd curled into the foetal position and was simply sleeping across the rusting tracks.

'Go on,' she said.

'Digital Forensics has been going through Jemma Vickers's office PC. It took a while to get access to the hard drive and most of the material on it is just work-related stuff, but they found an interesting email exchange with Lee on there. It looks like the two of them had some sort of falling-out recently.'

The wind howled again, and Paulsen pulled the phone tighter to her ear.

'What sort of falling-out?'

'Unfortunately, there's nothing to indicate what it was about. Just that Lee seemed to think Jemma was holding something back from him.'

Paulsen started to walk, as much to help her think as anything.

'It keeps coming back to that – that Jemma *knew* something important – but what?' There was silence on the other end at the rhetorical question and Paulsen nodded, almost to herself.

'You've done really well, Vanessa,' she said, sincerely.

'Thanks – I appreciate you saying that,' came the reply.

A little piece of Paulsen felt better for the exchange.

'I want to know what Jemma found out – whether it was Red Tide's identity or something else entirely. And why she'd keep it from her closest friend. Let's put all our effort into that.'

'I've got some good news on that front,' said Nash quickly. 'Steve Garland said Jemma had started using a new work phone recently – or least that's what she told him it was. I called her line manager at the bank, and she said nothing like that had been issued to her. Steve had a look and eventually found it concealed in a drawer in their bedroom – which he thought was odd. It's on its way back now.'

Paulsen processed the information for a moment.

'As soon as Digital Forensics have had a look through it, let me know what they find. There's one more thing you need to know . . .'

She explained to Nash where she was and what had happened to Craig Quilter.

'You're shitting me,' came the instant unfiltered response.

'I want a press blackout on this and Eddie Knox's death too. I doubt we've had time to get consent from Knox's next of kin anyway. You can tell the media office they're free to announce the discovery of the bodies and that inquiries are underway – but not to release any names or any possible connection to the Vickers investigation.'

'Any particular reason why, guv?'

'Lee might have a radio or TV in that cafe, and I don't want him spooked by any of this. We still can't rule him out for Jemma's murder and what you've just told me about a possible argument between them muddies that even more. Call Sami at the RVP and let him know too.'

'Okay, leave it with me,' said Nash. There was a pause. 'So how the hell *do* we find out who Jemma was talking to and where do we go next with this?'

Paulsen considered it for a moment.

'I can think of someone,' she said.

21

At the RVP Sami Dattani was updating Walsh and Rachel about the latest developments in Cedar House's investigation.

'Two men – both dead since this began? Christ on a bike, I don't suppose the landlord here would mind if we started cracking open some of the hard stuff now?' said Walsh.

'Something is clearly going on,' added Rachel. 'What's DCI Skegman's take on it?'

Dattani shrugged.

'That something is clearly going on. We've also found evidence of a row between Lee and Jemma recently. So, though we know that he can't have been involved in what happened to Knox and Quilter – he's still a potential suspect for her murder.'

'Don't suppose there's an update on Lee's father is there?' she asked.

'Still critical, the last I heard. Don't know any more than that.'

Walsh glanced at Rachel.

'What's your assessment of Lee's current frame of mind?' he said.

She crossed her arms – the pub was still freezing cold. The owner had finally agreed to let them turn the heating on, but it seemed to be taking forever to crank into life.

'I'm concerned – we don't really know why that shot was

fired or the extent of the injuries it caused. On the phone earlier, I heard DI Finn pleading with Lee to let Marco go. If he's seriously hurt, then we could be jeopardising his life by trying to wait this out.'

Walsh sighed.

'You know the drill – we're here for as long as it takes to find a peaceful resolution.'

'And what if Rachel's right about Marco?' said Sami. 'You might have to make a call on that whether you like it or not – or you could end up with a dead hostage, anyway.'

Walsh nodded in acknowledgement.

'On the other hand, Lee seemed to think it was just a flesh wound – that a first aid kit was enough,' he said.

'Lee's a cook in a cafe – not a doctor,' said Rachel.

'He's a former soldier who'll have some basic knowledge of field medicine,' retorted Walsh. 'Still, I take your point. Like you say we still don't know what caused that gun to be discharged or even if Lee himself was hurt in the incident as well.'

'At least the DI seems alright,' muttered Dattani.

Walsh appeared to have arrived at a decision and grabbed his coat from the back of his chair.

'I'll talk to the tactical commander and see what his assessment is; if we do have to go in – I want to know what his thinking is about it. It really is a last resort though; it could do far more harm than good, especially in a tight, enclosed space like that.'

'I just think Lee's in this for the long haul, guv,' said Rachel. 'He's made that very clear – that's his line in the sand. He may judge Marco as collateral, especially if he doesn't think he's too seriously hurt. Do you want me to talk to him again?'

Walsh nodded.

'Yes – we need a clearer picture of the state of play in there. If you can get him to put Finn on the line again, then maybe copper to copper you can find a discreet way to communicate.' He swung his jacket on. 'My every instinct about this is that we don't need to send a team in – that we can resolve this through dialogue.'

'What worries me,' said Dattani slowly, 'is if Lee *does* start to realise that this isn't going to be put to bed quickly. He's just lost his closest friend in the world – what if he decides he wants to end things on his own terms?'

His words hung between them all for a moment.

'You're a proper ray of sunshine on a cold day, son,' said Walsh, before turning and leaving.

Lee barely seemed to notice his phone ringing. He sat hunched forwards, head in hands, slowly rubbing his temples. Finn's attention was on Marco though. The young man's pupils remained dilated, and his head was lolling to one side now. As the phone's church-bell ringtone cut through the silence, Finn could only wonder why it had taken them so long to get in touch again and what that said about the investigation in progress. Lee's parting words to Rachel the last time had been to only call if there was a major breakthrough. He hoped that's what this was – for all their sakes.

'Answer it,' he called out sharply. 'They might have found something.'

As Lee slowly responded, Finn could see his eyes were red and bloodshot and he wondered if that was because the coke he'd taken earlier was wearing off. After rising to his feet, Lee walked over to the counter and took the call.

'Tell me you've got some good news,' he said wearily into the handset. He placed the gun down and turned his back on Finn to take the call.

'My mum . . .' murmured Marco woozily. 'I can't leave her alone.'

The words didn't seem to be directed at Finn particularly, but he could see a sheen of sweat glistening on the young man's forehead. Given how cold the cafe had become since Lee had turned the radiator off, it wasn't a good sign. Marco tried to prop himself up but couldn't manage it and fell back again, banging his head against the wall in the process. Finn winced. An incident room full of people conducting a murder investigation, he could manage. This situation was driving him crazy with frustration.

'Don't try and move,' he whispered. 'Just lie still. How are you feeling?'

Marco managed a weak grin.

'Like I should have taken the day off . . .'

Finn found a grim smile.

'You haven't discovered a thing,' said Lee into the phone. 'You're just fishing for information. Don't waste my time. I'm telling you nothing until you give me something concrete.' He ran a hand over his bony scalp and exhaled. 'Actually – there is one thing you can do – I want to speak to my dad . . .'

In the RVP, Rachel looked over at Dattani and held out her hands in a silent *what am I supposed to do with that?* gesture. He tried to think of something plausible for her to say but couldn't.

'He's not here any more,' she replied. 'He was finding the situation too stressful. Let's not give him anything more to worry about, okay?'

She glanced up again at Dattani for affirmation and he nodded. It was vague but would have to do. They both waited for a response and could hear Lee breathing heavily through the speaker.

'Where's he gone?'

'Don't worry about him – somewhere warm with good people. And you're wrong when you say we haven't found anything,' she said quickly. 'I can't get into the specifics but there *have* been some developments with the investigation. It would really help us to be able to interview you properly. You know so much about what happened in 2009, probably more than even you realise.'

Rachel and Dattani had had a quick conversation about whether telling Lee about Knox and Quilter's murders would have any benefit, but had agreed with Paulsen that withholding that information was the smarter move. There were still too many unknowns to be able to accurately predict how he'd receive the news and it wasn't worth the risk – at least at this stage. Letting him know that things were happening and unfolding didn't necessarily hurt though.

'Nice try – but I can tell you whatever you need to know over the phone,' said Lee.

Rachel automatically looked up as Walsh came through the doors of the pub. He saw the conversation in progress and immediately joined them.

'It's just worth bearing in mind that there are police officers here, dealing with *this* situation who could be working that investigation instead,' she replied, looking at Dattani.

'You said there'd been some developments?' said Lee. 'What kind of developments?'

Finn was straining to hear the other end of the conversation, catching fragments of Rachel's tinny voice through the phone. He was as interested as Lee in what was going on outside. He heard a groan and as he glanced round it was clear something was seriously wrong with Marco. His mouth had fallen open, and a small stream of clear liquid was dripping down his chin.

His eyes seemed to have rolled to the back of his head and his arms and legs were starting to shake.

'*We need help – Marco's seizing*,' roared Finn, mainly for Rachel's benefit. Lee turned to see what was happening and cut the call dead.

In the RVP, they'd all heard Finn shout. Walsh was already striding over to his desk. He grabbed his radio – the need to labour over what to do next, now gone.

'Trojan One from Silver,' he shouted. 'Strike, strike, strike.'

Finn's mind was racing – he was almost certain the team in the RVP would have heard him, and he could guess what was happening in there now. He hadn't had much choice but to do it this way and he knew they had perhaps only seconds.

'They can't risk a fatality – they'll send the Tactical Support Team in. Call them back *now* – tell them you're letting Marco go,' he barked. Lee was still staring at Marco's juddering body as if hypnotised by it. '*Call them!*' Finn yelled and Lee seemed to snap out of it.

'He goes – but you stay,' he snapped, and Finn nodded furiously.

Rachel took the call instantly. She listened, then shouted across the room.

'He's releasing Marco.'

Walsh snatched the radio up again.

'Trojan One from Silver – abort, abort, abort,' he shouted. There seemed to be an agonising wait before the radio crackled back.

'*Abort received and understood.*'

★

Finn could only guess how close the armed Tactical Support Team outside had been from smashing through the glass frontage of the cafe, ready to throw in a stun grenade. Beside him, Marco had stopped fitting and was unconscious again. Finn silently said a thank you to whoever was running the operation. The fine margins might well have saved Lee's life, if not his own – though Marco might yet prove to be a different story.

Lee put the phone down and picked up the gun, together with the knife he'd used earlier. First, he went to the front door and unlocked it, then he cut Marco's hands and feet free from their plastic ties. Finally, he reached into his pocket for the key to Finn's handcuffs.

'You take him over to the door – and don't try anything stupid. I'll have this pointing at you all the way,' he said, gesturing with the gun.

'He's got a head injury. It's going to take two of us to move him properly,' said Finn, rubbing his wrists where the cuffs had dug into the flesh.

'You'll manage – now stand up,' said Lee, and Finn stiffly obeyed. 'Go and open the door.'

Finn walked over and did as he was told. He saw a black-clad officer hurrying through the snow towards them. It was too risky to send in a paramedic and he guessed that this man was probably a trained medic too.

'Stay outside,' shouted Lee as he saw the officer approaching. 'Do you understand?'

The man nodded and held back. Lee motioned at Finn.

'Now take him out,' he snapped.

Finn went over to Marco, braced himself and lifted the stricken man over his shoulder. Slowly he made for the door.

'That's far enough,' said Lee as Finn reached the threshold.

The tactical support officer came forwards and carefully relieved him. Once the exchange was complete, Finn stepped back inside, closing the door behind him. He turned to find the Beretta pointing at his face once again.

'Just you and me now,' said Lee.

22

'Did I see you and everyone's favourite solicitor having a crafty tea break in YoYo's earlier?' said Jack Barton. Finn looked up from his desk with an expression that suggested this wasn't the moment to disturb him with trivia. 'What is it – have you found something?' said Barton instantly adjusting.

'Maybe,' said Finn slowly.

'You don't sound too sure.'

Finn leant back and took a sip from the tepid glass of water that had been sitting on his desk for most of the day.

'One of Karin's colleagues thinks he saw that white van speeding down his road on the nights of both abductions – and before you say there's a lot of white vans in south London – *I know* . . .' he growled.

Barton's craggy features widened into a smile.

'Which street is this?'

Finn pointed at his monitor on his desk, which was displaying a map of the area.

'Filimore Road – it's just under a mile away from Croydon Airport where we found the van this morning. I've been cross-checking it against the other sightings we pulled off the street cameras . . . and against some of the *potential* sightings the public have reported.'

'You like making things hard, don't you? You should have told me, and I'd have helped you,' said Barton.

'I think, by process of elimination, that I've been able to isolate one common area. One small patch that the van would have to have gone through each time – to make all those sightings make sense.'

'*All* of them?' said Barton.

Finn shook his head from side to side.

'About eighty per cent, I reckon – up to and including the final journey to where we found it this morning. But given some of those are probably different vans then that's a decent margin of error – the number plates weren't always visible.'

Barton squinted at the screen again.

'That's a big old area. If those kids are being held somewhere in there – it's needle-in-haystack territory. And nobody even got a partial plate?'

Finn shook his head and then rubbed his chin as he thought about it.

'What else have we got right now?'

Barton shrugged.

'Nothing much. The rest of the team are chasing ghosts, frankly – following up leads that aren't going anywhere useful.'

Finn nodded.

'So, let's tell Culley what we've found.' He pointed at the screen again. 'We need to get house-to-house inquiries underway across the whole area – and yes, I know that's going to stretch us. But if I'm right then maybe someone else saw that vehicle, and we can narrow down the search area even more. And if we're *really* lucky, then maybe they've seen or heard something even better than a van.'

'And if you're wrong?'

Finn smiled unexpectedly.

'Rolf will rip me a new one. Again.'

Barton grinned back at him.

'It must be at least an hour since the last time,' he said.

'What did you want anyway – other than to ask me where I go and spend my tea breaks?' said Finn.

Barton turned serious again.

'Sarah Littlewood's downstairs – you're doing that press conference with her, remember?'

A look of blind panic crossed Finn's face.

'That's not until . . .' He looked down at his watch. '*Shit!* I didn't notice the time.'

'Don't worry – I can go and talk to Culley and tell him about this if you want.'

Finn nodded gratefully and stood.

'Thanks, Jack . . .' He stopped as Karin entered the incident room talking to one of the other DCs. She saw Finn and Barton looking at her, winked conspiratorially at both of them, and then continued her conversation.

'I'm saying absolutely nothing,' said Barton.

It had been Culley's suggestion to hold a press conference. Finn hadn't been against the idea, especially after his encounter with Sarah at the Ricksons' earlier. She *needed* to do it – it gave her some agency at least and he felt like he owed her that much. At this point in the investigation, another request to the public for witnesses and information was no bad idea, especially if there was a rough area of interest to work with now.

Invitations had also been extended to the parents of the other two missing teenagers, but they'd declined to participate. Jemma's parents had now returned from their aborted trip to Venice and walked back into a nightmare, by turns furious and in pieces. Finn was privately pleased that they'd chosen to step back and let the police operation unfold – he was juggling enough balls as it was. The Ellises were simply broken by their son's disappearance – which was another reaction Finn had encountered before. There was none of Sarah's fury or the fluctuating emotions of the Vickers, simply overwhelming fear and worry. He didn't envy the FLOs working with both families, trying to hold them together and give them encouragement.

Sarah, therefore, had become by default the de facto spokesperson for all three teenagers. When Finn went down to meet her at the front desk there was no sign of her earlier fury. She'd brought her daughter Ella with her – and they both shared the same dead-eyed expression. It wasn't just her anger that had dissipated but hope too, it seemed.

The best-case scenario was that they found them all alive, and then they'd have to unpick exactly what had happened. He was also aware that with each passing hour Barton's earlier observation was correct – the likelihood was that they were now searching for bodies. The third possibility was arguably the worst – that they were *never* found, and all three families would have to live with the ambiguity of their children's fate for the rest of their days.

Some friends of the family had accompanied them, and they looked after Ella as Finn took Sarah to one side before they met the media.

'Are you sure you want to do this?' he said. 'I can read out a statement on your behalf if you'd prefer.'

Looking at her face he got the sense the impetus had died somewhere between home and Cedar House.

'I've been thinking about what will happen if you find Ollie's body,' she said slowly.

'We're not there yet . . .' began Finn.

'I don't mean the next few days or weeks, I mean the rest of my life. I'm a fighter by nature – as you may have noticed . . .' Finn's face softened, and he nodded. 'You don't have to worry about me . . .' she continued. 'I won't be doing anything stupid to myself – I still have another child to look after. But I also know I will never, *ever* be able to live with this.'

'If it comes to it. *If.* Then there are trained professionals who'll be able to help you,' he said. 'We won't abandon you – however this pans out.'

She shook her head.

'That's not what I meant – it's not the emptiness I'm scared of – it's the *anger*.'

Her eyes blazed as she said the words. 'I'm angry about everything right now – with myself for letting this happen, with the piece of shit who's taken him.' She stopped, visibly upset again. 'I've been angry with Ella – for no good reason. And I've even felt angry with Ollie – for *letting* this happen.' She shook her head. 'How ridiculous is that?'

For a moment Finn thought of his brother and the flashes of resentment he felt even now about his death.

'Not ridiculous at all. Human. And as I say, we're not there yet,' he repeated gently. 'This press conference might trigger something that helps us to find him though.'

She nodded and then suddenly turned sharply.

'The other question I've been asking myself . . . is what does that anger do to you as the years go by? How much of you corrodes – and what do you become?'

In the cellar, Lee could feel the blood running down the side of his face, the coppery taste of it on his tongue. Above all, it *hurt*. The open wounds stung like they were on fire, and he couldn't stop shaking either. He looked over at Oliver – now chained back up on the other side of the room. The promise to release him clearly an empty one. He'd tried to apologise at first but now he was just sitting on the floor, with his hands around his knees. Lee put a trembling hand up against his cheek and felt a loose strip of flesh hanging from it.

'There's cameras in here,' said Jemma quietly.

'Wha . . . what?' stammered Lee, almost panting the word. He looked across and saw her brown almond eyes burning with concentration. She looked beautiful, he thought, even in these circumstances.

'He knew where I'd hidden that knife – there's cameras in here somewhere. Must be like those ones the army have where you can see in the dark.'

Lee was beyond caring.

'It hurts – my face really hurts,' he said.

'I know – I'm sorry,' she said gently. The words sounded strong, but this time he could see the fear etched on her face too. She looked as terrified as he was by what had happened. She turned and looked over at the huddle on the other side of the room. 'Ollie – are you okay?'

There was no response. Even though he knew he hadn't had much choice, Lee couldn't stop himself from feeling furious. He'd actually *done* it – cut away at him like a piece of meat.

'He should have stabbed *him* with it,' he said savagely and then instantly regretted it. The act of snarling, moving his cheek had opened up the incisions even more, sending new waves of sharp splintering pain across his face. He could feel the blood streaming down his neck, on to his chest and sticking against his shirt. Still, he couldn't stop shaking either. He was in shock, he realised, and tried to hug himself, despite the chains restraining him.

'They must be over there,' said Jemma, pointing somewhere into the gloom. 'The cameras. He was kind of pulling you into a position, so you were facing that way. The sick fuck was filming you, I'm sure of it.'

'Why?' was as much as Lee could croak.

'I don't know – to watch back later? For kicks?' She almost

couldn't look at him he noticed, was almost recoiling from his wounds. 'Lee, I'm so sorry,' she said in a whisper. 'I wish I could do something to help you.'

'It's alright,' he said with a small smile, that sent another burst of stabbing pain across his face. Oliver seemed to be mumbling to himself, and the noise was almost too much for Lee on top of the pain.

'You've both got to hang in there,' said Jemma. 'We're still alive – that's what matters. The police must be looking for us – they could arrive at any minute. Keep that image in your heads – some cop pulling that mask off. I bet he's only a weedy little bastard underneath,' she said defiantly. But even as she rallied, Lee felt his own belief draining away and what he said next, he meant with every bone in his body.

'I think we're going to die in here, Jem.'

23

Today

Sarah Littlewood stared into her bathroom mirror as she washed her hands. Her face looked pale, her skin dry and lined. It was just gone four o'clock and she'd been feeling sick all day. First, there'd been the shock of Jemma's death. There'd also been that WhatsApp message she'd received on her phone. The implication of it was terrifying – the silence that had followed it from the sender, even more concerning to her. And then there was Lee – poor, broken damaged Lee, still holding Alex Finn hostage in that cafe, while his father lay critically ill in a hospital bed. She felt a streak of guilt; who was she to look down on Lee Ellis? She was as broken and damaged as anyone. Drying her hands with a towel, she took a deep breath and composed herself. If there was one thing she'd learnt over the last fifteen years – it was how to mask her feelings.

'Are you sure I can't offer you a cup of tea or something?' she said breezily, as she re-entered her living room a few moments later. Paulsen and Nash were sitting around a large circular glass table and politely declined the offer. Ella had gone out shopping and taken baby Kaitlyn with her, leaving them to it.

'Is there any more news from the cafe?' said Sarah, as she took a seat and joined them.

'Lee's released one of the hostages,' said Paulsen. 'Not Detective Inspector Finn, I'm afraid,' she added quickly in response to Sarah's hopeful expression.

'That's something I suppose. Hopefully, he'll come to his senses before anyone else gets hurt.' She smiled politely at them. 'So, what is it I can do for you?' she said.

'To be honest, we're struggling a little because there's only a limited number of people we can talk to about what happened fifteen years ago,' said Paulsen.

'We've found evidence that Jemma was investigating it, herself,' said Nash, and Sarah felt her heart sink. 'Did she mention that to you? We know you two got back in touch after she returned to the area. We've seen some of the correspondence between you on her phone.'

Sarah nodded. That was true. For a brief period, there had been some happier times – especially after Jemma had given birth to her own son. The two families had met up in the park from time to time as well as for the occasional lunch together.

'There's a lot that we had in common, obviously. But no, I had no idea she was doing that,' she said. 'She never mentioned it to me, anyway. I don't know *why* she would want to rake all that up, either – she always said she wanted to leave the past in the past.'

She could feel the scrutiny of both detectives as they tried to gauge the truthfulness of her answer.

'Something else you should know. Three people have died today. In addition to Jemma, a convicted criminal called Eddie Knox and someone you may remember from the original investigation: Jemma's former geography teacher – Craig Quilter.'

Sarah's face screwed up with confusion at the name.

'I *do* recall him . . .' she said finally and Nash nodded.

'Both men were investigated in 2009 as well. It's very early days – but we can't rule out the strong possibility that all three of them were murdered, and their deaths are connected,' she said. Sarah hadn't been expecting that. She felt her head spin and looked away, so they didn't notice.

'Is Lee right?' she said finally, turning back to them. '*Is* he still out there – the man who killed my son? Is that why Jemma was digging into it – why these people died today?'

'I can't tell you if it's the same person behind all this,' said Paulsen. 'Today's events could all be highly coincidental, but it seems pretty unlikely. That's what we're trying to figure out. Why this is happening and how it all joins up.'

'Did you accept Dennis Trant's confession in 2016?' asked Nash.

'Yes,' said Sarah simply. 'Alex Finn came to see me at the time and explained why he believed it was true.' She shrugged. 'I had no reason to *disbelieve* him. It all sounded perfectly credible.' She clasped her hands together on the table. 'It helped me a great deal with my own recovery. You never get over something like this – but it was an important moment for me. It was just a massive shame that Trant didn't live long enough to stand trial. That needed to happen too, and we were denied it.'

Paulsen nodded sympathetically.

'What about the other parents? What was their view?'

Sarah looked out of the window, remembering the countless conversations she'd had over the years.

'Jemma's family accepted it, as I recall. Terry Ellis took a lot of closure from it. So did George Rickson for that matter. People always forget the Ricksons – but they were affected by this as much as anyone.'

'I'm sorry,' said Paulsen. 'We don't want to cause you any unnecessary extra distress. We have no concrete proof that

Dennis Trant *wasn't* your son's murderer. But obviously, we have to explore every possibility, given what's been happening today.'

'Of course,' said Sarah, trying to absorb the implication of the conversation. Her mind was reeling but she was trying not to let it show.

'Is there anybody you can think of who would have had a reason to kill these people today?' said Nash.

Sarah looked at her as if she was slightly mad.

'Not a clue – honestly. I mean there was a lot of anger in the community at the time. Someone might not have forgotten. But Jemma . . .' She shrugged. 'That makes no sense to me at all.'

'There's nothing unusual that's happened recently then?' said Nash, and Sarah immediately thought of that WhatsApp message again. Someone out there knew far more than they should, and she couldn't fathom how. She faltered as the implication hit her again and she tried to cover the moment, but Paulsen had caught it and she cursed herself.

'I get a *lot* of nutters contacting me on social media – always have had. I'm a magnet for them. Some of it's pretty sick. It could be one of them, I suppose.'

'I'm so sorry – that's awful,' said Paulsen. 'But there's nothing recent that stands out?'

'Possibly, I'd have to look. It's more a trickle these days than a flood but it's never really stopped.'

'Any details you can pass on to us would be really helpful,' said Nash.

'Sure,' replied Sarah.

'But there's been nothing in the last few days?' said Paulsen. 'You're certain of that?'

Sarah nodded, and the detective didn't look entirely

convinced but she kept her smile fixed. Inside though, her heart was pounding.

Billy Rickson knelt down and used his front door key to slash open the tape sealing the cardboard box on the supermarket floor. Inside were thirty cans of tuna fish, which he dutifully started to remove and put on the shelf, barely noticing what he was doing.

'It was on TV earlier,' said a woman behind him. 'My husband's been to that cafe – used to have his lunch there before he went to the football on a Saturday.'

'Why don't they just shoot the bloke?' said the elderly man she was gossiping with. 'They always string these things out. Just gives individuals like that the attention they're after, in my view.' He sniffed dismissively. 'That's all it is really, isn't it? Attention-seeking.'

Billy turned and looked at the old man balefully, unable to find the words to match the jumble of emotions coursing through him. Fifteen years of shared pain with Lee Ellis, reduced simply to *'attention-seeking'*.

'Something the matter, son?' said the man noticing his stare. Billy spun back around and finished stacking the shelf. He picked up the empty box and walked back through the store. His manager was talking to one of the checkout assistants and, on a whim, he went over to join them.

'Sorry to interrupt, Lorraine, but I'm not feeling brilliant. I can't stop coughing . . .' he lied.

She looked at him suspiciously.

'I hadn't noticed,' she said.

'Would you mind if I left early? I haven't been feeling right all day, to be honest.'

'Jesus, Billy, we're short-staffed as it is.' She thought about it for a moment. 'Mind you, the last thing we need is you infecting everyone else. Go on then – get out, call me tomorrow morning – let me know how you're feeling.'

He thanked her and went through to the staff locker room where he got changed and then wasted little time heading for the exit.

His entire day had seemed like an out-of-body experience. He couldn't really remember a thing that had happened since he'd arrived for work and was glad to get away. The afternoon had settled into a cold bitter affair, but it felt good to be outside. The bright, white supermarket lights had gradually been giving him a headache. His phone vibrated in his pocket and he swore, hoping Lorraine hadn't changed her mind, then softened when he saw on the display who was calling.

'Auntie Sal,' he said into the handset.

'I'm worried about you,' said a warm, concerned voice. 'I've just seen on the news about Jemma Vickers. It's awful – I know how you felt about her – you must be in pieces?'

'Yeah,' was all that he could manage. It felt like there was so much emotion welling up inside that it had bottlenecked in his throat. He heard a sigh on the other end.

'You should have called me. You've been all on your own since your father passed. It must be so difficult for you, not to have someone to talk to. I wish you and Ella could sort yourselves out. Especially for little Kaitlyn . . .' she said but he didn't respond, giving the idea no encouragement. 'I'm always here if you want to talk, you know?' she added.

Again, there was so much he wanted to say but didn't know where to even begin – that sense of the past and the present colliding that had been his companion all day.

'Something happened earlier . . .' he said hesitantly, then stopped.

'What do you mean – what happened, Billy?'

Across the road, he saw a young woman pushing a pram along. As she looked up, he saw it was Ella. She was smiling, making faces at their daughter as she walked. She seemed far happier than when he'd met with her in the park earlier and a little piece of him begrudged her for that.

'Billy?' said his aunt.

'Can I call you this evening?' he said. 'I'm just out at the moment – we'll talk properly later, I promise,' he said and ended the call, his eyes still firmly fixed on Ella.

'Why does it feel like Sarah Littlewood was lying about something?' said Vanessa Nash. 'I can't back it up – and it doesn't make any sense to me either.'

Paulsen was listening but had one eye on the mounted TV in the corner of the incident room. A Sky News reporter was standing close to the cordon in South Norwood and was talking animatedly about the hostage release earlier. All too quickly the picture cut back to the presenter in the studio who was already moving on to the next story. Paulsen refocused on what Nash had been saying.

'Yeah, I felt that a bit too – but how do we know what *is* strange in Sarah's situation? Neither of us has been through what she has.' She shrugged. 'Who are we to judge her?'

Nash thought about it and nodded.

'I guess – but it still felt like there was something she wasn't telling us.'

Paulsen shook her head.

'We can worry about it later – has anything else come through while we were talking to her?'

Nash nodded.

'I'm still waiting to hear back from Digital Forensics about that so-called work phone Jemma was using. I'll give them a call in a minute and see how they're getting on.' She glanced down at her pocketbook. 'In terms of the rest of it, there's nothing much to add from the crime scene in Tooting – but Jemma's post-mortem has been scheduled for midday tomorrow. Forensics are still at Eddie Knox's flat. They've found nothing obvious so far – the early indications are that the whole place is clean. The killer knew what he was doing, and Knox seemed to know him too, given that he opened the door for him.'

'And the railway line?' said Paulsen.

'I spoke briefly to the forensic pathologist at the scene. She said there were some bruises on Craig Quilter's face and body that could be consistent with a beating – but equally, it could have come from the fall on to the track. There is one other thing that's come in, though – a resident in the building where Quilter lives says she saw a red Mazda speeding away when she was coming home from the shops. The timing's interesting because it was *after* our visit and *before* his body was found on the tracks.'

Paulsen looked up.

'Did she get a plate?'

Nash shook her head.

'No, and it could be absolutely nothing – but I'm checking the ANPR anyway.'

Paulsen nodded.

'We need to establish exactly what did happen – if Quilter jumped off that railway bridge, I'd say that makes him our prime suspect for the other two murders. If he was pushed . . .' She left the sentence unfinished. Nash was about to reply when her phone pinged. She glanced down and read the message and instantly Paulsen saw it was important.

'Have you got something?' she said.

Nash carried on reading for a second longer then nodded.

'It's from Digital Forensics. They've found a video clip on that phone Jemma was using. They think it was made by Red Tide – and she seems to have bought it on the Dark Web according to some of the email exchanges.'

'Correspondence with Red Tide?'

'No – if I understand this right – just someone selling the material second-hand.'

'So what's on this clip?' said Paulsen urgently.

Nash rolled her eyes.

'Sounds pretty grim. A seventeen-year-old kid being tortured by an older boy. Burning him with a cigarette, gouging at his eyes with a screwdriver. Apparently it's sustained and gets progressively more graphic. They've sent it over if you want to watch it?'

Paulsen pulled a face.

'I'll find a minute, but I think I get the gist for now. Any idea who these boys are?'

'No, except that they're all speaking German.' Nash looked up at her. 'What do you think it means?'

Paulsen looked out of the window at the silver sky outside and considered the information for a moment.

'We said earlier that Jemma was interested in Red Tide for a reason – something from her own experience that led her to him, and I think this might be it.'

'How do you mean?' said Nash.

'What exactly *do* we know about Red Tide? That he produces a tailor-made, high-end product that people are prepared to pay big money for. *Niche stuff* – that was how you described it earlier.'

'And you think this is what it is?' said Nash.

Paulsen nodded.

'You remember the state of Oliver Littlewood's body

when they found it? And also, the fact that none of those three kids in 2009 were sexually abused. What if Red Tide is shooting torture porn? And not just that – a very specific sort. In this case, teenagers – being forced to hurt *other* teenagers?'

24

'You know what this situation reminds me of?' said Walsh as he received a freshly brewed cup of tea from Sami Dattani. He sniffed the polystyrene cup suspiciously before taking a sip and continuing. 'Something I dealt with when I was a DI in Reading. A middle-aged man whose mother was killed in a mugging when he was just a nipper. He'd got it into his head that the police had nicked the wrong guy for it and spent years stalking the fella he thought *was* responsible.'

'What happened?' said Dattani.

Walsh shrugged.

'He turned up at the man's house with a knife one night and slashed his wrists in front of him. We detained him under the mental health act. Think he got released a few months later but you wonder where all that sits with him now.' He tapped the side of his head. 'The years that go by after something awful's happened and that's where the real damage gets done.'

Rachel picked up a tea from the cardboard tray Dattani had brought over and joined them.

'For what it's worth – I think we *might* – and I use that word carefully – be over the worst of this,' she said. 'The fact that Lee released Marco is encouraging. It's a de-escalation – the more time that passes, the more the wind might just be going out of his sails.'

'Doesn't that rather depend on how much coke he's snorted?' said Dattani.

'Hopefully, Marco can give us a bit more of an idea about his state of mind when we get the go-ahead from the medics to talk to him,' said Walsh. 'But I'll take a positive assessment with both hands right now.'

The young cafe owner was currently on his way to hospital, but the paramedics' early view had been cautiously optimistic.

'I think it works better for us now that it's just the two of them in there,' said Rachel. 'We know that they have a pre-established relationship. Finn's got a real chance now to capitalise on that.'

'Sorry to put a dampener on things again . . .' began Dattani. Walsh gave him a sideways look.

'That's starting to become a theme, son. Go on – knock yourself out,' he said.

Dattani looked at him sheepishly.

'With respect, I think Lee's a different case to the one you dealt with in Reading.'

'In what way?' said Walsh.

'By the sounds of it, that guy just couldn't accept the truth about the person who'd been arrested over his mother's death. But what if Lee's *right*?' Dattani looked up at the clock mounted on the wall behind the bar. It was just approaching half past four now. 'There's potentially a killer out there – someone who you could argue has been terrorising him all his life – in one form or another. I think he's partly locked himself in that cafe because it's the only place he feels *safe*. And he might have a point. There have been two more deaths – we don't really know what's going on, do we?'

Walsh stroked his beard while he thought it through. He was interrupted by one of his team, a middle-aged woman with bleached blonde hair who was striding over clutching her phone.

'Sorry to interrupt, guv – I've just been talking to DC McAlister. She's at the Croydon University Hospital.'

'What's happened?' said Walsh. 'Is it Marco?'

The woman shook her head.

'No, he's fine. It's Terry Ellis . . .'

Walsh was already ahead of her.

'You're kidding?'

'I'm afraid not. He died around ten minutes ago.'

'Ah, shite,' said Walsh with genuine regret. 'Tell McAlister to make sure that news doesn't get out – in case there's any press sniffing around the hospital.' The woman nodded and headed away. Walsh turned back to Rachel and Dattani. 'To state the bleeding obvious, we keep this information from Lee until he's out of that cafe.'

Rachel was looking thoughtful.

'Do we?' she said.

'Jesus – do you want him to blow his brains out, and quite possibly Alex Finn's too?' said Walsh.

'What exactly are you thinking?' Dattani directed his question at Rachel.

'That timed right . . .' she shrugged '. . . it might be what we need to end this.'

'And how the hell do we do that?' said Walsh.

'*We* don't,' she said.

'This ain't bad, is it?' said Nash. The big smile was back. She and Paulsen had retired to YoYo's to clear their heads after their discussion in the incident room earlier. It was Nash's first experience of the coffee shop and she was liking what she could see. Yolande came over and carefully placed a mug in front of Paulsen.

'Soya flat white, Mattie. I let it cool a bit, I know you don't take it too hot,' she said. Paulsen smiled appreciatively. With her other hand, Yolande plonked a cup down in front of Nash, splashing some of its contents into the saucer.

'Milky Assam,' she barked with a glare then headed back to the counter.

'What's her problem?' said Nash, mildly offended.

'Nothing – but she does take a while to warm to new people,' said Paulsen.

'How long did it take you?'

Paulsen thought about it.

'Nearly four years.'

Nash looked over at Yolande who was now back behind the counter, arms folded as if daring someone to make an order.

'Right.'

'She was also extremely fond of Jackie Ojo. We've kind of bonded over that recently.' Paulsen glanced down guiltily. 'And in that respect, I think I owe you an apology.'

Nash looked puzzled.

'How do you mean?'

Paulsen straightened up.

'It's been a difficult day. I've been pissed off with my family for reasons I won't bore you with, and for reasons they don't deserve. I've also been pissed off with the DI for getting himself into such a stupid situation. And I suppose – most of all – I've been pissed off with Jacks for getting herself killed. It all just seems to have come to a head today and I've taken it out on you, which isn't fair. You just happened to have been the person in front of me.' She held up her hands. 'And I'm sorry about that.'

Nash beamed instinctively in response.

'Don't be stupid. Now that you've explained it, it all makes perfect sense. It's a bit of a relief – I thought you'd taken against me.'

Paulsen produced an unexpectedly brilliant smile of her own.

'I take against *everyone*, Vanessa,' she said, and Nash laughed.

'I can believe that,' she replied.

Paulsen's face turned serious again.

'Now that I've got that off my chest – let's get back to the task at hand. I'm not bothered if Red Tide has operated in other countries. If he's been moving around, it might explain why he's gone quiet on a few occasions. It's also probably helped disguise where he's permanently based. With all that in mind – I think it's possible he *could* have been responsible for what happened here in 2009.'

Nash nodded.

'If you're right about the content he's been making then it fits – the injuries we know were inflicted on Oliver Littlewood, the cuts to Lee Ellis's face as well.'

'What if Red Tide used Lee or Jemma to inflict those injuries – like the lad in that German video?'

'That works too,' agreed Nash. 'And it might explain why someone might have used that as a motive to kill Jemma. But what about Knox and Quilter? How do they slot into this – why are they dead?'

Paulsen shrugged.

'I don't know. We've got some of the pieces but not enough to fully put it together.'

She stared at her undisturbed coffee for a second. 'I've been thinking about something Sarah said – about the Ricksons – that everyone forgets them. Billy Rickson was Lee and Jemma's best mate – I'd be interested to know what's going on in his head right now.'

Billy Rickson's head was pounding. The whole day was starting to catch up with him and the ache that had started with a low thrum was turning into full-on thumping pain. He'd continued to trail Ella and Kaitlyn as they'd slowly meandered down the high street, his gaze never far from the pram and its contents. By focusing entirely on his daughter, it shut out everything else. Jemma, Sarah, Ella, even the hammering beat inside his skull.

They say some events are life-changing but having a baby is *self*-changing and that had definitely been the case for him. Once Kaitlyn had come along everything else had become secondary. His self-pity, his confused feelings for Ella, his well-hidden crush for Jemma – all of it. His daughter had become the only thing that had really mattered to him, the one beacon of light – and now he'd somehow managed to almost screw that up too. His face hardened as he thought about it. No, that wasn't true, *he* hadn't screwed it up – others had. He'd found out the hard way that there *was* something else that mattered to him just as much as his daughter.

'The bastards . . .' he muttered under his breath.

He watched as Ella manoeuvred the pram into a Boots on the other side of the road and hung back to wait for them as the snow began to lightly fall, again.

Finn was back in handcuffs, but Lee was happy enough now to let him sit at one of the cafe's tables rather than on the floor. The pair were facing each other, the gun still in Lee's hand, the phone on the table between them. Above them, a neon light flickered and buzzed like a trapped insect.

'Do you know what really fucks me off?' said Lee.

'Burnt toast?' offered Finn. It wasn't a completely idle gag – things had improved between them since Marco's departure – and the quip was a gentle testing of the waters. The stony reaction to it told Finn all he needed to know. He was confident enough that Lee wasn't going to shoot him arbitrarily. But if – when – the Tactical Support Team *did* come crashing through, it was still hard to predict how the former soldier would react. Sieges rarely concluded well for the hostage taker and Finn was determined this one would end without bloodshed.

'It's those expressions people mindlessly repeat,' said Lee. 'You see them all over Instagram and Twitter – the same phrases over and over. The ones that sound clever but mean nothing.'

'I only really use social media for my job,' said Finn. 'So, you'll have to explain what you mean.'

Lee didn't seem to hear him and continued his train of thought anyway.

'Jemma used to come out with all that bollocks. Stuff like – *"Everything happens for a reason."* That became her way of rationalising what happened. Well, I'll tell you something – she was wrong – no, it doesn't. Life's cruel – shit happens because it does. People get run over or stabbed or die for any number of reasons and there's no purpose to any of it. Anyone who thinks otherwise is deluding themselves.'

Finn thought about it, could remember victims of crime he'd interviewed. Those who'd tried to find solace in the same concept. Truth be told, he'd always been a sceptic too.

'It *is* bollocks,' he agreed. 'I heard it a lot after my wife died but I can't say it helped me.'

'Well, there you go,' said Lee. 'I'll give you another one I hear all the time – *"People don't change."* He snapped out the words one after the other, barely hiding his contempt for them. 'Yes, they do. All the fucking time. In my experience, the sand is always shifting under your feet. I wish people *did* stay the same – I might understand the world a bit better then.'

There was some truth to that too, thought Finn. He couldn't help but think of his own life and the three deaths that had pushed him in so many different directions – his brother, his wife, and, most recently, his friend. It struck him that the version of himself he'd most like to be again was the one who'd first met Lee all those years ago. The man who'd fallen in love with Karin Bergmann when the future seemed limitless. But he was long gone and so was she.

'Yeah . . .' he murmured. 'I'll give you that one as well.' A thought struck him. 'Did Jemma change – is that what you're saying?'

Lee stared down at the gun.

'She couldn't accept the truth.'

'Which was?' Finn finally felt like he was on the brink of something important.

Lee looked up sharply, those cobalt blue eyes staring right into him.

'You're as broken as me – in your own way. Aren't you?' he said.

'What truth couldn't Jemma accept, Lee?' said Finn, ignoring him.

'That's your truth, isn't it? That there's not *that* much difference between us.'

'Help me here, tell me what you mean.'

Lee leant forwards.

'Admit *your* truth – in this room, right now – and I might . . .'

Finn looked again at the colourful tattoo that lined Lee's neck and throat and the vague hint of the scars underneath that they masked. If he wanted him to open up about what had truly happened in that cellar all those years ago then he knew he had to give him something in exchange.

'Fine – if that's what you want,' he said, putting his cuffed hands on the table in front of him. 'We're all carrying something. You think because I'm police, I'm not? I told you earlier I make mistakes like everyone else. The last one got a friend of mine killed. I thought I was in control of a situation. It turned out I wasn't, and she paid the price.' He closed his eyes, shut everything out for a moment, then opened them again. 'No one wants to change themselves more than I do. *That's* my truth.'

The only sound in the room was the buzzing light above. The phone rang and Lee snatched it up.

'Just checking in,' Finn heard Rachel's tinny voice say on the other end. 'And I wanted to say thank you for releasing Marco too. It's appreciated. He's on his way to hospital and should make a full recovery.'

'That it?' said Lee.

'Would you mind if I spoke to DI Finn again? Just to check he's okay?'

Lee thought about it, then stretched his hand across the table and put the receiver to Finn's ear.

'They want to know you're alright, again,' he said.

'It's me,' said Finn and listened to Rachel for a moment. 'I'm unharmed and I'm being treated well.'

Lee immediately retracted the phone and ended the call.

Rachel hadn't been stupid – she'd known she'd only have scant seconds and was aware of the risk of being overheard. So, she'd lowered her voice and whispered it straight away. And now Finn knew what they knew – that the only person Lee Ellis had left in the world was dead.

25

2009

The incident room had grown too hot for Finn. He was standing in the shade of the car park outside Cedar House in an effort to find somewhere cool to think clearly. In truth, it was even more sweltering outside. The press conference with Sarah Littlewood had come and gone. But the search for the white van had now intensified following his efforts in narrowing down its potential route through South Croydon. Culley had agreed to begin house-to-house inquiries and now all they could do now was wait and see if it produced anything.

'What are you doing out here?' said a familiar voice and he turned and saw Karin, wearing a pair of sunglasses that made her look like a Sixties movie starlet.

'I had to get out of that room – it's suffocating up there.' He pointed at the grey building opposite and she nodded in agreement.

'Too many unwashed male bodies,' she said. 'But it's just like that in the winter too, I can assure you.'

Finn smiled.

'I meant to say thank you, by the way. That tip-off about the van turned out to be really helpful – we're pursuing it,' he said.

Karin looked genuinely pleased.

'That's good to hear,' she said, then added lightly: 'Now

would be a good moment to suggest another drink, by the way.' He was about to reply when his phone rang interrupting them. He retrieved it from his trouser pocket, glanced down and saw Culley's name on the display.

'Sorry, I've got to take this,' he said with genuine regret.

She rolled her eyes in mock dismay, shook her head and began to walk away. Finn could only watch helplessly as he took the call.

'Where are you?' growled Culley.

'Just grabbing something from my car,' he improvised as Karin turned a corner and disappeared out of view. A little piece of him died inside.

'Get your arse back up here – something's just come in.'

'What is it?' said Finn a few moments later. He was breathing heavily – even climbing the short flight of stairs from the ground floor back to the incident room seemed to have soaked him in a new layer of sweat. Culley's usual side glance of disdain was missing though, and there seemed a genuine urgency about him instead.

'Local radio just ran a bit of the press conference you did with Sarah Littlewood – and we've had an instant response. Member of the public who thinks they saw that white van. It's interesting because of *where*.'

Finn followed as Culley walked over to the large, detailed map of south London that was spread across one of the walls.

'Right here . . .' He found the spot he was looking for and planted a finger on it. 'Dorsey Street.'

Finn saw the relevance immediately.

'That's bang inside the zone I identified earlier from the CCTV grabs,' he said.

'Exactly,' said Culley. 'The punter who called it in lives on that road and reckons he saw the van parked there on the nights of both abductions. He's a jogger – so he's been going out for late evening runs during the heatwave when it's been cooler.'

Finn looked at the map – he was starting to know the blobby shape of that area like the back of his hand.

'Karin's workmate reckons he saw it in Filimore Road . . . which is here.' He located it, then stretched out a finger to the street that Culley had just indicated. 'If these kids are being held somewhere on Dorsey Street – then that would be en route.' He stood back as if to double-check his logic. 'We need to get some manpower down there.'

'Hold your horses,' said Culley. 'Where's Jack got to?'

Finn looked around the room but couldn't see him.

'Probably taking a leak.'

'Find him – get your shit together, then get yourselves down there and take a look around. If this is the right street, then I don't want to alarm anyone – especially before we're ready. Let's be discreet – plain-clothed officers on the ground first. Once we're sure about the facts, we'll decide on our next move. I'll make sure there's a team ready to go in immediately if necessary – in the meantime let's find out who the properties on that road belong to and who's living in them.'

The doors swung open behind them, and Barton entered clutching a bottle of water. Both Culley and Finn immediately swivelled round to look at him.

'What?' he said.

Dorsey Street was a quiet row of large, expensive-looking Victorian houses. By the time Finn and Barton had driven across south London, the team in the incident room had begun looking through the land registry to find out who each one belonged to, and – just as importantly – what the plans for each property were. If it came to it and they needed to send a team in, then knowing the geography would be critical.

233

'It's quiet,' was Finn's first assessment as they stood at the top of the street.

'Which is probably exactly what you'd want,' murmured Barton.

Like everywhere else the place was bathed in bright sunshine. They decided to walk the length of the road, Finn watching the houses on the right, while Barton took in the ones on the left.

Money had clearly gone into these places. Some exotic-looking palm trees stood outside the front of a few; others had expensive, colourful porches with vivid red geraniums and purple hydrangea. Most had windows wide open in the heat, and Finn occasionally caught the eye of some of the occupants as he glanced inside.

'So, what do you reckon?' said Barton as they got to the end.

'Nothing obvious jumping out at me,' said Finn. 'You?' Barton shook his head.

'The guy who called it in lives at number fourteen. Shall we go have a chat?'

It was immediately obvious that it wasn't just the weather that had caused the man in question to go jogging late at night. With two young toddlers, his front room looked like a war zone. Finn guessed the evenings were about the only time of day he could escape for some exercise. He'd seen the van on both nights in question. It had caught his attention the second time because the vehicle's engine had been running, the back doors were wide open and there didn't seem to be a soul in sight.

'It looked like something was being dropped off,' he told them. 'Seemed bloody strange to me – anyone could have nicked it.'

Afterwards, the two detectives made a second sweep of the street and paid specific attention to the area, two-thirds of the way down, where their witness indicated the vehicle had been.

One particular house caught Finn's attention this time, not that there was anything eye-catching about it – but that was the point. The windows were closed, the blinds drawn, and the place looked deserted.

'What do you think?' he said to Barton.

The DC surveyed it for a moment.

'Owners could be at work. Kathy keeps telling me that we should shut the blinds and close the curtains in this heat because it keeps it cooler inside. It's doing eff-all for our place, I can tell you that now – it's like an oven when I get home.'

Finn looked across at the property next door. It was a large, detached house with a fair amount of foliage, and fencing separating the two buildings. He could see an old lady sitting in an armchair in the living room, a book perched on her lap.

'Why don't you use your questionable charm to ask her if she's seen or heard anything unusual,' said Finn. 'I don't think she's got three missing kids hidden away in there, somehow.'

'And what are you going to do?' said Barton.

Finn was already heading towards the other house.

'What do you think I'm going to do?'

Barton held out his hands.

'We're supposed to wait – you heard what Rolf said.'

'He told us to take a look and find out what's going on and that's exactly what I intend to do.'

'Are you sure you don't want me to come with you?' said Barton.

'I'm fine, Jack.'

Barton, almost reluctantly, began to walk away. Finn turned on his heels, checked all was still quiet and headed through the front gate. A small path led around the side. The whole place was sparse, though some effort had been made to keep the garden and patio at the back tidy. Unlike the front, there were no blinds or curtains drawn on the windows and he carefully peered inside. What he saw stopped him in his tracks and he felt his heart pound.

The cuts on Lee's face still stung viciously but he'd worked out that his best strategy was just to remain still. Oliver was also motionless on the other side of the cellar but for very different reasons. It was as if he'd accessed a part of himself that he'd no idea existed and now that the temporary demon that had possessed him was gone, he was in a state of shock at what he'd done. Most of all it had been for nothing – because he was still here, still chained to the same wall.

Lee wondered if the positions were reversed, whether he might well have done the same thing. Probably, but he was mutilated now and even if they did escape somehow – he'd bear these scars forever.

'We'll be alright, Lee?' he heard Jemma say softly as if she'd guessed his thinking. 'We'll go away when this is over – we'll treat ourselves. New York, somewhere like that. Just you and me.'

'Yeah – you can get your dad to pay for that,' he answered, imitating something of his old swagger and she smiled.

'I still think there's a camera down here,' she said. 'That he's watching us – listening to what we say . . .'

She peered around trying to spot some evidence of it.

'I'm sorry, man,' said Oliver suddenly looking up at Lee. 'I had to do it. I thought—'

'That he'd *really* let you go?' said Lee finishing his sentence and then regretting it. It felt like a hot iron was running down the side of his face.

'No – that he'd beat me to death with that bat or use the knife if I didn't. I'm sorry, okay – but I didn't have a choice.'

There was almost some aggression again in the final sentence and Lee remembered the snarl of fury on his face as he'd cut into him. He still found it hard to forgive, but he could see Jemma was watching him now too.

'It's okay – it's done,' he grunted.

The door at the top of the stairs swung open again and they all looked up with a start.

'How are we all doing down here? Rubbing along nicely, I hope?' said the man in the mask jauntily as he entered. It was a different tone to anything they'd heard from him before, but this time the sense of terror Lee felt was off the scale. 'I think it's time three became two . . .' he added in the same infuriating voice and then skipped down the stairs lightly like a TV chat show host making an entrance. Lee looked across at Jemma. What the hell was coming now?

The man walked over to the corner of the cellar where a large dark tarpaulin was spread. He lifted it away and underneath Lee saw some dusty furniture and several crates loaded on top of one another. He rummaged in one of the crates and pulled something out. When he turned, Lee could see what he was now holding and felt his stomach heave. In his hand was a long wooden hatchet. There was a chunky silver blade at the top, the white lettering of the manufacturer written down the handle.

Ignoring the other two he marched over to Lee, raising the hatchet as if to strike him down there and then.

'*Boo!*' he said and dropped his arm, reaching into his pocket instead, as Lee cowered in terror. He produced some keys and began to unlock the padlock on his chains.

'*No – no, no, no.no* . . .' said Lee, the words spilling out of him like liquid as he realised the implication immediately.

'Three becomes two,' repeated the man as if talking to a child. 'You decide who lives – or I'll use this on *you*.' He went back up to the top of the stairs, threw the hatchet down and it landed with a loud thump at Lee's feet.

'You've got ten minutes and if one of these two is still standing when I come back, I'll take you apart myself with that thing – limb by limb – do you understand?'

His voice was cold and soft now. The words literally hung over them and then he turned and walked out, locking the door behind him, and once again the room fell silent.

26

As Nash tried to find contact details for Billy Rickson, Paulsen was killing time at her desk, coat on, ready to leave. Normally, it would only take a few minutes to find the necessary information but for some reason, Nash seemed to be taking forever. While she waited, Paulsen checked her phone for messages. There was a WhatsApp from her brother Jonas.

16:45
Just spoke to mum – Dad now refusing to go into care. Call me!
There was another from Nancy.

15:37
Your mum called – sounds like she's having problems with your dad. She wants you to ring her. Drinking with workmates tonight – see you when I see you xxx

Momentarily foxed as to why her mother had called Nancy instead of her, she then saw the list of missed calls and voice notes she'd been left. Paulsen sighed, simultaneously worried about her parents and envious of her partner's more straightforward work life. Nobody in this room would be leaving at six for a quiet after-work beer this evening, that was for sure. Nash came over, looking slightly uncertain.

'What is it?' said Paulsen, dropping her phone back into her bag.

'I don't know – it might be nothing. I've got a mobile

number for Billy but there was no answer when I called just now. And there's something else . . . I found an address for what looks like his parents' place – but when I checked I discovered it's up for sale. I rang the estate agents, and they told me George Rickson had died recently, which was why the house was on the market.'

Paulsen leant forward.

'What happened to him?'

'A hit and run, a couple of months back – the Serious Collision Unit is still investigating. Do you think it might be relevant?'

Paulsen weighed it up – knew exactly the face Finn would probably be pulling now as he ran through the various permutations of this. But she wasn't Finn and the messages she'd just read were distracting her. Those voice notes could definitely wait until later.

'Maybe. Or perhaps it's just a coincidence. Did you find out where Billy lives?'

Nash nodded.

'That was the other interesting thing. Up until recently – with Sarah Littlewood. He's in a relationship with her daughter.' Paulsen looked up with interest. 'Or was,' continued Nash. He moved out a few months back. I've got an address and also for the supermarket where he works – we could just go straight there?'

Paulsen nodded and rose to her feet, glad to have some new impetus. But just as over breakfast, she had a sudden flash of her father alone in a care home and the thought cut her in half.

'I'll drive,' she said tonelessly and headed for the door.

A few minutes after five, Paulsen and Nash were at the Sainsbury's in South Croydon where Billy worked. A quick chat with his manager established that he'd gone home sick around an hour earlier. In and of itself, there was nothing particularly unusual about it. But on this day, any small kink in routine felt significant.

'You can't blame him,' said Nash as they left the store. 'Jemma Vickers gets killed this morning and Lee Ellis starts taking people hostage at gunpoint – I'm amazed Billy even turned up here today.'

She was right, thought Paulsen, and yet a nagging doubt remained.

'He's just lost his dad too,' she said. 'I suppose you can understand why he might be struggling at the moment.' She shook her head, wondering if she was overthinking it. The woman in the supermarket had mentioned his bereavement as well – and how close Billy had been to his father. *'Absolutely hero-worshipped him,'* she'd remarked.

'Maybe it's just what it looks like – he was ill and went home early,' Paulsen added but could feel a familiar irritation rising. Not with Nash, this time. Just at her inability to find her way through the fog of this. She was beginning to understand Finn's general air of detachment during an investigation now. If you weren't careful, your own emotions could colour your thinking all too easily. She shivered – the early evening temperature was starting to fall fast.

'Come on, let's try his flat,' she said.

Billy's headache had, if anything, got worse as the cold wind continued its icy assault. Across the road Ella was unlocking her car and beginning the process of moving Kaitlyn into the vehicle. He could see her mouthing soothing words as she went about it and felt a surge of resentment. It was ridiculous of course – because *he'd* chosen this exclusion from their lives, not her.

Jemma, Lee and the last fifteen years kept spinning round

his throbbing head. It was interesting how their lives had turned out. Jemma had gone to university and made something of herself. Lee went into the army, then returned – apparently broken by his past. And as for Billy, the worst of it was that he'd let his father down. George Rickson had been so proud of him, so sure he'd be a success. But he hadn't been. Instead, he'd carried all that survivor's guilt and never sought the help he probably should have.

For a time, he'd had a happy spell working for a hospitality firm. It had been full of young upwardly mobile types, and he'd felt at home there. The arrival of Covid ended that though, as the company – without events to service – went bust. Unemployed and alone, the various lockdowns had set his mental health back and he'd been grateful for the job at the supermarket when it had come along. It was just meant to be a stopgap – to pay the rent and keep him ticking over – but he'd been there for a while now. It was only when his relationship with Ella had begun, and Kaitlyn had come along, that his fragile confidence had slowly begun to rebuild.

And then Jemma had unexpectedly got in touch, asking to meet. The reunion had not gone well. Not long after that meeting, his father had died – the man whose belief in him had kept him going through everything. A mysterious hit and run, the police said – the driver, yet to be found. Immediately, a single thought had crossed Billy's mind. A seed of a suspicion that had grown into a cold hard certainty after that conversation with Jemma. At his father's wake they'd spoken again – but he'd seen something in her eyes that day – even as she'd offered her condolences, and he hadn't forgotten it.

Across the road Ella was checking on something in Kaitlyn's carrycot. In a few moments she'd start the car and disappear again. He remembered that feeling in the park earlier as he'd watched them go and couldn't face it again. It felt like he'd lost everything that had made his life worth living. His father, Jemma, a piece of himself even – and that he would never quite be whole again after today. He thought about the cold contempt in Ella's voice when they'd talked earlier and wondered if *they'd* ever be the same again – when the truth of a few things emerged. He wasn't quite sure what kind of future he was facing, but it felt cold and harsh, and right now he wasn't sure he wanted any part of it.

There was only one thing that *did* make sense to him any more, the only shining light left in a world going dark – and he desperately wanted to hold her close. The decision made, he pulled his baseball cap down over his face, sprinted across the road and reached Ella just as she'd climbed into the driver's seat and was grasping for the door. With one swift movement, he grabbed her with both hands, pulled her out and threw her on to the pavement. Before she could react, he jumped inside, slammed the door shut and accelerated away.

'What do you remember about the day that you found us?' asked Lee. The pair were still sitting at one of the cafe's tables. Finn sighed. The news that Terry Ellis had died was catastrophic. He could guess why Rachel had told him though. The more he knew, the more it informed the conversation they were having in here. And as he looked at the damaged, wretched man opposite, all he could feel was sympathy.

'Really? You want to go back to that day, *that* moment?' he said.

'Of course – because it *all* goes back to that, doesn't it? The Red Room.'

He said the final three words, almost reverently.

'Why do you still call it that?' said Finn.

'You *know* why I call it that,' replied Lee.

Finn nodded. The Red Room was how the teenage version of Lee had described the cellar in the conversations that had taken place in the days after they'd rescued him. In his mind, Finn could still see what it had looked like when the forensic team was at work and the full horror of what they'd found had been exposed.

'What do you want me to say?'

'The truth.'

Finn shook his head. Over the years when he'd met up with Lee and Jemma, he'd always told them he was happy to answer any questions they might have about what had happened. He'd seen it as a duty of care, and the day they were rescued was something that he'd gone through with them many times.

Now, it had the same feel of a young child asking for a favourite bedtime story to be repeated – so that they could enjoy tracing through its familiar beats and phrases. But he was in no mind to indulge Lee. That cellar was the last place on earth he wanted to revisit.

'Let's not go there,' he said gently.

'No – let's,' said Lee, snarling.

'You're not in control of this,' said Karin. *'Remember that.'*

'Alright,' he said reluctantly to both of them and took a breath. 'We'd found the house we thought you might be in. I sent my colleague to talk to one of the neighbours while I took a closer look.'

Lee was silent as he listened. One hand still holding the gun, the other gripping the side of the table with white knuckles.

'And what did you find?' he said, already knowing the answer.

Finn felt sick as he remembered. He could see it as clear as day in his mind's eye, looking through the window and seeing

244

a sports bag on the kitchen table – a can of pepper spray poking out of the top.

'I should have called for backup. Right there and then. That was the mistake.'

'But you didn't.'

'I tried the back door, and it was open.' He shook his head. 'If it had been locked, I probably *would* have called for backup – those were the fine margins. I went in and started to look around.' He swallowed. 'And the rest you know.'

'You don't get to stop there,' said Lee. 'Keep going.'

'Where's this getting us?' pleaded Finn. 'What aren't you telling me – what bit of this story do I *still* not know?'

Lee was inscrutable.

'I said, keep going.'

Finn looked over at the closed blinds covering the windows and wondered how close the Tactical Support Team outside were. He took another deep breath and continued.

'As I moved inside, a man in a mask jumped me. We grappled but he got away and made a run for the back door. I had a choice – and I chose you,' he said. 'I radioed my colleague and told him a suspect was escaping from the rear of the property. And then . . .' He faltered.

The memory was so vivid now. He could remember opening the door to the cellar and being hit by the rancid stench that rose from it. Something awful had happened down there – he'd understood that immediately. He'd found a light switch and a single yellowing bulb had illuminated a scene from hell. A young man lying on the floor. Dark crimson, sticky liquid everywhere. On the opposite side of the room Lee and Jemma, chained to the wall like medieval prisoners, eyes wild, shaking with terror. Later he'd learn that the actual murder had taken place much earlier and they'd been left alone with the body for hours.

Finn looked across the table and knew they were both sharing the same memory – that they were bound together by it. Lee was right, he realised. It did all come back to that.

'I'm sorry we didn't find you sooner,' he said hoarsely. 'But at least we got you both out alive.'

Lee looked down at the gun in his hand.

'You want to know what it is I held back from you all this time? Well, I'll tell you.' He fixed him with burning bright eyes. 'It wasn't our kidnapper who killed Oliver Littlewood – *it was me*.'

And there it was – the entire thing reframed in an instant. Finn looked at him aghast, lost for words. It was the one scenario that had never occurred to him – the one answer to every question surrounding Lee Ellis.

'What happened?' he said, and Lee explained the appalling choice he'd been given.

'That's how I got these,' he said, almost absently, pointing at the scars on his neck. 'He made Oliver do that to me – like a taster before the main event.' He shook his head and continued. 'I was never going to hurt Jem. That left Oliver and I didn't know what to do – and for a moment, I won't lie – I *did* think about it.' He paused. 'I went over to him – he was crying, begging me not to hurt him. I went too close, and he grabbed at the hatchet, tried to snatch it out of my hand. My feet got tangled in his chains and we fell.'

Lee stopped sharply – the pain written across his face.

'The blade . . .' said Finn, working it out.

'. . . must have severed some artery. It was obvious that it was bad straight away. He bled out in front of us and there was nothing we could do to help him. But it was an accident, I swear.'

'His body though? When I went into that cellar – there was far more than just one cut – it had been *mutilated* . . .'

Lee nodded.

'Jemma told me to do that. To make it look like I'd done as I'd been told. In that light it probably hadn't looked like an accident and we thought we were being filmed . . .'

Finn felt like he'd missed something obvious.

'There were cameras – that's what this was all about?'

'I was scared and desperate, so I did it and I've lived in fear all my life that one day that footage would turn up. Because it's out there somewhere – someone's *entertainment*.'

The words hung in the air and Finn stared at him trying to comprehend the horror of it. It was impossible to tell whether Oliver Littlewood had actually been dead at that point, and he guessed Lee's memory of the event was so distorted by the passing years it would be impossible to ever truly know.

'You were only eighteen.'

'And it's not the sort of thing you ever forget, trust me.'

Again, the image of that body and what had been done to it came back to Finn. He'd assumed it had been the work of some deranged psychopath, a paedophile, of Dennis Trant, but never the man sitting in front of him now.

'Why didn't you tell me all this before – I'd have understood – ruled out Trant years ago. He specifically confessed to killing Oliver – and the pair of you knew from the start it couldn't have been him.'

'Because we made a pact *never* to tell anyone,' said Lee fiercely. 'Because we didn't think anybody would ever believe or forgive and I didn't *want* anyone to know – particularly Sarah, Oliver's mum. But now that Jemma's gone . . .' He shrugged helplessly.

'I'm so sorry,' murmured Finn, a thousand questions already starting to form in his mind. 'You've been right all along – he *is* still out there, whoever did this to you.'

Lee fell back into his seat. He looked shattered.

'I've lost everything today. I heard what that cop said to you earlier,' he said almost incidentally. It took Finn a second to register what he meant and then it hit like a punch to the stomach – Rachel, on the phone, only minutes earlier.

'My dad's dead,' said Lee before he could react. 'And Jemma's gone too – they were all that were keeping me going.' He looked Finn bolt in the eye. 'Just promise me you'll find the bastard – and get it right this time,' he added savagely.

Then he put the gun to his head and pulled the trigger.

27

Everything seemed to happen in slow motion. For a moment, Finn remained seated as Lee's body fell sideways out of his seat, a huge gout of blood, bone and brain matter pluming across the cafe's tiled floor. As the sound stopped reverberating in his eardrums, his mind started working again. The shot would have been heard – both by the officers outside and probably also by the ones monitoring the building on a feed in the RVP. This time he suspected whoever was running things would instantly give the order to move in. He barely had seconds.

Pressing his handcuffed wrists down on to the table in front he levered himself to his feet. Turning, he saw the open door of the kitchen behind the counter. Small and self-enclosed it was about the safest place left and he made a beeline for it. But as he scrambled across the room, his foot slipped in the widening pool of blood. His momentum carried him over and he tumbled forwards on to the ground crashing hard against the bottom of the counter. Groaning, he saw Lee, lying opposite, the life now gone from those vital blue eyes. Even in these circumstances, the sense of failure was overwhelming. He wanted to scream in despair, then suddenly realised he *was* screaming.

Something smashed and he barely had time to turn to see it was the cafe's window shattering. He knew what was about to follow, closed his eyes tightly and curled into a ball as he heard a stun grenade clatter on to the floor behind him. For a split second, there was perfect silence and then a massive thunderclap ripped across the diner.

All he could hear was white noise, and all he could see was that last look on Lee's face before he'd pulled the trigger. Other images randomly flickered through his mind – Jackie Ojo's body in that house in Bethnal Green, Jemma Vickers, lying in the bloodied snow earlier. And the Red Room of course – so perfectly imprinted on his memory – as it surely always would be.

Lee Ellis had never stood a chance, he realised. From the day he'd been plucked off the streets of south London, the journey to this cafe floor had been almost inevitable. Finn had never known the true scale of what he'd been dealing with until now.

'*You didn't do this,*' said Karin. '*So don't waste time blaming yourself and concentrate on finding out who did.*'

Slowly the buzzing in his ears began to clear, and he could hear shouting now. Still, he kept himself tightly coiled in a foetal position, felt the ice-cold floor pressing against his cheek. There was pain too, from where he'd hit his forehead, and he could feel something wet running down over his eyelids but didn't care.

Now there were hands upon him, pulling and turning him over. He opened his eyes and saw a dark shape in the smoke looming over him.

'I'm okay,' he gasped and began to cough violently. The TST officer was continuing to shout, but Finn couldn't make out the words – everything just sounded like a slow, deep roar. But despite the chaos around him, there was an odd clarity too. Lee's final words had burnt themselves into him and he knew it was a request he couldn't refuse.

I'll find the bastard – and that's a promise, he thought.

★

Walsh had his phone clamped to his ear while he watched the feed of the cafe exterior on one of the laptop screens. Finn was now being helped out of the building by one of the TST officers. He was moving reasonably freely but Walsh could see what appeared to be blood streaking from a wound on his forehead. A pair of paramedics were already haring towards him.

Sami Dattani had taken himself into the corner of the pub and was calling John Skegman to let him know that the siege was over. Walsh finished his own call and joined Rachel.

'The cafe's secure – but I'm afraid Lee's dead. The TST commander says it looks like he shot himself.'

Rachel was genuinely distressed.

'It should never have come to that,' she said but Walsh appeared unmoved.

'It's regrettable, but he took two men hostage at gunpoint. We got them both out safely and that was always the priority.'

Rachel seemed to realise her first reaction could have been taken the wrong way.

'I didn't mean it as a criticism – I was blaming myself as much as anyone. *I* should have prevented this. I really don't think Lee intended to hurt anyone.'

Walsh's face softened.

'You know the reality of these scenarios – it's not like the movies, you can't always form a rapport with someone and talk them down. It sounds like he'd been struggling with his mental health for years. Sometimes this job just puts you in no-win positions.'

Rachel exhaled glumly.

'We could have gone in after the first shot was fired,' she said, challenging him and he nodded, accepting the point.

'Perhaps. But I'd back my judgement. And as it turned out

Lee *hadn't* shot Marco – so we were right to hold back. Don't worry, there'll be a mandatory referral to the IOPC.'

The Independent Office for Police Conduct was the police watchdog and every aspect of the operation at the cafe would come under scrutiny as was automatically always the case in these situations. Rachel knew Walsh was essentially correct though – they'd followed standard procedure to its natural conclusion and the IOPC investigation wasn't something to be feared. For all she knew, even if they'd got Lee out safely, he might still have made the same choice tomorrow.

'You know the worst of it?' she said. 'He died without getting any of the answers he was after.'

Walsh nodded slowly.

'I'm sorry, Rachel, but I appreciate everything you did today. His death's not on you.'

She didn't look convinced, and Walsh turned to Dattani.

'What about you, Sami—' he said, then stopped, because the DC had gone.

Finn was sitting in the back of an ambulance with a paramedic who was busy bandaging his head wound when Dattani found him. Across the road, there was a hive of activity around the shattered cafe entrance. The siege may have ended, but the forensic operation in there was just beginning.

'Guv – it's good to see you. How are you feeling?' said Dattani, getting as close as the paramedic's glare would let him.

Finn smiled weakly.

'Have you been in the RVP all this time, Sami? I got it into my head it was probably Mattie in there. Should have guessed she'd have something better to do.'

He was trying to quip casually, but the words came out heavy and leaden. Even as he said them, he knew – could feel

– he was in shock. He saw Dattani's concerned expression and realised he hadn't answered his question and pointed at his forehead. 'This is just a scratch. I'm fine, honestly.'

'I'll be the judge of that,' growled the paramedic. 'Any chance this conversation can wait until later?' he added.

Dattani stepped backwards holding an apologetic hand up.

'I'll let everyone know you're okay, guv,' he said.

'How's the investigation into Jemma Vickers's death going?' said Finn, ignoring the paramedic. 'I heard Rachel tell Lee there'd been some developments?'

Dattani nodded.

'Two more deaths – and you know them both as well. Eddie Knox and Craig Quilter.'

Finn looked shocked, then rose to his feet.

'No,' said the paramedic firmly. He was a tall heavyset man, who looked more than capable of enforcing the instruction if required.

'Just give me five minutes,' said Finn, undeterred, and promptly jumped out of the ambulance before the paramedic could argue.

At Cedar House, news that the siege had ended was already spreading quickly. But any relief at learning Finn was now safe had quickly been put to one side. The developing emergency regarding Ella Littlewood's daughter had over-taken everything else. John Skegman was with Paulsen in the incident room liaising with the CID team mobilising the search for the missing infant. He'd just activated a Child Rescue Alert, which would circulate Kaitlyn's details to both neighbouring police forces and the full spectrum of media outlets.

'This can't be a coincidence,' he said, joining Paulsen at her desk. She looked up and he answered her unspoken question.

'They're about to take Alex to hospital – but it's just precautionary. He's fine from what Sami told me.'

She nodded in acknowledgement.

'No,' she said. 'I can't see how this can be coincidental, but it makes absolutely no sense to me.'

'Did Ella get a good look at this guy?'

Paulsen took a deep intake of breath.

'Yes, she thinks it was Billy Rickson. He's the baby's father.'

Skegman's normally darting little eyes came to a dead stop as he made the connection.

'Jesus Christ,' he said, in lieu of anything else. 'The other kid from 2009 – why on earth would he do that?'

'I don't know. The couple split a while back – his decision apparently – and there was no issue with access. He wasn't at his flat when we called earlier. Uniform are with Ella, and we've got specialist officers on the way to talk to her, so I'm not making any assumptions until we know a bit more.'

'Any idea where he might be heading?'

Paulsen shook her head.

'We're just at the beginning of this – but so far he's not responding to calls.'

Skegman nodded.

'The helicopter should be in the air shortly – we know what vehicle he's using, so we're trying to pick it up with ANPR as well. But I'd imagine he'd be aware of that too and will try and lose the car as quickly as possible.'

One of the other DCs who'd been on the phone rose from his desk and came over.

'Sarah Littlewood's downstairs, guv. She wants to talk to someone – says she has some important information.'

Skegman and Paulsen exchanged a look, then – as one – headed for the door.

As she greeted her at the front desk, Paulsen wasn't sure

she'd seen anyone looking the way Sarah was right now. She could only imagine the emotions – the worst fear and pain this woman had ever experienced was revisiting her all over again. Most didn't suffer what she'd been through once, let alone twice in a lifetime. Ashen didn't cover it.

'I've not, I think, been entirely truthful with you,' she said slowly. 'There are some important things that I haven't told you about.'

Paulsen could feel Skegman glancing over at her but kept her gaze on Sarah.

'Do you know why Billy's taken Kaitlyn?' she said, and Sarah nodded.

'Yes,' she said and looked at them both squarely. 'I want to confess to a murder.'

28

Finn could feel himself recovering by the second. Adrenaline, it seemed, made for an interesting counteragent to shock. Dattani was now bringing him up to speed with the details of the two deaths that had occurred while he'd been in the cafe.

'We found nothing in 2009 that indicated either Knox or Quilter had anything to do with the abductions. Why would someone go after them *today*?' he said, harvesting the new information.

'At the moment we're not even sure Quilter *was* murdered – it's entirely possible that he jumped off that railway bridge,' said Dattani. Finn's head was hurting in more ways than one. He gingerly touched the bandage around his forehead – it felt like overkill – he wasn't sure the cut underneath it even warranted stitching.

'If it's the same person who killed Jemma Vickers, then honest to God, Sami, none of it makes any sense to me.'

'That's pretty much what the DCI said too.'

Finn found a smile from somewhere. If he'd had a bad day, then there was some consolation in imagining the number of balls Skegman had been juggling too. Dattani stopped as he saw Rachel and Walsh emerge from the pub and head down the pavement towards them. He just had time to identify the pair for Finn before they reached them.

'Detective Inspector – it's good to finally meet you,' said

Walsh with a tired smile. 'I'm glad you're okay – but shouldn't you be on your way to hospital?'

'Probably,' replied Finn. 'But it sounds like Cedar House could use a chat with me too – there's a lot I learnt in there that they need to know about. I also wanted to catch up with you both before I left – partly to say thank you, and partly to make sure I'm completely up to date with what you know as well.'

'Why did Lee shoot himself?' asked Rachel bluntly, skipping the introductions. 'He seemed so determined to stick this out until he had some answers.'

Finn recognised the look on her face and guessed she was blaming herself for what had happened. He wondered if she'd also deduced that Lee had overheard what she'd said over the phone to him regarding his father. Normally, two negotiators would be deployed at a hostage scene, but he suspected – given this had been a relatively small-scale incident – that one had been deemed enough here. As an acting DI, she may well have been part of the Accelerated Promotion Scheme and would have had some sort of negotiator training. How much live experience she'd had before today was hard to tell. He'd understood why she'd told him about Terry Ellis's death, though. Being brutal, it *had* proven a mistake but one he might well have made himself if the positions had been reversed. She was watching him closely and he made a quick decision about what to say.

'I think Lee was always going to do it. What happened was the culmination of an awful lot of things – some of which even I didn't know about myself until today.' He turned quickly to Walsh. 'How's Marco doing by the way?'

'Last I was told he was recovering well. It could have been different if he'd been in there much longer, though.'

Dattani's phone rang interrupting them, and he mouthed

an apology before stepping away to take the call.

'As you'll know – we're going to need to take a statement from you,' Walsh told Finn. 'There's no rush – it can wait until tomorrow. I really think you should get yourself to a hospital first.' Finn opened his mouth to argue but Walsh wasn't having it. 'You wouldn't be the first copper to think he's indestructible – and you probably won't be the last to find out you're not.'

Finn closed his mouth – to be fair, his head was starting to throb now. Dattani wheeled round, still clutching his phone. He looked mildly incredulous.

'What is it?' asked Rachel.

They were all looking at him now.

'It's Sarah Littlewood's granddaughter . . .' he began.

Skegman and Paulsen had taken Sarah through to the suite normally reserved for interviewing children and victims of crime. She'd declined a solicitor at this stage and given the sensitivity of the situation – with her granddaughter currently missing – Skegman had chosen not to carry out the interview under caution. She'd also been updated about the events at the cafe and had been visibly shocked when she'd learnt of Lee's death. They'd provided her with a cup of strong, sweet tea and given her a few minutes to get her head together before they began.

A distraught Ella Littlewood was back at her flat now. The detectives there had told Paulsen that she seemed both upset and confused that Sarah wasn't with her at such a critical moment.

In the incident room, Paulsen was preparing at her desk, flicking through the original files from 2009 for the umpteenth time. With every new development the day brought, the same black-and-white words seemed to take on a new meaning or slightly different nuance. The news Finn was safe had lifted her though and she was looking forward to seeing him again. She was also certain there must have been some very interesting conversations with Lee Ellis in that cafe.

'Shall we do this then?' said Skegman, joining her.

'Surely Sarah didn't kill Jemma?' said Paulsen, almost aggressively. 'It makes no sense.'

'Let's just wait and see what she has to say before we jump to any conclusions,' he replied.

'Every time I read these files, the more familiar I become with the details, the more confusing it seems to get,' said Paulsen. 'Why's all this exploded *today*?'

Skegman stared out of the window for a moment. It was only just gone six, but already it was pitch-black outside. He was aware the darkness wouldn't help the search operation for Billy and Kaitlyn Rickson, either.

'I don't know – and now we've got another problem,' he said. 'Lee Ellis was one of the few people who might have been able to answer that.'

Paulsen drained the dregs of a cold cup of coffee and grimaced, as Nash came over to join them.

'Ella's car's been found – a couple of miles away from where it was stolen. There's no sign of Billy or Kaitlyn I'm afraid.' She held up a couple of blurry pictures. 'But we've pulled these images off the CCTV cameras on the street.' She handed them to Paulsen and Skegman. They showed a young man wearing a baseball cap holding a carrycot, striding up the pavement.

'That looks like Billy, going by the profile pictures from his social media,' said Paulsen straight away.

'Where is this?' asked Skegman.

'Peckitt Street,' said Nash.

Skegman frowned, his little eyes on the move again. He

went over to the map on the wall of the room and searched it out. Paulsen and Nash followed him over.

'What is it, guv?' said Paulsen.

Skegman found the street and pointed at it.

'You've just been looking at the files, Mattie – doesn't this ring a bell with you?'

She looked at where he was pointing and suddenly it clicked into place.

'It's close to the spot where Jemma and Lee were abducted. Maybe only a street or two away. Why would he go there?'

Skegman turned to Nash.

'Make sure the team searching for Kaitlyn know the significance.' He shook his head. 'I hate to say it, but then go back – *again* – to the original statements. Perhaps there's something tucked in there that can give us a clue as to where he's heading.' Nash nodded and hurried away.

'Do you really think he'd hurt his own child?' said Paulsen. 'It feels the same as Lee – someone damaged, doing something extreme – and maybe just to make a point of some sort.'

Skegman shrugged.

'It's freezing cold out there. The safest way to safeguard that child is to get her back.'

Paulsen sighed.

'I'm sick of chasing my tail, guv,' she said. 'That's what it's felt like I've been doing all day.'

Skegman smiled wryly.

'That's essentially the job description of a senior officer – welcome to my world.' His expression hardened. 'Come on – let's see if we can't start putting some answers on the table.'

★

260

Sarah Littlewood looked almost at breaking point when they re-joined her.

'I'm sorry – finding out that Lee's dead has made this even more difficult than it was always going to be.'

Skegman smiled gently.

'At this stage, we're not recording anything and you're not under caution. Just start at the beginning and take as long as you need. If you want to stop – shout and we'll take a break.'

She nodded and took a deep breath.

'Jemma Vickers approached me a few months ago and asked if we could speak privately. When we met, she told me she'd never believed Dennis Trant was my son's killer. She'd seen pictures of Trant, and at the time Alex Finn had allowed her to hear the taped confession he made – she said she'd never thought that was the voice of the man who'd held them.'

'Why didn't she say that in 2016 then?' asked Paulsen.

'Because like all of us, she and Lee *wanted* to believe it was Trant – to put some closure on this. What he said in his statement was so convincing, and Alex and DI Culley seemed so sure . . .' She stopped and took a breath. 'I suppose none of us wanted to disbelieve it. But Jemma said as the years went by, it had nagged at her.'

'And what about you?' said Skegman. 'What did you think when she came to you with this?'

Sarah sighed and clasped her hands together.

'She was in that cellar with this guy and she was telling me – with absolute conviction – that she did not believe it was Trant who killed my son.' She looked at them both squarely. 'Oliver's death is the defining event of my life – something I can't live with any element of doubt about. And she was *so* sure.'

'So, she went digging into it – we know that much ourselves and I'm guessing she *did* find something?' said Paulsen.

'Yes – and in the end, ironically it was by pure chance. She spoke to George Rickson, and it was that conversation which raised her suspicions – about *him* specifically.'

There was a split second of silence as the two police officers took in the implication of what she was saying.

'Hold on – are you saying Jemma thought Billy's father was their abductor?' said Skegman and again, Sarah nodded.

'Initially, it was just a stray comment, something to the effect that Jemma "should have stabbed the guy when he had the chance".'

Paulsen's eyes narrowed, mindful of what they'd learnt about Red Tide earlier.

'What does that mean? We know Lee sustained knife wounds while they were held, but they never mentioned in their interviews afterwards that they'd had a weapon of some sort?'

'Apparently, when they were fed, they were given cutlery and Jemma got hold of a knife briefly.'

Skegman and Paulsen looked at each other uneasily.

'Did Jemma ever suggest to you that they'd been forced to hurt one another in that cellar?' said Paulsen carefully. 'Or even harm Oliver herself?' she added.

Sarah looked bemused.

'No – where on earth did you get that idea from?' she asked.

'We haven't yet,' cut in Skegman sharply. 'There are so many permutations to this – we've been thinking aloud a lot today, going through them all. And now that both Jemma, Lee and Trant are dead there are not many people we can talk to.'

Sarah nodded.

'I am aware of that, but if there was something I *really*

needed to know – particularly with regard to Ollie – I know they would have told me.'

'So, Jemma comes to you with her suspicions about George Rickson – what was your reaction?' asked Paulsen, getting back on point. She sensed from Skegman's quick intervention that she shouldn't have brought up the issue of whether the teenagers might have hurt one another.

'That she didn't have enough information to be certain,' replied Sarah. 'Maybe it was a slip of the tongue or a misunderstanding, or perhaps something Jemma had told Billy who'd told George that had got lost in translation. But then Jemma became more and more obsessed with the idea that Rickson fitted the right build and height. That he *sounded* like him too – and that it also explained why Billy was left on the street while they'd been taken.'

'So, what happened next?' said Skegman.

'She confronted George. She wanted to look him in the eye and see what his reaction would be. Rickson laughed it off, and that's what *really* sold it to her. He wasn't horrified or shocked. He didn't find the accusation absurd or unexpected. He simply laughed at her . . .'

'And what was your take on that?' said Paulsen.

'I'll be honest – I never liked George. There was always something a bit off about him – almost a sense that our children were at fault or weak in some way for allowing themselves to be taken. And then Jemma became so certain it was him, almost obsessed with the idea – and she wouldn't let go of it. I know she watched him for a while too – to be sure in her own mind. You didn't know her, but she was a very strong, determined person. Everything she did, she did thoroughly. We met and talked about it a *lot*. Eventually, it started to feel credible to me too.'

Paulsen had already guessed where this was going.

'The hit and run that killed George . . .'

Sarah didn't seem to react at first. Her expression remained focused, seemingly lost in the memory of those conversations.

'You have to understand what happened to Ollie,' she said, meeting Paulsen's gaze levelly. 'He was *butchered* in that cellar,' she whispered, the dam finally breaking, the emotion cracking through. 'If you had the chance to take revenge, to seek justice – wouldn't you? I owed my son that much.'

'What happened?' said Skegman quietly.

There was a long pause as Sarah composed herself again.

'Jemma and I met again. She said she was now one hundred per cent sure about Rickson and told me what she wanted to do and that she wanted my approval first – said she wouldn't act unless I was happy about it. I mean – this is Kaitlyn's grandfather we were talking about.' She dropped her head for a moment. 'I slept on it and then told her to go ahead.' She looked up defiantly. 'She planned it carefully, picked her moment then put Rickson down like a dog. I had a big gin and tonic that night and truthfully, it felt like a relief – until today.'

'You think Billy found out?' said Paulsen. 'That *he* killed Jemma – and that's why he's taken Kaitlyn? As revenge for what you both did to his dad?'

Slowly Sarah nodded.

'And you've been sitting on this information all day?' said Paulsen, trying to control her anger. 'People in that cafe could have died.'

'*Mattie*,' said Skegman sharply before turning back to Sarah. 'Do you have anything to back any of this up?'

'Yes – I know Billy now knows because he sent me this earlier and I don't know why else he would have done that.'

She reached into her bag, pulled out her phone and brought up the message she'd been sent. The word 'LIAR' clearly visible on the display as was the identity of its sender. Skegman and Paulsen exchanged a glance.

'Why am I coming forward?' continued Sarah. 'Because I can't go through this again. If anything happens to my grand-daughter, I won't be able to live with myself.'

29

'It all feels very credible,' said Paulsen as they regrouped with Nash in the incident room afterwards. She was looking at the CCTV image from the street in Tooting earlier. The figure in the baseball cap walking down the pavement with his back to the camera now suddenly looked all too obviously to be Billy Rickson. Like a jigsaw where one missing piece suddenly transforms the whole image. Skegman raised an ironic eyebrow.

'The only problem I can see is that they killed a man without a shred of evidence. Someone whose only crime might be that Jemma Vickers *thought* he sounded a bit like somebody who locked her in a cellar fifteen years ago. Someone whose face she never actually saw. Apart from that, it's all solid as a rock.' He finished his rant and looked slightly defeated by it. 'It's a mess, Mattie. And one we're going to have to untangle once we've found that baby.'

Sarah had now left the station and gone to be with Ella while they waited for news. The confession she'd made would have to be fully investigated before a decision on any potential charges could be made.

Paulsen collapsed into her chair, shattered. The day had felt like a giant obstacle course, throwing up one new hurdle after another and it didn't feel remotely close to being over yet. She checked the time and thought of Nancy out there somewhere enjoying a drink with her workmates, wondering too what was going on at home with her parents.

'Could George Rickson be Red Tide?' she said. 'The timings actually work. According to the information the Exploitation Unit passed on earlier, Red Tide's been inactive since Rickson died – so it's possible.'

'I don't want to start going down that road just yet,' replied Skegman. 'Red Tide might just have gone silent because he realised someone was looking into him. We'll investigate what Sarah told us thoroughly – but for now it's just a new line of inquiry. And need I point out – none of this answers any of the questions surrounding the deaths of Quilter and Knox.'

Paulsen sighed.

'It doesn't do much to help us find Billy and Kaitlyn either, does it? And while I'm at it – how worried should we be about that baby's safety?' she said.

'We can't assume anything because we don't know what state of mind he's in,' said Skegman. 'If he *did* kill Jemma this morning then I'd say all bets are off about Billy Rickson right now.'

'Really – you think he'd hurt his own baby?' said Nash.

'We've dealt with enough murder-suicides over the years to know what can happen – and need I remind you what Lee Ellis did earlier this afternoon? I'm not sure he *is* going to do that – but we need to find him, fast,' said Skegman. Nash nodded as she realised the implication of what he was saying. They'd asked Sarah where she thought Billy might have gone – but she'd been as stumped as anyone. Their initial attempts to track him via his phone had also failed because he'd clearly been smart enough to switch it off.

'While you were talking to Sarah, I was trying to play catch-up and find out as much as possible about Billy's world,' said Nash. 'And that's the interesting thing – it's been really hard. He lives alone now and has no immediate family – his mother died several years ago. His only surviving relative is an aunt in Buckhurst Hill.'

'Have you spoken to her?' said Skegman and Nash nodded.

'Yes and she's concerned. She talked to him on the phone earlier this afternoon and it sounded like he wasn't in a good place and hasn't been for a while. By all accounts, he's become very withdrawn since his dad's death.'

'And now we know why – because his girlfriend's mother was behind it. This is just a clusterfuck,' said Paulsen. 'Like a daisy chain of pain being passed on between all these people.'

'Did this aunt have any clue where he might be going?' said Skegman, turning back to Nash.

'No – but she was adamant that he wouldn't hurt Kaitlyn. For what it's worth he's got no history of violence at all that I could find.'

Paulsen held her hands out in frustration.

'Why would he be going back to the scene of the abductions – there's nothing there. He surely can't be going to that park they were heading for in 2009 – it's pitch-black and sub-zero temperatures. What else is in the area?'

The door to the incident room opened and Sami Dattani shuffled in, almost apologetically. He saw them in a huddle and came over to join them.

'Fuck me – what a day,' he said by way of greeting and Paulsen smiled back at him.

'Yeah – that pretty much sums it up,' she said.

'How's Alex?' asked Skegman.

'On his way to hospital – finally. Physically, he's okay – just took a minor graze to the head when the team entered the cafe. But I think he's quite shaken up.'

Skegman nodded.

'I'll give him a call shortly and see how he's doing. I'm guessing he took some persuading to go to hospital then?'

'Just a bit,' said Dattani and Skegman couldn't stop a small smile from forming.

'Did he talk about what happened in there?' asked Paulsen. 'Is there anything Lee told him that can help us?'

Dattani exhaled.

'Yeah – and you better brace yourself. Because what we all thought happened in 2009 . . . isn't quite what happened at all.'

And before he said another word, Paulsen already had a good idea about what was coming.

As Finn suspected, the trip to Croydon University Hospital was something of a waste of time. But that didn't mean it was unnecessary. He'd done enough work on himself over the last few years to know that his mind needed as much care as his body.

'I do believe you're actually learning,' chipped in his dead wife and he ignored her. He was still trying to understand everything Lee had told him in that cafe. His entire understanding of the abductions had been turned on its head. His sense of personal failure was total, which, hot on the heels of what had happened to Jackie Ojo, wasn't good.

'Stop it . . .' warned Karin and again he ignored her. The deaths today of two of the people he'd investigated in 2009 added another layer – a certainty that something important had been missed back then. But also, an odd feeling, that he already *had* the answer, somewhere in the recesses of his brain – he just needed to find his way to it.

The reason he'd been happy enough to come to the hospital in the end, was precisely to give his mind a break. He knew instinctively that despite his earlier protestations to Dattani, returning straight away to Cedar House would have been a mistake. John Skegman, in all probability, would only have sent him home – and the thought of sitting alone in his flat after the day he'd just had made him shiver. It would take a long time to shake off the image of Lee Ellis's head blowing apart in front of him.

There was also someone here he wanted to see. As the doctor who'd been checking him over gave him the all-clear – the bandage on his forehead now replaced by a plaster, which he intended to pull off at the first opportunity – Finn had asked him for directions. Now, he was walking through the long corridors and coloured zones by which the hospital was divided. He checked the signage for the ward he was look-ing for and made his way there. When he entered, he scanned the room until he saw the person he was after.

'Hello, Marco,' he said walking straight over. The young man greeted him with a broad smile of recognition. Finn could instantly see that he was in much better shape than when they'd last been together. There was life back in his eyes again, warmth too in the expression.

'It's good to see you,' he said, sitting up. 'I'm glad you made it out of there okay.'

'You've heard what happened with Lee?' replied Finn tenta-tively and Marco nodded.

'Yeah.' He shrugged, as if unsure what else to add. 'It's a real shame that it came to that. It's not what I wanted. Poor sod.'

'How are you feeling?'

'Head's ringing like Big Ben – apart from that, top of the world,' he said, fashioning a grin. For the first time, Finn felt he was finally meeting the real Marco Randelli. Someone considerably more relaxed than the angry, frustrated man he'd been locked up with all day.

'What's happening with your mum?'

'You've just missed her,' said Marco, nodding towards the

door at the far end. 'They delayed her surgery because of what happened today.'

Finn looked concerned.

'I'm sorry.'

Marco waved a hand.

'It's okay – they've rescheduled it for later this week, which I'm happy about. And then we'll have to see what happens afterwards.' His face clouded over, and Finn took a seat next to his bed.

'I know the road you're about to go on.'

Marco reacted, surprised, and Finn looked down.

'I've had my own experience – it's not an easy journey. But if there's ever anything I can do to help . . .'

Marco nodded and there was an awkward silence.

'So, what do you reckon?' he said suddenly, changing the subject. 'Was Lee right – did you guys blame the wrong bloke for what happened to him and his mate all those years ago?'

'I'm afraid I think we did,' said Finn. 'It's not much consolation – but I hope it's something I can still put right.'

Marco digested this for a moment.

'You know, despite everything, I really got the sense Lee respected you,' he said. 'I think that's why he wanted you in there today. To get the truth into your head. If he succeeded – then maybe that's some sort of positive to take away from all this.'

Finn considered it – frankly, everything felt a bit hollow right now.

'Thank you,' he said. 'Maybe.'

'And he hated the police,' continued Marco. 'I know that much – so I'd take his respect as a compliment.'

'Why do you say that?'

'When we were working together, he mentioned a few times that he'd been involved in something once – and now of course I know what that was. He said the cops back then were hopeless, but – as I say – I don't think he meant you personally.'

Finn was about to reply when he felt his phone vibrate. He pulled it out and saw Skegman's name flashing up and let it go to voicemail. Marco's words had triggered something. In hindsight, the investigation in 2009 *had* been a disaster – they'd rescued Jemma and Lee, but they'd got there far too late. Even now it felt like he could and should have saved Oliver Littlewood. Instead of simply blaming himself – perhaps he also needed to take a closer look at the work of one or two of his former colleagues.

Holding the carrycot in one hand, Billy was walking in semi-darkness against a driving cold wind. A silver full moon hung in the sky, shining ghostly white light down on the ground ahead. Glancing down at his daughter, for the first time all day he felt at peace and his headache had finally subsided. Fifteen years ago, this was the park he and his friends had whiled away a hot summer in, drinking and laughing. He missed them, he realised, as he trudged along the frozen grass. Not the people they'd become – but his mates, the ones he'd been inseparable from once.

The idea that it had been his father who'd bundled them into that van and attacked him with pepper spray was ridiculous. The possibility that his dad had also hacked Oliver Littlewood to death was simply obscene. His parents had been out there with the police searching for the missing teenagers at the time. He could also remember the conversations that had taken place over the years. George Rickson had been relentlessly supportive of his son – not just through his scant periods of success, but during the difficult times as well. '*It's not what life does to you, mate – it's how you get back up again,*' he'd said frequently. Not just good advice, but words to live by.

Kaitlyn gurgled and Billy stopped again to look at her crumpled little face, illuminated in the moonlight. Extraordinarily, despite everything, she seemed almost serene. He could guess the scale of the hunt that must be underway. He'd seen what happens in these situations, close-up, fifteen years ago. The full enormity of what he'd done earlier that day suddenly hit him too, and his heart missed a beat. This would be an altogether different kind of manhunt.

It had been his idea to meet with Jemma in Tooting that morning. Originally, he'd wanted it to happen here – or at least the place he was now heading for. It held a resonance for both of them – but Jemma had droned on about work and needing to be close to her office. So, they'd agreed to meet in a cafe instead. To talk – at least, that was the original intention. Except, that it had all spiralled out of control before they'd even reached the coffee shop. He hadn't been able to stop himself – had spat the accusation out on the street there and then: *'You murdered my dad,'* and immediately seen the guilt in her eyes. The sense of betrayal had been total. Of *all* the people who could have done this to him.

And then she'd used those bloody words again: *'You weren't in that cellar, Billy.'*

The full set of emotions he'd felt over the years – the rejection, exclusion and guilt had come to a head, and he'd lashed out. He'd raised his hands and the next thing he knew she was lying in the snow, bright red blood leaking from the back of her head. Conflicted, he'd panicked and fled, assuming the damage was just superficial. Then Sarah had visited him at his flat and told him that she was dead. He'd known exactly why she'd come too – it was a fishing expedition to see if *he* knew what they'd done. The woman's hypocrisy had been too much and that's why he'd sent her that WhatsApp message – because she'd been involved in this too. Jemma had confirmed as much before things had spiralled.

He reached some woodland and stopped, wondering if Lee was still in that cafe with Finn or whether he'd surrendered yet. Jemma had claimed he hadn't been involved in his father's death – and that she hadn't shared her suspicions with him yet. That was something to cling on to, he thought. Kaitlyn stirred again, and this time began to cry. He looked down at her face and immediately everything felt just that little bit better.

'*Shhh,* baby girl – it's just you and me now,' he said and started to walk into the woods.

30

2009

If Finn had been expecting any credit for rescuing the two boys, he was soon disabused of the notion by Chris Culley. Not that he actually cared. What he'd seen in that cellar had shaken him to the core. Jemma and Lee were currently being checked over in hospital, and their jubilant families were patiently waiting to be finally reunited with them.

In the immediate aftermath, Finn had left Barton to protect the scene while he'd tended to the two teenagers himself. They were moments he wouldn't forget. Shaking in fear, blinking unsteadily on their feet as they emerged into the light, he'd seen for himself how traumatised they were. When the time came to interview them properly it was going to need expert handling.

Breaking the good news to the families had been bittersweet. Their joy and relief had been palpable, but all Finn could think of was Sarah and Ella Littlewood. He'd have to look them both in the eye and Sarah would need to identify her son in the morgue later. The thought made him feel sick.

'I told you to wait for backup. I *explicitly* made that clear to you,' Culley droned on. 'But you decided you were going to be the hero. And now this fucker's free to do it all over again.'

'I saw an opportunity—' began Finn.

275

'Yes, you certainly did,' sneered Culley. 'I could have had people down there in minutes.' He shook his head in disgust. 'All you had to do was call it in and wait.'

'With respect guv,' said Barton, who was sharing the lecture. 'DS Finn made a judgement call on the spot – it may only have taken minutes for backup to arrive, but those minutes might not have been enough. We could have had another dead teenager on our hands.'

Finn felt like he was watching the conversation from the other side of the room. Culley stared at Barton sourly.

'We'll never know now, will we? We've got a missing killer free and still no idea who he is or even a trace of the murder weapon.'

'With respect, sir,' said Barton, showing very little. 'But the state of that cellar . . . I can't believe the CSIs won't find finger-print and DNA evidence down there.'

'Which all takes time, Jack – as well you know. We could have the bastard sitting in a custody suite instead.'

They'd established the house was a rental property that belonged to a Spanish businessman who spent most of the year in Barcelona. Normally it was rented out, but the estate agents he used said there hadn't been tenants in there for some weeks. In winter, the garden would need little attention, so it was a fair bet the place had been left alone for a while. What that told Finn was that the killer was someone both well prepared and well informed. With all the time in the world at his disposal, it was highly likely that the gruesome fate which had befallen Oliver Littlewood would imminently have befallen Jemma and Lee too.

He was also finally starting to shake off the sense of paraly-sis that had gripped him since he'd emerged from that house. He looked at Culley's pink little face as he carried on barking at them and decided – once and for all – that this man was an idiot. And there was only one rational course of action to take with an idiot – which was to shut out the noise.

'It's done – and I'll take responsibility for the decision I made,' he snapped back. 'There's no point giving Jack grief – all he did was follow my instructions.'

Culley seemed genuinely surprised by the pushback and looked at Finn as if he was beyond salvaging.

'Christ, you're a sanctimonious arsehole. Thanks for explaining the chain of command to me – the one that you so clearly have little time for yourself.'

A rather nervous-looking young DC interrupted them before Finn could dig himself any deeper.

'Sarah Littlewood's downstairs,' he said. Just the mention of her name was enough to take the wind out of both their sails.

'Perhaps you'd like to go and explain to that woman what *exactly* happened to her son,' hissed Culley.

An idiot and a coward, thought Finn.

'Yes, I will,' he said with a confidence that he didn't feel. 'And then when Jemma and Lee are ready to be interviewed, I'd like to be in the room too. If we're going to find this guy, they're our best bet now.' He left before the DI's spluttering indignance could get going again.

Culley watched him depart, shaking his head.

'Public school prick,' he muttered under his breath before catching Barton's look of contempt.

'Don't give me that face either, Jack. You can dress it up all you want – but he shouldn't have gone in there on his own and you know it.'

And with that, he turned and marched back to his office.

The walk down the stairs from the incident room was too long, Finn thought as he listened to his footsteps tapping on the hard floor. It was sweltering again of course, which didn't help. The heat had been unrelenting and briefly, he remembered that blast of stinking warm air that had greeted him when he'd opened the cellar door hours earlier.

They'd taken Sarah to the soft interview suite where someone had provided a jug of water and some glasses, which remained untouched. She looked accusingly at Finn as he entered.

'How did my son die?' she began, cutting him off before he could offer any condolences for her loss.

He knew she wanted the truth, however difficult it was, and he looked her steadily in the eye.

'We'll have to wait for the autopsy – but it looks like the cause of death was from multiple stab wounds – according to the forensic pathologist, quite possibly consistent with the use of a large blade such as a machete or an axe.'

He watched as the words sank in, embedded themselves and began to pollinate their significance. Sarah swallowed, still trying to maintain the tough exterior, and he willed her to let go of the effort.

'Tell me you've got the bastard,' she said finally. 'Tell me he's sitting somewhere in this building right now – that he has a name, and you know what it is.'

Finn shook his head.

'As you know we managed to rescue the other two, but it was at the expense of the suspect. He escaped when . . . we . . . entered,' he said. One day she'd know the truth and would approve of the decision he'd made. But that day was still to come. 'We have forensic teams crawling all over that house,' he continued. 'It's only a matter of time before we—'

He stopped as Sarah finally let go. Her whole body was shuddering, and her eyes had closed in silent agony. She put both hands over her face as a shield and this is what Finn had been dreading. It was hard to think of a conversation that could be more intimate. There were married couples that lived entire lives together without ever sharing a moment this raw.

He looked down at the table, focused on the jug of water, and waited for her. It felt like there wasn't a breath of air left in the room. For the first time since he'd returned to Cedar House that afternoon, he began to question himself and whether Culley might actually be right about what he'd done.

'I want vengeance . . .' said Sarah finally, dropping her hands back down on to her lap. 'An eye for an eye. Do you understand?'

He did, but he also knew she wasn't going to get it – at least not in the way that she wanted.

'We *will* find him,' he said, making a promise he shouldn't, not for the first time with this woman. 'And we'll bring him to justice.'

But the look on her face told him that still wouldn't be enough – that nothing would ever be enough.

After she'd left, back in the incident room, Finn found himself lost. He felt punch-drunk by the events of the day. There was a lot of work to do as well, but he couldn't concentrate. Grabbing a cup of water, he went to sip it in the cool of the corridor. He already knew that come somewhere around three in the morning he'd be lying wide awake, soaked in sweat, reliving everything all over again.

'Are you okay?' said Karin. He turned to see her walking towards him with a look of genuine concern. There was none of the usual playful sarcasm in her voice.

'I thought you'd left for the afternoon,' he said.

She shook her head dismissively.

'There's been a development with one of my clients, so I had to come back. I just heard what happened. Jesus – I'm so sorry, Alex.'

He tried to pin down how he was feeling. There was increasing guilt that he *had* screwed up. There was also the memory of the cellar of course, but most of all, a ringing in his head that just wouldn't stop.

'No,' he said. 'To answer your question – I am not okay.'

A couple of hours later she took him to a pub. It was out of the way, quiet, and the mood was very different to the last time they'd met for a drink. This most certainly wasn't a date. Despite the late evening sun, they chose to sit indoors – it felt appropriate somehow. Finn bought himself a double scotch and drank it with indecent speed. The burn as it hit felt like heaven.

'You looked like you could use that,' said Karin, sipping more demurely at a glass of wine.

'Just a bit,' he replied with feeling. If he were alone, he'd quite happily spend the evening drinking himself into oblivion. There were quite a few good arguments for that.

He told her what he'd done – what Culley had said and how self-doubt was now starting to eat at him. She absorbed it all quietly, even the horrors of the cellar.

'Sounds like Jack Barton was right,' she said after he'd finished talking. 'If you hadn't gone into that house anything could have happened. Those two teenagers probably owe you their lives.'

Probably – there was a lot in that word, Finn thought.

'If I'd just waited – then we'd have this man in custody tonight. I mean, I could have called Jack – he was only next door, but when I saw that canister of pepper spray . . .' He stopped and shook his head as he remembered. Karin reached across and took his hand.

'It's done. One thing I know from my job is when a situation has those kinds of shades of grey there's no point trying

280

to force a clear right or wrong.' She paused and shrugged. 'You'll always just torment yourself with the counterargument. Right now, I'm more concerned about you.'

Finn got a sudden whiff of his own stale sweat and hankered for a cold shower to wash everything away.

'I'll be fine,' he said, absently.

The look she gave him suggested she would be the judge of that.

'If we weren't here what would you be doing right now?'

He thought about it and blew through his lips.

'I don't know – sitting on my sofa at home feeling like death, probably. Waiting for a pizza to be delivered that I almost certainly wouldn't eat.'

She nodded, almost with approval.

'That's what I like about you. You don't dress things up – you're honest. You're nothing like the man I thought you were.'

He smiled, remembering the row they'd had at Cedar House earlier that week. So much seemed to have happened in the intervening time.

'So, what's your current assessment then?' he said.

'That you're not like most coppers, that's for sure. To be more accurate – not like most men I've met.'

'In what way?' he asked.

She arched an eyebrow.

'You're traumatised and yet still fishing for compliments? That's *definitely* like most men I've known. What I meant is you have at least a few teaspoons of emotional intelligence. You do like to internalise though and it's a bad habit. Too much brooding sat on your arse at home, I suspect.'

'You live alone too – don't you do the same thing?' he retorted.

She laughed.

'Being on your own's got nothing to do with it – it's about

the kind of person you are. You need some of those barriers of yours breaking down.'

Finn suddenly felt extremely tired.

'Maybe – but not tonight if that's okay. Feel free to smash away at them another time though.'

She nodded understandingly as their eyes met.

They didn't stay long. Afterwards, they lingered awkwardly outside the pub as they prepared to head off to their respective cars.

'We could have a meal next week,' he suggested. 'If you fancy it?'

'That would be nice,' she replied.

There was an awkward silence and he leant in to kiss her. She rolled her eyes and swerved out of the way.

'*Men*, honestly – you couldn't time a boiled egg,' she chided. 'That isn't what you need right now – *this* is what you need.' Before he had time to be confused, she pulled him close and hugged him tightly. Tentatively, he raised his arms, wrapped them around her, and held her too. They stood there for a while before disengaging.

'Plenty of time for the other, later,' she whispered before turning to go. 'And *I'm* picking the restaurant,' she added more firmly.

31

Today

'What on earth do you think you're doing?' said Skegman.

The question was directed at Finn who'd just walked into the incident room as if he'd only nipped out to the shops for half an hour.

'"Hi, Alex – good to see you're okay,"' he replied sarcastically. '"Not at all, boss – thanks for taking an interest."'

'What the fuck *are* you doing?' said Paulsen, coming over to join them, a big smile unfolding across her face.

'You're not going to hug me are you?' said Finn with mock concern.

'No chance,' she replied.

An unfamiliar young woman was standing awkwardly behind them.

'I'm DC Vanessa Nash,' she said introducing herself. 'We haven't met – it's my first day here.'

'You chose a cracking one to start with,' said Finn. 'I'm—'

'I know who you are,' interrupted Nash with a warm smile. 'The blood on your shirt rather gives it away – I'm glad you're okay.' He looked down, saw a great splash of dried burgundy just under his collar and nodded sheepishly.

'Seriously, Alex – you should be at home,' said Skegman.

Finn straightened up and turned to him. It was now nearly eight o'clock in the evening – but he had no desire to be anywhere else and was ready for the expected argument.

'There's stuff Lee Ellis told me you need to know,' he said. 'And there's stuff you've been investigating that I definitely need to know about – every last detail.'

Twenty minutes later, the exchange of information was complete. Paulsen and Nash had explained to Finn what they'd discovered about Red Tide, and he'd coloured in the details of what Lee had told him in the cafe. But it was Sarah Littlewood's confession and the working theory that Billy Rickson had murdered Jemma Vickers that had really blindsided Finn – not to mention the revelations about Billy's father.

'I have to ask, Alex – was George Rickson ever on your radar in 2009?' said Skegman.

Finn was genuinely stunned.

'No. Not once. But are you telling me the only evidence Sarah and Jemma had – *to execute him* – is some throwaway comment the man once made?'

Paulsen nodded.

'According to Sarah the fact that the kids had a weapon at one point was something only the killer could have known, and Jemma was a hundred per cent convinced by it. Or at least, it sounds like she *became* convinced by it.'

Finn considered this, remembering his interview with Billy Rickson on a hot summer's day years before. He hadn't taken to George Rickson then – but *had* he missed something important? He shook his head.

'We ran background checks on all the parents as a matter of routine – nothing flagged up about him.'

'We've obviously started to look into him,' said Paulsen. 'But we haven't found anything conclusive one way or another yet – but there certainly isn't anything jumping out to support what they did.'

'Where's Sarah now?'

'She went back home to be with her daughter,' said Skegman.

'Have you ever heard of this Red Tide before?' said Paulsen. Finn shook his head.

'No, but your theory that this is all about some sort of torture porn makes sense given what Lee told me just before he died. Do we know exactly what Jemma was doing on the Dark Web?'

Paulsen reached behind her and grabbed some paperwork.

'Yes, I almost forgot. Digital Forensics sent this through while the DCI and I were talking to Sarah.' She skimmed through the information for a moment. 'It's from the phone she'd been using to access the Dark Web. She'd gathered a lot of information on local teenagers who've gone missing in the last few years. Specifically, the ones who've never been found. She seemed particularly interested in a recent misper called Jarrod Thomas. He disappeared just before—'

'I know who he is,' said Finn, cutting in. 'Lee mentioned him too . . .'

He broke off, trying to make sense of it, but his tired brain was struggling.

'So, what – they both thought their abductor was responsible for these disappearances as well?' said Skegman.

'It can't be,' said Paulsen. 'If you add them all up over the years there's loads. I mean – it just *can't* be the same person?'

There was a silence as the implication sank in for a moment. Finn tried to focus his tired mind.

'Let's come back to that. I'm still trying to play catch-up. Explain to me exactly what happened to Quilter and Knox?' he said.

Paulsen told him how the morning had unfolded, precisely what had occurred and where her investigation was at.

'We know Knox was murdered and it's now looking

increasingly likely Quilter was too,' she finished to Finn's evident confusion.

'How come you're so sure? I mean I always liked him for this – even back then,' he said. 'It's possible *he* could have murdered Jemma and Knox and then jumped off that railway bridge.'

Paulsen was already nodding.

'We considered that – but we have a witness who saw a red Mazda speeding away from Quilter's flat earlier today. Forensics found several boot prints next to a puddle of vomit close to the bridge. We've been trying to trace the Mazda – and in the last hour we think we've got a match for it on the ANPR cameras near the railway track. It's looking like someone took him there deliberately and killed him.'

'Any idea who the car belongs to?'

'Not yet, but we've got a partial plate – so we should have more pretty soon.'

Finn fell back in his chair, he felt like he could sleep for a week.

'Why's all this happened *today* – it doesn't make any sense, after all this time?'

'That's what we were hoping you might be able to tell us,' said Paulsen but all Finn could do was slowly shake his head.

'More pressingly do you have any thoughts about where Billy might have taken his daughter – is there anything from 2009 that might give us a clue?' asked Skegman.

A memory flickered at the back of Finn's mind, something that had been said to him fifteen years ago.

'You say Billy dumped Ella's car close to where the abductions happened?' he said slowly and Skegman nodded.

'Just a couple of streets away. Why?'

Finn tried to push the weariness from his mind and remember the conversation.

'There was a place those three went that summer. Jemma mentioned it to me much later. A kind of . . . *secret den.*'

Both Skegman and Paulsen reacted immediately.

'And I don't suppose you know what and where this place might be?' said Skegman.

Billy stumbled through the woodland, grateful for the moonlight. Without it, the way ahead would have been pitch-black and even muscle memory wouldn't have helped. He hadn't been here for years. Even though he lived relatively close by he'd never felt the need for a nostalgia trip. Besides, he'd always assumed the place had long since been demolished. It still felt right to go there though. It was somewhere that held so much significance for him, somewhere, once upon a time, he'd felt truly safe.

He'd instinctively gravitated there because he needed time to think – there hadn't been a plan behind this, but it had just felt like the natural place to come. Everything had changed since the morning – since he'd killed Jemma. He shivered as he confronted that sentence finally. But it was true – he *had* killed her – and virtually nothing made any sense to him any more. The only thing that *did* make sense was Kaitlyn and now he just wanted to shut the world out and be with her for a while.

She was wriggling and crying loudly in her carrycot but it didn't matter because there wasn't a living soul within earshot. He reached out and cupped the back of her head with his palm and smiled gently.

'Hey . . . it's okay, sweet pea. Just you and me now.'

Her eyes brightened and her face broke into an unexpected smile and he couldn't help but smile back in return. That smile was enough to sustain him, to blot out everything else. He focused on her face, its endless little movements, sniffs and twitches were hypnotising. She sneezed and above he heard a flock of birds take off from the trees. Parts of the route were starting to come back to him even in the darkness. And with it, came back snippets of conversations from the past, the way Jemma used to snort when she laughed, how prone Lee had always been to a decent wind-up. He set off again with a new determination and after a few minutes he was there – almost stumbling upon it. The moonlight, revealing the silhouette of an old friend, still standing after all these years.

The small electrical substation had long been abandoned even in 2009. A crumbling, red-brick bunker of a building, it's where the three teenagers had shut the world out once. It was hard to tell in the dark of course, but the small cube-like structure seemed to be exactly the same. He walked quickly around the side and saw the large rectangular window he remembered, its glass long since smashed away.

He climbed through, carefully holding the carrycot and stepped into the gloom. Others had clearly been making use of the place – there were empty bottles and cans strewn all over the floor and the whole room smelt of piss. Long-disconnected bits of rusting equipment were still on the walls, next to shattered cabinets. An old-fashioned phone handle that Billy could remember playing with once hung limply next to the door on a curly plastic cord. Carefully placing the carrycot down, he sat next to it, leant back against the wall and breathed out. Around him, the ghosts of his dead friends smoked weed and drank beer and he wished with all his heart that he could turn back the clock.

In the incident room Finn, Skegman and Nash were standing behind Paulsen who was sitting at her desk, with Google Maps open on her PC screen. The large, expanded map of south

London pinned to the far wall didn't quite extend out to the area under their scrutiny.

'If you're right about the substation – then the likeliest bit of woodland would be Addington Hills which isn't too far from Lloyd Park,' she said.

Finn turned to Nash who was ahead of him.

'I'll get on to UK Power Networks and see if they have a record for anything in the area,' she said, already scurrying back to her desk.

Finn watched her go.

'She's done well,' said Skegman reading his mind. 'Survived trial by Paulsen today . . .'

Paulsen turned, glowered at them both and then refocused back on her screen. Finn smiled – not quite a baptism of fire, but most definitely a baptism of scowling, he imagined.

'I need to check in with the search operation. Give me five minutes, then come to my office, Alex,' said Skegman. His tone was reasonable, but Finn knew it was more than a polite request. The DCI departed leaving him alone with Paulsen and he took a seat next to her.

'So, they make you a detective sergeant and five minutes later you're after my job?'

'If you hadn't gone for the longest tea break on record, I wouldn't have had to,' she retorted, and he grinned. After the day he'd had, a little banter felt very welcome.

'How's it been?' he said, turning serious.

She considered the question.

'Tough, I won't lie. At times, I felt . . .' she faltered as if trying to analyse exactly what she *did* feel '. . . a bit overwhelmed, I suppose. Like I was always *just* about keeping on top of it – but sometimes not even managing that.'

Finn nodded.

'Don't be too hard on yourself – that's exactly how I feel most days. I think that is the job in a nutshell, to be fair.'

'Skegman said something similar.'

'Did he?' said Finn, smiling.

They were interrupted by Nash who'd returned swiftly and with some urgency.

'UK Power Networks found it straight away. There is an old substation in Addington Hills – and they've given me a grid reference for it too.'

Finn rose to his feet.

'I'll leave you both to it – I'd better go see what old misery guts wants,' he said. A thought struck him. 'How did you find working with him today?'

'Really supportive, actually,' said Paulsen.

'Fuck me,' muttered Finn and headed for the door. 'Should get myself locked up more often.'

'Don't be a pain in the arse, Alex,' barked Skegman almost as soon as Finn entered his office.

'I haven't even said anything yet,' he replied indignantly.

'You don't have to – I know you. You said you came back here to pass on the information Lee Ellis gave you. Well, you've done that now – so piss off home.'

The words might have been harsh, but Finn knew the intent behind them wasn't.

'John . . . I *know* Billy Rickson. Not as well as I knew Jemma and Lee, but we go back a long way – I can help you with this.'

'Thanks, but no thanks. After what you've been through it would be totally irresponsible of me to let you just waltz in and take control of this investigation.'

Finn suddenly realised this wasn't just standard duty of care stuff. If, God forbid, something went wrong, and that baby was hurt in some way then both Skegman and Finn's judgement would be called into question – again. And this time, neither of them might survive it.

'Alright . . . I won't argue with you. But I'll be in tomorrow morning at the normal time and that's non-negotiable.'

Skegman looked at him like he did very much want to negotiate the point. And as Finn prepared to stand his ground there was a knock at the door. Sami Dattani poked his head round.

'We've just had a call from uniform – a witness says they saw someone who matches Billy's description heading towards Addington Hills earlier this evening – says he appeared to be holding a carrycot.'

Skegman nodded.

'Alright. Thanks, Sami.' He rose to his feet. 'That nails it. Go home and get some sleep, Alex,' he said and strode towards the door. 'And yes – I *am* pleased that you're okay. Now, for the love of God – just fuck off.'

Finn flashed him a smile.

'Since you asked so nicely.'

Skegman followed Dattani down the corridor without further comment. Finn immediately pulled his mobile from his pocket and found a number. As he made the call, he quickly checked to see that the door had closed behind Skegman.

'Hello, Sarah,' he said. 'It's Alex Finn. I think perhaps we should have a chat.'

32

When Finn arrived at the Littlewoods' house, Ella immediately thought there'd been some sort of update in the search for Kaitlyn. It was interesting, he thought, that Sarah hadn't seen fit to mention to her that he was coming over, and Finn guessed that her daughter didn't know about the confession she'd made at Cedar House earlier. Ella Littlewood seemed to be holding up surprisingly well in the circumstances. Whether that was because she'd already been through the trauma of her brother's death, or because she simply trusted that Billy wasn't going to hurt his own daughter was difficult to say. But as he entered and nodded at the two FLOs with them, Finn found it hard not to recall the wan young child who'd accompanied her mother through those steaming-hot afternoons fifteen years before.

To spare Sarah any further potential embarrassment he suggested they take a walk and talk privately, which Ella seemed okay with. That was something else she'd grown up with, Finn realised. The relationship he had with her mother and how deeply embedded he was in this family's history.

'Christ, it's cold,' said Sarah as they stepped out of the front door into a blast of arctic air.

'We can stay here if you'd prefer. Talk in the bedroom?' said Finn.

'It wasn't me I was thinking about. This is no weather for a baby to be out in, is it?' she snapped.

'I promise you – everything that can be done *is* being done,' he said.

She stopped and fixed him with a look colder than anything the weather could offer.

'You've said that to me before.'

The words cut deep.

'I know,' he said simply, and they began to walk.

'I'm glad you're okay,' she said a few moments later, mollifying her tone. 'It must have been very difficult for you in that cafe with Lee.'

He could guess how hard Lee's suicide had impacted on her. Hot on the heels of Jemma's death, it was a lot for both of them to absorb.

'I can't deny it's been a pretty dreadful day and it's not over yet.'

The light of the full moon was giving their walk a slightly more picturesque quality than the occasion deserved.

'I suppose you've come to talk to me about what I told your colleagues earlier?' she said and he nodded.

'I have. But I also need to tell you something else first.' He exhaled, his breath visible in the night air. 'It's about *who* killed your son – and *how* that happened.'

And then he told her, together with the information Paulsen had discovered about Red Tide. He'd seen over the years just about every possible shade of grief, guilt and anger written on this woman's face. This time her expression was something different – part shock, part revulsion, part something else altogether.

'Someone *paid* to have Ollie killed . . . like *that*,' she said finally. 'By another teenager?'

'I'm afraid so.'

'Who?'

'We don't know. That's obviously something that's going to

be a priority to find out. Other agencies who've been looking into Red Tide haven't reported finding this specific material, so it doesn't appear to have been shared. My guess is that it belongs to a collector of some sort.'

There was a long silence, and he could guess the reason why. It wasn't just the identity of her son's killer that had come as a surprise, but also the idea that footage of it existed. Even now, it was sitting on a hard drive somewhere being replayed for kicks whenever its owner felt in the mood.

'I think I'm going to be sick,' said Sarah. 'Why didn't Jemma tell me? She let me think what happened was something else all this time. She lied – to me of all people.'

'Lee was ashamed, and Jemma was protecting him,' said Finn quickly. 'And there was fear too, of how the world – how you – would view him.'

'That's ridiculous,' snorted Sarah. 'The only consolation I have is that it sounds like the actual moment was accidental. But she let me think all this time that someone had butchered him when she knew the truth. Have you any idea how much of a difference knowing that would have made to me?'

Finn put himself in Jemma's position, remembered too the damaged, broken man he'd spent the day with in the cafe.

'I think – and this is just my opinion – that she understood Lee well enough to know he wouldn't have been able to live with himself if the truth had come out. It was an impossible calculation.'

There was just the sound of their footsteps crunching in the snow as Sarah considered it.

'Surely it would have helped your investigation to have known this before?'

The thought had occurred to Finn, but he was in no mood to judge Lee Ellis too harshly right now.

'Lee had to live with the memory of what he did. Put yourself in his shoes . . .'

'What do you think I've been doing for the last fifteen years?' she shouted. 'I've *always* been in that fucking cellar. I trusted both of them,' she said, her voice echoing around the deserted street they were walking down.

'Are you sure your view of Lee wouldn't have changed if you had known what happened?' said Finn. 'Think about it – properly think about it . . .'

There was a long silence as she did.

'I don't know. Maybe.'

'For what it's worth, I think the bond between them was closer than any other relationship in their lives including family and friends – even you.'

'And George Rickson – is *he* this Red Tide you mentioned?'

This was the bit Finn had thought about the most as he'd driven across south London from Cedar House. There were still lots of unanswered questions.

'Let me just clarify this so I can understand it,' he began. 'Jemma believed George was their abductor because of something he told them. Something George could only have known if he'd been in that cellar himself?'

He just about managed to stop himself from calling it the Red Room.

'Yes – at some point when they were in there, Jemma got hold of a knife,' said Sarah. 'After they were fed, I think.'

Finn nodded.

'Yes, I've got a vague memory of that – from the interviews we did afterwards,' he said.

Sarah shrugged.

'Their abductor took it back off her before she could use it. I can see why Jemma never mentioned it again – she can't have thought it was relevant. It was just a small random detail.'

'And George knew about this knife?' said Finn.

'Yes – that's why Jemma was so sure it was him. She said she'd only told the police about it. So, unless *you* mentioned it to someone?'

'No, of course not.'

An old lady walking an energetic terrier turned a corner and headed towards them. She seemed to sense the strained atmosphere and smiled awkwardly as she passed. They waited until she was out of earshot before continuing.

'Do you know if Lee and George had any contact over the years? Because that's the only way he could have found out,' said Finn.

'No!' snapped Sarah immediately. 'I don't think Billy and Lee stayed particularly close.'

'*Think?*' said Finn. 'Can you be certain of that? All it would have taken is one night, one conversation over the years where two old school friends caught up. If Lee had let that slip and Billy had then mentioned it in passing to his dad at some point . . . is it really that impossible?'

Sarah stopped as the implication of his words sank in and put a hand to her mouth. 'I never thought about it like that – I just assumed. I mean, maybe they did. Jesus – *I don't know.*'

'It's possible then. They both lived locally and could have bumped into each other in the pub or a shop at some point. I'm just saying – at some point over the last fifteen years they might have had a conversation about all of this.'

Sarah's mind was racing.

'Why didn't we ask ourselves that?' she whispered.

'As you say, it was a minor detail. We can't know everything that happened in that cellar. Why would Jemma have assumed that Lee had never mentioned it to anyone? I'm just saying that *may* be how George found out about it. It's also possible that Jemma was right – and Rickson *was* Red Tide.'

296

'What have we done?' she said, her voice trembling.

Finn stopped.

'Listen to me – you didn't play an active part in George Rickson's murder, and you've cooperated fully – told the police the truth. You don't have a criminal record – and with your history . . .' He shook his head. 'Given the circumstances, if you plead guilty, I'm certain that a judge would be looking at a suspended prison sentence. There's no way in the world you're going to prison for this.'

But she didn't seem to hear a word he was saying.

'What did we do?'

A lot was happening as Finn spoke to Sarah. Surveillance officers had found the electrical substation where they believed Billy had taken Kaitlyn Rickson. A drone was quickly deployed with thermal imaging cameras and established that an adult and an infant were sheltering inside. A few minutes later they realised they hadn't needed such a high-tech approach as the sound of a baby screaming at the top of its lungs echoed around the frosty woodland.

The surveillance team were now discreetly keeping watch while John Skegman held a hastily assembled briefing at Cedar House. Because the hostage was a baby, the approach they were taking was very different to the one Walsh had adopted at the cafe. There was no time to establish an RVP – with the temperature plunging, the priority was to resolve this as fast as possible.

'There's no reason to think Billy Rickson wants to hurt his daughter,' Skegman addressed the room. 'This is a man who recently lost his father and blames the baby's grandmother for his death. Having said that – he's our prime suspect in the murder of Jemma Vickers this morning – so nothing's off the table, either.' He turned and pointed to a newly printed map of Addington Hills, which had been pinned to one of the boards behind him.

'There are some advantages to the location that may help us. These are thick woods, and we'll be working under the cover of darkness. In terms of manpower, we'll keep this low-key. There'll be uniform and TSG teams on site, together with an armed response team – but they'll only be there as backup – as a last resort in case it looks like the baby's in danger of coming to any imminent harm. We'll also have an ambulance there as close as we can get it. I'll talk through the logistics of all this in a moment – but are there any questions so far?'

He looked around the room carefully. It had been a long, testing day and he wanted to make sure everyone's focus was where it should be with no immediate end to their shifts in sight.

'Do we know if the suspect's armed?' someone asked.

Skegman shook his head.

'It looks like Billy took the child on impulse. We know he was at work until mid-afternoon before he told his supervisor he felt ill. He can't have known Ella and Kaitlyn would have been in the area when he left, so it feels opportunistic.'

He turned to Paulsen.

'Mattie – you've done basic hostage negotiation training and I want you to lead on this.'

Paulsen looked thrown, but Skegman wasn't interested in a debate. 'We haven't got time to wait for someone and brief them on how we got here. We all know how cold it is – the forecast is for freezing temperatures overnight – that baby could die of hypothermia if she's out there for too long. Your head's in this and you know the background. There's no one better suited and I'll be on site with you running the operation.'

Someone slipped in at the back of the room and Skegman broke off, his face rapidly turning to thunder when he saw who it was.

'I'm happy to mind the store while you're out,' said Finn. 'If it helps . . .'

In the freezing dark, Billy was finally able to think properly for the first time. Or at least he had been until Kaitlyn started crying again. He gingerly picked her up out of the carrycot, unzipped his own coat and held her close and shut his eyes. In his mind's eye he was thinking of all the days he'd probably never have with her now – watching her take her first steps, say her first words, doing the school run later, arguing even, with the stroppy teenager she'd turn into. He'd sold that future with what he'd done that morning, denied Jemma's son a future with his mum too.

'I'm sorry, Jem,' he said, cradling his daughter close.

At some point he'd have to confront reality, he realised, because he couldn't stay in here forever. Kaitlyn would need feeding and changing soon and he wanted to savour every second of this while he could.

There was just enough moonlight coming in through the broken window to illuminate the room a little. Carefully replacing Kaitlyn back in the carrycot, he stood and scanned the floor looking for something, not entirely sure what, until he saw it – a large shard of dirty broken glass. He picked it up and examined it. One end rose to a razor-sharp point while the bottom was squared off, making it easy to handle. It would do the job. He sat back down next to Kaitlyn and placed the glass and his phone beside her too. He'd have company soon and he needed to think about what he was going to say and do next.

*

It took around another half hour before Skegman and Paulsen arrived on the fringes of the woods. Skegman had testily allowed Finn to stay in the incident room, largely because he didn't have the time to argue with him. The armed response unit had got there ahead of them and silently taken up positions on all sides of the substation. As per Skegman's instructions, the other teams placed themselves further behind, while an ambulance parked up on the main road, around a half mile away.

One of the surveillance officers was now leading Skegman and Paulsen through the trees, his torch light illuminating the faint sheen of drizzle that was falling.

'Alex would have been a better choice for this,' growled Paulsen as they made their way. 'He knows Billy Rickson – knew his father too. And frankly, he's more experienced than me.'

'We've been through this,' said Skegman. 'You can both bitch about my decision-making tomorrow – right now let's focus on what we're here to do.'

Now that they'd arrived, it all felt a bit real to Paulsen. Like cabin crew who'd done the training for what happens when a plane crashes but never expected to actually use the knowledge.

They could hear Kaitlyn's cries long before they got there and the sound focused her mind, reminding her what was at stake. They'd received a call from Nash, so they knew Billy had now turned his phone back on – and as the dark shape of the substation finally came into view it all had the bizarre sense of an appointment. She tried not to think about Lee Ellis and how *that* stand-off had ended earlier.

She took up a position only around fifty metres away from the crumbling brick edifice while Skegman liaised with the tactical commander of the armed response team before coming over to join her. The continued sound of Kaitlyn's howling, caught in the gusting winds, was both eerie and unsettling.

'Are you okay?' whispered Skegman.

'Oh yeah, I'll just roll over and grab myself another mojito,' she answered under her breath. He didn't respond and she didn't need to look at him to know he wasn't smiling. 'Yeah, I'm okay,' she confirmed. 'But I'd be a lot happier if I wasn't surrounded by men with guns.'

'They're only here as a backup – a last resort.'

She nodded.

'Then let's do this,' she said and, taking a deep breath, stepped forward.

33

For the briefest of moments, Paulsen had a flashback to a treehouse her father had built for her as a child. She'd retreated there often when she'd wanted her own space, when the kids at school had been too much. The sheer misery in Kaitlyn Rickson's howling brought her back into the moment. Irritated by the lapse in concentration she refocused, lifted her phone and made the call. It was answered immediately – he'd been expecting it, she guessed.

'Hello, Billy,' she said. 'My name's Detective Sergeant Mathilde Paulsen from the Metropolitan Police.'

'Hi,' he replied, almost politely. She was staring so hard at the substation that it was as if she could see right through the bricks at the man behind them.

'We need to get Kaitlyn somewhere warm. Whatever's upsetting you, we can talk about it. But we've got to get Kaitlyn out of the cold as quickly as possible,' she said. 'Will you help me do that?'

'No,' he replied in the same, sightly unnerving tone.

'Do you want to tell me what this is all about?' said Paulsen carefully but there was no reply. She was pretty certain that he hadn't planned this out, so she needed to be careful not to push him into any corners. Another blast of wind buffeted against her, and she waited for it to subside.

Skegman's earlier point that the location gave them some advantages came back to her. He was right in part, but the substation was also effectively a bunker. She had no idea what Billy's state of mind was or what he was capable of doing. They didn't know why he'd taken the baby or whether he was capable of harming her – but what she did know was that there wouldn't be a quick and easy way in if they needed to move fast. She pushed the phone hard against her ear again.

'Billy? I'm asking again – what's this all about?'

'There's stuff you don't know about,' he replied hoarsely. 'About my dad – and how he died.'

'Don't be so sure of that – Sarah Littlewood came in to talk to us earlier today. She confessed that she and Jemma Vickers had conspired to kill your father. I'm guessing that's what you're referring to – so there's no need for you to continue with this. We already know what happened.'

'Is she under arrest?'

Paulsen rubbed her brow.

'No,' she replied. 'But we'll be investigating what she told us – and if she's guilty of something then she'll be treated like anyone else.'

That was certainly true, but she also knew that there was little chance of a custodial sentence.

'Why didn't you arrest her – she tells you what they did – admits it, and you do what? *You just let her go?*' he shouted. There was another strong gust of wind and Paulsen was struggling to hear him properly now.

'Billy – can I come in there and talk to you face to face? It's really difficult speaking like this and there's a lot we need to discuss. I'd like to see that Kaitlyn's okay as well.'

As if on cue the baby started screaming again. Each cry cut through like a knife – the infant sounded audibly distressed. Paulsen worried for a second that Billy had actually hung up on her and she checked the display on her phone, but the call was still connected. She looked around in frustration at

Skegman who watched behind her with concern. Don't give me that look – this was your idea, she thought. She lifted the handset back up again.

'Please, Billy – I'm not armed, and I just want to talk to you.'

'Alright, walk round to the left-hand side – you can get in from there,' he said, and she felt a surge of relief. It might only have been a small breakthrough, but it was one, nonetheless. She turned again to Skegman, mouthed *'I'm going in'*, waited to see he'd understood and then she followed Billy's instruction. She found the large, smashed window frame at the side and peered through it. Billy was sitting against the far wall, and she saw the carrycot on the floor next to him.

'You can climb through but stay by the window,' he said. He lifted his hand so she could see the shard of broken glass he was holding. The sight of it made her heart miss a beat but she knew she couldn't let the fear show and concentrated on getting herself through the gap.

'There's really no need to do this,' she said. It wasn't any warmer in there, but the constant gale had been giving her earache and there was instant relief once she was inside.

'Stay where you are,' said Billy, by way of greeting. 'And don't come any closer.'

Paulsen could immediately see he was in a highly distressed state. She couldn't take her eyes off the dirty piece of glass in his hand, a chunky-looking wristwatch sitting incongruously above it. She didn't know whether he intended to harm Kaitlyn, himself, or use it in self-defence if he had to and she didn't want to find out. Calmly she explained the conversation that had taken place at Cedar House, and he began shaking his head immediately.

'My dad never hurt anyone – the whole idea's just a joke. They wanted someone to blame, and they made him their scapegoat. They had *no right*,' he said tremulously.

'There'll be a proper investigation into what happened, I promise. But please – you're not really going to use that glass, are you? Don't you think that there's been enough death today? First Jemma and now Lee?'

Billy looked up at her with confusion and then she realised the mistake she'd made.

'What do you mean, *Lee?*' he said slowly.

Finn was finishing a bacon sandwich in his office, and it felt like the single most beautiful thing he'd ever eaten. He washed it down with a mouthful of foamy coffee and allowed himself to savour the moment. Wiping his fingers on a napkin he turned his attention back to his PC screen. There was a polite knock at the door and in a complete break with Cedar House tradition whoever it was didn't barge straight through.

'Come in,' he shouted, and Vanessa Nash tentatively entered, holding some paperwork.

'Are you okay?' she asked.

Finn had a fair idea he probably looked like death warmed up.

'Better than I was an hour ago – put it that way,' he replied. 'Don't suppose there's any more from either the Knox or Quilter crime scenes is there?'

She nodded.

'That's why I'm here – we've had some luck with that red Mazda. One of the ANPR cameras gave us both a partial number plate and an image of some of the occupants.'

Finn looked up with interest and she passed him the piece of paper she'd been holding. The picture wasn't great, but the heavyset features of a man in the back seat were distinguishable, as was the torso of someone next to him.

'The car was stolen earlier this morning – the driver didn't even know about it until we called him – he's still at work, but we've run that image through the facial recognition software and got a name – Harvey Russell. He's a thug – been in and out of prison for a variety of robbery offences, but there's a lot of GBH and ABH too. We're trying to track him down, obviously.'

Finn absorbed the information.

'Any history with Quilter? With *any* of this? Is he Red Tide?'

Nash shook her head.

'That was my first thought. The thing is, according to his record Russell was working as a contractor in Canada between 2007 and 2010. He actually did time over there for six months before they deported him.'

Finn forced his tired brain to think it through.

'Could he have killed Knox today? Do we have any idea yet how much time separated his death from Quilter's?'

'Broadly, but it doesn't look like they were too far apart,' said Nash.

Finn nodded. 'The key question for me continues to be what Knox and Quilter's connection was to all of this. They were both pretty much eliminated from our original investigation. At the time we didn't find anything conclusive on them and we thought we were looking for just one man. Now I'm starting to think it's all a bit more complicated than that.'

'How do you mean?'

He leant forward. 'I'm not sure of the detail yet – how it all connects up – but I think they both knew Red Tide's identity.'

'And Harvey Russell silenced them?'

Finn mulled it over.

'Question is: did Russell do it to protect himself . . . or someone else?'

★

In the substation, the news of Lee's death had hit Billy hard. If Paulsen had ever been unsure whether she had the maternal instinct, now she knew. She was fighting an almost overwhelming urge to run over and pick the carrycot up, but Billy was still holding the shard of glass in a trembling hand. Kaitlyn's intermittent cries just made it even more difficult.

'This place is surrounded by armed men,' she said slowly. 'But I promise you – not one of them wants to use their weapon. They'd all rather be at home in the warm, filling their faces with food and watching TV. But getting your daughter to safety is their priority – they won't hesitate to gun you down if they have to.' She let that sink in for a moment. 'Alternatively, we can just walk out of here.'

He looked up at her and she tried to see if her words were having any effect.

'I killed Jemma,' he said in a low voice. 'I didn't mean to, and I didn't want to – I kind of loved her. I always have. But she wasn't thinking about me when she murdered my dad, was she?'

His face screwed up in pain and Paulsen held her breath. She still, in her heart, didn't believe he would hurt Kaitlyn, but he was out of his mind with grief. She hadn't forgotten Skegman's warning earlier about his mental state and where this could potentially go – where it *had* gone with Lee Ellis.

'I think a judge would be sympathetic to a plea of manslaughter by reason of diminished responsibility,' she said honestly. 'Because that's what I think it *was*. Can you genuinely say you were thinking straight this morning?' She fixed him with her gaze, trying to inject as much empathy as she could into it. 'It's up to you what happens next. But don't you think that little girl deserves a future too?'

He looked down at Kaitlyn, the broken shard of glass

trembling in his hand. Paulsen couldn't read him, had no idea if she was getting through or not, but every second felt torturous.

'I would never hurt my daughter. I just wanted to be alone with her for a bit,' he said almost matter-of-factly, and she felt the relief course through her.

'I know.' Her mouth was dry as a bone. 'Please – can I take her now? We need to get her into the warm,' she added quickly. He nodded slowly, and she walked over and carefully picked up the carrycot. Instinctively, she whispered *'shhh'* at the pink little face peering up at her.

'Do you want to drop that now?' she said quietly. Billy was still holding the broken glass. He looked down at it almost in surprise and let go. Paulsen fumbled with one hand and pulled her radio from her pocket. She called Skegman and told him they were coming out and that Billy was unarmed.

'Are you ready?' she said to him afterwards. He nodded and rose to his feet. For a brief second, they faced each other in a shaft of moonlight and got their breath back.

'I'll go first, and you follow – nice and slow,' she said and then walked up to the broken window. Having finally got hold of Kaitlyn, she was in no rush to hand her back. Carefully, still holding her, she negotiated her way through the gap. Outside, she waited until Billy was behind her and then turned to him again.

'Put your hands above your head and don't make any sudden movements, okay?' she said. He did as she instructed, and they began to walk.

As they came round to the front Paulsen saw Skegman and a paramedic standing around thirty feet away. Despite being so close, she could feel her heart thumping in her chest, aware of the marksmen hidden in the dark, whose sights would be trained on them. She was almost there now, just another few steps and this would all be over.

Everything that happened next was like an extended blur. There was a sudden flash of bright white light in the corner of her eye, and then she heard the whipcrack of a shot.

34

Paulsen instinctively pulled Kaitlyn out of the carrycot and dived for cover. She could see Billy, wild-eyed and terrified on the ground close by, and could hear Skegman shouting frantically into his radio.

'Stay down,' she yelled at Billy. 'Are you okay?'

He nodded.

'It missed me.'

Before she could say any more, she heard a voice in her ear. She turned and saw a green-tunicked paramedic already reaching out his hands to take the baby from her. Gratefully she passed the bundle over as Skegman sprinted over to join them. Armed officers were now streaming out of the woods. Other uniformed officers were also emerging, swarming in their direction.

'He was unarmed – I thought they were only here as backup. What the hell just happened?' Paulsen screamed at Skegman, unable to contain both her fear and relief.

'One of the marksmen thought Billy was holding a weapon,' he replied. 'Said he saw a blade reflecting in the light behind you and believed he was about to use it.'

Paulsen was livid.

'*What* blade?' She looked round at Billy, now engulfed by armed men and thought it through. 'His wristwatch,' she said, remembering it. 'It must have been the moonlight reflecting off it.'

Billy was now on his feet, handcuffed and petrified. As they began to lead him away, he turned and looked over at Paulsen. Someone gave him a shove.

'Be gentle with him,' she shouted, but they didn't seem to notice.

'Mattie . . .' began Skegman.

'And *you* shouldn't have put me in that position,' she said whirling round to confront him.

'You did brilliantly – but you need to take a moment now,' he said, punctuating the words.

She took some big gulps of the icy night air and her heart finally felt like it wasn't trying to punch a hole through her chest.

'I thought I was going to get that child killed. He had this piece of glass . . .' She coughed and Skegman put an arm around her. Even in the context of the situation, part of Paulsen was slightly taken aback– she'd never seen him do anything like that before.

'You did *brilliantly*,' he repeated slowly.

'I radioed you – told you he was unarmed,' she heard herself gabble. 'Billy could have died – or that bullet could have hit the baby.'

'But it didn't,' he said. 'There's plenty of time to debrief later. First things first, are you okay – or do I need to get you checked over?'

Paulsen shook her head. It was only then that she noticed how badly she was shaking.

'I'm fine – or at least I will be. But I want to know why a trained marksman mistook a wristwatch for a knife. How does that even happen?'

Awkwardly Skegman removed his arm from around her shoulder.

'The whole team knew he was unarmed, and no one gave

the order to shoot,' he said. 'We'll get to the bottom of it later, I promise.'

'You're damn right we will,' said Paulsen, calming down now and starting to think properly. 'Because either that guy is a terrible shot or he disobeyed a direct instruction.'

The marksman's name was Ross Matthews. Back at Cedar House, it was now approaching ten in the evening. Matthews had stuck to his story, insisting that even accounting for the night vision technology fitted to his ballistic helmet, he'd thought he'd seen a weapon being raised. Making a split-second decision he'd fired just as Billy had taken a step forwards and the bullet had only missed him by millimetres.

Finn listened to the account of what had happened, grateful for several things. Firstly, that this time history *hadn't* repeated itself and Sarah Littlewood had been spared a whole new chapter of pain. Strong as she was, losing her grandchild might have been more than even she could handle. He was also thankful that Billy had come through unscathed. To have lost all three people from that fateful afternoon in 2009 would have been too much to bear. He was now downstairs being processed in the custody suite while Kaitlyn Rickson had been returned to her mother.

'I think everyone needs a decent night's sleep,' said Skegman. 'Christ knows I do – we can come at this fresh again in the morning.'

Finn looked around the room and couldn't disagree.

'Matthews needs looking at,' growled Paulsen. She was a lot calmer now but wasn't going to let go of what had happened easily.

'You know how it works, Mattie,' said Skegman. 'There'll be an internal investigation – for now though, we need to move on.'

Paulsen didn't look happy, but Finn nodded in agreement.

'We still have three deaths to investigate,' he said. 'We also need to stand up whether Jemma Vickers murdered George Rickson and establish exactly what Sarah Littlewood's role in that was.' He ran a hand through his hair. 'And then we'll need to make a decision on whether to charge her.' He'd already made up his mind on that – if and when the moment came, he wanted to be the one to do it. He owed her that much.

'Billy confessed to me in the woods that he killed Jemma. I didn't get the sense it was premeditated either. He was devastated.'

'I didn't think it would have been,' said Finn. 'There was too much history between them. What do you think happened?'

'My guess is that he just wanted to confront her about his dad, and things got out of hand,' said Paulsen.

Finn nodded. From what he'd seen that morning the main damage had been done when Jemma's head had hit the frozen pavement. It was all too easy to imagine a confrontation in those icy conditions spinning out of control.

'Does he need to be on suicide watch overnight?' said Skegman.

'No. But I want to make sure he gets the necessary support from the relevant agencies,' replied Paulsen. 'I'll talk to his lawyer in the morning.'

'Which leaves us with Knox and Quilter,' said Nash.

Finn explained the work he'd been doing in his office while the others had been dealing with the situation at Addington Hills.

'What are you saying – that this Harvey Russell is Red Tide?' said Skegman when he'd finished.

'I'm keeping an open mind, put it that way,' Finn replied. 'He doesn't strike me as the type to have the brains to organise all of this. Someone might have paid him to throw Craig

Quilter off that railway bridge and quite possibly murder Eddie Knox as well.'

'So we're back where we were then – who?' asked Paulsen.

Finn was about to reply when something Marco had mentioned came back to him.

'He said the cops back then were hopeless.'

'Everything we did in 2009 got us nowhere,' he said slowly. 'If those two *were* actively involved in what happened back then – then what exactly did they do, and how did we miss it?'

When he got home Finn took a shower and tried to clean the day off him. The sadness he felt about Lee and Jemma wasn't going to wash away so quickly though. His whole relationship with the pair had been reshaped by Lee's revelation that he'd been the one responsible for Oliver Littlewood's death. Every conversation he'd ever had with them now informed by that truth. But unlike Sarah, he couldn't find it in his heart to get angry about their deceit – if that's what it was. In the cafe, he'd kept asking Lee what had really happened. He now realised he should have been asking himself the same question much sooner.

It was only here in the quiet of his own home that he appreciated what else had been tugging at him all day. It had been during the original investigation in 2009 that he'd first begun dating Karin. He wondered if that's why this investigation mattered so much to him, why he'd kept in touch with Jemma and Lee over the years – because it was a touchstone to the past. On some level he connected them with her. From somewhere in the back of his mind he could remember a glass of warm wine and his wife-to-be telling him she thought he was an arse, and he smiled.

'*Still are,*' she said.

'I know,' he replied.

After he'd finished in the shower, he put on a dressing gown and sat down on his sofa. As he'd expected, despite feeling shattered, the last place he felt like going was to bed. Even assuming he was going to get some sleep – he didn't fancy the dreams that were probably even now brewing in his subconscious. Instead, he picked up his phone and rang Sarah. If there was one person who was feeling the same way, it would be her.

'Hello, Alex,' she answered wearily. Her tone was warmer though this time, and it struck him that he never really knew what to expect when he spoke to her because he didn't really know what their relationship was. They weren't friends in the classic sense, but it was a relationship of sorts, one that had endured over time. A *connection* might be a better way of describing it, he thought.

'I just wondered if you were okay?' he said. The words sounded inadequate, not remotely enough to cover the complexity of where they found themselves.

'Thank you for getting Kaitlyn back safely,' she said. 'But no – I can't say I'm doing brilliantly tonight – it's been a hell of a day. I just keep remembering that conversation I had with Jemma. The one where I gave her the go-ahead to do what she did to George.' He heard her swallow. 'I was grateful at the time because I'm pretty sure if she hadn't done it, I probably would have.'

'Perhaps that's why she did it – to save you from yourself?' said Finn. As he said the words, he was almost certain he was right. The Jemma he'd got to know would have thought it through, would have wanted to spare Sarah any additional emotional trauma. Simultaneously he cursed her for not bringing her suspicions to him first. He remembered Lee's scorn for the police in the cafe, and it stung him to think that Jemma had shared that feeling.

He heard Sarah sigh.

'The idea that I've ended up destroying Billy's life . . .' she said. 'He was the son of the man I thought had killed Ollie and I just didn't care about his feelings. Part of me was even grateful when he moved out.'

For a moment there was silence, both of them lost in their thoughts. Finn stared up idly at the picture of Karin on his mantelpiece. He liked that one of her, the angle of it – the faint trace of a smile she seemed to be throwing back at him.

'There's something I want to ask you,' said Sarah. 'And I need you to answer me honestly – no more *"we'll do the best we can"* stuff, okay?'

'Go on,' he replied.

'Do you think you'll *ever* catch this guy? The real culprit, I mean – if it definitely isn't George.'

He remembered the promise Lee had made him give just before he pulled the trigger.

'I've been giving Red Tide a lot of thought tonight,' he said. 'He's a broker, essentially. Someone who fills a gap in the market for people with a very specialised taste. Lee was convinced he'd never gone away.'

'You mean this has been going on all this time?' said Sarah. '*Other* teenagers being forced to do the same thing?'

'We think Jemma was looking to that possibility – did she not mention that to you?'

Sarah shook her head.

'She may have been waiting until she found out something more concrete. There was a boy who went missing before Christmas called Jarrod Thomas. You might have heard his name on the local news. Lee thought he'd been taken by their abductor too. We found a reference to him on a phone Jemma used to access the Dark Web.'

'But that's impossible, surely?' whispered Sarah. 'There

can't be more of them out there – I never even considered that.'

'A hundred and seventy thousand people go missing every year in the UK– seventy thousand of those are teenagers or children and two per cent of those are never found,' he replied. 'That's a lot of kids unaccounted for.'

'You still haven't answered my question,' she said. 'Will you ever catch this guy?'

He thought about it and decided there was no point sugar-coating the answer.

'I honestly don't know.'

35

Paulsen slept heavily until around five in the morning. It was pitch-black outside and her bed was warm and comfortable. On any other day, she'd have enjoyed the feeling but the sound of that bullet whistling past wouldn't leave her. The memory of that wriggling bundle in her arms amidst the chaos hadn't gone either. Oddly, the whole experience had made her think of her father again. Kaitlyn Rickson's short existence could so easily have come to an abrupt end in that wood. Meanwhile, Christer Paulsen's journey was drawing to its undignified, inexorable close. Life was unforgiving at whichever end of its road you were.

She looked across at Nancy, envious of the solid hour of sleep she still had before their alarm sounded. With no danger of dozing back off herself, she slipped out of bed and quietly peeked through the curtains. It had snowed again heavily overnight, and a blanket of white gave the scene a Dickensian look under the bright street lamps. She went through and made herself a cup of coffee and took a seat on the sofa in the living room. After the havoc of the last twenty-four hours, the stillness of their flat was welcome. She felt exhausted from the previous day and the new one hadn't even properly begun yet.

She grabbed her phone and weighed it in her hand. Since he'd retired and before he'd received his diagnosis, her father used to enjoy catching up on his reading in the early hours.

She'd enjoyed more than a few private phone conversations with him at this time, but those days were long gone. The memory of them made her heart heavy.

By the time she'd finally returned home the previous night, it had been too late to call her family and she certainly hadn't been in the right frame of mind. But there was someone else she suspected was awake right now and probably drinking coffee alone, too. More in hope than expectation she fired off a quick message.

'You up?'

It took only about a minute before her phone began to ring.

'Hello, Mum,' she said softly.

She apologised for not getting in touch sooner and decided against explaining in too much detail what had been happening. Instead, she let her mother vent – and there was a lot to listen to. Her father had cut his arm open after smashing it on a glass door. It only required minor stitching, but the incident highlighted the family's problem.

'This is the hardest thing I've ever had to do,' said her mother. The words stung because Paulsen knew she was a woman who rarely allowed her pain to show. Evelyn Paulsen was normally the epitome of stoicism. But here, now, in the early hours of the morning, was the raw truth.

'How bad's it been?'

'There's just enough of him in there to know what's going on. But he gets so angry now. And you know your father – you can count on one hand how many times he's ever lost his temper. So, this comes from his heart, Mattie. Putting him into care – it's a *betrayal* and I know he feels it that way too whatever anyone else tells me.'

'So don't do it then,' said Paulsen in a small voice.

They both knew it was a plea from the heart, not the head.

'I'd give everything in my power not to, but I can't cope.

This *has* to happen, and I think a little piece of me is going to die when we do it.'

Paulsen had no answer for her, no solution, not even a hollow silver lining she could offer. Afterwards, the tears came and initially she didn't even notice Nancy's hand on her shoulder. But then she stood and wordlessly they held each other as outside the snow continued to fall.

Despite his fears, Finn slept like a log. There were dreams too; he was aware of them when he woke, but perhaps fortunately, couldn't remember any of the detail. It didn't take long for the memory of the previous day to descend like a cloud, though. The more he thought about it, the more he was sure the point of the siege had been to build to that confession – even if Lee himself hadn't realised it.

As usual, Finn tried to restore his equilibrium by getting back to some normal routines. He was naked, shaving in his bathroom when the doorbell rang. Swearing under his breath he wrapped a towel around his waist and went to answer it.

'Sweet Jesus, you look like Father Christmas,' said a familiar Glaswegian accent. Finn glared at Murray Saunders, wiped some of the shaving cream off his chin and let him in.

'What are *you* doing here at this hour?' he said testily. It had only been twenty-four hours since he'd left him on a snow-covered Clapham Common but it felt like a week. The Scotsman beamed at him and raised a supermarket tote bag.

'I've come to make you breakfast, what else?'

'I don't need you to make me breakfast,' he said as Murray made himself at home. 'I *like* my breakfast – I make myself a *good* breakfast.'

'You go finish scraping your face and chuck on some clothes, and I'll get cracking in what passes for your kitchen,' said Murray, the annoying smile getting ever wider.

Twenty minutes later Finn stared down with dismay at the greasy pile of sausages, bacon and fried eggs that had just been placed in front of him.

'Don't give me any grief,' said Murray. 'It'll make a change from whatever combination of nuts and birdseed you normally eat. You're a man, not a squirrel for fuck's sake.'

'Well, go on then,' said Finn with resignation. 'You didn't really come over here just to clog my arteries – get it off your chest, whatever it is.'

Murray shrugged.

'You think I don't watch the news? Didn't see what happened yesterday? I'm just checking that you're okay.' His voice hardened. '*Are* you okay?'

Finn explained what had happened, from its origins in 2009 to the showdown in Addington Hills the previous night. Murray listened and ate at the same time.

'I wondered if there might be some personal element to it,' he said when Finn had finished.

'So, what's your grand assessment then?'

Murray looked up and regarded him for a moment, like a doctor with a patient.

'You're not good with death, Alex – you and I both know that. And after what happened to Jackie Ojo, you needed this like a hole in the head.'

Finn winced.

'Perhaps not the best choice of words,' he said.

'Aye – sorry,' said Murray.

'I'm fine,' said Finn, taking a sip of his coffee.

'I've heard that before. The trouble with you is you've got too many ghosts. Your brother, your wife, Ojo and now these two poor people.'

'It's not like I had much choice,' said Finn.

'No, but you blame yourself, anyway,' replied Murray,

sitting back in his chair. 'You think that if you'd made different decisions along the way then some of them might still be alive.'

Finn surrendered on the breakfast he'd barely touched and threw his cutlery in the centre of the plate.

'Of course I do.'

Murray leant in.

'So today, this morning, this moment, right now . . . what's biting at you?'

Finn knew that the question was the real reason why Murray had come. As usual, his friend had wanted to get to the heart of it, deployed banter to soften him up, then gone for the jugular. He met him head on.

'I worry that I won't be able to catch this Red Tide, that I won't be able to keep my promise to Lee and that I'll let Sarah Littlewood down again.'

Murray nodded.

'I get that. Ever heard of a guy called Maxwell Maltz?' he said brightly. Finn gave him a tired look. 'He was an American cosmetic surgeon – wrote a few books too. He said, *"You make mistakes, mistakes don't make you"*.'

'The trouble is – my mistakes tend to be lethal,' said Finn. 'And I can't afford to make another one.'

Murray looked him in the eye, all trace of his earlier humour suddenly gone.

'I'm not a policeman but I know one thing: you won't catch this guy with that attitude. Whatever's happened before, forget it and shake it off fast – or you'll be dead in the water before you even start.'

Around an hour later Finn made his way to Cedar House. Irritatingly, the conversation with Murray had helped. Facetious as the man could be, his insight was sharp as a nail and cheaper than a therapist too. He'd been starving on his way in though and dropped into YoYo's for a second, healthier breakfast of coffee and porridge.

He scanned his phone while he ate, curious to see what coverage the media had given to the previous day's events. It was odd how it had all been swallowed up. There wasn't much on the siege – journalists, generally, not interested in suicides, while the abduction of Kaitlyn Rickson had been resolved before it could become a major story. Knox and Quilter's deaths merited a few cursory paragraphs, which gave little detail away. Something connected all this up though, and he – of all people – should be able to see it, he thought. Someone somewhere was reading the same headlines and *could* see it.

'I thought you'd be giving cafes a swerve for a while after yesterday,' said a familiar voice.

He looked up and saw Paulsen. She was carrying a take-away coffee and what looked like a croissant in a paper bag. The lack of a coat suggested she'd only popped over the road from Cedar House.

'You're in early?' he said.

She nodded and sat down opposite him with a slightly distracted air. Finn considered himself a decent reader of Paulsen's various moods. A standard morning tended to bring a scowl of welcome – this looked like something different.

'I woke early,' she said tersely before pulling the lid off her coffee and taking a sip.

'I'm not surprised. Have you recovered from last night?' he asked. 'It sounds like it was pretty intense out there.'

She frowned.

'No, I'm not sure I have – but not for the reasons you think – I emailed HR this morning.'

Finn looked surprised.

'*HR?* I don't understand.'

'I asked them to send me Ross Matthews's service record. Turns out he's got quite a history of fuck-ups,' she said.

'Well, there you go—' Finn began but she waved him down.

'And he also spent a long time working for someone you know.' Finn felt the hairs on the back of his neck go up even as she said it.

'AC Culley.'

36

'You're fucking kidding me,' said Karin. 'Show me.'

They were lying in bed and the news had come through in the early hours. Finn passed his phone over to her.

'Oh, you're fucking kidding,' repeated Karin as she read the confirmation.

'I'm really not,' said Finn.

Overnight Britain had voted to leave the European Union. Both of them had believed the Brexit vote would be comfortably won by Remain. *'Storm in a teacup, you'll see,'* Finn had said just before they'd turned the lights off the previous night.

'Well, that's us done, isn't it?' said Karin, passing the phone back to him. 'I expect they'll want to deport me back to Germany by Thursday.'

'I was hoping for Wednesday – it'll give me time to get someone else in by the weekend,' said Finn and she casually raised a middle finger at him.

'Seriously, this is going to be a disaster,' she said, then saw the preoccupied expression clouding over his face. 'You're more worried about this morning, aren't you?'

He nodded glumly.

'I haven't seen Chris Culley in seven years – I can't say I'm looking forward to it. Our relationship was never the same after Oliver Littlewood. Not that it was that good before, to be fair.'

'But isn't this what you've been waiting for – closure?'

Finn lay back on his pillow and stared up at the ceiling.

'Why's this Dennis Trant suddenly decided to confess to this? It's as if being a paedophile's not enough for him – like he has to add a notorious unsolved murder to his CV too,' he said.

Karin looked over at him, surprised by the sudden passion in his voice.

'You're still blaming yourself, aren't you?'

Finn shook his head.

'It's not that – it's just interesting timing. There was an abduction a few weeks ago that had a similar feel and I went back through the old files, put in a few calls – just to be sure that there wasn't a connection – and now someone terminally ill conveniently steps forward and takes responsibility for what happened back then? He didn't live anywhere near the area – and those three kids were taken from the same streets from the same tightly knit community. Something smells off.'

'Or maybe it's exactly what it appears to be – someone approaching the end wanting to set the record straight.'

Finn didn't look convinced.

'Maybe.'

'Try to keep an open mind, Alex.' She leant across and kissed him. 'Just for once.'

A couple of hours later Finn was sitting in the main reception of Belmarsh prison in south London. He was trying to work out why he had butterflies about seeing Culley again. It wasn't Culley himself, he thought – it was all the memories from back then that had been stirred up by Trant's confession. The Red Room, the man who'd escaped that day, the other potential victims he didn't know about as a result – the ones whose deaths were on his conscience.

He looked out of the window and at the world beyond the prison car park. A couple of young twenty-somethings were walking past the gates carrying placards that read 'Stop Brexit' and 'European and Proud'. Finn guessed they were going to the big anti-Brexit demonstration that was taking place in Parliament Square later. Behind them was a familiar face.

A few moments later Chris Culley charged through the doors of the prison entrance like a rhinoceros, saw Finn and stomped over without any smile of recognition. He looked much the same – though Finn noted with some satisfaction that he'd put on a little weight.

'Alex,' he barked.

'Commander Culley,' said Finn formally, rising and extending his hand. 'Congratulations on your recent promotion.'

Culley looked like he'd prefer to be just about anywhere but here.

'I see Dennis Trant's come to your rescue then,' he said curtly. 'Seven years too late – but now we can finally put this to bed I suppose.'

Okay, thought Finn. That's how this is going to be.

'I'm keeping an open mind,' he said.

'Always were on opposite sides of the fence, weren't we?' said Culley.

'We had a professional relationship – which is all it needed to be,' replied Finn as diplomatically as he could manage. Culley snorted with contempt.

'Professional, my arse. You never liked me – which I never cared about. But you never respected me either – which *did* piss me off. Because it got in the way, frankly.'

Finn nodded. 'That's fair enough – but I could say exactly the same about you.'

Culley's piggy little eyes flared with anger. If anything, his face seemed to have got pinker and rounder in the intervening years too.

'I thought you were arrogant – without ever having earned the right to be.'

Finn didn't reply. This had all got very unpleasant far too quickly.

'So, what do you make of Trant's confession?' he said, trying to cool the temperature a bit.

Culley took a second to change gear.

'It feels credible – the man's terminally ill, he's got nothing left to lose. He wouldn't be the first in that situation to want to get a few things off his chest before the end. What's your take?'

Finn shook his head.

'Something doesn't feel right. I've seen nothing in this guy's background which suggests he's capable of hacking someone to death. And Trant's a paedophile but none of those three teenagers was sexually abused, need I remind you?'

The two men stared at each other.

'Shall we get this over with?' said Culley.

Dennis Trant was too ill to be a man playing games, was Finn's first thought when he saw him. He was skeletal and didn't look too far from the end. Like a lot of sex offenders, he was unmemorable. Not the creepy-looking perv you'd warn your kids to be careful of, or a man you could say might have been handsome once. Trant was more the invisible sort you could sit opposite on a long train journey and never notice or remember. The dangerous type.

After the formalities were out of the way, Culley took charge and Finn was happy to defer to him. He wanted to watch Trant while he spoke, look behind his eyes and try to gauge whether this was someone to take seriously or not.

'I was the senior investigating officer in 2009,' began Culley. 'DI Finn was also on the team at the time,' he added almost as an aside. 'Between us, we are *extremely* knowledgeable about what happened back then, so if you're about to spin us a load of old bollocks, we'll know – do you understand?'

Trant nodded, not batting a hairless eyelid. Stuff had happened to this man while he'd been inside – Finn could see that without being told. It was written into his expression, the weariness of his gaze, the stillness.

'I have had a lifelong interest in young people,' said Trant simply. There was a wheeze to his voice and the effort of speaking was obvious. 'But until that summer – I'd always been someone who just *watched*.' He took a sip of water and swallowed it noisily. There was a slight tremble to his hand, Finn noticed. 'But that was the year, things changed.'

'Why then – what triggered it?' said Finn.

Trant shrugged.

'It was hot. Everyone in their T-shirts and shorts, maybe. Or perhaps – *just because*. Even I can't give you a good answer to that.'

'Give us some details then, Dennis. We're not here for your life story,' said Culley irritably. 'If you actually did the things you're claiming – prove it.'

Trant looked at him, sizing him up, not making much effort to hide what he was concluding either.

'I can see you're in a hurry, Commander Culley,' said Trant. 'Trust me, no one's time is more precious to them than mine,' he said with more than a hint of detectable bitterness. And then he began to talk.

He described the abductions with perfect accuracy – the white van, the house and the cellar. He knew what the three teenagers had been wearing and had answers for most of the outstanding questions. He claimed Oliver had become difficult, screaming and shouting hysterically and he'd had no option but to kill him – simply to contain him. He'd known where the police had found the van, and he told them that he'd used a hatchet, which he'd disposed of by the time he was interrupted.

'The afternoon when *you* came along,' he said, locking eyes with Finn. And even though he'd only met Trant for the first time that day, Finn felt the distinct crackle of a shared memory passing between them.

As he left the interview room later – he struggled to make sense of it. The man simply knew too much and yet something still didn't feel right.

'He knows a hell of a lot . . .' he said to Culley, outside in the prison car park. 'But I still have a few questions.' He wondered if he was trying to convince himself as much as anyone. Culley looked at him, astonished.

'Alex – there's a reason in the last seven years I've become a commander and you're still at Cedar House making up the numbers.'

Finn beat down a flash of anger – not at the jibe, but because he wasn't being listened to. That felt familiar with this man.

'I admit he just gave us a huge amount of detail only the killer could know. But there were some gaps in there too.'

'What gaps?' snarled Culley.

'We think from what Jemma Vickers told us that he probably had cameras in that cellar – but we found nothing. No devices of any kind for that matter – if he was filming everything then where was it going?'

Culley shrugged, unimpressed.

'He moved the equipment – just like he disposed of the murder weapon.'

'Exactly – but when, how? It's like he *knew* we were coming.

And why did he hold those kids for several days without laying a finger on them? We never even found print and DNA evidence of him there. I've sent you everything I've done this week on this – there's nothing that puts him in south London at that time.'

Culley sighed.

'I read it – there's nothing there that says he *wasn't* in south London either. And you know as well as I do, that we never found *any* print and DNA evidence in that house.'

'And if Oliver was kicking off – why not just gag him, why hack him to death like that?'

Again, Culley looked as if he couldn't quite believe what he was hearing.

'Because he's a psycho. That's the trouble with you – you've always been too literal. Brain like a textbook. You tell me – is Trant the same height and build as the man you saw that day?'

It was a difficult question, Finn thought. Trant was emaciated and dying but he was about the right height. A younger, fleshed-out version might just have been the person he'd fought with.

'Possibly.'

'And can you account for the detail in the statement he gave? There's stuff there that's *never* been in the public domain. He knew what that cellar looked like – the crates covered by the tarpaulin, even which wall they were stacked up by. And he said the murder weapon was a hatchet, which he disposed of later – a weapon we never recovered, which also happens to match the pathologist's findings too.'

Finn hesitated. He was about ninety-five per cent there, but the five per cent was nagging at him.

'No, I can't,' he said finally. 'And I *do* believe what he's just told us – I just don't think we should automatically take him at his word either, that's all.'

Culley rolled his eyes.

'It's *over*, Alex. Your next job is to charge him – he'll never make it to court, but it'll give those families some much-needed closure. Today's a win – take it and move on. And with luck, you and I will never have to meet again.'

37

The conversation with Paulsen in YoYo's had increased Finn's uncertainty about the original investigation and how it had been managed. He was now standing in Skegman's office, and the DCI was listening to his argument with considerable scepticism.

'I'm not saying Chris Culley is Red Tide, I'm just saying there's a few things that are starting to bother me about him,' said Finn.

'You do get just how screwed our reputation is right now?' said Skegman. 'Now you want to start investigating an assistant commissioner because you've added two and two and made five?'

Finn shifted uncomfortably on his feet; he'd always known this was going to be a hard sell.

'Just park your resistance to the idea for a moment. He was in the perfect position to steer that investigation fifteen years ago. I'd spot the signs now – but back then I was a bit greener.'

Skegman's eyes were flitting around the room as if the answer might be found scrawled on the walls somewhere.

'What are you saying? That he headed up some sort of conspiracy involving Quilter and Knox?'

Finn looked down at the floor.

'That's the bit I can't make work – he did everything he could to point the finger at Knox and to try and divert me away from Quilter.'

'And how does Harvey Russell figure into this? Surely he should be front and centre of our thinking right now? We have witnesses who saw him driving away at speed from Quilter's flat and then a screen grab of him close to the railway bridge.'

Finn nodded. A full-on search was underway for Russell but had so far turned up nothing.

'My guess is if he was involved in yesterday's deaths then he's gone underground. I also think it's more likely he was acting on someone else's instruction rather than being the person pulling the strings.'

'That's a guess.' growled Skegman. 'And the marksman who fired the shot last night, Ross Matthews – are you folding him into this too?'

'Possibly. Quilter and Knox's murders suggest someone cleaning up after themselves. It's certainly looking increasingly like Red Tide is more than just a one-man band – whoever it is.'

Skegman remained deeply unconvinced.

'Ross Matthews is a marksman who's had a few issues in the past. Last night wasn't the first time he's made the wrong judgement call. I get that you had a difficult day yesterday – but you're not thinking any of this through properly. It's all woolly as hell.'

The energy seemed to drain out of Finn.

'I know. And you're right – it *is* all wafer-thin,' he said shaking his head. 'But I remember how Culley was when Trant confessed. Relieved – he wanted the whole investigation sealed in a crate and thrown to the bottom of the sea at that point.'

'He was thinking about his career, that's why. And how *do*

we think Trant knew so much? We've been working on the assumption that he must have seen footage of some sort?'

Finn nodded.

'That would partly explain it. Or someone gave him the details of what happened to Oliver Littlewood – someone who was intimately acquainted with that information and wanted to hide their involvement once and for all. Who better to use as a patsy than a dying man with similar tastes? And Trant gets to claim the notoriety.'

Skegman stood and looked out of his window for a moment while he thought about it.

'Logically – I can see that if Culley was behind this that would answer a lot of questions,' he said slowly. 'But he's a highly decorated officer who's done some seriously impressive work since he left this station. You've worked with him – do you genuinely believe he's capable of doing the things Red Tide has done? And have you at least asked yourself *why*?'

Finn tried to think it through dispassionately. Culley was an irritating pain in the arse for sure, but he'd never seen anything that suggested he was anything more than that. But that didn't mean much either – he'd caught many a killer who'd hidden very effectively in plain sight. Experience had also taught him you never really knew what was going on in *any* man's mind.

'You talked to him yesterday – how did he strike you?'

Skegman shrugged.

'Not happy at having all this exhumed, that's for sure.' He stopped as he realised what he was saying. 'Which given everything that was happening was a little odd for a senior officer.' He looked across his desk at Finn. 'Alright, I can see where you're coming from. There are a few bits and pieces around him that smell strange. I'll give you a *little* bit of licence to dig – to rule him out if nothing else. But, be discreet for Christ's sake, Alex.'

Finn smiled.

'Discretion's my middle name – and I know exactly where to start.'

An hour later Finn had driven out to Chislehurst on the London/Kent border. The further away from Cedar House he'd got, the deeper the snow on the ground seemed to be. He chided himself as he parked up. Staying in touch with people had never been a strength of his – even those he liked. Life could be like a river at times, sweeping over you, washing people into your past whether you wanted them gone or not. And then he felt another stab of guilt – because life wasn't like that at all actually – you always had the choice to stay in touch.

He was walking through the driveway of a large, detached house that right now looked like a rather picturesque Christmas card. This particular old friend was clearly doing okay, thriving even, and it pleased him to see it. He looked for a doorbell but there wasn't one and used the wrought-iron doorknocker instead.

'Fuck me, you look exactly the same – still a great long streak of piss,' said a familiar voice as the door opened. Finn couldn't prevent a smile from spreading across his face. Jack Barton certainly looked a bit different. He'd lost all his hair for a start and had filled out considerably since his days at Cedar House.

'And when exactly did you become Shrek?' he said.

Barton bellowed with laughter.

'Come in, you silly sod, and tell me what's so important that you've dug me up.'

Finn felt a blast of warm air as Barton led him through to a beautifully appointed living room. A roaring log fire was

336

burning while groaning bookshelves lined the walls, together with some tasteful-looking artwork. The whole place felt instantly comforting. His old friend had left Cedar House in 2010 and taken a job with Surrey police where he'd stayed, by choice, as a DC for the rest of his career. Finn hadn't been surprised; Barton had always made it clear he held little appetite for rising through the ranks.

'You haven't done too badly for yourself,' said Finn, admiringly.

'Decent investments and a good pension, mate,' said Barton. 'Don't worry, your time will come.'

'How's Kathy?' asked Finn.

'Gone, I'm afraid. Last year – cancer. The only good thing was that it all happened very quickly. She didn't suffer – not for long, anyway.'

Finn felt another wave of guilt – Barton had sent flowers to Karin's funeral together with a heartfelt message that had meant a lot at the time, and he'd completely missed this.

'I'm so sorry to hear that, Jack. I know how much she meant to you. It's a horrible thing to go through on your own. As you know, I've been there too.'

Barton nodded and patted Finn on the shoulder.

'I know you have.' He brightened. 'Can I get you anything? Tea, coffee? I've got some decent single malts as well . . . I remember how much you like a dram.'

Fin smiled. 'It's half past ten in the morning.'

Barton grinned back at him. 'Which is exactly why I'm offering.'

Finn rolled his eyes and then turned serious. 'Nice as this is – there's stuff I need to tell you,' he said. Barton motioned at a large sofa and the pair sat down. Finn explained why he was there, taking his old friend through the sequence of events that had begun with the discovery of Jemma Vickers's body in

Tooting the previous morning. Barton looked increasingly shocked as he listened.

'How could we have got it all so wrong?' he said as Finn finished up.

'That's why I'm here – I don't think we did. I think somewhere along the way we were being steered.' He shared his suspicions about Culley.

'You two always did wind each other up but isn't this taking it a bit far?' said Barton.

'What do you remember about him back then?'

'Jesus, Alex – I can barely remember why I go and open the fridge door these days.' He focused on the question. 'Everything was done by the book as I recall. We interviewed pretty much anyone who'd ever had any connection to those kids; I trawled through hours of CCTV footage trying to find that van. Logically – we should have come up with more than we did. It was always frustrating that Culley *didn't* get more involved. I remember that much – he was the SIO, and yet he was never around.'

'What are you saying?' said Finn and Barton shrugged.

'I'm not sure I know myself – but in hindsight what was he doing that was more important? An investigation of that size and he left it to a DS and a DC to effectively run alone.'

Finn focused, trying hard to remember.

'And Harvey Russell – I don't suppose that name rings any bells with you?'

'This guy you think killed Quilter and Knox? Sorry – he's a new name on me. He certainly wasn't in the frame fifteen years ago. You think Culley's behind him?'

'It's one possibility – put it that way.'

Barton exhaled.

'It does sound like whoever committed the murders yesterday was organised. An assistant commissioner would have the contacts to do that – and the cash, for that matter. And if there was even a chance George Rickson was involved and his son knew something, then I can see the logic in trying to silence Billy. Especially if you've got a friendly marksman in your pocket.'

Finn stared at the orange glow of the flames, heard the wood crackling in the heat and nodded.

'So how do I go about doing this?'

'You tread carefully. I know what happened to you last year – I still have half an ear on the jungle drums. That DS who got killed, the bent DC in your team? And I know what top brass are like. You go after Culley and get it wrong and they'll come after you hard.'

Finn nodded – that thought had already occurred to him.

'I can't do this on my own – will you help me, Jack?' said Finn.

Slowly, Barton nodded.

Finn spent the rest of the afternoon in his office. He'd brought Paulsen in on what he was doing but had kept it from the rest of the team. Given the sensitivity, the fewer people who knew the better. She'd given him a wide berth, working quietly at her desk until there was something tangible to bring to him. It was just after three when he finally emerged. She saw him crossing the incident room and anticipated his question before he reached her.

'There's nothing new to tell you, guv. Though . . .' She checked her watch. 'Jemma Vickers's post-mortem is happening this afternoon so we might get something from that later.'

As she spoke, she saw what he was holding in his hand, a poster of a teenage Black youth. 'Who's that?'

'This is Jarrod Thomas, the boy Jemma was looking into. Lee mentioned him to me in the cafe too.'

'And?'

'There's nothing that's unique about him particularly – but I called the Missing Persons Unit and they say there has been a small spike in mispers in our neck of the woods, compared to other regions. Specifically, kids in their late teens.'

'What are you saying?'

'What Red Tide is selling is pretty unique – and when something's unique there's a market for it. If Red Tide did take at least some of them, then where did they end up?'

'Are you saying there's *bodies* out there – on our patch – that haven't been found?'

'Let's not jump the gun. The Missing Persons Unit believe the vast majority – if not all of them – are runaways. But it's worth taking a deep dive through all the mispers who might be the right kind of age and profile. Cross-check with the Exploitation Unit and see if they can help us narrow the field.'

'What are we looking for?' said Paulsen. 'Are you still trying to link this back to Culley?' she said discreetly. Finn looked uncertain.

'I want to know if there just might be a pattern to it, first of all. And from there we can start putting potential names into the frame.' He looked at the picture on the poster again thoughtfully. 'Where's Jarrod Thomas right now, Mattie? What happened to him?'

38

It took Paulsen around an hour to find it. And even then, she'd had to look at the map several times to be sure. When she brought it to Finn, it took him back fifteen years, when as a young DS in the same incident room, he'd identified the rough area where Jemma and Lee had eventually been found.

'*Sidcup?*' he said, slightly incredulously.

'Sidcup,' repeated Paulsen. 'Not precisely obviously – and you wouldn't spot it unless you were specifically looking. But there's certainly *something* going on round there.'

She went through some of the mispers in the system. A seventeen-year-old boy travelling to a football match in 2010. A nineteen-year-old barmaid who never came home from her shift in 2013. The sous-chef who'd left for work and never arrived in 2017.

'I mean there's plenty of others *not* in this area and they're not all the same age as the three from 2009. But it just caught my eye – when you actually go through them – just a few too many bunched up in this patch.'

She was right, thought Finn – the faintest trace of a pattern *was* there, either a home address or a last sighting that connected them.

'Sidcup . . .' he said. 'Interesting.'

'Does AC Culley have any connection there?' said Paulsen.

'Carry on looking at it – the more of these you can find, the more you can cement this, the better.'

She was about to ask again about Culley when she saw the look on his face and decided better of it.

Half an hour later he came and found her at her desk, and that expression hadn't changed.

'I've been running some background checks and found a property that you could broadly put at the heart of the area.'

Paulsen frowned.

'That's convenient,' she said. 'Running background checks on who – Culley?'

He passed her an envelope with an address scribbled in biro on the back.

'It's a small cottage in one of the villages close to Sidcup – I want you to get a search warrant as quickly as possible.'

'Who does this belong to?'

'Don't worry about that – just let me know when you've got it and get yourself ready to go. Take Nash and a TSG team with you too. I want *everything* searched including the land outside – you'll need heavy-duty digging equipment because it won't be easy in these conditions.'

For a moment she was struggling to take it all in.

'What am I looking for?'

Finn's jaw tightened.

'What do you think? Have a SOCO team with you as well.'

She nodded, understanding.

'Are we likely to encounter any resistance?'

He shook his head.

'No – if I'm right, the place will be empty. At least I very much hope it will be.'

'And where will you be?'

'Skegman's across all this, but I want you to keep it on a need-to-know basis at this point. So just the people you're taking – and if you find *anything*, anything at all – call me straight away.'

Paulsen looked up at him, confused.

'Guv, I don't understand – who does this cottage belong to and where will you be?'

And so he told her, and her eyes widened.

It was around seven by the time Paulsen's application for a search warrant was granted. After discreetly assembling the necessary personnel, she held a quick briefing at Cedar House before setting off with Nash.

'Another night, another set of dark snowy woods – brilliant,' she muttered under her breath as they closed in. That wasn't quite true. The cottage was part of a loose assortment of properties that lined a country road between Sidcup and Foots Cray. It was a small-looking place with a huddle of thick-set trees behind it. There wasn't much street lighting but, once again, the moon was doing a decent job of illuminating the landscape.

As per Finn's instructions, TSG and SOCO teams were accompanying them, together with a specialist search unit carrying detection equipment. They held back while Paulsen and Nash made an initial reconnaissance sweep in their car. After passing the building slowly, they came to a stop at the side of the road and the pair watched for a few minutes but could see no obvious signs of life.

Paulsen radioed the TSG commander, and the six-man team joined them on foot. She then walked up to the front of the cottage as the TSG unit spread to the sides and rear. She gave them a few seconds to get into position then knocked at the door. When it became clear no one was coming, an officer carrying an enforcer stepped forward and began to smash his way through.

A few minutes later they were inside. Having established the place was empty the search team got to work. Immediately it was obvious that no one was living there. It was tidy, but vacant, almost like a holiday home – the only signs of life a jar of instant coffee in a cupboard together with a packet of half-eaten biscuits.

'I don't know if this place belongs to Red Tide but there's something about it that I don't like,' said Nash, who'd followed her in. Paulsen looked around the sparse living room and couldn't help but agree. It was cold and smelt of damp and you couldn't shake the feeling that *something* had happened here. One of the search team officers came through and joined them.

'We've found something round the back you should see,' he said urgently. They followed him out and saw multiple torch beams flickering around the garden like a light show. It was a large unkempt area, which backed on to some woodland. A group were congregating around one small section at the point where the snow-covered grass met the trees.

'What is it?' asked Paulsen.

The man angled his torch and she saw what looked like a six-foot-long ridge as if the ground there had sighed and fallen in on itself.

'What the hell's that?' said Nash, at her side.

'I know what I think it looks like . . .' murmured Paulsen.

Just a few miles away Finn was sitting in his car, waiting. There were two uniformed officers with him, the heat between them steaming up the windows. He checked his watch – it was just approaching eight. The silence was interrupted by the buzzing of his phone. He took the call from Paulsen and listened as she relayed what they'd found.

'What do you think?' he said.

'I don't want to pre-empt – I mean people bury their dogs in their gardens, don't they? But it doesn't look good,' she replied.

'Tell me the minute you have any kind of confirmation,' he said. And as he ended the call, felt a hot surge of frustration. If there was evidence, Paulsen would find it. All he had to do was sit tight. And yet . . .

'*Don't do anything stupid – just stick to the plan*,' warned Karin.

But he was also remembering Lee's final tortured moments once again, the pleading in Sarah Littlewood's voice the previous night on the phone and felt his anger rise once more. He'd hidden that quite well he thought – the growing rage as the day had progressed. What was that saying – '*Those who ignore their history are doomed to repeat it?*' He could almost hear it coming out of Murray's mouth. Fuck it, he thought.

'Be ready – I'll call you when I need you,' he said to the two officers in the back and got out of the car. He crossed the road and walked through the gates of the house in front, feeling the snow crunch underfoot.

It was time to end this once and for all and he reached for the wrought-iron doorknocker.

'Two visits in one day – what have I done to deserve this?' said Jack Barton a few moments later.

'Thanks for seeing me again, mate – I appreciate it,' replied Finn with a warm smile.

At the cottage, the search team had now deployed a portable x-ray unit, together with ground-penetrating radar. The early assessment was that the earth looked like it had been dug relatively recently, probably just before the current cold snap. Temporary floodlighting was also now in the process of being erected. Nash had gone back to join the team searching inside and as she watched, Paulsen felt an ominous sense of inevitability about what was unfolding.

The officer using the x-ray unit suddenly beckoned to her.

She went over and looked at the small display screen. Clearly visible was the unmistakable shape of a human body and her heart began to pound. That image was someone's son or daughter, and she had a fairly good idea about how they'd probably died. She was just reaching for her phone to call Finn when one of the other SOCOs waved at her.

'I think we've got another one,' he shouted.

'I thought it might be a good idea to talk tonight, now that you've had a chance to think about it,' said Finn as he was being led through the hallway. There was a blast of stuffy air as they entered the living room and he could see the fire in there was still burning healthily, a fresh pile of logs on the hearth in front of it.

'I've been thinking about nothing else since you left, to be honest,' said Barton. 'It seems to me what you need is some hard proof.' He walked over to an antique wooden cabinet. 'Can I get you a drink this time? I know I could bloody use one,' he added, and Finn nodded.

'What kind of proof did you have in mind?' he asked.

Barton opened the cabinet and reached down, but when he turned around it wasn't a bottle he was holding. In his hand was a hatchet.

'This kind?'

39

'You were right about Culley – he was a fucking idiot,' said Barton amiably. Neither man had moved a muscle. 'He even rang me yesterday to tell me that you were digging into all this. He wanted to make sure we were on the same page about what happened back then. Poor old Rolf – only ever bothered about his career.'

'It was you – wasn't it?' said Finn quietly. 'Screwing the investigation from the inside back then. You're Red Tide.'

Barton laughed.

'If you want to call me that. It's all a bit Scooby-Doo though – Red Tide's more of a *franchise*.'

The words and their truth hung in the air between them for a moment.

'Before you do anything stupid, you should know I've brought backup with me,' said Finn calmly.

Barton looked at him like he was slightly slow.

'*I know*. I went and took a peek at you earlier, which is why I brought this beauty back down from the loft.' He held up the hatchet as if admiring a particularly fine bottle of vintage wine. Even after such a long time, Finn could see rust-coloured bloodstains on its blade. He wondered if that belonged to Oliver Littlewood and how many other people it had been used on since then.

'Backup's only useful if you can call it in,' continued Barton. 'So, throw your phone and radio on to the floor for me.'

Slowly, Finn reached into his pocket and did as he was told. Barton stepped forward and kicked them both across the room. Behind them, the fire crackled noisily.

'How did you work it out?'

'Two things,' said Finn.

Despite the calm tone of the conversation, both men were standing legs apart, balancing on the balls of their feet, ready for any unexpected movements.

'Go on.'

'Lee told me in the cafe that he thought there were cameras in that cellar – that he was being filmed. That's why he mutilated Oliver Littlewood's body. But as you'll recall – we didn't find anything in there, not a trace of a camera – and I left *you* to protect the scene. And of course, we never found the murder weapon either.'

Barton smirked.

'And the second thing?'

'One of my team did a deep dive into our back catalogue of unresolved mispers. We'd have probably missed it if I hadn't visited you earlier – but the coincidence was too much. I remember you looking for property in Sidcup back in 2009. Why would you own what seems to be a holiday home relatively close to where you live? We're searching it now, by the way.'

If the news bothered Barton, it didn't show. Instead, he laughed.

'Well done, mate. You put it together. You got me. Only took fifteen years, eh?'

It became swiftly clear to Paulsen that they were severely under-resourced for what they'd stumbled upon. Two more potential shallow graves had now been found and given the freezing conditions this was going to be a long, painstaking process. The sheer size of the space also suggested that three could be a bare minimum. Finn's phone was now frustratingly ringing out and she was in the process of firing off a WhatsApp message to him when Nash emerged from the cottage and joined her.

'What now?' she said, as she caught the expression on her face.

Barton seemed to be in two minds about whether to take the time or simply swing his arm round and end Finn with one blow of the hatchet.

'Red Tide is a business, Alex,' he said. 'You'd be surprised how many people around the world are willing to pay for *original content* – as the kids say these days.' He gestured at the living room. 'You really think a copper's pension provided all this? Where better to protect yourself from scrutiny than from inside the police? It's not hard – a bit of banter, you keep a low profile, do the job and everyone thinks you're a solid citizen.'

'You were a good officer,' said Finn slowly, remembering.

'Thanks *guv*,' said Barton with a grin.

'How did you keep all this from Kathy for so long . . .' Finn faltered, as realisation set in. 'There never *was* a Kathy, was there?'

'No – turns out it doesn't take much to fool a room full of hardened detectives.'

Barton's whole face seemed to have changed and the gentle mocking tone Finn remembered from all those years ago now sounded cruel and malevolent.

'And I'm guessing you were behind Dennis Trant too?'

Barton smiled.

'Correct. He had nothing to do with any of this – but I knew him from the forums. I kept an eye on things over the years and learnt you'd started digging back into it in 2016. When I

349

found out Trant was terminally ill it seemed too good an opportunity to miss, and he was bang up for it. The idea of misleading the police right at the death, so to speak – and of claiming a bit of late notoriety appealed to him.'

'And what about Quilter and Knox?'

'Both part of the same community. We met on the Dark Web too – I was actively looking for people in the area to recruit. We then planned the whole thing months in advance just like a police operation. Knox picked out Littlewood and tracked him for weeks. Quilter did the due diligence on the pair at his school, and I found the house – then steered the investigation away of course.'

'Why those three . . .' whispered Finn.

'Because that's what the client wanted – three young healthy adults. Two boys and a girl, preferably who knew each other,' Barton replied, his smile widening. 'But needs must when the devil drives . . .'

Finn knew Barton wouldn't be telling him all this if he had any intention of letting him go. And he'd seen a long time ago what that hatchet could do. He needed to keep him talking and hope the two men in his car would start to get suspicious.

'I don't understand – you were the one who gave Knox's name to Culley. If you were working together, why did you do that?'

Barton nodded as if receiving a compliment.

'A bit of calculated misdirection. I told Eddie I was going to use him to bait Culley – and I told him and Quilter what they needed to say and do to stay out of trouble. It worked like a charm. We had you and Rolf in a tailspin – you didn't know your arses from your elbows.' He grinned again. *'None of it makes any sense, Jack! It doesn't add up, Jack!'* he parroted.

'You played me,' said Finn.

'Yeah. Exactly. But then you were quite distracted back then, as I remember.' He leered.

Finn felt slightly sick as he remembered some of Barton's teasing about Karin. It hadn't been harmless banter, more a subtle way of keeping him off-balance.

'So, who took those kids off the street – and who was in that house wearing the mask?'

'Everything was a combination of the three of us. Quilter kidnapped Oliver Littlewood and Knox picked up Jemma and Lee thanks to some useful intel from Quilter. We took turns inside the house, so we'd all have alibis. On the day you went the full tonto it was Knox in there. I tried to warn him, but he didn't pick up my messages in time. Fortunately, I was able to tidy up after him before forensics got there.'

He held up the hatchet proudly. Before he could say any more, they were interrupted by a low buzzing noise.

'That's my phone,' said Finn. 'The backup I brought with me, probably wondering if I'm okay.'

Barton's expression hardened.

'Well now – what *are* we going to do?'

Nash had brought Paulsen into the cottage's kitchen to see what they'd found. The light in there was almost yellow from a single bulb that was hanging without a shade. An old, battered wooden table had been moved to one side and the fraying rug it was standing on folded back. The TSG commander was moving the surrounding chairs out of the way to give them some more space. Paulsen could see exactly what had caught their attention – a neat square hatch door with a single metal handle.

'We thought we'd wait for you,' said Nash.

'Thanks,' said Paulsen drily.

'You paid Harvey Russell to kill Knox and Quilter yesterday, didn't you – to silence them?' said Finn, trying to keep the conversation moving.

'You wouldn't be trying to spin this out would you, Al?'

'What's the point in killing me?'

Finn's eyes were now solely on the hatchet. The slightest movement would give him a split second of warning and a chance to react.

'Knox and Quilter were panicking – Jemma's death had freaked them both out. I could guess what was happening at Cedar House too – the old files being dug out, every last detail being pored over by some twelve-year-old DC. Culley's call yesterday rather confirmed that.'

'You thought Knox and Quilter might crack and sell you out, then?'

'Exactly. These kinds of relationships are loose – marriages of convenience if you like – but easily dealt with if you know men like Russell and have the resources to pay them.'

Almost as soon as he'd finished speaking, he made his move. Finn saw it late and jumped backwards as the hatchet came swinging round. If the intention had been to try and catch him by surprise it only partially worked. The blade caught him in the chest, and he felt sharp hot pain spreading out across his torso. If he hadn't moved when he did, it would probably already be game over.

'What's this going to achieve, Jack – we're *at* the cottage. We'll find the evidence,' he gasped.

'I'm ex-Job, mate. I know how to disappear – don't you think I haven't got a go bag already packed?'

Finn was in agony now. The slice across his chest felt like it was on fire, and the blood was leaking out freely now. As Barton advanced again he put all his effort into backing off. It was futile though; there wasn't enough room to maintain the distance and sooner or later he was going to get cornered. Barton grinned and winked at him.

'Come on, mate, let's bury the hatchet,' he said and then with a snarl jumped forward.

The TSG commander went down first as a rank, sickly sweet smell rose out of the hatch and wafted into the kitchen. Paulsen peered into the inky gloom after him and could see the flash of a torch beam for a moment, then a bright glare as he found a light switch.

'*Clear,*' he shouted after a couple of seconds, and she immediately began to descend the stairs to join him with Nash following closely behind. The space was small and the first thing she saw was a wooden table with an empty stained jug on it. The commander was standing stock-still, staring at the opposite side, and she turned to see what he was looking at.

Chained to the wall was the emaciated body of a young Black man, possibly in his mid to late teens, though it was hard to tell. The bones of his ribcage were showing through almost translucent, thin flesh and long red welts lined his body. It took Paulsen a second but then she realised where she'd seen his face before – on that flyer Finn had been holding earlier. His name was Jarrod, she remembered. Very slowly, his head began to lift.

Finn had managed to swerve again, leaving Barton to slash at the space where he'd been standing. Neither of them were talking now, both concentrating furiously on the other. Inch by inch, Barton was getting closer. Finn was trying to ignore the agonising sting coming from his chest, though the pain combined with the heat from the fire was making his head spin. He backed up against a side table and his hand curled around a vase. He threw it at Barton, who dodged it with ease, and it shattered into pieces behind him.

Finn continued to edge away and was close to the fire now as Barton lunged again. This time he fell backwards on to the hearth and could feel the flames licking at his neck. He grabbed one of the logs and suddenly knew what to do with it. Jumping up with what remaining energy he possessed, he hurled it through the bay window. As it smashed, welcome cold air flooded in. They both knew the men in the car would surely have heard the noise. Barton had a simple choice now – either finish him off or make a run for it. There wasn't time for both. He hurled the hatchet at Finn, and it embedded itself in the wall only inches from his head. With no other card left to play the ex-detective turned and ran.

Finn chased after him through the hallway and into the kitchen where he could see a back door at the far end. He knew he should just retrieve his phone and call for assistance. The place would be flooded in minutes and there'd be nowhere for Barton to escape. But he'd made a promise to both Lee Ellis and Sarah Littlewood. He caught up with the older man and pulled him on to the hard kitchen floor. Instantly he pinned him down, punching him hard in the face as blood sprayed from his nose. He punched him again and then for a third time. The pain in his chest was almost unbearable but he continued raining down the blows.

'*Just stop,*' said Karin.

And then he did. Panting and sweating, he looked down at the bloodied, unconscious face of the man who'd once been his friend and finally lowered his fists.

40

One week later

The cold snap had passed as quickly as it had come. The ominous steel skies from the previous week replaced by cotton-wool clouds and the occasional glimpse of sunshine. Mattie Paulsen was standing in a small suburb of Norwich feeling a strange sense of detachment. Or denial – she wasn't sure which.

'You okay, Mat?' said her brother.

'What kind of answer do you want to that, Jonas?' she replied tonelessly. Her eyes were fixed on the large Victorian building in front of them. Behind them, her mother was shepherding her father out of the back seat of Paulsen's car.

'It's one of the best places in the county – he'll be looked after properly here,' whispered Jonas.

'So he should be, for what they're charging,' muttered Paulsen. 'And it looks soulless,' she added.

'Once he settles in, it'll be fine—' Jonas broke off as an anguished howl interrupted them.

Tears were streaming down Christer Paulsen's face. A pharmaceutical scientist for most of his life, he still *looked* like he should be running a lab somewhere – but his family knew that man was long gone. He was shaking his head and mumbling now, digging in, refusing to move from where he was standing. His wife, Evelyn, was trying to cajole and persuade him, visibly struggling to hold it together herself. The whole tableau was just about every nightmare Paulsen had envisaged for this moment.

Randomly, she remembered Jarrod Thomas, the teenager they'd rescued from the cottage the previous week, somehow still clinging to life in an intensive care unit in London. She wondered if that's what had been deadening her feelings today, why the emotional avalanche she'd feared still hadn't come. Once you'd witnessed something like that, everything else – even this – took on a different perspective.

'You take care of Mum – I'll handle Dad,' she said to Jonas, channelling her inner detective sergeant.

Evelyn now had a hand clamped over her mouth and seemed to be finally defeated by her husband.

'I'm sorry – I thought I'd be okay today, but I can't do this,' she said, breaking up.

'Come on, Mum,' said Jonas, gently guiding her away. A middle-aged woman was emerging from the care home, striding towards them with a big friendly smile of welcome. Christer seemed unsure whether to stay rooted to the spot or whether to follow his wife. Paulsen walked purposefully towards him, meeting his terrified gaze head on.

'Hey, Dad,' she said casually.

Did he know what was happening? Was it just the unfamiliarity of where they'd brought him? Or would he be sitting quietly in a chair in a few minutes, oblivious of his family? Then she saw it for herself, in those once-wise, beautiful eyes of his – *he knew*. Somewhere in there he understood what was going on. Still, she didn't crack, instead doubled down on her determination to get this done smoothly for the sake of all concerned.

'I want to go home,' he said in a small voice.

'Would you like some coffee?' she countered and dug into her bag. She produced a green box with a big black 'Z' stamped across it. 'I've got some Zoega Skanerost – your favourite.'

He stared at the carton as if hypnotised by it.

Over seven decades this man had cared for and supported her, not batting an eyelid as she'd found her sexuality or the career she'd wanted to pursue. Now he was looking at a carton of coffee, like a dog staring hopefully up at a biscuit in its owner's hand. Somewhere, the *real* version of him would be proud of the strength she was summoning, would be egging her on. She smiled conspiratorially at him.

'Come on – let's go inside, eh?'

She put an arm around him and slowly they began to walk.

Extra officers had been drafted in to help the team at Cedar House with the mammoth job the discovery at Barton's cottage had created. In total, eleven bodies had been found at the 'House of Horrors' as the media had rather unoriginally dubbed it. A laptop had been recovered too with more than enough evidence to convict Barton. Harvey Russell had also been found by police in the West Midlands together with his red Mazda. Fibres taken from the back seat of the car had matched with the clothing worn by Craig Quilter and slowly the loose ends were being tied up.

Finn was now sitting in his office looking through some of the evidence that had been gathered. His chest was still sore from where Barton had attacked him, but it had only been a flesh wound and was healing slowly. Finn hadn't been fooled that Barton was only working with Knox and Quilter and that others might yet still be operating in the area. Even with the ringleader under arrest, this investigation still had the feeling of a bottomless pit.

There was a knock at the door and John Skegman entered without waiting to be asked.

'I thought you'd like to know, I've just had AC Culley on the phone. He's obviously very interested in how the Barton investigation's unfolding.'

'What does he make of it all?' said Finn, curious.

'Same as you – angry with himself for not spotting the signs, angry at being so easily fooled – and downright fury at the betrayal. But he did specifically ask me to relay his congratulations on the arrest. I got the impression there's quite a lot of contrition there about you.'

Finn felt a twinge of guilt. He and Culley had never liked one another and probably never would, but that's all it was – a personality clash. Barton's arrest had reframed their whole relationship. It sounded like Culley was having a similar reappraisal.

'I think I might have underestimated him a bit,' he admitted.

'You mean the part where you thought he was a deranged killer?' said Skegman, sitting down. 'It's not like you to have a history of disrespecting your commanding officers, is it?' he added.

'Incredibly hard to fathom why . . .' replied Finn, deadpan.

'He's more than happy to cooperate with the investigation – I mean he doesn't have much choice, but I think he wants to make sure this is done properly, and that there are no mistakes. No further mistakes, anyway.'

Finn nodded.

'Maybe we've got the station back into a little bit of credit with all of this?' he said. 'It's certainly got plenty of media coverage and if Culley's paying me compliments then the winds are certainly changing higher up the ladder.'

Skegman flicked a stray bit of dirt off his sleeve as he thought about it.

'Possibly. But given that we were in the doghouse partly because of a corrupt DC – it's ironic that it took the arrest of another former officer here to achieve that. But a win's a win wherever it comes from, and I'll take it.'

'There are only two of those bodies that we still haven't identified. There's some mispers going back to the 1990s we're looking at for potential fits,' said Finn and then shook his head. 'Barton must have been doing this for years – how did he fool us all?'

'Because he was very good. And that's the point, Alex. Sometimes the only closure you get is from understanding that you can't change the past.'

Finn let that sink in for a moment then nodded.

'I think that goes for quite a lot of things.' He checked his watch and raised an eyebrow when he saw what the time was. 'I'm out for the rest of the afternoon, by the way – Sami's in charge.'

'Something important?' said Skegman and Finn nodded.

'I've got a funeral to attend.'

The funeral in question was a double service for Lee Ellis and his father. It had been organised by a close friend of Terry's in lieu of any other family. Sarah Littlewood was amongst the mourners, and she greeted Finn warmly when she saw him waiting outside the church. Jack Barton's arrest, it seemed, had finally brought her some genuine closure. The wake was held at a local social club and gave Finn the chance to properly catch up with her.

'Should you be buying a drink for a woman you're going to be arresting next week?' she asked as he passed her a large gin and tonic.

'You're going to be okay,' he replied, and she held up a hand to stop him.

'Don't give me the speech again – just let me know when you're coming and I'll make sure the kettle's on.'

He smiled, aware it was gallows humour. There was still work to do on the investigation into George Rickson's death and the precise role Sarah had played in it. Barton had confirmed under interview that Rickson hadn't been involved in the abductions. That at least had been important for Billy but Sarah would have to live with the consequence of what she'd done.

Finn looked around – the other people in the room, judging by their age, looked like they were Terry's friends. There were some younger ones too and he wondered if they'd been old army colleagues of Lee's.

'Have you been invited to Jemma's funeral?' said Sarah tentatively.

Finn shook his head.

'I haven't heard anything – it's obviously entirely up to the family, but I'd like to be there,' he said and Sarah nodded. 'How are you?' he asked. 'Really, properly – how *are* you – now that the dust's settled a bit?'

She thought about it.

'Still here for my daughter and granddaughter. They're what have always kept me going. You don't realise how strong you are until you have no option – that's probably the best way of describing it. George Rickson ... is something I'm going to have to make sense of and I'll need to look Billy in the eye at some point. He's still the father of my daughter's baby – it's just a mess. I also keep thinking of that conversation with

Jemma – if I hadn't given in to that need for revenge – two people might still be alive.'

'Does Ella know what you did yet?'

Sarah nodded.

'It's complicated – she understood my reasons, but I wouldn't say she condoned them. She's in shock – it's going to take a long time for us to work through this.' She took a lungful of air and breathed out. 'So, that's me – how are *you* doing?'

Finn found the question slightly harder than he expected to answer. He'd spent a lot of time thinking about Jack Barton over the last week.

'We caught him – that's the main thing, stopped him from hurting anyone else. Who knows how many more there would have been?'

'That's not really what I asked,' she said, and he nodded in acknowledgement.

'I blamed myself for years for letting your son's abductor get away that afternoon. Lee blamed me too – but now we know the truth. That the man responsible was a serving Met police officer subverting everything I was doing from inside the investigation. In hindsight we did bloody well to rescue those two.' He faltered. 'None of which changes the fact I didn't get there in time to save Ollie – for which I will *always* be profoundly sorry.'

Sarah took a step forward, taking him by surprise.

'Come here,' she said and hugged him tightly. 'Stop blaming yourself. Thank you for everything you *did* do, not what you didn't.'

And as he held her, Finn felt a burst of emotion. He and this woman had been on such a journey together. She'd screamed at him, hurled abuse, pleaded and begged, cried her heart out too. The full spectrum. It struck him though, that he finally understood their relationship – that he could finally call her his *friend*. They held on to each other tightly for a few more moments then disengaged.

'Don't be a stranger, eh?' she said, softly.

'Not a chance,' he replied.

41

After the funerals, at John Skegman's insistence, Finn finally took some much-needed leave. For the first time since Karin's death, he left the country. Berlin was just as viciously cold as he remembered it. He spent a day there, wandering around, remembering a few previous visits. He liked the city – could even imagine himself living there at some point. It wore its scars openly in the form of memorials and brightly painted fragments of concrete and cinder block. If it were a person, he could identify with it.

The last time he'd come had been with Karin in the final months of her life. She'd sat him down in a coffee shop near Hackescher Markt and expressed her concerns about how he'd cope after she was gone. She'd been right to worry as it had turned out.

After one last walk along the Spree, he headed to Gesundbrunnen Station and caught a train. Three hours later he arrived at his final destination in the coastal city of Stralsund and that's when it hit him again – the pain, he'd done so well to contain and control over the last few years. He let the emotion burn through him and then began walking down some familiar streets.

'Alex. It's good to see you,' said Olga Bergmann, twenty minutes later, greeting him with a kiss on the cheek as she opened her front door. Karin's mother was eighty-three now, though she looked a good decade younger.

'I'm so sorry about Otto,' he began, but she waved him away.

'Now we are both bereaved. Which makes your visit much appreciated.'

Part of the reason for coming here was to see how she was coping. Her husband had died the previous year and Finn hadn't been able to make it over for the funeral – work, as usual, had got in the way. But he could see the answer to his question for himself as they entered her tidy, well-tended home. Colourful abstract paintings – landscapes, he fancied – adorned many of the walls.

'These are nice,' he admired.

'My work,' she replied with obvious pride. 'After Otto died, I had time on my hands and it's something I've wanted to try for a while. I needed something to distract myself with and as it turns out – I'm not too bad at it either! There's a young lady in the city who wants to put on an exhibition.'

Finn found it rather life-affirming to see someone getting a little professional success so late in life and clearly enjoying the taste. But the melancholy that had shrouded him since leaving London was also still there. He had no idea Olga possessed such a talent and Karin would have been gobsmacked – but she'd never get to see these paintings and he found that thought unexpectedly distressing. Even now his loss found new ways to surprise him.

'So, Alex, why have you *really* come?' asked Olga. 'Lovely as it is to see you, you haven't travelled all this way to eat lebkuchen and admire some pictures.'

Finn took a deep intake of breath.

'I've been thinking about Karin lately. I mean, I never really stop obviously, but her ashes, specifically . . .'

After her cremation, Finn had given the urn to Otto and Olga to scatter in her home town. It had seemed right, and he'd been happy for them to choose an appropriate final resting place. But the recent funerals and the memory of their first dates back in 2009 had stirred up his emotions and he'd felt a calling to come here. Olga's eyes widened with alarm.

'It's a bit late if you want them back,' she said and Finn couldn't help but chuckle.

'No, that's not it. I just wondered if I could see *where* . . .' He tailed off, and she extended her hand and put it on his.

'Of course,' she said.

A few moments later they were standing in a beautifully maintained high-fenced garden at the back of the house. Thorny rose bushes lined its sides and a large careworn apple tree dominated one end.

'Over there,' said Olga pointing at the tree. Finn had seen it before, in warmer conditions – back when he and Karin had been married. He'd eaten long summer lunches in its shadow, had drunk wine and kissed his wife under its branches too.

'Of course,' he said, nodding approvingly. 'Where else.'

'You take as long as you need,' said Olga before turning and going back inside.

He stood facing the old tree for a moment, then crossed the grass, reached out a hand and touched it.

'It's time, isn't it?' said Karin. *'To finally say goodbye.'*

He stood in the perfect silence, his hand still on the bark.

'Yes, my love. I think it is,' he said.

Nancy had taken Paulsen to the cinema in an attempt to lift her mood. Listening to her whinge on the walk home, she realised she'd been successful in distracting her, but victory had come at a price. They'd seen an average action movie in which the heroine had defied the odds, common sense and the laws of physics to save the day. Now, Nancy was getting the usual lecture as to why Paulsen would choose the next film they went to see.

'Chases in real life don't work like that,' she said irritably.

'You mean you *don't* leap from rooftops on to the top of moving trains then?' replied Nancy.

'Not with my knees. Truth is, usually one of you gets too knackered to continue and that's how these things end.'

Nancy raised an eyebrow.

'Really?'

'Yeah – happens all the time.'

'And what do you tell your bosses?'

Paulsen considered it.

'He just seemed to disappear, guv.'

They both laughed.

'It's nice to see you smiling again, Mat,' said Nancy.

'What else am I going to do?' replied Paulsen more soberly.

'You haven't said much since you came back from Norfolk. Are you okay?'

'Not really. But there's not much I can do about Dad's situation is there? It is what it is – and unfortunately, the worst is yet to come.'

They carried on walking in silence for a few moments.

'And how are *we* doing, do you think? We haven't really talked about that for a while,' said Nancy carefully. It was a conversation she'd been wanting to have for some time, and this finally felt like the right moment.

'What's that supposed to mean?' said Paulsen, surprised. '*We're* fine, aren't we?'

'Yes. I mean, insofar as we're trundling along. We go to work, eat, sleep, drink and grab a couple of weeks in the sun every year. But . . .'

'But what?'

'Don't you want any *more* from it all?'

Paulsen stopped and so did Nancy.

'Do you?' said Paulsen.

'What's happening with your dad has certainly made me think about everything. Also, the fact that you nearly got shot the other week,' said Nancy. 'That focused my mind as well.'

'Think about *what*?' said Paulsen, still bemused.

'That maybe, it would be good . . .' She paused, as if reluctant to actually say the words.

'Just spit it out.'

'That it might be nice to do the whole marriage and kids thing . . .'

There was a split second between Nancy uttering the words and their meaning sinking in. A smile began to tiptoe across Paulsen's face and then, even to her own surprise, developed into a full-on sprint.

After his trip to Germany, Finn took a few days to take stock of his life. Despite being comfortably middle-aged now, he still felt hungry to achieve things. He was a better police officer today than he had been in 2009. He knew the job better, but he was an older man too. Everything he'd been through since Karin had died – the mental health crisis he'd suffered; Jackie Ojo's death; the realisation he'd got so much wrong, for so long, with Jemma and Lee – had added to his sum knowledge. Whether he'd wanted those life lessons or not, he was stronger for them.

He spent an evening with Murray and allowed himself to be mercilessly mocked all night and then thanked him for his friendship. The Scotsman's intervention the previous week had been small but critical in helping Finn find his way to Barton. The feeling persisted that for all the sharp humour there was something vulnerable beneath the surface there – but that was one for another day. The night with him, hot on the heels of his visit to Stralsund, had helped him reset following his experience in the cafe with Lee. He was ready to go again. There was just one thing that didn't feel quite right, and it took him a while to identify it. And when he did, he smiled.

The following evening, he made his way to a familiar wine bar in Clapham. He hadn't had much cause to come here for a while and even the sight of it brought back some sad memories. He bought two glasses of wine and then found a table. A few minutes later Mattie Paulsen swept in and smiled as she spotted him sitting alone.

'I took the liberty of ordering for you,' he said rather stiffly as she made her way over. 'I hope that's okay?' Paulsen took off her coat and sat down. She took a cautious sip from the flute of white wine in front of her.

'Mmmm, citrussy – with a hint of apple pie.'

'Really?' said Finn.

'No idea,' said Paulsen. 'But it's cold and hitting the spot nicely, so thanks.' She looked around the bar with interest. 'So, this is where you and Jackie used to come for those piss-ups of yours.'

Finn looked embarrassed.

'I wouldn't call them piss-ups, more chewing the cud, setting the world to rights – that sort of thing.'

Paulsen gave him a cynical look.

'A giant bitch-fest then?'

Finn shifted on his seat like a naughty schoolboy.

'That too – but only about the truly deserving. Mainly John Skegman if you must know.'

Paulsen grinned.

'Sounds like Jacks,' she said. 'Anyway – before we get on to that – which sounds fun, by the way – I've got something to tell you.' She left a pregnant pause. 'I'm getting married.'

She said it simply and bluntly as was her way. Finn – as was *his* way – looked momentarily awkward, then smiled.

'That's brilliant – congratulations, Mattie.' A thought struck him. 'Did you propose, or . . .'

'I didn't go down on one knee if that's what you're getting at. It was more of a mutual thing.'

Finn, surprisingly, found himself mildly shocked by the news. It was more to do with the general glow about Paulsen. Glowing wasn't really a word you associated with her. For an instant, Lee's sermon in the cafe about people's inability to change came back to him. It wasn't true – Paulsen had changed considerably in the time he'd known her. The woman in front of him now was visibly more at ease with herself than the young DC he'd first met.

'I'll also be sticking around Cedar House for a bit too,' she continued. 'I'd like to be settled for a while, both personally and professionally.'

Finn raised an eyebrow.

'You were looking to leave last year. And you've built up a really healthy CV too – if you did want to try for something.'

Paulsen shrugged.

'I happen to like working with you, believe it or not. We're underdogs, aren't we? Outliers – the ones with reputations.' She smiled again. 'Just how I like it really. Why would I want to go anywhere else?'

He looked pleased and lifted his glass.

'I can drink to that,' he said and chinked his glass against hers.

'So what have *you* been up to this week, then?' she asked.

He thought about his flying visit to Germany, the meal with Murray – and all the thinking he'd done in between.

'Not a lot. Just resting, I suppose,' he part-lied.

Paulsen eyed him suspiciously.

'You seem very relaxed.'

'I'm always relaxed,' bluffed Finn.

'No – you're definitely not,' she replied tartly.

He looked out of the window for a moment. The snow had gone, but it was still a freezing cold night out there.

'Okay then. Like you, I've been pondering the meaning of it all. Long story short – it's time to start moving forwards with my life. I think that's what this business with Lee Ellis really rammed home to me: that you can get very lost in the past if you're not careful. There comes a point where you have to make the break.'

Paulsen was eying him closely as he spoke.

'I've heard you say stuff like that before, but this is the first time it sounds like you actually mean it.'

Finn looked offended.

'I'm not *that* bad a liar, am I?'

'Yes, you are,' she said and sipped some more of her wine.

'Nancy asked me something, just before I left. She was a bit puzzled about tonight. I mean we don't tend to do this, do we – *socialise*, I mean?'

'No,' said Finn agreeing. 'We do not.'

'She wanted to know if we were meeting as friends – or just workmates.'

Finn seemed to consider the question himself for a moment.

'And what did you say?'

Paulsen caught his eye and smiled.

'I said I'd tell her tomorrow.'

The End

ACKNOWLEDGEMENTS

I've always been slightly fascinated by those news stories that allude to something much bigger but only merit a hand-ful of lines in the newspapers. Hostage situations that are 'successfully resolved' by police after a couple of hours or train journeys held up by 'passenger incidents.' We've all read them, worked around them even – a short inconvenience for most of us as roads are closed or trains are cancelled. But for someone, somewhere - the biggest and most important day of their lives where everything has coalesced – and that was really the starting point for this story.

Once again I'm hugely indebted to police advisor Stuart Gibbon who fielded every possible query on hostage and siege scenarios to the mechanics of dealing with dead bodies buried under frozen ground. Big thanks too to my editor Beth Wickington for being a great voice of reason on this book when it was needed, and to my agent Hayley Steed for her ever-constant support and encouragement.

Thanks as well are due to Paul Romain for some invaluable local knowledge which helped me plunder a few more loca-tions in south London that I hadn't yet mined for this series. And finally, as is traditional, to my friend Nishat Ladha who always gets a sneak preview of what I'm writing, gives the best feedback, and remains the best friend anyone could wish to have.

An ordinary day. An ordinary street. A gruesome delivery waiting on the doorstep that's going to set off a spine-chilling chain of events . . .

The fourth instalment in Will Shindler's critically acclaimed DI Alex Finn and DC Mattie Paulsen series is available now!

Sadie Nicholls has been found dead
and her little boy is missing.

Is it more than a coincidence that a
similar crime was committed at the
same house nearly 20 years ago?

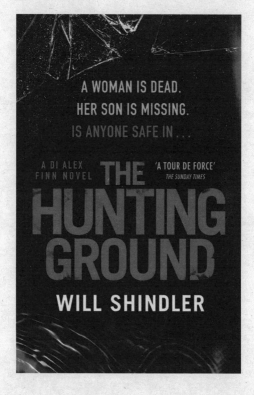

A WOMAN IS DEAD.
HER SON IS MISSING.
IS ANYONE SAFE IN . . .

A DI ALEX
FINN NOVEL

'A TOUR DE FORCE'
THE SUNDAY TIMES

THE
HUNTING
GROUND

WILL SHINDLER

Read the thrilling third book in the unmissable DI
Alex Finn and DC Mattie Paulsen series now!

Karl is forced to make an impossible choice at knife point.

Stay and die, or walk away from Leah and take a thug's word that they both will live.

Should Karl trust a villain and leave his daughter with a knife at her throat?

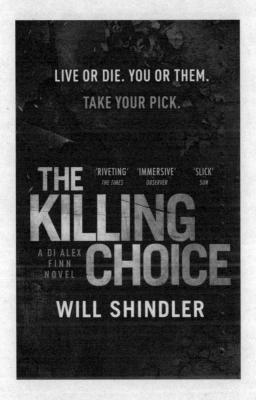

The second book in the phenomenal series featuring DI Alex Finn and DC Mattie Paulsen is available now!

A close-knit team of fire fighters emerge from
a fire without a body and quit the service.

Five years later one of them is set
alight at his own wedding.

Someone knows what they did that night.

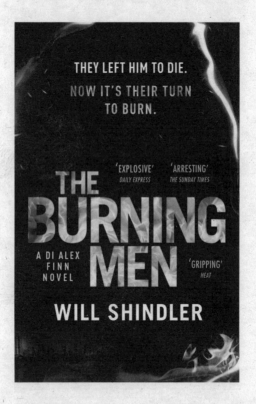

THEY LEFT HIM TO DIE.
NOW IT'S THEIR TURN
TO BURN.

'EXPLOSIVE'
DAILY EXPRESS

'ARRESTING'
THE SUNDAY TIMES

THE
BURNING
MEN

A DI ALEX
FINN
NOVEL

'GRIPPING'
HEAT

WILL SHINDLER

Read the first book in the gripping DI Alex
Finn and DC Mattie Paulsen series now!